Mrs. Bennet's Favorite Daughter

by

Jann Rowland

One Good Sonnet Publishing
Publishers of Fine Romance and Fantasy Fiction

By Jann Rowland

Published by One Good Sonnet Publishing:

PRIDE AND PREJUDICE VARIATIONS

Mrs. Bennet's Favorite Daughter
Flight to Gretna Green
With Love's Light Wings
Mistletoe and Mischief: A Pride and Prejudice Christmas Anthology
Another Proposal
A Matchmaking Mother
The Challenge of Entail
The Impulse of the Moment
Mr. Bennet Takes Charge
A Gift for Elizabeth

This is a work of fiction based on the works of Jane Austen. All the characters and events portrayed in this novel are products of Jane Austen's original novel or the authors' imaginations.

MRS. BENNET'S FAVORITE DAUGHTER

Copyright © 2020 Jann Rowland

Cover Design by Jann Rowland

Published by One Good Sonnet Publishing

All rights reserved.

ISBN: 1989212220
ISBN-13: 9781989212226

No part of this book may be reproduced or transmitted in any form or by any means, electronic, digital, or mechanical, including photocopying, recording, or by any information storage and retrieval system, without permission in writing from the publisher.

To my family who have, as always, shown
their unconditional love and encouragement.

PROLOGUE

*G*rimacing, Colonel Anthony Fitzwilliam flexed his left hand, willing it to return to its former strength. But the wish was futile, for the limb was damaged, its use reduced from what it had once been. Though he had cast aside the sling which had been his constant companion these past weeks, the weakness remained, the return to full strength still nothing more than a distant spot on the horizon.

The sound of a soft chuckle reached his ears, and Fitzwilliam looked up to see his superior watching him, his expression part sympathy, part amusement. "My apologies, Fitzwilliam—I should not laugh. It is simply that I have been in your position, and I understand the frustration."

Fitzwilliam gave him a sour look. General Harold Berger had been Fitzwilliam's direct superior for several years, and a better man one could not find. Though his family was German, the Bergers had lived in England for more than three generations, a respectable, though not prominent, family. General Berger had entered the army as a young man at a low rank and obtained his promotions through the auspices of hard work and military capability. He was one of the few officers of higher rank who deserved the position he held, in Fitzwilliam's estimation. He was also one of the few generals in England who was not a direct scion of a noble family.

"The worst of it," said Fitzwilliam, annoyance welling up within his breast, "is that it happened on a training ground, of all places. I have been to war, I have fought on the peninsula, I have faced the best troops the tyrant has to offer and emerged without a scratch. To be injured in a training exercise is not only humiliating but the height of stupidity."

"Yes, you have informed me of that much," said General Berger, his amusement never dimming. "As I recall, you have also informed me many times that the French could not shoot straight if their lives depended upon it. If that is so, you cannot attribute your survival to any skill on your part, can you?"

Fitzwilliam flashed his superior officer a grin. "When you put it that way, I suppose you must be correct. It does not change the fact, however, that I have been reduced to the role of a spectator while the regiment continues to train around me. It does not sit well with me."

"Again, I am unsurprised," said General Berger. "It is for that reason I asked to speak with you today."

"Oh?" asked Fitzwilliam, feeling a hint of suspicion fall over him.

The general nodded and leaned forward. "You have no doubt heard the rumor of our deployment to Spain?"

"Yes, I have," replied Fitzwilliam. "Is it confirmed?"

"All but confirmed. There is talk from the war office that Wellington intends to make a concerted effort in Spain next year, and he will need fresh men to bolster the armies already in place."

Fitzwilliam nodded and sat back in his chair. "Once more into the breach?"

"Indeed." General Berger regarded him for several moments before he said: "To be honest, my friend, your injury has hampered your regiment's training efforts, which must now be of the utmost priority since we will see battle next year."

"I agree," said Fitzwilliam, looking down at his injured arm with disgust. "Unfortunately, there is little I can do at present until this blasted arm heals."

"Which is the reason for our conversation." The seriousness in the general's voice pricked Fitzwilliam's interest, leading him to wonder if there was not something else afoot. "The truth of the matter is, I have been considering your situation, and now that our deployment is confirmed, I cannot afford to have a colonel who cannot complete his duties. Thus, though it pains me to have to do it, I have little choice but to replace you."

Fitzwilliam frowned—he should have known something of this nature was imminent. There was little to be done, though Fitzwilliam had no desire to be assigned away from these men he had commanded for so long. To send them into battle without leading them himself felt like a betrayal, though Fitzwilliam knew it was not his fault.

"Do you have anyone in mind?"

General Berger nodded and said: "Colonel Warwick has been made available. It is my hope you will assist him in becoming accustomed to his new post before you report to your own new commission."

That surprised Fitzwilliam, for he had not thought he would be reassigned so quickly. "New posting?"

"If you accept it," said the general. He leaned forward and said: "At present, it is clear you are not fit to drill a regiment of regulars, but I believe you will serve with distinction as a commander of the militia."

Fitzwilliam had never been so surprised in his life. "Militia? But I have always been a member of our fighting forces—I have never even considered a life in the militia."

"This I understand, my friend. At present, however, there is little you can do to help us, and that will not change for several months. If you accept this posting in the militia, the enlisted men in that regiment can only benefit from the presence of an honored military veteran, and you can still feel useful. We both know a posting behind a desk would not suit you."

That was true, Fitzwilliam reflected—General Berger knew him well. There was something else at play here, however, and Fitzwilliam was certain he knew what it was.

"I sense my father's hand in this business," said Fitzwilliam, peering at his superior. "Did he request this transfer?"

General Berger chuckled and shook his head. "I informed my superiors you would comprehend the situation at once. Your father is aware of the upcoming deployment and is concerned, and as you have been injured, it was a perfect time for him to intervene."

"I am uncertain I appreciate his interference."

Stiff with anger though Fitzwilliam was, General Berger did not take any notice. "The earl is your sire, Fitzwilliam—of course, he worries for you, and if he is in a position to provide assistance, I do not blame him for an instant."

"It does not look good to the other men."

"No one else knows of it."

"They can guess," retorted Fitzwilliam. "It is no secret that my father is a peer."

"Then let them guess. It is nothing to them."

Fitzwilliam did not wish to agree, but the general did not allow him to protest.

"Let us be frank, Fitzwilliam. You do not need this posting; you have told me of your estate. The men all know your situation does not require you to serve in the army—they all know you do it because of your sense of duty. You have served your country with distinction. Perhaps it is time to pull back, to allow yourself to think in a position which will not require the focus and attention that your current one does. If you do so, it may be you will decide you prefer to allow this chapter of your life to end in favor of the next."

The general's words were powerful. For some time now, Fitzwilliam had found himself fatigued with the way of life he had chosen. Not that he had regretted it—the general was correct about his sense of duty. Fitzwilliam had served willingly and without hesitation. Maybe this posting would help him transition from an officer of His Majesty's army to a gentleman farmer.

"Tell me of the position," said Fitzwilliam at length. "Why is it in need of a commanding officer?"

"Because the previous officer's father called him home when his elder brother died in a hunting accident," replied the general.

"And can the position not be filled from within the ranks of the militia?"

"Of course, it can," said General Berger, his countenance alight with amusement. "If you refuse it, the war office will assign a new militia colonel, as usual."

"Then it is being held for me in particular," replied Fitzwilliam.

General Berger shrugged. "Yes, I suppose it is."

"And where is the regiment stationed at present?"

"Outside a small town in Hertfordshire. The town is called Meryton. It is a market town, like many others, and the local society is filled with small estates and country gentlemen. I would not say there is anything remarkable about it, though it lies only half a day's journey from London."

"The society there is likely to be medieval," said Fitzwilliam, thinking of the woman who had once made such a statement to him. The memory brought Fitzwilliam's thoughts to her brother, and he said: "I wonder if his estate is anywhere nearby."

"You have a friend there?"

Fitzwilliam shook his head. "Bingley is not a friend of mine, though he is a good sort. Rather, he is my cousin's friend, a man descended from a line of tradesmen, now seeking to enter the ranks of the gentry."

"Then I commend your cousin," said the general. "There are many men of society who have not the slightest connection to the peerage and yet disdain men of this Mr. Bingley's lineage."

Knowing General Berger was speaking from experience, Fitzwilliam nodded, saying: "Darcy is a good man, though he can be a little inflexible. Bingley's background does not bother him in the slightest—the content of his character is much more important."

"Then it is possible you will have acquaintances nearby."

Laughing, Fitzwilliam fixed his general with a mock glare. "Desist in your attempts to persuade me, sir! Hertfordshire is a large county—it is not likely Bingley lives near this Meryton at all."

"Perhaps not. From what I have heard, however, it is a pleasant country. It is near Luton on the Great North Road, only a few hours north of London, so it cannot be too savage."

"That is true," replied Fitzwilliam.

"Then you will accept the posting."

Fitzwilliam considered it for a moment, his hesitance prompting him to speak in slow and concise words: "If I should accept and wish to return to the regulars when I am healed, will I be denied?"

"I shall write your recommendation myself," said General Berger with a laugh. "Should you wish to return, I should think there will be generals lining up to bring you into their commands."

"In that case, I shall accept," said Fitzwilliam.

General Berger rose and offered his hand, which Fitzwilliam did not hesitate to grasp. "Though I regret the necessity, I believe you have made the correct decision. Warwick will arrive within three days, and when he has, I should like you to acquaint him with your command. When that is complete, you can report to Meryton and take command of your new regiment. It has been my pleasure to know you, Fitzwilliam."

"Thank you, General," replied Fitzwilliam. "The feeling is very much mutual."

After a few more moments of conversation, Fitzwilliam left the general's office. The first order of business was to speak to his direct subordinates, exemplary men whom it would be a sadness to leave. But while Fitzwilliam regretted he was to go away, a part of him wondered how he would settle into this new regiment, in the less strict environment of the militia.

And he wondered about the town to which he was being dispatched. Then Fitzwilliam decided he would speak to Darcy at the earliest opportunity. If Bingley was close, Fitzwilliam would appreciate the ability to visit the man, for he was a good man, what little Fitzwilliam knew of him.

CHAPTER I

*Y*oung ladies, when anticipating an introduction to another lady of whom they have heard much, will often become excited to the point of unruliness. When those young ladies are prone to such behavior in the first place, it is almost a certainty.

Such was the situation one morning at the estate of Longbourn, home of the Bennet family near Meryton in Hertfordshire. The fact that Longbourn was considered one of the principal estates in the neighborhood was a testament to the dearth of any large estates nearby and not to its own prominence. There was one much larger, but its owner, having inherited the property some years earlier and not having any use for it as a home, had allowed it to sit empty, such that most residents nearby did not much consider it when ranking the nearby properties.

That had all changed the previous summer, for, on a midsummer day, the second of the year's quarter days, a young man of large fortune from the north of England had taken up the lease on the estate. That the man, a Mr. Bingley by name, had not arrived at his residence until August was a matter of much annoyance among the locals. The smallness of the neighborhood, coupled with the fact the rest of the families were established, long-term residents, meant that any addition to or change in their ranks was a matter of much interest and speculation. Thus, while they had all known the gentleman had taken the lease—the local solicitor's wife was among the foremost gossips in the neighborhood—the curiosity of the locals was to remain unsatisfied for six weeks.

When Mr. Bingley finally did arrive, he came alone, though his two sisters soon joined him, accompanied by the eldest sister's husband. Upon being introduced to the man, the neighborhood universally proclaimed him amiable and handsome, a man made even more attractive by the subsequent rumor that he had to his name an income of five thousand a year. Many a young maiden's heart swelled with hope, and most began to scheme how they could attract the young gentleman to admire their charms.

Alas, it was Longbourn's eldest daughter who drew the eye of the gentleman, and within a few weeks, it was widely acknowledged that he had eyes for no other. What the other ladies of the neighborhood thought of that circumstance was unsurprising, and while no one could think ill of such a sweet creature as Miss Jane Bennet, there was envy aplenty.

That morning, however, the young ladies' excitement was for another reason altogether. While Mr. Bingley's sisters, Miss Bingley and Mrs. Hurst, were by now well-known in the neighborhood—though perhaps not universally admired—it was not their arrival which was so anticipated. Word had come, through Mr. Bingley himself, that the sister of one of his close friends, a Miss Georgiana Darcy, was to join the Bingleys at Netherfield. It was also said her brother was to join them some time later, but that business had delayed him. While the coming of *another* wealthy young gentleman might be an occasion for further rejoicing, that event was still far enough distant, and Miss Darcy's arrival, imminent, that it had, as yet, made little impression on the neighborhood.

Miss Elizabeth Bennet, Longbourn's second eldest daughter, was a bright, intelligent young woman of twenty, possessed of a pleasing form and figure, a wealth of dark, chestnut hair, a pretty face, and a pair of the finest dark eyes in the county. The Bennet sisters were all pretty girls, though the middle sister, Mary, was not so blessed as her sisters. That Jane Bennet was the undisputed beauty of the neighborhood had never bothered Elizabeth, for not only had she always had her share of admirers, but her sister was of such a sweet, modest disposition, that no one could be envious of her.

That morning, however, Elizabeth's two youngest sisters were foremost in her mind. Kitty and Lydia were only seventeen and fifteen years of age, and while their elder sisters were proper and demure, if lively and playful in Elizabeth's case, the youngest still had not grown out of their childish boisterousness, a tendency to laugh too loud and long, and an unfortunate penchant to speak when they should be silent. Elizabeth, who took a significant interest in their education and in molding them into creditable young ladies, watched their current behavior with annoyance.

"I wonder what Miss Darcy is like," said Lydia, her voice, as was her wont, at least two levels too loud. "Perhaps she is a haughty young miss, one who will look down on us for our humbler station."

Lydia's partner giggled at her statement. "If she is anything like Miss Bingley, I cannot imagine her being anything other than proud and disagreeable."

Had Kitty's statement not been true, Elizabeth might have stepped in to bring them to order. As it was, however, Elizabeth did not much like Miss Bingley herself, though Jane protested that Miss Bingley had always been kind to *her*. Then again, Jane never thought ill of anyone if she could avoid it.

"If she is a friend of Miss Bingley's," said Lydia amid her giggles, "she must be proud and above her company. I wonder how much dowry a woman must possess before it renders her character unbearable."

"Lydia!" exclaimed Elizabeth, feeling her sister's words had gone too far. "That is enough of that."

While Lydia appeared ready to retort, a look from her mother quelled her outburst. "Lizzy is correct, Lydia. It is gauche to speak of a young lady's dowry, especially when you are not acquainted with her."

"You should also refrain from judging her before you have met her," said Elizabeth with a grateful nod to her mother. "By all accounts, Miss Darcy is not Miss Bingley's particular friend. Rather, *Mr.* Bingley claims Miss Darcy's brother as *his*, meaning she is the sister of his friend. That is a significant difference."

While Lydia still appeared to resent being called to order, she subsided, much to Elizabeth's relief. Though Lydia was not yet out, there were some events she attended, and many opportunities for her to make herself and her sisters look ridiculous. There had been, Elizabeth thought, some slight improvement in her behavior over time, but she also needed much more progress before she would be a credit to the family when in society.

With her mother, Elizabeth had long possessed the closest of relationships, for Elizabeth was the most like her mother in figure and form, though their characters were not at all alike. Mrs. Bennet had not been born a gentlewoman. The daughter of the town's solicitor, she had come to the attention of the master of Longbourn as a girl; drawn to a pretty face coupled with good humor, Mr. Bennet had proposed. It was only after their marriage that Mr. Bennet had realized his wife had not been blessed with the greatest of intelligence or sense.

It might have turned out differently if Mr. Bennet had not spoken to his wife, teaching her what she needed to know about being a gentlewoman and how to behave like one. Mrs. Bennet was a woman who, though she understood her limitations, was a good mistress and good mother for her children, and while she still worried for their futures (the state was entailed to a cousin, a man unknown to them), Mr. Bennet's diligence in ensuring his wife and daughters would have something on which to subsist should the worst happen assured her that while she might suffer a diminution of her status, she would never be unprotected.

Though she had never spoken of it with her mother, Elizabeth had long suspected her mother saw something of Mr. Bennet in her, for while mother and daughter were not at all alike, father and daughter were akin to two peas in a pod, possessing the same intelligence, a similar sense of humor, and similar tastes in literature. Of all her sisters, Elizabeth enjoyed the best relations with her parents, though none of the Bennet sisters had any doubts about the love their parents held for them.

Soon the sound of a carriage approaching the front door interrupted Elizabeth's thoughts and the moment was upon them. Mrs. Bennet arranged the girls as was their custom when visitors arrived, and when the youngest girls settled, they presented the picture of a proper, genteel family. Seeing this, Elizabeth nodded to herself, satisfied their visitors could have nothing about which to complain.

The first sight of Miss Bingley, however, reminded Elizabeth why there was reason to concern herself with the impression they presented to their neighbors. Miss Bingley was a tall, graceful woman, not lacking in feminine attraction, presenting impeccable form and dress every time she ventured into society. It was unfortunate the woman's virtues did not also include a friendliness of manner, a sunny disposition, or a lack of haughtiness. Though Miss Bingley was the daughter of a tradesman and well below anyone in the neighborhood by society's standards, she seemed to consider herself above them by virtue of her twenty-thousand-pound dowry.

By contrast, Mr. Bingley, her brother and the master of Netherfield Park, was a genial, friendly man, eager to please and be pleased, accepting of all and sundry. It was Elizabeth's observation that Mr. Bingley had become enamored with Elizabeth's elder sister, Jane upon first meeting her, for by now, having been in the neighborhood for some weeks, he could not be separated from her for any reason any time they were in the same room with each other.

In a sudden insight, Elizabeth realized that Miss Bingley would not be at Longbourn that morning if she had a choice. It was, no doubt, Mr. Bingley's insistence which brought her here. The notion that the gentleman was firm in his convictions was welcome to Elizabeth, for sometimes comments made within her hearing had suggested that was not always the case.

"Mrs. Bennet," said Mr. Bingley, taking the lead in greeting his nearest neighbors. "How wonderful it is to see you all here today."

"Welcome, Mr. Bingley," said Mrs. Bennet, dropping into a curtsey. "We are, as always, pleased to welcome you to Longbourn."

"Excellent!" declared the enthused gentleman. "We bring a visitor today who wished for an introduction to you."

Gesturing a little behind him, standing between the Bingley sisters—Mr. Bingley's eldest sister, Mrs. Hurst, had also come—the Bennets caught their first sight of a young and diffident woman. She was tall, though not so tall as Miss Bingley, possessed of light, flaxen hair, and when she looked up from the floor, they could see she had bright blue eyes and a pleasant countenance. She also appeared very young.

"Please allow me to introduce Miss Georgiana Darcy," said Miss Bingley, only a hint of displeasure about her mouth betraying her lack of enthusiasm for this task.

Then Miss Bingley named each Bennet in turn and introduced them, after which they settled into their visit. With keen interest, Elizabeth invited the girl to sit next to her, which once again raised Miss Bingley's dander. With nothing she could do, she sat nearby, determined to ensure no Bennet corrupted her guest's sensibilities.

"Miss Darcy," said Elizabeth, "It pleases me to make your acquaintance at last. Miss Bingley has had much to say of you."

"And my brother, Miss Darcy," Miss Bingley interjected, directing a simpering smile at the girl. "Charles has been eager for your coming too."

It was all Elizabeth could do to stifle a laugh at Miss Bingley's blatant attempt to forward her brother as a potential match for Miss Darcy. The exchange also confirmed Elizabeth's initial observation of Miss Darcy's shyness, for the girl blushed and lowered her head, mumbling something which Miss Bingley took for agreement. The woman beamed at Miss Darcy and turned a sneer on Elizabeth. It was a challenge, Elizabeth decided, one she had no intention of accepting.

"I understand you are from the north, Miss Darcy."

"Oh, yes," said Miss Darcy, her head rising as she gazed at Elizabeth with sudden animation. "My brother's estate is called Pemberley, and William says it is the most beautiful place he has ever seen. Though I have not traveled so much as William, I, too, find it lovely."

It seemed there was no subject which Elizabeth could have introduced which was as guaranteed to provoke the girl's response as talk of her home, and for a while, they conversed with perfect civility. Then, when Elizabeth chanced to mention a piece she was learning on the pianoforte, she learned how mistaken she was, for Miss Darcy responded with more animation and vigor. Soon they were talking together like old acquaintances, and by the time the half-hour had passed, Elizabeth was convinced she had gained a lovely young friend. That Kitty and Lydia did not have as much time with Miss Darcy was not palatable to the two girls; it seemed to Elizabeth, Miss Darcy was a girl who did not possess the high spirits of her sisters, and thus she was not so comfortable with them.

"My brother is Mr. Bingley's closest friend," said Miss Darcy not long before they were to depart.

"So we have heard, Miss Darcy," said Elizabeth, showing the girl a wry smile. "Mr. Bingley has spoken of your brother often."

Miss Darcy seemed to understand Elizabeth's humor, for she chuckled a little. Miss Bingley, who had been occupied by Elizabeth's mother, looked at them with no little asperity, but she had no means by which she could extricate herself.

"Mr. Bingley *does* rely on William, but he is an excellent man. What you may not also know is my cousin, Colonel Fitzwilliam, is the new colonel of the local regiment. It was he who escorted me here when he came to take his command."

"Has he?" said Elizabeth, interested to hear this piece of information. "Though we had heard some rumors to the effect that a new colonel had been appointed, we had begun to wonder if there would ever be a replacement for Colonel Forster, for he departed for his father's estate three weeks ago."

"Anthony has long been in the regulars," said Miss Darcy, "but a recent injury has rendered him unfit for battle. He is to command this regiment until he has regained his full health, and then he will report back for another assignment."

"Then I hope to make his acquaintance soon."

"I am certain that will be possible," said Miss Darcy. "The regiment has been much involved with local society, have they not?"

"Too involved of late," replied Elizabeth. "Though the captains are capable men, I do not think they hold as much respect with the men as a colonel would. Your cousin will have an arduous task in restoring discipline ahead of him."

"I know there is nothing Anthony cannot do, for I have every confidence in him. Anthony shares in my brother's guardianship over me; William and I have been close to him a long time."

"Then it is beneficial for you to have such a beloved elder relation so nearby."

Miss Darcy allowed that it was, and soon after, the Bingleys indicated their need to return to their home. As Elizabeth watched Miss Bingley shepherd her party from the room, she did not even consider the woman's eagerness to depart. Instead, Elizabeth was considering the wonderful friend she had made that day, for Miss Darcy was a charming girl. It seemed interesting new people had, indeed, come into the neighborhood, and Elizabeth was anticipating her meeting with the two gentlemen of whom Miss Darcy had spoken. She was certain they would be as interesting as those she had already met.

That afternoon, Fitzwilliam rode for Netherfield, his thoughts of the regiment he now commanded mirroring those Miss Elizabeth Bennet had expressed, though unknowingly. It was not much of a surprise, he supposed, for the regiment had been without a commanding officer for more than long enough to expect discipline to lapse; Fitzwilliam was surprised the situation was not worse than it was. Returning order to his command was a nuisance, though he supposed he should be philosophical and acknowledge it could be worse

In all honesty, he should still be at camp, ensuring his commands were being followed, rather than bound for Netherfield. But Fitzwilliam had promised Darcy when he had brought Georgiana to Hertfordshire that he would not leave her to Miss Bingley's scheming, and Fitzwilliam, sharing in her guardianship, was no more eager to allow Miss Bingley to fill Georgiana's head with her idea of good behavior.

"I suppose a respite will not hurt," said Fitzwilliam to the accompaniment of his horse's canter. "The regiment will not fall apart if I am away for an hour or two."

Jupiter, his horse, nickered at his words, and Fitzwilliam patted the animal's neck. A fine stallion his father had purchased when Fitzwilliam went into the army, they had been through many ordeals together. It had been Jupiter's calmness, not to mention his vicious streak, which had preserved Fitzwilliam from injury or death more than once. He was now more than a mount—more like a close acquaintance or colleague, a friend from whom Fitzwilliam could never imagine being parted.

As the estate rose in the distance above the tops of the trees, Fitzwilliam considered the place. It was an excellent property, he decided, just what Bingley needed to become accustomed to managing an estate. Fitzwilliam had no notion that Bingley would settle here, but there was nothing the matter with the neighborhood.

When Fitzwilliam arrived in front of the manor, he threw the reins to a stable hand, instructing him as to Jupiter's care, and strode into the house. There the reminder of the drawback residing at the estate greeted him almost as soon as he entered.

"Anthony!" exclaimed Georgiana upon seeing him stride into the room. In her manner was an unmistakable sense of relief for his presence, the reason for which was, of course, Miss Bingley's presence by her side. Fitzwilliam refrained from scowling, knowing this was why Darcy had asked him to look in on his precious sister.

"Hello, Georgiana," said Fitzwilliam, accepting her embrace. "It seems you have emerged from your first brush with Meryton society unscathed. You were to visit one of the local estates today, were you not?"

"Fitzwilliam!" exclaimed a voice behind them.

Turning, Fitzwilliam accepted Bingley's hearty handshake in greeting, noting the man was in an ebullient mood. Given what Fitzwilliam had heard of his interest in a young lady of the neighborhood—from the man himself—Fitzwilliam was not surprised.

"The Bennets were wonderful, Cousin," said Georgiana, returning Fitzwilliam's attention to her. "There are five daughters, Cousin. Five! Though I only spoke with one of them for the most part, I found them all friendly and obliging. I hope that we shall become excellent friends."

"And the one with whom you spoke at length?" asked Fitzwilliam, denying Miss Bingley the opportunity to say something caustic.

"Miss Elizabeth is so friendly!" cried Georgiana. "We talked about Pemberley and music, and she is ever so intelligent and amusing!"

"It is no shock she wished to speak of Pemberley," said Miss Bingley, seeming eager to speak. "She can see that you are a young lady of quality, and she has heard of your brother's coming. Mark my words, Georgiana—she means to attract Mr. Darcy's attention by whatever means necessary."

So caught up in her diatribe was Miss Bingley that she did not notice the look exchanged between cousins. The woman's words were nothing less than a faithful representation of herself, but she was not self-aware enough to recognize it.

"Upon my word, you are harsh, Caroline," exclaimed Bingley. "The Bennet family is genteel and not in the habit of chasing after men. I cannot imagine a less faithful portrayal of a young woman as what you have just said."

"What of Miss Bennet's pursuit of you?" demanded Miss Bingley of her brother.

Bingley shook his head. "That is an even less accurate account. Miss Bennet is everything good. To say she has chased after me is ridiculous. I must wonder if you have had your eyes open at all when in her company."

"The fact is that Miss Bennet is not suitable."

"In what way can you consider her unsuitable?"

"She is naught but the daughter of a country gentleman," snapped Miss Bingley.

"And *we* are nothing but the scions of a line of tradesmen," rejoined Bingley, causing his sister to gasp. "Our father was not ashamed of what he was, Caroline, and you should not forget about our heritage either."

"Charles," said Miss Bingley with exaggerated patience, "the salient point is our father wished us to join the ranks of the landed."

"A process I have begun."

Flashing a glare of impatience, Miss Bingley replied: "It is a good start, but nothing more. Miss Bennet is a sweet girl, but she cannot assist us to gain standing in society."

"If I cared about such things," said Bingley, "I might agree with you."

Miss Bingley attempted to protest, but Bingley interrupted, saying:

"At present, this conversation is premature, Caroline, for I have not known Miss Bennet long enough to understand if I wish to make her an offer. But know this: if I decide I *do* wish to offer for her, I shall; all your displeasure will not prevent me. Even the notoriously fastidious Fitzwilliam Darcy will find nothing amiss with Miss Bennet—and the entire family—and if he did, it would not cause me a moment's concern."

"Sensible, as always, Bingley!" said Fitzwilliam, amused at the direction the conversation had taken and how the warring siblings had forgotten about their audience. "I believe I wish to meet these people when the chance permits. They sound like an excellent family!"

"They are!" said Georgiana and Bingley in tandem.

Miss Bingley, seeing she was outnumbered, scowled at them all. But then, as if her displeasure had been nothing more than their imagination, she shifted to a simpering smile.

"I should think you will agree with me once you meet them, Colonel Fitzwilliam."

"That is possible, I suppose," replied Fitzwilliam. "However, given what I am hearing from Georgiana and your brother, I cannot imagine finding them anything other than people worthy of knowing."

"Surely you would not wish for your cousin, for example, to be taken in by people of base natures! Yet that very thing is what I am trying to protect my brother against."

The wide-eyed credulity with which the woman spoke did not mislead Fitzwilliam. Far from it. While he might have wished to laugh at her stupidity, he forced himself to answer with honesty.

"On the contrary, Miss Bingley," Fitzwilliam enjoyed the manner in which her face fell, though it was not gentlemanly, "should Darcy fall in love with one of the Bennet sisters, I could do nothing but support him. Though my family has done what we can to support our near relations, I understand Darcy is lonely and in want of the companionship only a wife could bring. Should he find it, I will applaud."

The sickly green cast to Miss Bingley's countenance was more fuel for Fitzwilliam's amusement, though he fought hard to avoid laughing. Then the woman said: "Mr. Darcy's happiness is paramount, to be sure. Now, if you will excuse me, I should see to dinner."

When the woman left the room, a grinning Bingley turned to him and said: "I thought Caroline would faint when you spoke of your cousin and one of the Bennet sisters."

"You have my apologies, Bingley," said Fitzwilliam, his grin anything but contrite, "but I had no intention of offending your sister."

Bingley shook his head. "I have tried to tell Caroline that Darcy has no interest in her, but she will not listen. Perhaps this visit will make it clear to her in a way even she cannot misunderstand."

"It would be best if she learned it without delay," replied Fitzwilliam. "She is wasting her time with Darcy. Now, I would appreciate the opportunity to meet these sisters of whom you speak, but my duties are heavy at present, for the regiment requires discipline."

"Did you not receive an invitation to Sir William's soiree three nights hence?" asked Bingley. "If you have not, it would surprise me. Sir William is not the sort to exclude anyone from his parties."

"Ah, yes, I remember Captain Carter mentioning something of that nature. Then we shall attend, and I shall count on you both to introduce me. Who knows? I might find my future wife among the Bennet sisters."

Laughter was Georgiana's response. "How you jest, Cousin. Given the size of the estate, I cannot imagine any of the Bennets has a dowry you require in your future wife."

"You forget, Georgiana," replied Fitzwilliam, enjoying their jesting, "with Thorndell, I can choose a woman of less means. If she is special enough, I may just settle for a close relationship with a poor woman, rather than the riches of a cold one."

"A man after my own heart," said Bingley. "Stay for dinner, Fitzwilliam. I should like to exchange stories of what I would like in a wife. If nothing else, it will annoy my sister."

The three laughed and Fitzwilliam accepted. Bingley, he was discovering, was a man whose company Fitzwilliam could enjoy as much as his cousin did. Though this posting still irked him, Fitzwilliam was enjoying himself in Hertfordshire. There were many worse places in which he could find himself, including on the front lines facing down French bayonets.

CHAPTER II

*O*n the day of the party at Lucas Lodge, the Bennet family traveled
the short distance to their near neighbors, the Lucases, and were
welcomed in the manner of friends of longstanding. The family
was one not born to the status of the gentry; the patriarch, Sir William,
having gained his knighthood upon giving an address to the king, had
moved his family into their current dwelling with the money and
notoriety which had come from that venture. Sir William was a hearty,
kind man, one who took it upon himself to be the leader of the
community in civility; society was his delight, and he often treated
others to boasts of his exploits in St. James's Court. His wife was a
similar character, a woman who delighted in gossip and was mean of
understanding. Between Lady Lucas and Mrs. Bennet existed a firm
friendship, though Mrs. Bennet possessed enough sense to avoid
gossip.

Of children, they had five, two daughters and three sons, and while
two of the sons and one daughter were younger—Maria being Lydia's
age—Elizabeth was well acquainted with the elder two. Samuel, a few
years older, was often absent, for his interest in society was akin to his
father's, though he craved that of a higher level. The eldest child,
Charlotte, was a few years Elizabeth's senior, and Elizabeth's closest

friend other than Jane. It was Charlotte who welcomed Elizabeth that evening, full of smiles and exclamations of delight.

"Lizzy! I am so happy to see you!"

"As I am to see you," replied Elizabeth.

The two women fell into a conversation that consisted of their recent doings, as they had not met in some days. It was then that Elizabeth informed her friend of meeting the newest resident of Netherfield and her knowledge of the new colonel of the regiment. To say her foreknowledge impressed Charlotte was an understatement.

"I am all astonishment, Lizzy!" said Charlotte. "I knew of the young lady's coming to Netherfield and of the new colonel of the regiment, but my father could find nothing of the connection between them."

Elizabeth laughed. "It is rare, indeed, that something is known in Meryton which was not first discovered by your father."

"It is interesting that this Miss Darcy was first seen at Longbourn to visit *you*, Lizzy."

Frowning, Elizabeth said: "I cannot understand why. Why would it mean anything at all?"

"That is what confuses me," said Charlotte. "Had she been Mr. Bingley's sister, it would be obvious, given the admiration the gentleman shows to Jane."

"That is true," replied Elizabeth. "Perhaps that is all it is. As Mr. Bingley admires Jane, he wishes to promote her to all his friends. In Miss Darcy's own words, Miss Darcy's brother has long been one of Mr. Bingley's closest friends."

At that moment, the Bingley party's arrival interrupted their conversation and Elizabeth had all the pleasure of introducing her new friend to the old. The two ladies expressed their pleasure and stood speaking for some moments. Then, Charlotte's mother called her away to see to some task, leaving Elizabeth alone with Miss Darcy.

"I am pleased to renew our acquaintance, Miss Darcy," said Elizabeth.

"As am I, Miss Elizabeth," said Miss Darcy. "Though Mrs. Annesley is wonderful, she is a companion, not a young woman with whom I can converse with no restraint."

"And this you do not find at Netherfield?" asked Elizabeth with a laugh. "With Miss Bingley and Mrs. Hurst in residence, I would think there would be many opportunities for lively conversation."

Miss Darcy blushed, but she ventured: "Miss Bingley *is* attentive, but she is not what I would term a friend. Her brother is my brother's friend — that is the only connection between us."

"I dare say Miss Bingley would not appreciate that characterization," observed Elizabeth, at the same time noticing the sour look the woman in question was giving them.

"Perhaps she would not," replied Miss Darcy. "But it is the truth, nonetheless."

Miss Darcy paused and glanced about to see if there was anyone near enough to overhear. Seeing no one, she leaned close to Elizabeth and added: "Though Miss Bingley has attempted to induce me to keep this neighborhood at arms' length, I am pleased to have found many friends. It will be a great relief when my brother arrives."

Though Elizabeth smiled to acknowledge her friend's declaration, she decided it politic to change the subject. "Do you expect your brother soon?"

"William may come as early as next week," replied Miss Darcy. "There is some business that prevented him from coming before now, but I expect it will be completed soon."

With a nod, Elizabeth introduced another topic and they began to speak of other matters. Pleased with each other's company, they stood together for some time. Others came and went, some to beg an introduction, some to speak with her, while Miss Bingley attempted to draw Miss Darcy away twice. Miss Darcy, however, refused to be parted from Elizabeth's side.

"When you came to Longbourn, you mentioned your interest in the pianoforte?" asked Elizabeth when the subject of music arose.

"I enjoy playing, but my talents are not at all out of the common way."

"Do not let her mislead you," interjected Miss Bingley, who was close enough to hear them speak. "Miss Darcy's performance on the pianoforte is divine. I have rarely heard better."

With her eyes, Miss Darcy pleaded for Elizabeth to leave the subject alone, and taking pity on her friend, Elizabeth changed it. "In my family, Mary and I are the only ones who play to any great extent. Jane can play a little, but Kitty and Lydia claim they have no aptitude."

"Have you had access to masters?" sneered Miss Bingley, her tone showing how unlikely she seemed to think it was.

"We have," replied Elizabeth, not allowing the woman to ruin her good cheer. "I shall not call my performance capital, for I do not take enough time to practice. But Mary and I have both had masters to aid us."

It seemed to Elizabeth that Miss Bingley regarded her with a hint more respect, though her understated snort of disdain suggested otherwise. The woman then moved away, disgusted she could not draw Miss Darcy away for her own purposes. When they were alone again, Miss Darcy looked back at Elizabeth with some relief.

"Thank you, Elizabeth." Then she gasped and put a hand over her mouth.

"It would please me if we referred to each other by our Christian names, Miss Darcy. If you are agreeable."

With a shy smile, Georgiana agreed. "Miss Bingley praises me to the skies whenever she has the chance. I believe I have some skill, but I cannot bear her fawning, which I know is nothing more than the desire to get my brother's good opinion and secure a proposal from him."

Elizabeth could not stop the laugh which bubbled up in her breast. "That seems like a strange way to go about inducing a proposal."

"Then you know little of London society," said Georgiana. "Though I am not even out yet, I have seen it many times."

"If it were me," said Elizabeth, "I would prefer a gentleman propose to me because he cannot resist me. I do not know why anyone would think praising a man's sister might be a way to his heart."

The giggle with which Georgiana replied indicated her agreement. "Nor do I, Elizabeth. Nor do I."

"There shall be entertainment this evening I should expect," said Elizabeth, turning the conversation back to the previous subject. "Shall you amaze us all with your exceptional skill and taste?"

The look of panic which came over her friend's face surprised Elizabeth, though, given the girl's shyness, Elizabeth supposed it should not have. "Oh, please say nothing to our hosts. I could not possibly play before all these people."

"Of course, you need not if you do not wish it," soothed Elizabeth. "Charlotte, however, will insist I do my part, for she seems to have some perverse need to see me make a fool of myself in front of everyone."

"I am certain your playing shall be perfectly lovely," replied Georgiana.

About this time the members of the militia regiment began entering the room, having arrived some time later than Elizabeth might have expected. At their head was a tall man with an erect bearing, broad of shoulder and a pleasant, though not handsome countenance. Sir William greeted them as was his wont, and the officers dispersed to the various corners of the room. The tall man looked about and spying the girl by Elizabeth's side, said something to Sir William and approached them with a wide grin.

"Hello, Sprite," said he to Georgiana, catching her up in an embrace. "I see you have made yourself at home here."

"Anthony!" hissed she, though her annoyance was betrayed as feigned by the grin with which she regarded him. "You will ruin my pretensions of maturity with such displays!"

"Ah, I should never wish to do that," replied he. Then he turned to Elizabeth, his manner expectant.

"Anthony," said she, turning to Elizabeth, "may I present my friend, Miss Elizabeth Bennet. Elizabeth, this is my cousin, Colonel Anthony Fitzwilliam. Though he gives the impression of a reprobate, my cousin was assigned to the dragoons, and has been transferred here to command the local regiment."

Elizabeth curtseyed to the gentleman's bow, noting the aspect of good humor in his countenance. "I am pleased to make your acquaintance, sir. Georgiana has spoken almost as much of you as she has of her brother."

"Ah," said Colonel Fitzwilliam, winking at his cousin, "it seems I am forever second in her affections."

"Is it not natural? After all, you are only her cousin."

"That will not induce me to cease trying to be first!"

They laughed together, Elizabeth appreciating the man's wit and amiability. The colonel, Elizabeth soon decided, was a man of Mr. Bingley's ilk, though he was more playful, and, at the same time, more serious than the other gentleman. That he was intelligent Elizabeth understood at once, but his ability to charm soon disarmed her, and she found herself enjoying his company.

"I must own, sir," said Elizabeth after some minutes in his company, "that I am surprised at you."

"Oh?" asked Colonel Fitzwilliam, catching her jesting tone. "Why is that?"

"Because I have it on good intelligence that you are the son of an earl. Should you not disdain us all as unsuitable, provincial, and uncouth?"

Colonel Fitzwilliam guffawed and exclaimed: "If you wish for *that* sort of behavior, you must wait for my cousin to arrive, for he is accounted as haughty, while I am agreeable to all."

"Anthony!" exclaimed Georgiana swatting at him. "William is everything amiable."

"Once you come to know him, Cousin," said Colonel Fitzwilliam, clearly unrepentant. "When first introduced, Darcy is uncomfortable among strangers and has difficulty making a good impression."

"Now I must meet him," said Elizabeth. "Perhaps I can induce him to smile where few have succeeded before."

"If anyone can it is you," replied Georgiana, while Colonel Fitzwilliam fixed her with an interested look.

"Yes, perhaps you can," added Colonel Fitzwilliam. Then he grinned and said: "I would not have you believe Darcy is a man given to airs, Miss Bennet. He can be taciturn at times, but he does not mean to give offense. Whether or not he means it, often offense follows him, for he *is* uncomfortable in company he does not know."

"Then I shall refrain from convicting him," said Elizabeth. "But I shall reiterate my eagerness to meet him. If he is anything like his sister, I am certain he will be an acquaintance well worth knowing. Now, Colonel, you have not informed me of your impressions of the militia. Having served in the regulars, it must be very different."

"That is true," replied Colonel Fitzwilliam. "The militia is very different."

"In what way?" asked Elizabeth, interested to hear his perspective.

"For one, it is not as . . ." the colonel paused and smiled. "Well, serious, I suppose though that is not quite it either. To understand you must remember that the purpose of the regular army is to go to battle an enemy. The militia is tasked only with the defense of the homeland, though in that, they also share the duty with certain elements of the regulars."

"I can understand how that might be different and 'serious,' as you put it," replied Elizabeth.

The colonel nodded. "I would not have you believe the men I command are inferior. It is a different sort of man, to be certain, but the officers I command are estimable." Colonel Fitzwilliam paused and winked, saying: "I would want them to acquire much seasoning before I would wish to put them in command of any men going to battle."

Elizabeth could see how that would be desirable; she had thought herself that the officers known to them were pleasing in general, but many seemed more like boys with little experience.

"And the fighting soldiers?"

At this question, Colonel Fitzwilliam grimaced a little. "Yes, well, the fighting men need much training."

In this vein they continued to speak, the colonel giving Elizabeth some insight into the workings of the militia regiment. Elizabeth found the matter interesting, for none of them had ever met many men who were true soldiers who had seen battle. The colonel's accounts reminded Elizabeth that it may be best to take what she had learned and inform Kitty and Lydia, who were unabashed in their admiration of the militia, that these soldiers in their midst were not the battle-hardened veterans they imagined them to be.

A little later, Elizabeth was witness to Colonel Fitzwilliam's brand of discipline. Though the officers had been well behaved in most settings where Elizabeth had met them, at times they became a little too rowdy, their laughter a little more raucous than was advisable. That evening was just such an occasion.

The sound of their laughter and the sight of several officers speaking with several young ladies of the neighborhood caught the colonel's attention. Lydia and Kitty were not among them, Elizabeth noted with relief — her sisters were not far away with their mother in close attendance and were talking with admirable composure to another pair of officers. When another burst of laughter along with the obvious flirting of one of his men caught his further attention, Colonel Fitzwilliam excused himself.

"Pardon me, Miss Elizabeth, but it seems I must impart some of that seasoning I mentioned."

With a bow, the colonel stepped away, and within moments, the sound of his voice reached them. "Watson, Davies, I see you are making the acquaintance of the local ladies."

The officers in question straightened at the sight of their commanding officer. Though Elizabeth could not hear their reply, Colonel Fitzwilliam nodded and smiled at them.

"Will you introduce me?"

The introductions proceeded and the colonel spoke charmingly with those young ladies, though she could see he was taking care to include his officers. Elizabeth's heart swelled with respect for this jovial gentleman, for it seemed he wore command like a well-fitting glove and knew what to do in any situation.

"Well, Elizabeth?" asked Georgiana, drawing her attention back. "What do you think of my cousin?"

"He seems like an excellent man," said Elizabeth with no hint of exaggeration. "The way he handled his officers was masterful."

"Anthony has always said it does no good to humiliate his subordinates in front of others. Later, when they are alone, he will have a word with them, warning them about their behavior, and that will be the end of the matter."

Elizabeth nodded. "Yes, I can see how that would be effective." Not having known Colonel Forster well, Elizabeth could not speak to his style of discipline, but Colonel Fitzwilliam's actions made it clear he would tolerate no misbehavior among his officers. It boded well for the stay of the militia in the neighborhood, for they had all heard stories of the havoc a company of militia could wreak on a small community.

A little later, Charlotte came to chivvy Elizabeth to the pianoforte, and while Georgiana giggled at Elizabeth's raised eyebrow, she spoke of her eagerness to hear Elizabeth's performance and shooed her away. Not unwilling to perform for the company, Elizabeth agreed and soon began to play.

Whatever Miss Bingley had to say about the local society, Fitzwilliam decided that it was more hyperbole than the truth. Take the Bennet family, for example. While Fitzwilliam had spoken to Mr. Bennet for only a few moments, he saw nothing objectionable in the man. Mrs. Bennet was lovely, both as a woman, though she was five and forty if she was a day, and in her behavior, which was gracious and welcoming. The girls were all lively except for Mary, who seemed more like Darcy than her sisters. Miss Elizabeth, in particular, was a delight.

Further provoking Fitzwilliam's approval was the young lady who he had learned was Miss Elizabeth's closest friend. Though Miss Lucas was not as animated as the second Bennet sister, she was sensible and interesting, and Fitzwilliam enjoyed the few moments he spoke with her. After a time together, she excused herself, leaving Fitzwilliam standing alone, watching Miss Elizabeth as she played the second of her songs.

"Well, Colonel Fitzwilliam," said a voice by his side, "have you come to my way of thinking yet? Of course, you must! For who, having known excellent society, cannot agree when witnessing this spectacle?"

Years as a soldier honing nerves of iron prevented Fitzwilliam from jumping at the sudden sound of a voice in his ear. Miss Bingley—for it was she—stood a little behind him, regarding him with that little sardonic smirk she often used. Then she turned and glanced about, her gaze raking over those present before her eyes found him again, eyebrow raised in challenge.

"There is, I suppose," said Fitzwilliam, "something of a countrified air about most of them, for most here do not move in the circles to which I am accustomed."

Miss Bingley's smile widened at this evidence of his agreement.

Seeing this, Fitzwilliam returned her smile, though understated, and added: "But there is no harm in them. If you travel enough, Miss Bingley, you will find that most small country societies are similar. It would take behavior far more egregious than this to induce me to call them uncouth."

The smile running away from Miss Bingley's face, she sniffed and looked about, her eyes coming to rest on the performer. Fitzwilliam glanced over, noted that Miss Elizabeth's song had ended, prompting the applause of the company. She smiled and thanked them, and then turned the instrument over to Miss Mary, who began to play in her stead.

"Yes, it has seemed to me you have favored Miss Elizabeth tonight." The woman laughed, a harsh sound, and said: "Can it be that you have found your future wife in this insignificant speck of a town?"

Fitzwilliam laughed at her sally, saying: "That is amusing, Miss Bingley, for it proves how soon a woman entertains thoughts of matrimony. I like Miss Elizabeth very well, indeed, for she is a bright light. But while I have not known her long, I believe I may state with no hesitation that I do not believe she would be right for me."

"I cannot but find your reply sensible," said Miss Bingley, seeming to believe she had scored a significant victory.

"Perhaps it is," said Fitzwilliam with a shrug. "There is nothing the matter with Miss Elizabeth, and should something develop between us, I suspect we would do very well together.

"The more I think about it, however, the more I suspect Darcy would find her irresistible."

It was a musing comment, one he had made without thinking about in advance. Miss Bingley was horrified, her face turning chalk-white at the thought. The sight diverted Fitzwilliam, but he did not wish to torment the woman, though her behavior was, at times, more predatory than demure.

"That is nothing more than nonsense," said she, her tone sharper than he thought she had intended. "Mr. Darcy has far more sense than to entangle himself with someone of Miss Elizabeth's ilk."

"You speak of her as if she is a scullery maid, Miss Bingley," said Fitzwilliam, fixing her with a significant look. "Though Meryton is a small community and I doubt she spends much time in town, she is a gentleman's daughter, with all the status that entails. Do not make the mistake of believing her unworthy because she does not make frequent appearances in London's sitting-rooms. To many—Darcy included—that would be an advantage rather than a detriment."

"I see," said Miss Bingley, though it was clear she did not.

The way Miss Bingley was glaring now at Miss Elizabeth — who was currently speaking with Captain Carter — Fitzwilliam wondered if he had just done his new acquaintance a disservice. Then again, Fitzwilliam had every confidence in Miss Elizabeth's ability to defend herself against the likes of Miss Bingley. Perhaps it was kinder to be cruel for the moment and point out the flaws in her thinking.

"I cannot speak for Darcy, Miss Bingley," said Fitzwilliam, pulling her attention back to him. "But I will remind you I know my cousin better than any man alive. Yes, I suspect Darcy will enjoy Miss Elizabeth's company, for she is intelligent and interesting, something Darcy claims he does not find often in young society ladies. If nothing else, she has some of the finest eyes I have ever seen, and I suspect Darcy will agree with me."

"That is interesting, Colonel Fitzwilliam," said the woman, projecting false joviality. "I would never have imagined it."

Miss Bingley stepped away, leaving Fitzwilliam watching after her, wondering what he could do to prevent her from making a fool of herself. Not that she was entirely reprehensible — on the contrary, there were some definite benefits to her situation. But there were also drawbacks. Had she not been so intent upon climbing society's ladder, Fitzwilliam might have considered pursuing her himself, for her dowry would be a welcome addition to his coffers when he took up the reins of his estate. But her occasional nastiness was not an attractive trait, nor was her tendency to denigrate others to bolster her image.

"What did you say to Miss Bingley, Cousin?" asked Georgiana as she approached him, scattering his thoughts asunder. "I dare say she fled from you with her tail between her legs, and is, even now, sitting with her sister looking about as if everyone in the room has mortally offended her."

A glance at Miss Bingley proved his cousin's words, and Fitzwilliam could not help but grin at the sight. "Yes, she appears to be less than amused. But then again, she always appears that way, does she not?"

"I suppose she does," said Georgiana, "though her glares at Elizabeth have increased in intensity. Did you say something to her to provoke such a response?"

"Yes, Georgiana," said Fitzwilliam, giving his young cousin a rueful smile. "I am afraid I did. In a moment of inattention, I informed her that I thought Darcy will admire Miss Elizabeth when he meets her. You can imagine how she would have taken that assertion."

"William and Miss Elizabeth?" asked Georgiana, seeming dumbfounded. "William never pays attention to *any* woman."

"That is true," said Fitzwilliam with a low chuckle. "But consider that William always claims that young ladies possess little intelligence and less ability to speak of matters of any interest. Can you ascribe either failing to Miss Elizabeth?"

"No," said Georgiana, deep in thought.

"Then add her lively character and her beautiful eyes and you have a recipe for an attachment on Darcy's side, at least. Whether Miss Elizabeth would like Darcy, I cannot say as I have only met her today. But I cannot think she would be indifferent to him."

Georgiana did not reply to Fitzwilliam's assertion, and soon she had taken up a position beside Miss Elizabeth and began speaking with her again. Fitzwilliam considered what he should do when Darcy arrived. His cousin would see through any attempt to induce him to take a liking to the lady and would balk. But perhaps a little subtle praising of the woman's virtues would induce his cousin to consider her through eyes unprejudiced. Suddenly, Fitzwilliam could not wait for Darcy to arrive.

CHAPTER III

A few days after the party at Lucas Lodge, a note arrived from Netherfield. It was addressed to Jane, and, as their mother remarked, had been written in a very elegant hand. When Jane opened the missive, she smiled with pleasure.

"It is from Miss Bingley. She has invited Lizzy and me to Netherfield for dinner tonight."

"Both of us?" asked Elizabeth with some surprise. "I had the distinct impression at Lucas Lodge that she did not much care for me, for her behavior turned cold, though I could not understand why."

"I saw nothing of it, Lizzy. Either way, the invitation includes us both."

Of course, Jane would see nothing of it, for she was inclined to see the best in others. Elizabeth knew her sister was not a simpleton, nor was she unobservant. However, Jane believed others were good, and she little liked it when poor behavior was proven to her. It was the one trait of her sister's which both delighted Elizabeth and exasperated her.

"I suppose," said Mr. Bennet, regarding his two eldest daughters with affection, "that you will wish for me to send for the coach."

"Of course, they must go by coach," said Mrs. Bennet. "It looks like rain outside, and though I know Lizzy would prefer to walk, I cannot have my daughters appear at Netherfield looking like vagabonds."

"Yes, that would be inadvisable, indeed," said Mr. Bennet, winking at Elizabeth. "Then I suppose you must bow to your parents' great wisdom and travel in our poor carriage, Lizzy."

"Oh, Papa," said Elizabeth, shaking her head at his teasing. "I like to walk, but you know I should never answer an invitation such as this with an intention to traverse there on my own feet."

"I should be quite put out with you if you did!" exclaimed Mrs. Bennet, showing a hint of that excitable nature she sometimes displayed. "I have taught my daughters better than that, Mr. Bennet—please remember that."

"Never would I have suggested anything different, Mrs. Bennet," replied the master, fixing his wife with a fond look. "Our girls are both well-mannered and beautiful, and I dare say none of them have ever done anything to embarrass us. We are as blessed as anyone in the district."

Nothing he said could have drawn greater approval from Mrs. Bennet, for she was proud of her progeny and took great satisfaction that she had produced the most beautiful girls in the neighborhood. With a shake of her head, Elizabeth exchanged a look with Jane and rose from the table, their breakfast completed.

That afternoon, as they prepared to depart, Mrs. Bennet came to Elizabeth's room to speak to her. As was her wont, she spent a few moments fussing over Elizabeth's appearance, adjusting her dress or inspecting her hair, but when she finished, she nodded with satisfaction.

"You look wonderful, my dear. There is little doubt you and Jane will represent our family well."

"Is there ever any occasion in which we do not?" asked Elizabeth.

"No, there you are correct. You both are wonderful girls—as good as any who have graced rooms finer than anything Netherfield can boast."

Mrs. Bennet paused and chewed her lip for a moment, and then fixed Elizabeth with a wry smile. "It seems to me—though I would not injure you by supposing you, my most perceptive daughter, have not noticed it—that Miss Bingley does not favor our family."

With a sigh, Elizabeth nodded. "I have noticed, Mama. Not only is she supercilious and even nasty at times, but I noted her particular disgust for me at the party at Lucas Lodge."

Mrs. Bennet huffed. "The woman has a very high opinion of herself.

It shows a lack of understanding; it is difficult to imagine that she considers herself higher than the daughters of a gentleman."

"Wealth gives those who possess it all the leave they require to think meanly of others. I have heard it said that Miss Bingley possesses a handsome dowry."

"It is nothing compared to what your friend, Miss Darcy, possesses, or so I have heard."

"Which proves that wealth does not always provoke great pride," replied Elizabeth.

Mrs. Bennet nodded. "Then I shall trust you to support your sister, for Jane will see nothing untoward in Miss Bingley's behavior."

With a sigh, knowing it was true, Elizabeth nodded and kissed her mother's cheek, promising to support Jane against Miss Bingley should it be necessary. A few moments later, the sisters had boarded the Bennet carriage for the brief journey to Netherfield.

At Netherfield, the three ladies greeted them, though it appeared the gentlemen were not present. Mrs. Hurst was as detached as she ever was, greeting them with perfect politeness but no warmth, whereas Georgiana was the opposite, her eager greetings testifying to her delight at seeing them. For her part, Miss Bingley watched them, though Elizabeth could not decide if she thought Miss Bingley expected them to ask after the gentlemen. If she expected it, she was to be disappointed. She did not mention their absence, and Elizabeth and Jane were too polite to ask after them. Thus, it was from Georgiana that Elizabeth learned the reason for their nonattendance.

"Mr. Bingley and Mr. Hurst are attending dinner with the officers tonight," said Georgiana when they seated themselves together in Netherfield's sitting-room. "My cousin invited them the day after the Lucas Lodge party."

The implications of the invitation to dine, the very day the gentlemen were to be absent, were clear at once to Elizabeth. She thought Georgiana understood herself, for she darted a quick look at the sisters, who were speaking with Jane, before turning back to Elizabeth.

"It has seemed to me that Miss Bingley has anticipated this evening greatly, though I cannot say what she expects to happen. I cannot accuse her of ulterior motives, but something in her behavior is not what I would expect."

"Perhaps she wishes to know us better," said Elizabeth, attempting diplomacy. "When Mr. Bingley is together with my sister, neither has any attention for anyone else."

Georgiana laughed, drawing Miss Bingley's attention — and her sneer at Elizabeth. "Yes, I suppose you must be correct." Then Georgiana's countenance turned serious again. "I hope, however, you are not as trusting as your sister appears to be, Elizabeth. I do not accuse Miss Bingley of anything specific, but some of the comments I have heard these past few days tell me she is not a friend to her brother's interest in your sister."

"That, my dear Georgiana, I have known since almost the first moment of our acquaintance."

The five ladies stayed in this attitude for some time, and while Elizabeth received annoyed glances from Miss Bingley from time to time — for it appeared the lady liked her friendship with Georgiana no better than she had before — she appeared to concentrate more on Jane than Elizabeth. Enjoying her conversation with Georgiana as she did, Elizabeth attempted to take little notice of Miss Bingley.

"It is now definite that my brother will arrive next week," said Georgiana after they had been sitting together for some time.

Elizabeth smiled at her young friend. "You must anticipate his arrival very much."

"I do," confirmed Georgiana. "My brother is the best of men, you see, and I am very fond of him. William is not a voluble man — in many ways he is much like I am." Georgiana's countenance attained a hint of a blush. "He has much more confidence than I have ever possessed. Once you come to know him, however, I am certain you will see him in the same light as I do."

"With such recommendation as this," said Elizabeth, amused at Georgiana's hero-like worship of her brother, "I cannot wait to meet him. Perhaps we can, between us, assist Mr. Darcy in becoming more comfortable with the neighborhood."

A beaming smile was Georgiana's response, followed by an emphatically stated: "Yes, that is it. With your ability to make everyone about you comfortable, I cannot imagine it is beyond your ability to assist my brother too."

Elizabeth laughed. "Then I shall do my best, Georgiana, for I would not wish him to find us all wanting."

While they remained in the sitting-room before dinner, Georgiana continued to speak of her brother. Had it come from Miss Bingley, Elizabeth might have considered another motive for the excessive praise which Georgiana lavished on her brother. In her friend, however, Elizabeth could see a devotion one often saw in a younger sibling for one much older, and as such, she listened to Georgiana's account; if even half of what Georgiana said was true, Mr. Darcy must be a fine man, indeed.

A little later, they were called in to dinner. It had been, Elizabeth expected, ordered with an eye toward making an impression—or perhaps overwhelming what she considered her simpler guests—for Miss Bingley's meal was of three courses. Elizabeth, seeing this and noting Georgiana's amusement, fixed her friend with an amused grin and a roll of her eyes. Then Miss Bingley's conversation became intrusive, proving Elizabeth's suspicions.

"I understand you do not have much family, Miss Bennet," said the woman after the servants had cleared the soup away and placed the second course before them.

"And I have heard that you have a large one," said Elizabeth, deflecting the woman's inquisition with a grin. "Or I believe I heard Mrs. Hurst speak of cousins, aunts, uncles, and all sorts of other Bingley relations."

"That is true," said Mrs. Hurst, much to her sister's exasperation. "Our father had four brothers reach adulthood, and my mother's family is, likewise, large. There are so many that it is sometimes difficult to keep track of them all."

"That must be wonderful," said Georgiana, a wistful note in her voice. "While the Darcy family have connections aplenty, we have few near relations. Our nearest Darcy family is several generations removed, and my mother only had two siblings—my uncle, the earl, and my aunt, who lives in Kent."

"It is sometimes a blessing and sometimes a curse," said Mrs. Hurst with a fond look at Georgiana. "Though I can understand why you would wish for more with such a small family."

"Your mother's relations must bring you great pleasure," added a simpering Miss Bingley. "How fortunate you are to be related to an earl!"

"I have never thought of it," replied Georgiana, her shrug showing her uncle's position was of little consequence to her. "My uncle is everything good, and we are very close to his family. If I was not reminded of it, I declare I would not remember his position in society!"

An awkward silence fell over the table, much to Elizabeth's satisfaction; Miss Bingley should know better than to speak with such fawning attention. Taking pity on them, Elizabeth directed the conversation back to Miss Bingley's original question.

"The Bennet family, Miss Bingley, is not large either." Miss Bingley perked up at Elizabeth's statement. "My father has a sister, who lives in Devonshire with her husband, and we do not see her often because of the distance. On my mother's side, she has a brother and a sister, both of whom live nearby."

"Oh?" asked Miss Bingley with exaggerated nonchalance. "Their estates are also situated near Meryton?"

With a smile, hilarity welling up in her breast, Elizabeth replied: "Yes, my uncle's estate is near to Meryton. As for my aunt, she lives in Meryton itself, for her husband is the solicitor there."

"A respectable profession," said Mrs. Hurst.

"Of course," said Miss Bingley. Her reply was nearly a sneer. "What is the name of your uncle's estate? If he lives close by, I am surprised we have not yet made his acquaintance."

"Oh, our uncle does not reside at his estate at present, Miss Bingley," said Jane. "Uncle lives in London at present, for he is engaged in business there."

The smile with which Miss Bingley regarded them was now both triumphant and cruel, and her manner became ever haughtier. "Your uncle is in business, is he?"

"Yes," continued Jane, blind to Miss Bingley's growing self-satisfaction. "Uncle is an importer and owns a large warehouse in Gracechurch Street, near Cheapside. At present, he lives near to his warehouses, for he finds it convenient to live nearby."

"I can see how that would be desirable," said Miss Bingley, fixing Jane with a look which reminded Elizabeth of that a cat might have when stalking a mouse. "Then you do not see him much, I suppose, for he must be a busy man, though I suppose those of this community would welcome him with open arms."

It seemed Miss Bingley's last statement confused Jane, who had detected her supercilious tone. Elizabeth, however, understood the woman perfectly and interjected herself into the conversation, eager to prick her insufferable bubble of self-conceit.

"Actually, we see our aunt and uncle often, Miss Bingley, for they visit us in the summer and at Christmas. However, we shall soon see them with more frequency, for my uncle is to move into the neighborhood next year."

"Oh?" asked Miss Bingley, her enjoyment fading a little. "Does your uncle mean to purchase an estate? Or perhaps he will move his business to Meryton?" Miss Bingley snorted. "I suppose those living in the town would appreciate the arrival of a new family, and, more particularly, a new shop."

"You are mistaken, Miss Bingley," said Elizabeth, enjoying the exchange, "for my uncle need not purchase an estate; he already owns one, as I have already said."

This caught Miss Bingley by surprise. "Then he has chosen to live in London while he owns an estate? That is singular."

"No, Miss Bingley, again I must contradict you. My uncle, you see, is descended, though several generations removed, from a line of gentlemen. His father was the solicitor in Meryton, but Uncle Gardiner had no interest in the law and instead made his fortune in business. Aunt Gardiner is the granddaughter of a gentleman, and her father was a parson."

Elizabeth turned to Georgiana and smiled. "She is also from Derbyshire and has much praise to give to your home." Then Elizabeth turned back to Miss Bingley. "Uncle made his fortune and purchased an estate last spring, but as he is not giving up his interest in his business, he decided to take a year to prepare to transition it to a manager who will continue its operation in his stead. In the meantime, he leased the estate for a year until he can take personal control of it."

To Elizabeth's eyes, it appeared Miss Bingley had caught her inference, for she blanched. Elizabeth regarded her for a moment with satisfaction before speaking again.

"We appreciate your brother's interest in Netherfield, Miss Bingley, for my uncle wished to ensure it would be managed by an honorable man, one who would see to its prosperity in his stead. Netherfield has stood empty for some years now, forcing my uncle to spend much of the spring in residence trying to correct some of the issues which had resulted from the master's lengthy absence. My father has offered his assistance, but having someone in residence is a boon.

"I suppose, in some respects," said Elizabeth, twisting the knife even further, "your brother's situation is much like my uncle's. I assume your brother will follow Mr. Gardiner's example and purchase his own estate when the lease expires. I wish him the best of luck, for Mr. Bingley is an excellent gentleman."

"Thank you, Miss Elizabeth," said Miss Bingley. "We have always been proud of Charles."

So satisfied was Miss Bingley that she did not raise the subject again. They finished their dinner with amicable comments of a blander nature, and if Miss Bingley did not contribute as much, Elizabeth did not repine her reticence. Neither, it seemed, did Georgiana.

"I am quite put out with you, Elizabeth," said Georgiana when they had retired to the sitting-room, where Miss Bingley turned her attention on Jane. "When you informed us of your uncle's ownership of this estate, I almost burst out in laughter!"

"It was all I could do to keep my own countenance," replied Elizabeth. A glance confirmed Miss Bingley was oblivious to what they were saying. "It was clear from the moment she began to speak that she wished to discover something she could use to persuade her brother away from Jane."

"Then it was a spectacular failure," replied Georgiana. "She has always had a high opinion of herself. It may be she will be more bearable now that you have pierced her conceit with such precision."

Elizabeth doubted this was true, for she suspected Miss Bingley's opinion of herself was sufficient to withstand the beating Elizabeth had given it. But she did not say this to her friend, instead turning the conversation to other matters, which included them all after a time. It would not do to anger Miss Bingley and alert her to the subject of their discourse. Though Elizabeth suspected the woman would not return the favor if the situation were reversed, she, at least, would not behave in such a manner. Her mother had taught her children to behave better than that.

The dinner with Bingley and Hurst was proceeding as Fitzwilliam might have expected, for Bingley had little to say which did not consist of his admiration for the eldest Bennet daughter. He was an agreeable man, though perhaps a little fixated on certain matters. Then again, had Fitzwilliam the admiration of a woman of the quality of Miss Bennet of which to boast, he might well trumpet it from the rooftops too.

"What do you think of Miss Bennet, Fitzwilliam?' asked Bingley after a time of this. "Do you not think her the most beautiful creature you have ever beheld?"

"Oh, aye," said Fitzwilliam, stifling a laugh at the sight of Hurst's rolled eyes. "She is in possession of an uncommon beauty, to be certain."

"And a dear, excellent creature too," said Bingley with a sigh. "I cannot thank the heavens enough, for never had I expected to find such an excellent woman in such a place as Meryton."

"Come now, Bingley," said Fitzwilliam with a hearty laugh. "Do you speak censure of this fine neighborhood?"

"No, not at all," replied Bingley, his attention focusing again on his surroundings, where he had been contemplating his lady's perfections only a moment before. "Meryton is all that is pleasing. I simply did not expect to find a woman I could see making my wife."

Hurst snorted at his brother's declaration. "I dare say you have said that about no fewer than a dozen other young ladies."

"I have never announced my intention to make any of them my wife," replied an injured Bingley.

"Perhaps you have not gone so far," replied Hurst. "But what of Miss Cartwright? Miss Colford? Miss Herbert?"

By this time Bingley was blushing to the roots of his hair, much to Fitzwilliam's amusement. Hurst, it seemed, was not so interested in the conversation as he had suggested, for he turned back to his plate at once. After a moment, Bingley collected himself and glared at his brother.

"Maybe I have spoken out of turn in the past. But Miss Bennet is different."

"As you please," said Hurst. "Only take care, for you know it will anger your sister to hear you speak so of a country miss with no fortune or connections."

Bingley grimaced and shook his head, turning to Fitzwilliam. "As you have likely guessed from Hurst's inelegant statement, Caroline does not think well of Miss Bennet."

"She was friendly enough," replied Fitzwilliam.

"Oh, Caroline deigns to associate with her in Meryton, for there is no one else she considers worthy. But if we were to meet in London, Caroline would hold Miss Bennet at arms' length."

"That is the truth!" guffawed Hurst. "Your sister has a high opinion of herself—there is no mistaking that!"

"It is all so vexing!" exclaimed Bingley. "I cannot understand what Caroline is thinking. That Miss Bennet is the daughter of a country gentleman I well understand, but she *is* the daughter of a gentleman. Does that not make her acceptable in society's eyes?"

"Is she acceptable in *your* eyes?"

"Without a doubt," replied Bingley without a hint of hesitation. "I would consider myself fortunate should I obtain her affections."

"Then it seems to me," said Fitzwilliam, "that yours is the only opinion that matters. Society would agree with you, Bingley, for birth trumps fortune. Some will think you mad for marrying a girl with no attention to her fortune, but you will have the comfort of an affectionate wife. Should I advise you, I would urge you to care little for the opinion of society and act in a manner that will constitute your own happiness."

"I am interested to hear you say that," said Bingley, fixing Fitzwilliam with a look that was faintly amused. "Only last night

Caroline informed me with no hint of doubt that you would advise me against Miss Bennet."

Fitzwilliam snorted, diverted himself. "Though it pains me to say it, Bingley, your sister does not know of what she speaks. Not only would I never presume to question your judgment in such matters, but I am also aware of the benefits of affection in marriage."

"Can I also assume that Darcy would agree with you? Caroline was most emphatic in her assertion that Darcy will warn me away from Miss Bennet as soon as he comes."

"What do you think, Bingley?" asked Fitzwilliam. "Does such officious behavior sound like my cousin?"

"Well . . ." said Bingley slowly, "he has advised me against certain ladies in the past."

"If you will recall," interjected Hurst, "Darcy informed you of a rumor he had heard of Miss Colford. Her family lives near his aunt, so he would have some knowledge of them. If Darcy had not stepped in, you might not have heard of the family's financial difficulties until it was too late."

"That is true," said Bingley, his eyes coming into focus. "And regarding Miss Townsend, he only informed me she did not seem too enamored of me."

"And he was correct," said Hurst with a laugh, "given her engagement only a month after you stopped calling on her."

Bingley nodded, warming to the subject. "As I recall, Darcy had little to say any other time I asked him about a young lady. In fact, I remember him telling me once to consider her carefully, but that I should allow nothing to stand in my way should I be convinced of my love—and hers."

"It seems you have your answer, Bingley," said Fitzwilliam. "If Darcy thought a woman held you in no affection, I believe he might intervene, but only to make his opinion known. Should you decide in favor of Miss Bennet—or any other woman—I doubt Darcy would do anything other than congratulate you."

Bingley nodded, his countenance suffused with pleasure once again. "Yes, I can see you are correct. Perhaps I shall ask Darcy's opinion, but I shall hold to my right to decide my future."

"Excellent, Bingley! Then I suspect you will be a happy man. Should your sister not appreciate your choice, it is *yours*. She can have nothing to say."

"Thank you for that, Fitzwilliam, Hurst," said Bingley, nodding to each in turn. "I believe you have given me the best advice I have ever received."

The conversation turned to other matters then, though Bingley was still inclined to bring Miss Bennet into it whenever the woman crossed his mind. That she did so every few minutes was amusing. Fitzwilliam thought the lady's calm demeanor and kindness would do well for his friend.

CHAPTER IV

Elizabeth's account of her handling of Miss Bingley brought much amusement to her family. Mrs. Bennet, in particular, took offense to Miss Bingley's probing questions.

"Well, it is good you diverted the lady so neatly, Lizzy," said she with a sniff when the matter was made known to her. "If it had been me in your place, Miss Bingley should not have escaped without a stinging set down."

The Bennets were a tight-knit family, the bonds of affection strong between them. Though they had rarely had occasion to defend their position, the neighborhood in which they lived being dotted with families of similar circumstances, the fact remained that Mrs. Bennet had not been born to a gentle family. Few remembered that fact, but when others raised it, the family united in defending their position and rebuffing whatever criticism came their way.

"There is little need to concern yourself with what a woman such as Miss Bingley has to say," said Mr. Bennet. "For her to look down on any of us is absurd, considering her father was a tradesman and her brother does not yet own his estate."

"That does not make her any less acceptable in my eyes," said Jane.

"No, Jane, nor would I suggest it should," replied Mr. Bennet. "We were speaking of Miss Bingley, not our family. With your uncle engaged in his own business—and making a highly successful go of it, I might add—we Bennets cannot cast stones at anyone of similar circumstances. I only suggest that Miss Bingley should refrain from thinking herself above us when my family can claim a line of gentlemen which extends more than two centuries."

To that, Jane nodded and turned her attention back to her meal. Jane had not misunderstood Miss Bingley's comments the previous day, for they had spoken of the matter on their return journey to Longbourn. Elizabeth did not wish her sister to think poorly of Miss Bingley if she did not so wish, but she did hope that Jane would be wary of her. Though Jane had said nothing, Elizabeth believed her sister would watch Miss Bingley, though it was not in her sister's character to behave with any unkindness toward her.

"There is another matter which will be of some interest to all my family," said her father, returning their attention to him. "For we are to have a visitor, it seems, and soon."

"A visitor?" asked Lydia. "Other than Aunt and Uncle Gardiner, we never host anyone at Longbourn."

"That is true," replied Mr. Bennet, grinning at his youngest. "We would all welcome more frequent visits from my sister, but as the distance is great, that is not possible. No, the person of whom I speak is a man unknown to me, yet he possesses a close connection to us all."

This cryptic statement prompted a reaction, just as Elizabeth was certain her father had wished. The gentleman watched them all with some amusement for a few moments, laughing at some of the more outrageous guesses offered by his youngest daughters. Then when the tumult died down a little, he assuaged their curiosity.

"Though you have made some interesting deductions, none are correct." Mr. Bennet glanced at Lydia and with laughing eyes said: "Lydia, do you believe I am not known to Colonel Fitzwilliam? And why should he stay with us when he is situated with his officers, in very comfortable accommodations, I might add?"

"Then who is it, Papa?" asked Elizabeth.

"Our visitor is to be none other than Mr. Collins, my heir and the future master of this estate."

If there was any subject likely to provoke a response from Mrs. Bennet, Mr. Collins was that subject. Though Elizabeth could not remember it, her father had told her of the nerves his wife had displayed early in their marriage. And had Mr. Bennet not done anything to help her overcome her fears, Mrs. Bennet would have been right to fear for her future, for genteel poverty was not a matter at which one should laugh.

The Bennets' circumstances, however, were not so dire as this. All five girls had dowries, though it was true they were not on the scale of those possessed by Georgiana, or even Miss Bingley. Lydia and Kitty's dowries were still smaller than the rest, but with Mr. Gardiner's help, Mr. Bennet was adding to them, and with the interest return from some investments their uncle had suggested, they all had fortunes large enough to support themselves should the worst come to pass.

"I cannot say that I am eager to host Mr. Collins," said Mrs. Bennet, nodding to Mr. Bennet's news. "But he *is* your heir, and thus it is prudent we give him our attention. Do you know what kind of man he is? I should not like to accept a ruffian into my home."

"No, I do not think he is a ruffian," replied Mr. Bennet. "Mr. Collins's father was one of the most disagreeable men I have ever known, but even he was not a lout. This Mr. Collins seems like him in some ways, but different in others. I cannot say I expect his society to be agreeable, but he should not tax us too much.

"In fact, he is a parson and holds a respectable living in Kent. Given his choice of words in his letter, I suspect he is not the most intelligent of men, and his continuous words and praise of his patroness, one Lady Catherine de Bourgh, is almost laughable. But other than perhaps a propensity to induce us to laughter, I hope he will not be objectionable."

"Very well. I shall have the guest room prepared for his arrival."

"Excellent, my dear," said Mr. Bennet. "I believe you can expect my peacemaking cousin on Monday at the stroke of four if he keeps to his stated schedule."

It was later that day that Elizabeth received some intelligence of the character of their future guest, though it was not in a manner she might have expected. Longbourn was host to the visit of several officers of the militia that morning, among them Colonel Fitzwilliam. The colonel, Elizabeth knew, was a busy man with all the concerns of the regiment. Even so, it seemed he possessed the ability to visit the homes of those in the neighborhood on occasion, and for that, Elizabeth was grateful, for she found him more interesting than the rest of his men.

"Lady Catherine de Bourgh, you say?" asked Colonel Fitzwilliam after Elizabeth had informed him of their upcoming visitor. "And this man who is visiting is your cousin?"

"Yes," replied Elizabeth, intrigued by the colonel's reaction. "Mr. Collins is my father's heir, for Longbourn is entailed. Have you heard of this Mr. Collins?"

"No, I know nothing of the gentleman, but given what I know of his patroness, I believe I can guess as to the man's character."

At Elizabeth's obvious interest, Colonel Fitzwilliam chuckled and nodded. "It appears I have surprised you, Miss Elizabeth. The one piece of information you do not possess is that I am acquainted— painfully—with Lady Catherine de Bourgh. You see, the lady is my father's sister."

"Your aunt!" exclaimed Elizabeth. "What a curious circumstance."

"With that, I cannot disagree," replied Colonel Fitzwilliam. "I had not thought to meet Lady Catherine's new parson until my visit in April. My cousin Darcy and I visit her at Easter every year, though it is a pleasure we could both forgo without regret. Since Lady Catherine is a widow, my father has charged Darcy with assisting her with her books and other estate tasks during the spring, while he takes it upon himself to do the same in the autumn."

Colonel Fitzwilliam grinned and added: "If I am not very much mistaken, I believe my father is to go there in October, some time after the harvest."

"Given your words," said Elizabeth, taking care in how she phrased what she wished to say, "am I correct in guessing you are not fond of your aunt?"

"It is as easy to be fond of Lady Catherine as it is to be fond of a hedgehog, Miss Elizabeth. The hedgehog is undoubtedly less prickly than my aunt."

Caught by surprise, Elizabeth laughed at the colonel's characterization of his aunt, which the gentleman did not hesitate in joining. The thrust of Colonel Fitzwilliam's comment, she readily understood.

"Given your aunt's demeanor, you expect my cousin will not be a man of much character?"

"Of his character, I cannot say," replied Colonel Fitzwilliam. "What I *can* say is my aunt prefers to surround herself with those who will not dare question her authority. Mr. Collins, therefore, will either be a man too frightened to do anything without her ladyship's express approval or one engaged in licking her boots at every opportunity. Which I cannot say for certain, though I suspect the latter is more likely."

"Then I shall consider myself forewarned," replied Elizabeth, laughing along with him. "At the very least, this Mr. Collins should provide us much amusement.

* * *

The drudgery of the militia was more mindless than Fitzwilliam had ever thought. In the regular regiments, there was always something with which to occupy oneself, for there were always more tasks than time to complete them, and the men were a more serious sort, who had joined knowing what they were about. The militia, however, was not the same caliber of men, populated by those, instead, who wished to present a dashing image to the ladies, or who could not stomach the thought of battle.

Fitzwilliam filled his days with whatever he could. There was, of necessity, much to do, given the lack of a commanding officer before his arrival. Though Colonel Forster had not left the company in a shambles as Fitzwilliam had feared, it was clear discipline did not meet the standards he demanded. Learning that one must take greater care with these part-time soldiers, Fitzwilliam had worked to improve not only the discipline but also the morale of the men under his command. Despite these duties, Fitzwilliam still found he had the time to not only exercise his arm but also to partake of some of the society in the neighborhood, though day visits, such as that he made to Longbourn, were rare.

Only a day after that visit, Fitzwilliam learned of a piece of information that not only surprised him but rendered him unable to determine how he should respond.

"A missive has arrived from Lieutenant Denny, sir," said his assistant when he entered the room that morning. Denny was the only officer Fitzwilliam still had not met, as Colonel Forster had granted the man leave to see to a situation which had arisen in his family, and the lieutenant had stopped at London for a few days at the behest of his father. From all he had been told, Denny was much like the others in essentials, but Fitzwilliam had always preferred to judge a man himself without resorting to the accounts of others.

"He is to return Tuesday, is he not?" asked Fitzwilliam.

"Yes, sir," replied his aide, Sergeant Danvers. "He confirmed the date of his return and writes that he has found a new recruit for the vacant lieutenancy."

"Has he?" mused Fitzwilliam. "That is welcome news. The commission has been vacant for some time, has it not?"

"And Richards has been vocal in his wish to have it filled," replied Danvers. "Though he resigned it, as you know, he has not yet received the proceeds as the post is still vacant."

"Then that is welcome news, not only for the other lieutenants but also for Richards. Does Denny say anything of the recruit?"

"Not much other than the name," replied Danvers. "The man is called a Mr. Wickham, and he has resided in London for some time, though Denny does not say what his occupation was."

It was all Fitzwilliam could do to keep his countenance. "Wickham, you say?"

"Yes, sir."

"Very well," said Fitzwilliam. "When he arrives, I would like to see him at once."

It was clear Danvers saw nothing out of the ordinary in his command. For several more moments, they spoke of other matters, and soon Danvers saluted and let himself from the room, leaving Fitzwilliam alone with his thoughts.

Wickham! Of all the names he had thought to hear, Wickham would not be among them, nor would he wish to ever hear from the man again. The thought of Georgiana's tears after Ramsgate was still enough to bring Fitzwilliam to a blinding rage. A part of him relished the opportunity to put the fear of God into the reprobate and send him on his way with his tail between his legs.

The more practical side of Fitzwilliam considered the matter while keeping his feelings for Wickham firmly in check, knowing this was a chance to exert some control over one George Wickham. Would Wickham bow to the inevitable, or would he turn tail and run as he so often had in the past?

The longer he sat and thought about it, the more Fitzwilliam realized he did not know quite what he would do until Wickham was standing before him. The urge to run the man out of town on a rail was strong. Much would depend on Wickham's demeanor when he came. More would depend on Fitzwilliam's reaction to seeing the libertine again.

The day of the awaited arrival came, and the Bennet family gathered outside as Mr. Collins's coach pulled up to the front door of the house. To call it a carriage was generous, for it was nothing but a hired gig. True to Mr. Bennet's assertion, the time was almost precisely four in the afternoon, a matter which provided him some amusement.

"It seems my cousin is punctual to his time, if nothing else," observed Mr. Bennet.

"You already knew Mr. Collins was a silly man," accused Elizabeth.

Unrepentant, her father winked. "I will own, I possessed some foreknowledge. Beyond my impressions of Mr. Collins's letter, near the end of his life, I received a letter from my cousin. Though I will not bore you with an account of the accusations he leveled at me, accusing me for his lot in life, his lamentations concerning his progeny and his statement that he was not the son he had always wished to sire informed me that to the father, at least, he was a disappointment."

Mr. Bennet shrugged. "As I have never trusted my cousin's judgment, I thought this was sour grapes on his part. It seems, however, he may have been more truthful in this matter than I ever knew him to be in his life."

By that time, the gig came to a stop, and the parson descended from it. Mr. Bennet welcomed him, and he bowed, giving Elizabeth the first impression she had of him. He was tall, though not on Colonel Fitzwilliam's scale, a little rotund around his middle, and moved with a stately, affected air. Elizabeth could little imagine meeting a less appealing specimen of manhood, for his greasy hair dangled about his head, looking as if it had been years since he washed it, his face was round and homely, and his eyes approximated the hue of used dishwater. Elizabeth could not imagine him possessing any intelligence at all. Then he spoke and removed all doubt.

"Mr. Bennet," said he in a voice with a nasal, haughty quality, "I thank you for your welcome and for your swift response to my offered olive branch. It shows some greatness of mind that you accepted it, for it is not what my father taught me to expect of you."

While the entire family regarded the man with disbelief at his insulting speech, Mr. Bennet, giving the appearance of enjoying himself, nodded and gestured toward the house. The parson accepted with alacrity and allowed Mrs. Hill, their housekeeper, to lead him to his room. As the sound of his loud stomping footsteps echoed on the stairs, Elizabeth turned to a chuckling Mr. Bennet and fixed him with a look of some annoyance.

"Well, what do you think, Lizzy?" asked he, a twinkle in his eye.

"I think this visit will be far more interminable than any of us expected," was Elizabeth's acid reply.

"Lizzy has my agreement," said Mrs. Bennet, looking at the stairs as if they offended her. "I have little desire to host a simpleton, and even less, one who I expect will be everything objectionable."

"And yet, he is here, and we have little choice."

With that, they were forced to be content, for Mr. Bennet's statement was nothing less than the truth. While it was the truth, however, Elizabeth had little notion of enduring the man more than she felt she must. Her sisters, she suspected, were forming similar designs to avoid Mr. Collins as much as they could. The execution of that resolution would prove to be more difficult than any of them thought.

By the time the dinner hour was upon them, the members of the family were beginning to feel a little better about the situation. Mr. Collins had disappeared into the guest room and did not emerge until called for dinner. Though Elizabeth was uncertain if they could expect such behavior the man's entire stay, for the moment she was content. When he emerged, however, no one could do anything but repine his civility.

"It seems you have a comfortable home, Mrs. Bennet," said Mr. Collins, turning his words to the mistress as was proper.

"Thank you, Mr. Collins," said Mrs. Bennet. "While it is not a great estate, it is our home, and we are prodigiously fond of it."

"Yes, I suppose you must be," replied Mr. Collins. The man peered about the room for a moment and commented: "Have you made the arrangements I see before me yourself?"

Mrs. Bennet looked about at the dining room, which she had redecorated some five years past. "This room is my work, Mr. Collins. I do not feel the need, as some may, to redecorate according to the whims of fashion; thus, I have left many of our other rooms as they are. It is wasteful to make changes on such extravagant notions."

"With that, I must agree," said Mr. Collins, though his tone was absent. For a moment he inspected the paper on the walls before saying: "Did you consider a darker green, Mrs. Bennet?"

Taken aback, Mrs. Bennet echoed: "A darker green?"

"Yes," said Mr. Collins, nodding his head slowly at first and then with more vigor. "Had my patroness advised you, I believe she would have guided you toward darker colors. Lady Catherine has decorated her dining room in the most tasteful forest greens and dark browns. It is the finest dining room I have ever beheld."

"That is interesting, Mr. Collins," said Mrs. Bennet, from her tone attempting to maintain her temper. "But I have always observed that light colors in a dining room are to be desired, for I believe it helps with digestion."

It was an absurd statement, Elizabeth thought, but no more so than Mr. Collins's own silly pronouncements. Mr. Collins, it appeared, was not listening to Mrs. Bennet, for his responding nod was absent. It was not long before his attention found another focus.

"What a lovely set of silverware this is, Mrs. Bennet. Might I ask if it belongs to the estate?"

The surprise with which Mrs. Bennet had regarded the parson's last question was nothing compared to her shock at his next. Mr. Collins looked at Mrs. Bennet, expectation in his manner, undeniably unaware he had just asked a question so gauche; Elizabeth did not think she had heard anything similar in polite conversation. It was a moment before Mrs. Bennet responded, but when she did, it was in a tone so cold it would have warned anyone else to be silent.

"No, Mr. Collins. These are mine, inherited from my mother, and when I pass on, I intend to leave them to *my* eldest daughter."

"Ah, that is a shame," replied Mr. Collins, though he did not even glance at Jane. "Would it be too much trouble to ask you to show me the utensils that belong to the estate?"

"I shall make sure we use them tomorrow, Mr. Collins," said Mrs. Bennet, her glare again making no impression on the parson. "In fact, for the duration of your stay, I shall ensure we use that set at every meal."

It seemed Mr. Collins was not devoid of all measure of sense, as he frowned at Mrs. Bennet's tone. A moment later, however, he shrugged, seeming to think he had misheard. Elizabeth glared at the parson, wishing she could incinerate him by the force of her gaze, then turned a raised eyebrow on her father. Her mother, she knew, did not possess an endless well of patience—Mr. Collins was taxing what she possessed beyond endurance.

"In your letter," said Mr. Bennet, understanding Elizabeth's entreaty, "you mentioned your patroness. As I recall, your ordination was a recent event?"

"Yes, it was," replied Mr. Collins, preening at Mr. Bennet's mention of it. "The culmination of years of study and effort it was, and Lady Catherine, wise as she is, saw what I accomplished and installed me in the living at Hunsford as soon as she met me."

There was more than a hint of self-congratulation in Mr. Collins's tone as one might have expected. What surprised Elizabeth, however, was that Mr. Collins praised his patroness regarding her ability to see in *him* a man worthy of notice. It seemed her father saw the same, for he did not hesitate to further question the man on the matter.

"And this Lady Catherine of whom you speak, is she a prominent woman?"

"As prominent and wise as any lady in the land!" explained Mr. Collins with rapturous enthusiasm. "Why, it is her ladyship's design which brought me to your door."

"Then I shall ensure to write to her and thank her for her generosity."

Everyone in the room understood Mr. Bennet's irony except for Mr. Collins, for the man nodded with earnest vigor. "That is wise of you, sir. For Lady Catherine informed me herself, with her peculiar brand of condescension, that it is not proper for contention to exist between families. 'Mr. Collins,' said she, 'you should act at once to bridge this distance, for there should be no contention among us.' As wise as Lady Catherine is, I should never dream of contradicting her words, which led me to return to my study that very day and write the letter by which I introduced myself."

"How good of the lady to quote the Bible to you, sir, though I will note a little study would have given you the same notion the lady was kind enough to supply."

Mr. Collins looked at Mr. Bennet for a moment before saying: "The Bible, sir? Lady Catherine's instructions resulted from her own wisdom I am absolutely certain."

Even Mary winced at this sign of Mr. Collins's lack of knowledge concerning the book of holy scripture from which he preached every Sunday. It seemed Mr. Collins had met all Mr. Bennet's expectations of amusement, for he continued to bait the man, provoking him to greater heights of absurdity. Mr. Collins did not seem to understand everyone at the table was exasperated with him or laughing at his inanity.

Not long before the end of dinner, Mr. Collins made one more matter known to the family, causing much consternation among the ladies. It was given in as pompous and nonsensical a manner as of any of Mr. Collins's other statements, though he spoke it in a tone which was just short of negligent.

"How long do you mean to stay, Mr. Collins?" asked Mrs. Bennet, her meaning clear to Elizabeth to be a query about how long she would be required to endure him.

"A fortnight, madam, if it pleases you." Mrs. Bennet was *not* pleased, but the parson would not understand it, even if Mrs. Bennet hit him over his thick head with it. "Lady Catherine has sent me here with a specific purpose, one I have delayed too long in fulfilling."

"How fortunate you have such an involved patroness," said Mrs. Bennet, her tone showing her lack of interest.

"You see," said Mr. Collins, "it is the duty of every clergyman holding a living to set the example of matrimony in his parish, and I have been remiss in seeing that I attend to my duty. Lady Catherine suggested an . . . alliance, in her beneficence, which makes some sense. For myself, I believe I know what I wish for in a wife and shall begin the search at once for a woman who can fit my needs."

Horrified, none of the Bennet sisters spoke again. Mr. Collins did not seem to notice, for he relished his meal, even smacking his lips as some tasty morsel went into his mouth. When his mouth was free of encumbrance, he conversed with Mr. Bennet, though the Bennet patriarch, by now tiring of Mr. Collins's brand of silliness, did not answer often.

When the meal was completed, the ladies withdrew to the sitting-room, leaving Mr. Bennet with the parson. Elizabeth did not fail to notice her father's longing looks at them, but in this instance, she left the duty of entertaining their guest to her father with pleasure. In the company of their mother, the five sisters trudged away from the dining room, each thinking the same thought: surely Mr. Collins would not turn his attentions on any of them!

"What an imbecile," said Lydia, the first to speak when they reached the sitting-room. "How any woman could endure him for three minutes, let alone an entire lifetime, is beyond my understanding."

"I hope he does not wish to marry *me*," fretted Kitty, looking back toward the dining room with fear.

"Mr. Collins is a parson," said Mary in her prim tone. "As such, he must be respectable."

"Respectability, dear Mary," said Elizabeth, "is bestowed upon a man who earns it with his actions, his character, and his ability to show his nobility of character to others. I wonder that Mr. Collins became a parson, for it seems as if he has little knowledge of the Bible."

To that, Mary could say nothing.

"Well, Mr. Collins is a disagreeable man," said Mrs. Bennet. "But you need not concern yourself, girls. Even should Mr. Collins fix his attention on one of you, your father and I will not require you to marry him. I would prefer you to remain old maids than marry such an objectionable man as he."

The five sisters murmured their agreement and fell silent, though the specter of Mr. Collins remained foremost in their thoughts. It was perhaps not surprising that when Mr. Collins lingered with Mr. Bennet, they one and all decided it would be best to retire early.

CHAPTER V

$\mathcal{U}$pon entering the breakfast room the following morning, the Bennet sisters discovered Mr. Collins had not yet descended to break his fast. Whether this was an anomaly, they could not know at the moment, but on face value, it appeared the parson was not an early riser. Given his profession, one could not have predicted such behavior, but on the first day, there it was.

What they did not escape was the reproachful glares and aggrieved complaints from their father. "It seemed you were all content to abandon me to a dullard last night," said he in a tone accusatory, though with his customary brand of humor. "Well, I shall have my vengeance, for I do not mean to make myself available at all times. No, you shall all have your turns hosting Mr. Collins, for I insist upon it."

"I have already informed the girls that we will not force them to marry Mr. Collins," said Mrs. Bennet.

Mr. Bennet released his false afflicted air. "Of course, you will not. If you had thought otherwise, I would be quite surprised."

"No, I did not think otherwise, Papa," replied Elizabeth.

"Then you should not concern yourself. There is something odd about my cousin," mused Mr. Bennet, "something on which I cannot quite put my finger. Whatever it is, I did not gain the impression he means to focus on one of you girls for his future wife. There is something else on his mind, though I cannot state with any surety what it is."

While Mr. Collins was not punctual to their mealtimes—and he made no apology when he arrived to break his fast as the family was rising—he was most attentive at all other times. The man lingered over his breakfast for some time—longer than Elizabeth thought was necessary. When he finished, he took it upon himself to attend 'his fair cousins,' as he put it himself, and none could convince him his civility was unnecessary.

"My, your stitches are uneven, are they not, Cousin Elizabeth?" remarked he not long after they were all seated in the sitting-room. "Perhaps you should practice more, for my patroness always speaks of the efficacy of practice in effecting an improvement in one's skills."

"Thank you, Mr. Collins," said Elizabeth, not at all offended by his faux pas. "Lady Catherine's wisdom in this matter cannot be disputed. Though I do not enjoy embroidery, as a rule, I would agree that practicing would improve my stitches."

Mr. Collins, however, paid no attention to Elizabeth's reply. "Really, Cousins, must you laugh so loud?"

In Elizabeth's opinion, Kitty and Lydia had not been bothering anyone; they could when they put their minds to it, but at present, they were rather quiet. Lydia appeared on the verge of some retort, but a sharp look from Elizabeth put an end to it, and she sulked instead.

"That is better," said the parson. "If you have not heard it said that children should be seen and not heard, let this be a lesson to you. There is little to be gained from making a raucous display when you should sit quietly in the presence of your betters."

For the girls this was the final indignity, for after fixing Mr. Collins with a hateful glare, Lydia rose and called Kitty after her, leading her sister up the stairs. The sound of the door slamming behind them as they entered what Elizabeth thought was Lydia's room was a testament to the offense they felt. Mr. Collins did not seem to understand it for what it was, for he smiled and nodded with satisfaction, and turned his attention back to Elizabeth.

"It appears your mother has done little to restrain the high animal spirits of your sisters. I should advise in the most strenuous manner possible that she should not overlook their education." Mr. Collins paused and directed a critical look at Elizabeth. "In fact, it may be best if she attended to you all or hired the services of a woman to oversee you if she is not capable of it herself. Your sisters will not grow to be a credit to your family if you do not teach them to behave."

A stinging retort was on the tip of Elizabeth's tongue when Mary said: "Shall you not sit with me, Mr. Collins? I was reading in Deuteronomy yesterday and came upon a passage I cannot quite make out. Perhaps your knowledge of the scriptures and insight as a parson would help."

Mr. Collins waved Mary off. "Then I would recommend you listen closer to Sunday sermons, Cousin Mary. I am not in the habit of explaining every minute detail of the scriptures to those who do not bother to take their attendance with the seriousness it requires."

For a moment, Mary could find no reply, so surprised was she. Then she too rose and, giving the parson an imperious glare, retreated from the room. Mary was better behaved than her younger sisters, and the slamming of her bedroom door behind her was not so loud. Elizabeth fancied her sister's footsteps on the stairs were heavier than Mary's usual tread.

"It seems your sisters have all taken my advice to improve themselves," said Mr. Collins with satisfaction. "That is well, for if Lady Catherine were here, she would advise them in the most serious manner to listen to the words of their superiors, lest they are despised wherever they go."

Then Mr. Collins turned to Jane. "Tell me, Cousin, do you play the pianoforte?"

"Only a little, Mr. Collins," said Jane. "Though I enjoy it—"

"No, no, that will not do at all!" exclaimed Mr. Collins. "Why were you not taught? Have my cousin and his wife abrogated their responsibilities to this great degree? Have I come to a family who has no talent, no training, and little in their heads other than fashion and novels?"

"Jane," said Elizabeth, rising to her feet and looking at her sister to avoid strangling the parson. "Shall you not assist me in my room? I believe I have forgotten something there."

Though Jane's sense of politeness urged her to disagree, she caught the stony nature of Elizabeth's glare and agreed. While Jane made some quiet attempt to excuse herself from the parson, Elizabeth hurried her from the room and led her upstairs. When they gained her room, Elizabeth closed the door—without slamming it, though it was a near thing—and rounded on her sister.

"Thank you, Jane. If we had stayed another moment in that room with that odious man, I would not have been responsible for what I said to him!"

Jane sighed and sat on Elizabeth's bed. "Mr. Collins is . . ."

"A disgusting and unendurable man," finished Elizabeth.

Even Jane could not gainsay Elizabeth's statement. "It is well that our parents have already made it clear they will not require any of us to marry him."

"I would not anyway," rejoined Elizabeth. "I should rather end a scullery maid than endure Mr. Collins my entire life."

Jane nodded with agreement and they fell silent.

When Mrs. Bennet returned to the sitting-room after speaking with Mrs. Hill, it surprised her to see Mr. Collins sitting alone. The parson, far from showing distress at his solitary state, appeared to be basking in self-satisfaction, though she could not understand why that might be.

Maggie Bennet was a woman who was under no misapprehensions about herself. Well aware of her limitations, she instead chose to focus on those traits she considered to be strengths, and among those was the ability to manage the house and be a good hostess. Maggie also thought she had done a credible job of raising five beautiful and intelligent daughters.

What she was not was an intelligent woman. It was one reason she had always been so close to Elizabeth, for she saw in Elizabeth that quickness of mind that had attracted her to her husband, a trait passed on from him to his second daughter. Maggie had always known that even if she did not understand something, Elizabeth's quick mind would grasp it. Her ability to share her knowledge with Maggie in a way she would understand had always made her grateful to her daughter for her assistance.

Even with these limitations, Maggie Bennet knew a dullard when she saw one, and Mr. William Collins was the stupidest man she had ever met, and the most objectionable. Part of her wished to consign him to his own company and occupy herself elsewhere, for she knew with an instinctive surety that he would offend her within minutes. But the attentive hostess in her would not abandon her guest, no matter how objectionable she found him. At least, she would not abandon him without attempting friendly relations.

"Where are my daughters, Mr. Collins?"

Catching sight of her, Mr. Collins gave her a look of satisfaction. "They have taken my advice and absented themselves to effect the improvements I suggested."

That sounded worrisome, for Maggie could imagine nothing Mr.

Collins could say to improve her girls. It was more likely he had offended them and driven them all from the room.

"Now, if you please, Mrs. Bennet, I wish to speak to you on a subject most dear to my heart."

Though feeling all the effects of skepticism, Maggie decided it was best to humor him. "Very well, Mr. Collins," said she, settling herself in her favorite chair. "How may I assist?"

"I wish to know something of the neighborhood, Mrs. Bennet. The families with whom you dine, the number and attributes of any daughters they have, and so on."

"You mean to make yourself agreeable to our society while you are here?" asked Mrs. Bennet.

"Of course," said Mr. Collins, "for it is the duty of a clergyman to adapt himself to the society in which he finds himself, whether high or low. There is another matter of which I am interested, but I shall make more of that known anon when I know something of the people who live here."

A sudden memory entered her mind of Mr. Collins speaking the previous evening, and she said: "As I recall, you are here to search for a wife."

"To put it with indelicacy," replied Mr. Collins.

Thinking hard, Mrs. Bennet considered the gentleman before him. He was objectionable to be certain, but on a certain level, he was also respectable, possessing a good living, not to mention his future inheritance of the place she now called home. Though there were many ladies in the neighborhood who were eager to find husbands, loyalty dictated she speak of her own daughters first. Mary was pious and knowledgeable concerning Bible-related matters, and Mrs. Bennet had always thought she would make a good parson's wife. Maggie thought Mary a little more disposed to Mr. Collins than her other daughters, given what she had said the previous evening.

"There are many young ladies near Meryton, Mr. Collins," said Mrs. Bennet.

"Yes, yes," said the gentleman. "I am sure there are. But I do not wish to hear of them all—only those who possess that certain something that all men wish to find in his wife."

Maggie was confused, but she attempted to reply, nonetheless. "If you are looking for a wife who will suit you as a parson, my middle daughter, Mary, would suit. Mary is pious and studious and often visits our tenant children. I think she would make an excellent parson's wife."

Whatever response the parson offered, Mrs. Bennet would not have expected him to laugh. But he did, shocking her yet again.

"My dear Mrs. Bennet," said Mr. Collins. "I do not believe you understand me. For the future Mrs. Collins, I wish to marry a woman of good standing, a woman of means, one who possesses what any man in my position would want—dowry and connections. Your daughters may be amiable, but you cannot think I would ever offer for one of them. They possess little dowry, am I correct?"

"Their dowries are not large," confessed Mrs. Bennet, growing more offended by the moment.

"Exactly," said the man with a nod. "Furthermore, though you are proud of them, as any mother would be, I cannot think their chances of capturing husbands are great at all."

"Whatever can you mean?" demanded Mrs. Bennet, now growing cross.

"Why, because of those deficiencies attendant to their situations. Some of these are no fault of their own but certain others are without a doubt."

"My daughters are wonderful girls, Mr. Collins," said Mrs. Bennet from between clenched teeth. "They are pretty and amiable, have excellent dispositions, and have been brought up in the proper manner. Though they do not have extensive dowries, as you say, I cannot but think they would make any man who asks to marry them proud."

Mr. Collins laughed again—again! The sight of the man and his merriment brought Mrs. Bennet close to the breaking point. What she would not give for a bottle to break over his thick head!

"The affection you hold for your daughters is admirable, but you cannot be blind to their deficiencies. Miss Jane is tolerably pretty, I suppose, but she cannot even play the pianoforte, has little talent otherwise, and rarely opens her mouth. Your youngest daughters are improper hoydens in need of a firm hand and your middle daughter is a bluestocking and the most likely spinster in the making I have ever seen. And the worst is your second daughter, who speaks as if she were a man, talking of matters she cannot understand, besides being ill-favored and the furthest thing from tempting to a man that I can imagine. I suggest you prepare your daughters for spinsterhood, Mrs. Bennet, for it is unlikely they will ever marry."

Shooting to her feet, Mrs. Bennet glared down on the parson, unwilling to allow him to insult her dear daughters. "Then it is fortunate for you, Mr. Collins, that you do not consider my girls good enough to be your wife, for I cannot imagine ever agreeing to any of them marrying you."

Then she turned on her heel and marched from the room, head held high, not caring what Mr. Collins thought. As she climbed the stairs to her room, Mrs. Bennet was counting the days until they could dispense with the parson's company. He was the most loathsome man she had ever met!

The fourth time Mr. Bennet heard a door slam above him he looked up from his book, wondering what was happening in his house. The first one had been the loudest, the third the softest, but all had been unusual in what, he thought, was a tranquil home. Could something have happened that morning?

As Bennet considered the matter, he decided to refrain from investigating. If his presence was required, his wife would call him, and as she had not appeared, it was better to leave well enough alone. Besides, Bennet had little desire to draw his cousin's attention. Let the ladies have the pleasure of his company for a time—Bennet had endured enough of the man the previous evening.

That decided, Bennet turned back to his book and immersed himself in its pages.

The ubiquitous presence of Mr. Collins made it difficult for anyone to enjoy their home. When out of their rooms, the Bennet sisters were treated to an unapologetic Mr. Collins dogging their every step—it seemed to Elizabeth the man was not even aware of how he had offended them. Retreat to their rooms was possible, but not desirable, for no one wished to spend all their time hidden away in their bedchambers.

Thus, not long after luncheon, the Bennet sisters decided among themselves that they would escape the man's presence by walking into Meryton. Even that, however, was a failure.

"Then I shall accompany you into the town," said Mr. Collins when he learned of their intention. Jane and Elizabeth shared a glance—it had been their wish to free themselves from him. "It will be just the thing, for there, you might introduce me to those of the neighborhood, so I may be about the task which brought me to your door."

"It was my understanding it was your patroness's wish to restore relations between us," was Elizabeth's acid observation.

"Of course," said Mr. Collins, waving his hand as if shooing away an insect. "But it was also to find a wife. I suspect this will be an excellent location in which to begin my quest."

Elizabeth did not think there was a young lady in all Hertfordshire who could endure him, but there was nothing to say, and she refrained from giving him any further reason to speak. Not that he needed any. Seeing her mother glaring at the parson as if to bore holes in him, Elizabeth wondered if he had offended her too. Before they left, her mother contrived a moment to speak to her.

"You may tell your sisters they are safe from Mr. Collins." Mrs. Bennet turned a glare on the man as he was pulling on his gloves and looked away from him as if he were of no consequence. "He is looking for a woman of fortune to become Mrs. Collins and has expressed his . . . disinclination to pursue any of you."

"I had determined that much myself, Mama," said Elizabeth, kissing her mother's cheek. "But I thank you, regardless. It is good to have it confirmed by his own mouth."

"If you see my sister, give her my regards," said Mrs. Bennet, before exiting the vestibule.

The entire length of their walk to Meryton, Elizabeth did not think Mr. Collins was silent for two seconds together. He spoke of his patroness, his wishes for his visit, the people he thought he would meet and the places he would dine—dining seemed to be a matter of much interest to Mr. Collins, unsurprising, given the state of his belly. Underneath it all was an odd sort of self-congratulation mixed with a healthy measure of disdain for them all, Elizabeth thought. That they returned it in full measure meant Elizabeth did not feel it necessary to concern herself with Mr. Collins's opinions. However, during their walk, she ensured each one of her sisters knew what their mother had discovered from the man the previous day.

"Good!" spat Lydia when Elizabeth shared it with her. "Though I should take immense pleasure in laughing in the face of a proposal, Mr. Collins is not worth the effort." With that sentiment, Elizabeth could not but agree.

Meryton's principal street was busy that morning. The Bennet sisters visited some of the shops—a still pontificating Mr. Collins following behind—enjoying their outing as much as possible given the circumstances. During their activities, they met a certain number of friends, to whom they introduced Mr. Collins like the chore it was. For Mr. Collins's part, it seemed he did not appreciate those to whom he was introduced—though he greeted them all with his peculiar brand of civility, there was little warmth in his tone.

After some time of this, the Bennet sisters had determined it was time to return to Longbourn when they met a person who had been absent of late. The sisters were not among the coterie of ladies who hung off the officers' every word, and thus, they did not concern themselves with the officers' doings. But Lieutenant Denny was a friendly man impossible not to like, as he was a favorite of all. That morning, he had come to Meryton with a friend.

"Miss Elizabeth," greeted the officer as he and his friend stepped toward them. "How do you do today?"

"Very well, Mr. Denny. Welcome back to Meryton; I understand your family called you away for a time."

"Thank you," said Mr. Denny. "Now I am returned, and I could not be happier. And I have brought a friend with me."

With an expansive gesture, Mr. Denny motioned toward his friend and said: "Please allow me to introduce my good friend, George Wickham. Wickham is to join the regiment, so you will see much of him in the coming weeks and months."

Mr. Wickham bowed and greeted them all with perfect manners, showing his pleasure at having met them. As he did so, Elizabeth studied him. Mr. Wickham was a tall man, lean and handsome, moving with fluid grace, his air practiced and gentlemanly. His hair was a dark brown, his eyes a light blue, and his countenance suggested good humor and an open disposition. In Elizabeth's experience, there were few men as blessed as Mr. Wickham.

"This is an auspicious beginning, Mr. Wickham," said Elizabeth after they had exchanged pleasantries for a few moments. "The commander of the regiment has changed of late—I am certain you have heard?"

"So Denny tells me," replied Mr. Wickham. "I am eager to meet him. That was where we were to go when we happened upon you ladies."

"Then we shall not keep you, sir," replied Elizabeth.

With a few more words, the Bennet sisters farewelled the officers, and after a quick conference among themselves, turned their footsteps toward home. The unwanted person of Mr. Collins following, they made their way toward the road leading back to Longbourn.

"Well, Wickham?" said Denny, pulling Wickham's thoughts from the fetching picture of five lovely young ladies walking away from them. "There are beauties aplenty in Hertfordshire—did I not tell you?"

"That you did," said Wickham absently, watching the tall blonde as she moved away. Now that was a woman worth a second look. And the brunette who spoke to him was her equal in beauty, and playful too. Wickham could think of a few activities in which he would like to engage with her.

"But what of fortune? Are any of them dowered enough to keep a man in comfort?"

Denny laughed. "We cannot all be fortune hunters, Wickham. I do not know the state of the Bennets' fortunes, but the estate is not large. Beyond that, you must speak to the ladies themselves."

"Ah, but it would not do to scare them away, would it?"

"No, I suppose not," replied Denny. "Anyway, let us go to the barracks."

Wickham went along with his friend with a will, reflecting on what had brought him here. A favor called in from a former friend had furnished him with enough funds to make the purchase of the commission—it had annoyed Wickham the man had refused to give him the money as would have been his preference. Military life, he thought, would not suit him, as he had no interest in the discipline such a life would entail.

A chance meeting with Denny had changed his mind, at least for the moment. It seemed the militia was not strict in their adherence to such things, and the stories of society and the potential for fun informed Wickham that it may be a pleasure to spend some time in the company of such people. It would not be his profession for long, but at present, with few funds and fewer prospects, Wickham thought he could endure it.

The colonel's assistant met them as they entered the regiment's headquarters and informed them that Wickham was to report at once to his commanding officer. That was not unexpected, Wickham supposed, though he might have wished for some evidence of a more relaxed commanding officer. Denny slapped him on the back and promised to meet with him once he had made the colonel's acquaintance, then left to return to his own quarters.

The building was a fine one, though perhaps not new. Then again, militia companies such as this one were at the mercy of their hosts for their accommodations, and this was as good as any, he supposed.

The sergeant led Wickham to a door and with a smile, gestured inside. Wickham, confident as ever of making a good impression, strode through and approached the desk, where a man was sitting, writing on some papers. The door closed behind him and Wickham waited for the man to notice him, wondering at the delay.

Then the colonel looked up. "Hello, Wickham."

CHAPTER VI

A simpleton could have seen the shock etched onto Wickham's features. Though it had not been his intention to surprise the man in the manner he had, Fitzwilliam reflected now that it had been for the best. Not only would he not put it past Wickham to run at the sight of him, but it gave Fitzwilliam the opportunity to see him in an unguarded moment, attempt to determine what Wickham's purpose was for joining the regiment.

Shock, as he had already noted, was present in Wickham's features—shock at seeing a man he feared and detested, followed soon after by the realization that he had put himself into the power of one who knew what he was and would not hesitate to use that power to good use. Then came the fear, uncertainty, and panic, wondering just what Fitzwilliam would do. Finally, Fitzwilliam thought he caught a hint of acceptance, though perhaps colored by determination. But determination for what? To flee at the first opportunity? To attempt to bring his fellow officers to his side, to ensure his fellows accepted his stories before anyone could dispute them?

If he thought that, he was a greater fool than Fitzwilliam had ever suspected. It would be the work of a moment to see him discredited and thrown from the militia in disgrace, his commission—and the money used to purchase it—confiscated and gone forever.

The thought caused Fitzwilliam to frown, which destroyed much of Wickham's bravado, he noted with an absence of mind. How had Wickham acquired the funds to purchase the commission? The last Fitzwilliam had heard of the man after Ramsgate, Wickham had been destitute because of his failed bid to lure Georgiana and steal her fortune. Fitzwilliam filed that thought away for future investigation.

Under the weight of Fitzwilliam's pitiless glare, Wickham struggled for some time to say anything, though it was clear the words would not come. Seeing this, Fitzwilliam's amusement grew ever darker. At length, Wickham found his voice, though his attempt to speak was as ineffectual as the way he lived his life.

"I had not expected to see you here."

"That much is evident," was Fitzwilliam's reply. "If you had known I was seated behind this desk, would you still have braved entry?"

Wickham did not respond, and Fitzwilliam realized there *was* no response. Though Wickham might not own to it, Fitzwilliam had always known he was a coward, better suited to preying on the defenseless than standing up to a man who would return his assaults blow for blow. When Wickham fell silent a second time, Fitzwilliam knew he would need to speak next, for the man appeared ready to flee.

"The question is, what are we to do with you?"

Wickham's silence persisted for an instant, and then the man responded with words Fitzwilliam might have predicted in advance. "I shall resign the commission."

In that instant, Fitzwilliam made a snap decision. If he allowed Wickham to walk out the door, he would never amount to anything, his most likely future being an unmarked pauper's grave. Though the thought of attempting to reform George Wickham into a man of whom his Uncle Darcy might have spoken with pride was no less than repugnant, Fitzwilliam knew it was the correct path to take.

"Sit, Wickham," said Fitzwilliam when he noticed the man about to rise. "Let us not be too hasty. Shall we not speak like rational adults?"

Wickham gave a nervous laugh. "As I recall, the last time we met you promised to run me through."

The chuckle which escaped Fitzwilliam's lips was involuntary and caused Wickham to blanch further. "Yes, I said that, did I not? I had forgotten."

"I have not," replied Wickham.

"In some respects, the urge to run you through is still with me, Wickham, but at present, I would prefer speech instead of action."

"To what end?"

Fitzwilliam sighed and leaned back in his chair, watching the man as one watches a rabid dog. "I shall not bore you with diatribes about how you have lived your life. Not only would it do no good at all, but I am also aware you would become angry and declare your life was yours to do with as you please.

"But let us face the facts." Fitzwilliam leaned forward and stared into the other man's eyes. "You are seven and twenty and are without occupation. If I allow you to resign your commission, where will you go? What will you do? Do you have some means of supporting yourself of which I am not aware?"

His lip curled with the old bitterness Fitzwilliam knew he had always harbored for his life and what he saw was Darcy's good fortune. For a moment Fitzwilliam thought he might speak, rail again at Darcy for denying him his due or complaining bitterly over his lot in life. In the end, he did not open his mouth, for he must know Fitzwilliam would not stand for the repetition of such grievances.

"It is as I suspect," said Fitzwilliam. "My uncle educated you at great expense, gave you advantages no one of your station could have dreamed of receiving. Yet, you squandered those advantages in gambling, wenching, and carelessness, and now you have nothing. To be blunt, if I allow you to walk out that door, your ways will lead you to poverty and death."

"Why should you care?" demanded Wickham, at last showing a hint of the spirit Fitzwilliam knew he possessed under his bravado, for all he usually shunted it aside in favor of his cowardice. "Do you not wish me dead for the trouble I have caused your cousin? Do not my actions toward Georgiana leave you wild to follow through with your threats?"

Fitzwilliam sighed. "I have never wished you dead, Wickham, my threats notwithstanding. My Uncle Darcy esteemed you, though you did not deserve it. It is for that reason and that reason alone that I offer you this chance."

"What chance is that?"

"The chance to make something of your life," said Fitzwilliam, fixing Wickham with a pointed look. "What I propose is that you stay in the militia and learn something of life in the army. Should you wish it, once you have a taste of what it is like, I can see about getting a transfer to the regulars if you decide it is the life you wish to lead."

"Why should I wish to join the regulars?" asked Wickham with a sneer. "I do not fancy being the target for every soldier in Bonny's army."

With a laugh, Fitzwilliam agreed, saying: "No, I suppose you would not at that."

Wickham's eyes narrowed and he said: "Why are you here anyway? You have spent your career with the dragoons, as I recall."

"You are correct," replied Fitzwilliam. "But an injury left me unfit for duty, and with my regiment due to be deployed to Spain, my superiors gave me this command while I heal."

"You have all the luck, it seems," muttered Wickham.

"In some ways, you may be correct. I will note, however, that I have fought against the French before. A colonel is less likely to die in the crown's service than, say, a lieutenant, though there is still some danger."

"Then why do you think I would accept such a posting?" demanded Wickham.

"Because it pays better," replied Fitzwilliam, knowing Wickham was a man for whom such things would matter most.

"Not nearly enough to bother," rejoined Wickham. "No matter how well the regulars pay, serving therein will not make a man wealthy."

"No, it will not," replied Fitzwilliam. "Come, Wickham, by this time you must understand it is not likely you will ever attain your goal of fabulous wealth. You have sought after riches all the years of your life and are no closer to procuring them now than when you were fresh out of university."

Wickham glared, but he did not respond.

"Let us come to the point. The militia is not a taxing environment, though I expect the men under my command to do their part and complete their duties. But the militia also does not even pay enough to meet an officer's immediate needs. Most of these men have families who assist in their support. Do you have such a means?"

It was clear from Wickham's stony look that he had no such means, which Fitzwilliam already knew. "Perhaps you mean to further supplement your income by gambling with your fellow officers, but you never had much luck in such things. The regulars, however, pay well, enough for a man to support himself. Then, when the war is over, you may go on half-pay, and while it will not be much as a lieutenant, there is also the possibility of advancement."

"Where will I have the funds to purchase higher commissions? There is no way to save enough to allow me to purchase them."

"Perhaps I might persuade Darcy to assist."

Wickham snorted his disdain. "Darcy told me the last time we met that he had no intention of further funding my activities. Furthermore, I would need to survive the war to ever take advantage of that half-pay of which you speak."

"Perhaps a posting in a northern regiment, unlikely to suffer deployment?"

"You know as well as I that is no guarantee."

"That is irrelevant," said Fitzwilliam, tiring of the conversation. "Let us be plain then, Wickham. Do not even offer to resign your commission, for I will not accept it. I owe my uncle enough to try to make something of you. What you become is your choice, for I will force nothing on you other than to see you remain in this company. From here, you will proceed as far as you wish on your own merit. But I will not allow you to walk away when this may be the last chance you have at a useful life."

It was clear Wickham did not appreciate what he was being told, but he did not respond, drawing on whatever well of restraint he possessed. Fitzwilliam nodded with approval.

"As I said before, I will expect you to complete your duties. But not all will be drudgery, for there is society aplenty in this town, and we do not run our officers to the point of exhaustion. One thing upon which I will insist is your behavior regarding the townsfolk. Regiments such as this are not always welcomed with open arms—this community has been very good to us. That means no credit and no dallying. Am I clear?"

The man appeared as if Fitzwilliam had just forced a lemon down his gullet, but he gave a curt nod.

"Though I cannot stop the men from gambling, I insist upon temperance. If you choose to join the men at cards, you will ensure you do not gamble away all means of support. Remember moderation, Wickham.

"If you abide by these strictures and do your best, I will be willing to assist you in selling your commission. Perhaps you may prefer to emigrate to the Americas. I can assist you with that should you wish it; I might even persuade Darcy to help."

Thoughtful, Wickham nodded again, this time with less asperity. Deciding he had had enough of Wickham for the moment, Fitzwilliam stood and offered his hand. Wickham looked at it for a moment, then accepted it, though hesitantly.

"Speak to Sergeant Danvers, and he will show you to your quarters. Denny is your friend, is he not?"

"He is," was Wickham's terse reply.

"Then have him introduce you to the rest of your fellow officers. When that is complete, send him to see me." Wickham gave Fitzwilliam such a foul look that he laughed. "Do not concern yourself, man—I have no interest in besmirching your name. I have not met Denny and should like to do so at the first available opportunity.

"I would have you remember, Wickham," added Fitzwilliam, fixing a stern look on the man, "that as I have taken you into my regiment, your behavior now reflects on *me*. Not only have I no interest in ruining your reputation with Denny or the townsfolk or anyone else, but I also have a vested interest in your good behavior. Do not make me regret my decision."

Implicit in Fitzwilliam's words was the promise that if Wickham caused him regret, Wickham would share in it. The grim nod with which he responded told Fitzwilliam that Wickham had understood his warning. With a nod, Wickham turned to leave.

"One more thing," said Fitzwilliam before his new lieutenant reached the door. "Georgiana is staying with Darcy's friend at an estate close to Meryton. I trust I do not need to inform you of what awaits you should you attempt anything further with her?"

"No, sir," replied Wickham, though it was clear it surprised him to hear Georgiana was nearby. "I have no intention of so much as speaking with her."

"Good. Then we shall get on famously."

Wickham nodded and let himself from the office. With a sigh, Fitzwilliam sat behind his desk, wondering what he had done. Had he made the correct choice? At present, he could not say, for he had little faith in Wickham. If he had allowed him to walk out of the office, however, Fitzwilliam knew Wickham would never have amounted to anything. Though he did not like the man, Fitzwilliam knew this was Wickham's best and, perhaps, last chance. Thus, he would do what he could to ensure Wickham was kept under control. Perhaps he would surprise them all.

Another sigh escaped Fitzwilliam's lips and he drew a sheet of paper from his desk drawer and began composing a letter to Darcy. His cousin would wonder if he had taken leave of his senses and would journey to Meryton at once. Fitzwilliam wondered himself if he had not lost his wits. Expecting Wickham to reform must be the maddest thought he had ever had.

It was clear on the return journey from Meryton that Mr. Collins was displeased with what he had seen. The moody way in which he stomped along the path, the choice epithets she could hear muttered under his breath informed Elizabeth, if his glares at everyone and nothing did not. Kitty and Lydia avoided him by carrying on about Mr. Wickham, how handsome he was and how he would appear to excellent advantage when he donned regimentals. Elizabeth regarded them with exasperation, though in part she was amused at their antics — as they were not yet out, they would have far less contact with the officers than they would wish.

Mary and Jane walked a little ahead, speaking in low tones, leaving Elizabeth with Mr. Collins. It seemed the parson had singled her out among her sisters, for he turned to her at once and began to ply her with questions.

"What an interesting little town you have here, Cousin."

"It is our home, Mr. Collins, and will one day be yours. Meryton is, perhaps, not the center of fashion and society, but the neighborhood's worth is in its people, is it not?"

Mr. Collins huffed, though it sounded like a snort. "I suppose you must be correct. But those we met this morning must not be all the neighbors you can boast? There must be others, those from more . . . prominent families?"

Knowing to what he was referring, Elizabeth felt hilarity build up in her breast, though she refrained from laughing. "If by prominent you refer to those of the peerage, I must inform you there are none of that sort nearby. The nearest man of any prominence, I believe, would be Baron Harlow, who lives some miles to the south and east, beyond Hatfield. We never see him here."

"And others of wealth and fortune?" demanded Mr. Collins. "Is this neighborhood devoid of such people?"

"There is more to people than wealth," Mr. Collins," said Elizabeth, her tone chiding. "You, as a parson, do not tie a person's worth to the state of his pocketbook or his prominence in society, do you?"

"Of course not!" snapped the parson, though Elizabeth could see his displeasure still hovered over him like a cloud. "Our Lord is no respecter of persons and loves the pauper as much as the prince."

"Then we see matters alike, Mr. Collins," replied Elizabeth. "Once you come to know the people of the neighborhood, I know you will see them as I do. We are not a high and mighty bunch, but neither are we savages.

"Take my closest friend, Charlotte Lucas, for example. There is no firmer friend than Charlotte, for she is everything good, gracious, kind, and lovely. Should she be despised because she does not possess the riches that society seems to hold so dear?"

"Is she *very* poor?" asked Mr. Collins is a sulky tone.

"Of course, she is not," snapped Elizabeth, beginning to become cross with him. "In all measurements that matter, Charlotte is an excellent woman, and I am convinced that any man who attains her hand would find blessings aplenty for the simple fact of having her as a wife."

Mr. Collins glared at Elizabeth with suspicion. "Are you attempting to put forth your friend as an acceptable match?"

"I do no such thing," said Elizabeth. In the confines of her mind, she added: *I would not see her bound to such a man as you!* "The only thing I am suggesting is that Charlotte is a good woman and a wonderful friend, and I do not think it right that men should overlook her qualities in favor of great wealth. If they do, they will miss out on a gem of the highest value."

"Yes, I can see why you would say that, Cousin," said Mr. Collins, though Elizabeth knew she had not moved him in the slightest. "It is unfortunate that so many men dismiss her with nary another thought because of her circumstances. But that is the way the world works. It is not my responsibility to change it—rather, I must live in it."

As a parson, Elizabeth thought Mr. Collins had some forum in which he could trumpet proper values, even if others were unwilling to listen. His words, though proper in some respects, were nothing more than lip service, for the man was so fixed on a wealthy wife that it blinded him to all other considerations. Elizabeth had no interest in changing his mind, for not only did she not wish to turn his attention on her, but any length of conversation with the man was liable to provoke an aching head.

"Is there no one in this neighborhood who possesses that which a man seeks in the woman he marries?"

"As I said, Mr. Collins," replied Elizabeth, eager to end this conversation, "we are simple people. Most of my friends possess dowries but if you are looking for a woman with a dowry of twenty thousand pounds, you will know disappointment."

When Elizabeth opened her mouth to end their discourse once and for all a sudden thought struck her. Though the thought which had crossed her mind was one she should not contemplate, it also possessed the possibility of provoking great amusement. Mr. Collins stumped along, his head bowed in thought, a thunderous moue of disappointment drawing his eyebrows together. Perhaps it was unkind of her mention it, but the lady was most deserving.

"Now that I think on it, Mr. Collins," said Elizabeth, drawing his pouting eyes back to her, "it has come to my mind that there *is* a young woman in the neighborhood who might meet all your requirements."

An instant transformation came over the parson. "There is?" asked he, excitement in his voice.

"The Bingley family has come to the neighborhood of late to live at Netherfield Park, an estate owned by my uncle. Mr. Bingley is an amiable man—he has shown a great deal of interest in my sister, Jane. One of his own sisters is married, but the other is yet single and with no prospects of changing her status of which I am aware."

"Yes? And her dowry?"

"Oh, it is not proper to speculate about a woman's fortune," demurred Elizabeth. The exact number she knew, though that presupposed the gossips of Meryton had received the correct information but she was not about to inform Mr. Collins.

"That is correct, I suppose," replied the gentleman, deep in thought. "You say your sister Jane has been the target of his attention?"

"Mr. Bingley visits often and rarely has any attention for anyone other than Jane. Furthermore, Miss Bingley claims Jane as a friend, and I am well acquainted with her as well."

"Then will you introduce me?" Mr. Collins's excitement was unmistakable.

"Mr. Collins," said Elizabeth, no trace of facetiousness in her voice, "nothing would give me greater pleasure than to introduce you to Miss Bingley at the earliest opportunity."

"Excellent," replied he.

For the rest of the walk, Mr. Collins was silent, a great improvement on his usual tendency to fill any void with his bland pronouncements and nonsensical musings. The thought of riches seemed to have overwhelmed that inclination, for he peered off into the distance, seeing nothing, muttering to himself about how he would go about wooing the unfortunate Miss Bingley.

For Elizabeth's part, she could not wait to tell Charlotte of Mr. Collins, to introduce her to him and to share her bemused opinion of the gentleman. Further, the thought of haughty Miss Bingley fending off an amorous idiot in Mr. Collins was beyond any amusement Elizabeth had seen in her neighborhood in the last twelvemonth. How she would laugh!

CHAPTER VII

$\mathcal{M}$eryton was a market town much like any other. A wide thoroughfare comprised the center of the community, on which sat merchant shops that might exist in any other town in the kingdom. It was not unattractive, but it was not Lambton either, with its winding, cobbled streets and old country charm.

Had Darcy been of a mind to pay much attention to the town in which he found himself, he might have looked about with interest, regardless of his thoughts of the plainness of the location. Bingley's estate was nearby, meaning Darcy would spend at least the coming two months here, and it was always beneficial to know the residents to effect good relations with them.

Darcy, however, had little attention for such considerations. The late August sun was beating down on him, the day hot and muggy, and the news he had received from his cousin did nothing to improve matters. It was likely that Fitzwilliam had penned his letter in the expectation that Darcy would drop everything and rush to Hertfordshire, and he was correct. While Darcy could have come to Netherfield days earlier, he had been enjoying the last few days without Caroline Bingley's suffocating presence, even though London was not pleasant at this time of year. News of Wickham and the libertine's proximity to Georgiana changed all that, for Darcy could not rest without seeing personally to his sister's protection.

The directions Fitzwilliam had given him were precise, and Darcy found the building the militia was using as their headquarters with ease. It was a low building, paint peeling from weatherworn panels of wood, no sign other than the officers in evidence as to the building's present use. There was also no way to tell what it had been used for before the regiment took control of it.

Presenting himself within as instructed, Darcy followed a junior officer toward the back to a plain, nondescript door, and when the sound of his cousin's voice called for them to enter, Darcy followed the man into the room. It was plain and utilitarian, not much different from the building which housed it, though his cousin's presence behind the desk was a welcome sight.

"Ah, Darcy," said Fitzwilliam with his customary smirk, then nodding in dismissal at his officer. "You made better time than even I thought."

"Enough of your insouciance," said Darcy, his voice gruff from the dust of the road, but also prompted by simmering annoyance. "Have you taken leave of your senses?"

With a chuckle, Fitzwilliam shook his head and gestured to a chair in front of the desk. "It is good to see you too, Cousin. It is about time you deigned to join your sister at Netherfield. If not for some excellent friends she has made, she would have been quite at Miss Bingley's mercy."

No doubt as Fitzwilliam had intended, Darcy's interest was aroused at the mention of his sister's friends—Georgiana had always been so shy, making friends was difficult. Intent on receiving answers, however, Darcy directed the conversation back to his concerns, perhaps a little harsher than he had intended.

"I wish to know of Wickham, Fitzwilliam," said Darcy, speaking in a slow and uncompromising tone. "Do you not recall how he attempted to make off with *my sister* only two months ago? And now you propose to allow him to remain here, where he is only two miles from her? How can you account for such foolishness?"

"If you would allow me," said Fitzwilliam, "I will tell you my reasoning. It would be best to remember, Darcy, that I am not cowed by your authoritative manner, nor does your displeasure affect me. I am also one of Georgiana's guardians, and I am aware of the need to protect her. I would not be doing this if I did not have excellent reasons."

Though the urge to castigate his cousin was strong, Darcy refrained. "Very well, then. Tell me why you have allowed Wickham to remain."

The slight smile with which his cousin regarded him annoyed Darcy further, but at least Fitzwilliam did not further delay. "Tell me, Darcy—have we ever had a better opportunity to control Wickham than we do now?"

"And you think you can control him."

"Yes, I understand he has always been ungovernable. But he has never been a soldier under my command either. At present, Wickham has two choices: he may restrain himself and fulfill his duties to *my* satisfaction—else I will see him in the stockade—or he sneaks away in the middle of the night. Deserting in a time of war, even from the militia, is a serious business."

"Or, there is a third option," added Fitzwilliam, his gaze as sharp as Darcy's. "You can call in his debts and see him incarcerated in Marshalsea where he should have been all these years already."

Darcy could not suppress the grimace provoked by Fitzwilliam's pointed comment, for his cousin had been warning for years about Wickham, urging him to have the debts called in. There was little argument to make on the subject, for after the events of Ramsgate, Darcy knew he was correct.

"I see you have decided to be sensible," observed Fitzwilliam, his smug tone annoying Darcy all over again. "Then let me explain some of my other reasoning to you, for when Wickham appeared in this very room, I was tempted to run him through and end his association with the family forever."

"As I recall, such threats were a large measure of your reaction when you learned of Wickham's actions at Ramsgate."

"I do not deny that," said Fitzwilliam. "But when faced with him, when faced with the possibility this might be his last opportunity, I knew throwing him out on his ear, however much I wished it, would not do."

"When you suggest this is his last chance, I suspect you are referring to the opportunity to make something of his life?"

"I do," confirmed Fitzwilliam.

Darcy snorted with contempt. "When has Wickham ever taken *any* opportunity to make something of his life?"

"If you will forgive me, Darcy," replied Fitzwilliam, "your father indulged Wickham and never made him acknowledge and correct his mistakes. After your father's death, you paid him a substantial sum of money *and* paid his debts in Lambton, rather than removing it from the money he received from you. I know that as a man, you should not need to teach him to pay his debts, but perhaps if you had done so, though he would not have liked it, some measure of responsibility might have sunk into his thick head."

Passing a hand over his eyes in weariness, Darcy slumped back in his chair. In this also Fitzwilliam was correct—how many times had Darcy taken himself to task for how he had handled the situation?

"You know I do not blame you for Wickham's transgressions, Darcy," said Fitzwilliam, his tone compassionate. "You sought to spare your father—I might have done nothing different. This approach, however, has not done Wickham any good. Quite the opposite."

"Then you mean to reform him," said Darcy.

Fitzwilliam snorted his amusement. "Like you, I have little notion it is possible to reform Wickham. What I *can* do is exert some authority over him. My captains know to watch him, though I have not told them everything, and I have warned him against accumulating debts and trifling with the ladies of the neighborhood. At the very least, I mean to ensure Wickham attends to his duties, for a little work will do him no harm."

"And if he proves ungovernable?"

The vicious smile with which Fitzwilliam responded was more like the cousin he knew. "Then we raise the specter of his debts, which we know are substantial. If that still does not work, we always have the option of transporting him to Botany Bay—I would suggest the Americas, but Van Diemen's Land is more distant, which I think would suit us all well. If he is here, we know where he is and need not search for him if he does not behave as he ought."

"Then we will do it your way," said Darcy. "But if he so much as looks at Georgiana, I will see him in prison."

"Believe me, Darcy," said Fitzwilliam, "if he does, I shall reach him first. If I had known treating Wickham in this manner would raise your bloodlust, I would have done it long ago."

"What are your impressions of the neighborhood?" asked Darcy, eager to dispense with the subject of Wickham for the moment.

"I have enjoyed the society in the brief time I have been here," said Fitzwilliam with a shrug. "If you ask the same question of Miss Bingley, you will receive a different answer."

"I might never have guessed," said Darcy, shaking his head. Though the company of his friend was welcome, Darcy was not eager to stay in a house managed by Miss Bingley.

Fitzwilliam grinned, an evil quality in it, knowing Darcy was walking into the lion's den. Then he shrugged and continued:

"The residents are simple, but we have both complained many times of those who consider themselves sophisticated." Darcy nodded, knowing Fitzwilliam knew of his disinclination for the company of most of those of society. "Most are small estate owners with all that entails, and while there is a knight living in the neighborhood, he is the least polished of them all.

"But they are acceptable, regardless of what Miss Bingley might say." Fitzwilliam paused and grinned. "Your friend seems to find the locals acceptable, for he is already extolling the virtues of his latest angel. I must own that she is one of the most beautiful women I have ever seen."

"Another of his infatuations, no doubt," said Darcy. If he was nothing else, Bingley was predictable. "If he began soon after he arrived, Bingley should already be tiring of her."

"This young lady appears to be different," replied Fitzwilliam. "There is nothing I can say against her, for she and her family are all well mannered and good, everything a gentle family should be."

"But is she suitable?" asked Darcy. "What are her connections and fortune?"

"I neither know nor is it my concern, Darcy," replied Fitzwilliam. "I cannot imagine she possesses a fortune which is even a fraction of Georgiana's, but she is in no other way unsuitable. Besides, it is Bingley's concern, is it not? If he does not find her situation objectionable, what can it be to us?"

"Nothing, of course," replied Darcy. "Bingley may do as he pleases. It has long been my habit to ensure the woman Bingley admires is not some lady eager to dip her fingers into his pocketbook. Bingley has almost been taken in by a mercenary woman several times."

"If that is all you mean to do, then go to it. Otherwise, I would suggest you do not become involved, Darcy. It would be officious if you were to do more, and you may just find yourself in agreement with Miss Bingley."

With a laugh, Darcy acknowledged his cousin's hit.

"And it may just be that you will find another who interests you." Darcy fixed his cousin with a questioning glance, and Fitzwilliam obliged his unspoken query, saying: "Miss Bennet has a younger sister who is unlike any other woman I have met."

"How so?" asked Darcy, his interest aroused.

Fitzwilliam leaned back, putting one booted foot on his desk. "For one, she is the most intelligent woman I have ever met. Have you not always lamented how young ladies can speak of nothing more interesting than fashion or the weather?"

At Darcy's nod, Fitzwilliam grinned and said: "Miss Elizabeth Bennet does not fit that mode. Why, at a party a few days ago, she had some interesting things to say about the Luddite unrest in the north."

"Did she?" asked Darcy, eyes wide. "Is she a bluestocking?"

"Miss Elizabeth is intelligent enough to be a bluestocking," said Fitzwilliam, shaking his head, "but she shows no such tendencies. She gives her opinions in a sensible manner, and when she disagrees, she can argue her perspective with the best debaters at Cambridge. Though she is playful and clever and can see the foibles in others, she laces her observations with such good humor that offense is completely disarmed. And add to this, she is as pretty as her elder sister, and you have an intriguing woman, indeed."

"And her sister, Bingley's angel?"

"The epitome of sweetness and goodness, a woman much too good for this world." Fitzwilliam paused and laughed. "I am sorry, Darcy — I know that sounds terribly melodramatic. Miss Bennet is an excellent woman if one is inclined toward impeccable, though gentle, manners as Bingley clearly is. Miss Bennet and Miss Elizabeth are the jewels of the neighborhood. In my opinion, however, Miss Elizabeth rises high above all, even her sister. The other sisters are fine in various ways, but none can hold a candle to the bright flame of Miss Elizabeth."

Darcy regarded Fitzwilliam, amused at his cousin's extolling of the family. "There are more?"

"Five, if you can believe it. Each quite different from the others, though the two youngest are still young and silly. Miss Elizabeth, however, can never be termed anything remotely approaching silly."

"It seems to me you admire Miss Elizabeth," said Darcy, never having seen his cousin act this way about a woman before.

"Oh, you know me," said Fitzwilliam with an airy wave. "Though I possess my own estate, I must have a woman of fortune to augment my holdings. I have no interest in her. But I can well recognize a gem of the first order when I see one."

Though the cousins sat and talked for some time, Darcy's mind was on other matters. Fitzwilliam, jovial and easy in company though he was, could also be a difficult man to please. If he claimed this Miss Elizabeth was an excellent woman, Darcy had no doubt she was. Perhaps his time in this town would not be as dull as Darcy had expected.

"Darcy!" exclaimed Bingley when Darcy arrived at Netherfield sometime later. "It is good to see you, man. I was beginning to think you would not come at all."

"I apologize for my tardiness, Bingley," replied Darcy. "But I would never abandon you to the tender mercies of local society."

Bingley laughed. "Oh, it is not so bad. There are some here with whom one may not wish to associate, but those people exist everywhere, do they not?"

"They do," replied Darcy, thinking of what his cousin had said.

"Now, let us see you to your room before Caroline discovers your presence." Bingley grinned again. "I believe she is speaking with the cook to ensure tonight's dinner is worthy of a king."

The room to which Miss Bingley had assigned Darcy was the best Caroline Bingley had available—or at least that was what the woman would say, Darcy knew. Snell, his valet, had preceded him there and had a bath ready for him, excellent man that he was. After Darcy had cleaned and dressed in a new suit for the evening, he was preparing himself for the chore of attending Miss Bingley, when there was a knock on his door.

"Brother!" exclaimed Georgiana upon entering the room at his command. "At last you have come!"

Georgiana threw herself into his arms, and Darcy held her close, wondering at the change in her demeanor. When she had left London for Hertfordshire—to Darcy's concern, given Miss Bingley's presence—she had been a timid, sad creature, one who said little and attempted to avoid being noticed. The girl who stood before him now reminded him of how she had been at twelve, a happy, carefree girl. Georgiana had taken their father's death hard, and while she had always been a shy child, it was only after that she had become so inward-facing as to be mute in the company of others.

"I am glad to see you so well, Georgiana," said Darcy. "But I shall own I cannot account for it."

"It is wonderful here in the country!" exclaimed Georgiana. "And I have made excellent friends."

"Oh?" asked Darcy, surprised to hear it. "You have only been in the neighborhood for two weeks. Is that enough time to have such close acquaintances?"

Georgiana blushed, returning a little to the shy girl he had known before. But then she raised her head and said: "Perhaps I have not been here long. When you have met the wonderful friends I have, you will understand. Miss Elizabeth is vivacious and friendly, just what a young woman ought to be."

"Miss Elizabeth?" asked Darcy, interested to hear that name on Georgiana's lips. "She is your friend?"

"Are you acquainted with Miss Elizabeth?" asked Georgiana, confused.

"No, of course not," replied Darcy with a laugh. "It is only that Fitzwilliam spent several minutes praising her to the skies, so much so that I wondered if he was becoming enamored of her."

Georgiana fixed him with a smile which seemed to mean much but say little. "Oh no, William, Anthony is not in love with Miss Elizabeth, though if he was, I could understand why. But she *is* delightful, and he can see how she has been an excellent friend to me. She is so intelligent and confident! One cannot help but feel more poised when she is near, for she imparts of her self-assurance to all around her."

"Another member of my family praising this woman!" said Darcy, surprised once again. "I believe I shall need to make her acquaintance, for your words have intrigued me."

"Meet her you shall," said Georgiana. "Though I do not go to Longbourn every day, I go often. Do you know she also showed me around Meryton? Meryton is not Lambton, but they have some of the quaintest shops I have ever seen!"

For some moments as Darcy made his final preparations, he listened to Georgiana prattle on about Miss Elizabeth Bennet. The praises were so like what he had heard from Fitzwilliam, it seemed unlikely such an exquisite woman could exist.

But Georgiana's sudden liveliness was so unexpected, so contrary to her character, and Fitzwilliam had been so adamant, that Darcy was certain there must be something to their words. Perhaps she was not an angel with furled wings and a halo over her head, but some of what they were saying must be true rather than hyperbole.

Then the memory of what brought Darcy to Netherfield returned to him and sobered him, and Darcy knew he must speak with her of Wickham. Reluctant though he was to ruin her mood, Darcy needed to know what she thought of it.

"Georgiana," said he, "I apologize for raising this subject, but I assume you are aware of Wickham's presence in Meryton."

The curl of Georgiana's lip in contempt was unlike any reaction Darcy had expected. "Anthony informed me of it last night."

"Are you not concerned for his proximity?" asked Darcy,

perplexed.

Georgiana made a cutting motion with her hand and shook her head. "This news affects me not at all, Brother. Anthony promised me he would watch Wickham, and I am wiser now. Should he attempt his wiles with me again, I shall give him a piece of my mind."

"Then there is little more to say," replied Darcy, amazed by the sudden maturity his sister was showing. "It may not always be possible to avoid him—when he is nearby, I shall ensure he does not bother you. It would also be for the best if you avoided being alone, in Meryton, for example. Let us not give Wickham the opportunity to importune you with no one else in proximity. I shall assign Thompson to accompany you when you leave the house."

The smile with which Georgiana responded was bordering on vicious. "Mr. Wickham fears Mr. Thompson, does he not?"

"He does," replied Darcy, returning her grin.

"Then I welcome his protection. But you need not concern yourself for me, Brother, for Mr. Wickham will never dupe me again."

"I am glad to hear it."

Soon, the siblings took themselves downstairs, joining the rest of the party in the sitting-room. Fitzwilliam had arrived while Darcy had prepared for dinner and was conversing with Bingley and Hurst. Miss Bingley looked up when Darcy arrived, and though he could detect her annoyance at missing his arrival, soon her smile turned predatory.

"Fitzwilliam, do you not have a regiment to command?" asked Darcy, hoping to avoid Miss Bingley's cloying attentions for a few more precious seconds.

"I do," said Fitzwilliam, not a hint of repentance in his manner. "But the food is much better at Netherfield, and Bingley claims he is content to indulge me."

"I am," replied Bingley, good humor flowing from him.

"You should take care, my friend," said Darcy, motioning to his cousin. "He will eat you out of house and home if you allow it."

Fitzwilliam threw Darcy a mock glare while Bingley guffawed. Miss Bingley, it seemed, was not about to allow Darcy to ignore her any longer.

"Welcome, Mr. Darcy. I apologize for not being on hand when you arrived, but it seems I was not informed."

The look Miss Bingley threw at her brother suggested he had countermanded her orders to the staff and was angered by it. If she hoped to cow him, however, it was a miserable failure, for Bingley ignored her. Miss Bingley continued as if nothing had happened.

"I hope your room is comfortable, Mr. Darcy. When I chose the room, I left explicit instructions with the staff to prepare it to your specifications. If there is anything amiss, I can assure you I shall have harsh words for the maids."

"That is unnecessary," replied Darcy, reflecting she could have no idea of what his specifications consisted. "Everything is lovely, Miss Bingley. Thank you for your diligence."

The woman preened at Darcy's compliment, but she was not quick enough to continue to monopolize the conversation, for Bingley spoke up.

"You have come at an auspicious time, Darcy, old chap," said Bingley, the way in which he spoke suggesting some mischief or another. "We are planning a ball for next week, and I know how much you love to attend a dance."

Fitzwilliam snickered and Georgiana giggled—even Hurst's amused snort met his brother's quip, though Miss Bingley looked upon him with exasperation. Darcy, however, was not about to allow Bingley to tease him.

"On the contrary, Bingley, though dancing is not my favorite pastime, I have nothing against the amusement."

"That is well, for I wish to make a good impression upon my neighbors."

With interest, Darcy looked upon his friend. "Having good relations with your neighbors is always an excellent strategy. But I am confused, Bingley, for I had understood there was no option to purchase—as you will only be here less than a year, do you need to hold a ball?"

"Whether or not I need to is irrelevant," was Bingley's firm reply. "These people have been friendly and obliging and have accepted us with open arms, and I mean to show them my appreciation. But you are correct—Mr. Gardiner, the owner of the estate, means to take up residence at the end of the lease, so I will not settle here."

The sight of Miss Bingley's blush caught Darcy's attention, which he found curious, for he did not know what embarrassed her. Speaking of the matter, however, would encourage her to attempt to dominate the conversation, so Darcy addressed Bingley again.

"Where does Mr. Gardiner live now?"

"In London, or so I have heard," replied Bingley. "It is my understanding he owns a successful business there and means to hand it off to a manager while he assumes the role of a gentleman. It is also said he has relations in the neighborhood, though I know no more than this."

Miss Bingley's blush deepened at her brother's statement, intriguing Darcy even more. Could the woman know something about this mysterious owner and his relations? Interested though he was, Darcy kept firm to his intention to avoid giving the woman any encouragement.

"It is my intention to deliver the invitation to our nearest neighbors, the Bennets, in person tomorrow. Perhaps you would like to accompany us? It would be an excellent opportunity to meet some of the locals."

"Yes, I believe I should like that," said Darcy without thinking about it, much to Miss Bingley's disgust.

"Excellent!" exclaimed Bingley.

"Brother," said Georgiana, "I wondered if you will allow me to attend."

Darcy shared a look with his cousin, but Georgiana was not about to allow them to decide without further making her case. "It is only a country event, and the people in the neighborhood are excellent. I know I am not yet out, but I should like to attend very much."

"Perhaps we might allow it," said Darcy.

Before he could say another word, Georgiana squealed and threw herself into his arms again. It appeared this was becoming a regular occurrence, though Darcy could not dislike it. Seeing her so happy was a balm to his soul.

"But," said Darcy, extricating himself from his gleeful sister, "you must know there will be restrictions. You are *not* yet out, so we will insist on restricting your partners to close friends of the family, and you will go to bed after dinner."

"It is well worth my agreement if I may attend. I am so excited! Elizabeth will be so pleased!"

Once again Georgiana had dropped that name into the conversation, and while Miss Bingley did not seem to appreciate it, Darcy was growing more curious by the moment. So interested was he in every word which passed his cousin or Georgiana's lips that he quite forgot about his intention to speak to Bingley concerning this woman he was pursuing. The morrow could not come soon enough, for Darcy wished to meet Miss Elizabeth Bennet for himself.

CHAPTER VIII

$\mathcal{S}$ometimes George Wickham felt he would have no luck at all if it was not rotten luck.

"Here, what are you waiting for, Wickham?" asked one of his fellow officers. "Will you call or fold?"

"I believe I must bow out," replied Wickham, throwing his cards onto the table.

Another time, Wickham might have attempted to bluff his way through to win the hand, but given the current circumstances, he could not afford to lose. Funds were scarce and with Fitzwilliam watching his every move, Wickham knew he would be hauled onto the carpet if it became known he had accumulated markers with his fellow officers. Prudence was a concept unfamiliar to Wickham, but given the situation, it seemed there was no choice but to learn how to practice it.

With a nod to the other men at the table, Wickham rose and flipped the innkeeper a copper for his drinks and made his way from the inn. Behind him, unbidden, came his only friend in the militia, a man whose enthusiastic words had landed Wickham in this mess in the first place. The thought caused Wickham to shake his head—it was not Denny's fault. It was whatever cursed luck had led to Fitzwilliam, of all men, becoming the commander of the regiment he had decided to join.

"That differs from your usual practice, Wickham," said Denny as they walked out into the night. "I have never seen you give up on a hand—or a game—so quickly in the time I have known you."

"One simply must understand when the time comes to limit one's losses," was Wickham's blithe response.

Denny regarded him for a moment, his expression searching, and then shrugged. "Then I suppose you have learned something, my friend, for you would not have concerned yourself with such things before."

Wickham nodded, for there was no point in disputing his point. As they walked in the stillness of the night, Wickham felt the warmth through his jacket, heard the far-off cry of a wolf, wondering if the poor animal felt as caged as he did.

The thought of running had crossed Wickham's mind, for such a life as this did not suit him. Two truths which he could not deny held him back: the first was that he had little ready capital, no way of acquiring it quickly, and nowhere to go, and the second was that Fitzwilliam would set off after him in a trice. When Fitzwilliam caught him—Wickham was under no illusions he would escape the vengeful man's pursuit—then he would truly be in the soup.

No, his only recourse was to endure the situation at present and attempt to discover some way out. George Wickham had never in his life had his choices so thoroughly curtailed as they were now, and the truth of that statement annoyed him to no end. But there was nothing he could do at present. Perhaps there was some lady in Meryton who would provide him with what he needed—a fortune to share and a bed to keep warm. Fitzwilliam could not hold him back if he was to marry.

With that thought in mind, Wickham pushed his pique aside and turned to Denny. "There has been little society in this neighborhood since I arrived."

Denny laughed. "Perhaps not, but to hear our fellow officers speak of it, there will be plenty to come."

"Are you familiar with many of the families here?"

"Not as much as some of the others," replied Denny. "If you will recall, my father called me home not long after our arrival here."

"But you have some knowledge."

"I suppose I do," replied Denny.

"Then what is the lay of the land? Are there any ladies worth pursuing?"

Once again, Denny released an amused chortle. "That is what I have always liked about you, Wickham—you are entirely predictable. Still looking for some way to make your fortune, are you?"

"A man must always watch for ways to improve his lot," replied Wickham piously.

"That is the truth, my friend. The sad fact is there is little fortune in this neighborhood. Most of the estates nearby are small, and few of the ladies have much dowry."

Wickham wished to scowl at this news, but he held his countenance. Then Denny mentioned a potential lifeline.

"There is, I understand, one young lady of some fortune in the neighborhood."

"Oh?" asked Wickham, feigning nonchalance. "And who is she?"

"A woman whose brother has leased an estate nearby of late," replied Denny. "His name is Bingley, and his sister is said to have a fortune of twenty thousand pounds. Before you hare off in pursuit of this woman, you should know that she is said to possess a disposition sour enough to make any man flee in terror."

Denny laughed at his own joke, but Wickham decided against responding. There had been many times when he had tamed even the most caustic tongues, and he did not think this Miss Bingley would be any different.

Subsequent inquiries on the subject changed Wickham's outlook, especially one piece of crucial information on which he happened by chance. The officers of the regiment were a talkative bunch, and while the cynical might say they were all intent upon securing whatever prizes existed for themselves, most had no compunction at all against sharing what they knew of the local ladies.

"Oh, aye," said a Lieutenant Sanderson, a rosy-cheeked boy who was about as capable of wooing a woman as a boy of fourteen. "Miss Bingley is something of a legend around these parts, even though she has only lived here for fewer than two months."

"That bad?" asked Wickham, attempting not to wince.

"She can flay the skin from a man's bones from forty paces with naught but her sharp tongue. Poor Richards, before he left, made the mistake of approaching her at a party; she sent him away with his tail between his legs for his trouble. All you will receive from Miss Bingley is frostbite and a stinging set down. I would avoid her if I were you."

But Wickham learned the most disheartening piece of information from his superior, Captain Carter. Though Wickham had not asked Carter concerning Miss Bingley, her demeanor or her dowry, another fact Wickham had not known became clear when the man made an offhand comment.

"Bingley is an agreeable man, friendly and obliging. His sister is not his equal but if a man steers clear of her, he should be well enough. And I understand he has friends staying with him now."

"Friends?" asked Wickham, wondering if there might be another possibility.

"Yes," replied Carter. "A woman of considerable fortune, or so I understand. I have not met her, though I have heard she is still full young."

A sinking feeling appeared in the pit of Wickham's stomach, which only became worse at Carter's next statement. "It is also said her brother will join them soon. In fact, he may already be here."

Wickham nodded and made some innocuous comment, his thoughts turning inward. Darcy! This Bingley must be his friend, and Georgiana must be staying with them. Of all the cursed luck!

Caught up in the misery of the situation, Wickham considered the matter for some moments, wondering what he should do. Pursuing Georgiana was out of the question, and given the Darcys' proximity to Miss Bingley, it would be difficult to make any inroads with her either. What a foul situation this was!

In the end, Wickham decided there was nothing he could do other than to watch and act according to what he saw. If this Miss Bingley was as his fellows told him, Darcy might not have any interest in her. The bastard was never interested in *any* woman! Though he had made it his mission in life to put obstacles in Wickham's path, surely, he would not prevent Wickham from bettering his lot? While Darcy would not allow eloping or compromising her, if Wickham succeeded in winning her affection, little likely though that seemed, Darcy would not interfere.

It was all he had.

Darcy's first sight of Longbourn was positive. Rising over the surrounding trees he caught a glimpse of the manor house as the coach in which they traveled departed the road through the village and entered a drive, which was even and well-maintained. The house itself was a typical manor house of the lower gentry, its walls constructed of reddish stone, ivy climbing its surface, lending it an air of distinction and respectable age. Around the back of the manor was a large open grassy area, surrounded by groves of trees, and the hint of a small garden. It was nothing to Pemberley—it did not even compare favorably with what he had seen of Netherfield. It was, however, a picturesque location, its state of repair speaking to the industrious nature of its inhabitants, the pride of one's possessions, and the respect for one's forebears.

"What do you say to that, Mr. Darcy?" said Miss Bingley. A glance at the woman told Darcy her impression of the sight before them was not as complimentary as his had been. "It is quaint, I suppose, but these people are nothing compared with those with whom we *should* associate."

For a moment, Darcy considered what he might say in response. While he could speak of his own impressions, Darcy knew it would not stifle the woman's vitriol. Thus, he decided brevity was the best option.

"It is a picturesque setting, Miss Bingley. Other than that, I shall wait to meet its inhabitants before I come to any conclusions."

That the woman did not appreciate his cautious statement was without question. Darcy's bland response had achieved his objective, for Miss Bingley sniffed with her usual measure of disdain. A moment later, the carriage jerked to a halt in front of the manor and Darcy exited, handing his sister from within while Bingley provided the same service to Miss Bingley, much to her annoyance.

The interior of the estate did not contradict Darcy's initial impression. The entrance was clean and spacious, the décor understated, but fine. There was a hall at the far-left end of the room leading further into the house where the housekeeper led them to a door on the right, which led to what Darcy assumed was the estate's main sitting-room.

When the housekeeper led them within, the family—five younger women along with an older couple, as Georgiana had informed him— rose to greet them. Bingley performed the introductions in his usual cheery manner, and while Darcy noted the names, it was Miss Elizabeth, of whom he heard so much, who caught his attention.

The laughing eyes of which both his cousin and Georgiana had spoken were crinkled in amusement, a circumstance Darcy suspected was a common occurrence. Her fine, mahogany hair had been tied back in a simple style, and her dress, of a much simpler design than Miss Bingley's elaborate costume, suited her from the cut to the color. Had Darcy met her without hearing any earlier intelligence of what to expect, he might not have given much thought to her at first. Forewarned as he was, Darcy examined her, though as unobtrusively as he could, and he concluded that she was not only intelligent and interesting but the entirety of her figure, face, eyes, and character made her irresistible. Within moments, Darcy knew he would enjoy coming to know her—and this without having exchanged anything but the barest of greetings!

"Mrs. Bennet," said Bingley as Darcy was musing about his first impressions of Miss Elizabeth, "we have come today to invite your family to attend a ball we will hold at Netherfield on Tuesday next."

With a flourish, Bingley produced the invitation and passed it to the estate's mistress, who looked down at the elegant card. There were many small society wives, Darcy knew, who were of mean intelligence, indifferent temperament, and of flighty dispositions. Mrs. Bennet was, it seemed, none of these things, for after reading the card, she looked up at Bingley and smiled.

"Thank you, Mr. Bingley, for your gracious invitation. We should be happy to attend, although," the mistress turned her gaze on two of her girls, who, based on the order of introduction, were the youngest, "as Kitty and Lydia are not yet out, their presence is yet to be determined."

The way the youngest pouted, Darcy suspected she was at a difficult age and not afraid to show her displeasure, though the next youngest was also unhappy. That she did not protest, however, showed her mother had taught her some manners. To Darcy's vast surprise, Georgiana's voice interrupted his musings.

"I am to attend, Mrs. Bennet, and I am not much older than Miss Lydia, though my brother has insisted on some restrictions. Perhaps Miss Kitty and Miss Lydia may attend under the same?"

It was clear Georgiana's words had surprised both parents. Mr. Bennet exchanged a glance with his wife, and when the gentleman shrugged, Mrs. Bennet turned and asked her the details. Within a few brief moments, Mrs. Bennet learned of Georgiana's restrictions and gave her permission for the two youngest Bennets to attend, much to their pleasure. Both girls were effusive in their thanks, and for a few moments, they sat together chatting about the upcoming amusement and what they might expect.

After this, Georgiana approached Miss Elizabeth, and they exchanged a few friendly words. It surprised Darcy once again, for this differed greatly from the shy, withdrawn girl she had been since the incident that summer with Wickham. Then they turned toward Darcy and approached.

"Brother, this is my close friend, Miss Elizabeth Bennet," said Georgiana when they stood before him.

"Yes, Georgiana," replied Darcy, injecting a hint of humor into his voice, "I do remember the introduction."

Miss Elizabeth laughed. "You did not inform me your brother possessed teasing manners, Georgiana."

"Teasing? My brother?" Georgiana shook her head, fixing Darcy with a sly, devious look. "Anthony is the teasing one. William is accounted as being more serious than jocular."

"Is that so, Mr. Darcy?" asked Miss Elizabeth. "Given your cousin's propensity for mischief, I would think you would have developed your own, if for nothing else than to match his witticisms."

"I am not devoid of the ability for jesting, Miss Elizabeth," replied Darcy, "despite anything my cousin or my sister might say. There are, however, times for banter and times to be serious."

"Oh, aye," replied Miss Elizabeth. "One cannot go about life with nothing but a grin on one's face, for life can be a profound business. But I must say that I much prefer to laugh than the reverse; the cares of life are so much easier to bear when faced with a laugh. Do you not agree?"

Charmed, Darcy replied: "I do. Gravity is appropriate in certain circumstances, but what are we here for if not to enjoy our lives?"

"Then what do you enjoy, sir? Do you have favorite pastimes, authors, music, or the like that we may discuss?"

As it turned out, there were several tastes Darcy had in common with this lively young miss. While they were both devotees of Shakespeare, they differed in their tastes, Darcy preferring the histories while Miss Elizabeth loved the comedies. Neither was a lover of poetry, though both agreed there was some merit in it, and while Darcy preferred Bach and Handel, Miss Elizabeth loved Mozart and Beethoven. Of the more physical sort of activity, Darcy was an avid rider, and while Miss Elizabeth informed him she could ride when pressed, she much preferred the exercise gained by using her own two legs. While they had yet to discuss any weightier topics which Fitzwilliam had informed him were her specialty, Darcy liked her very much after only a few moments of conversation.

In time, the sound of a ponderous voice nearby interrupted their conversation, one that had been droning like the buzz of a bee on the edges of Darcy's consciousness for some time. Turning, Darcy saw a tall man, dressed in the black garb of a cleric, standing close to Miss Bingley, speaking in a weighty voice. Miss Bingley, it appeared, was not pleased.

"Yes, that is correct, Miss Bingley. The parsonage which I call my home is an excellent building, standing as it is in a grove of oak trees, with a picturesque view of my patroness's estate in the distance. The parsonage itself is neither too small nor too large for a man of my position in society and while those who do not know me might wonder if it is too much for a bachelor such as myself, they do not understand that I mean to marry as soon as may be. With a wife and several children running about, why, it might become too small after a time!"

The parson laughed, the only one understanding his words to be a jest. "As such, it is fortunate that I am the heir of this fine estate, for I can provide a fine position which any woman must covet. My cousin, though he appears healthy at present, will become infirm before long, I have little doubt, so my inheritance cannot be far off. It is a desirable estate, do you not agree?"

Though it was clear to Darcy that Miss Bingley did *not* agree, the lady refrained from speaking, though her poisonous look at the parson spoke volumes. The parson, however, did not notice, and when the lady tried to move away, he moved to intercept her, his words not ceasing for an instant.

"Let me tell you of my patroness's estate, Miss Bingley, for it is a jewel of a place, situated on a bit of rising land, and by no means lacking in windows. Why, I have it on good authority that when she redecorated the dining room of late—a room which must be the pinnacle of all such chambers now—she spent in excess of one hundred pounds on the materials."

It was a curious subject for a parson, for, in Darcy's experience, most talked of the evils of covetousness or lust for wealth. As he continued to speak to the unfortunate Miss Bingley, Darcy turned back to Miss Elizabeth, surprised to see her watching the scene with amusement, which, when she noticed Darcy's attention on her, changed to the rosy cheeks of embarrassment.

"I believe the gentleman was introduced as your cousin, Miss Elizabeth?" asked Darcy.

"Yes," replied she, her cheeks still flaming, but turning her attention back to Darcy. "Mr. Collins is my father's heir and is visiting us for a time."

"He seems a little . . ." Darcy paused, searching for the word. "Well, his words do not convey the usual messages the clergy try to impart."

Miss Elizabeth snickered and rolled her eyes. "No, they do not. Furthermore, Mr. Collins is a man . . . let us say he is not the most sensible of men. When he arrived, he informed us he is searching for a wife. My sisters and I cannot be more grateful we are not in contention for the position."

Miss Elizabeth delivered the comment with such wryness, Darcy could not fail to laugh—his sister joined in the merriment. "Yes, I can imagine how that would be a relief."

Darcy turned to consider the parson and his unwilling audience again. "Is this the first time Mr. Collins has been introduced to Miss Bingley?"

Once again Miss Elizabeth's cheeks attained a reddish hue. "It is." Darcy and Georgiana both looked at her askance, which increased her blush all that much more.

"Mr. Collins asked me about those of the neighborhood," explained she, though in a slow cadence, clearly still embarrassed. "It seems he wishes to marry a woman of fortune to further improve his own position. The difficulty for Mr. Collins is that there are no ladies here who possess large dowries."

"Except for Miss Bingley," said Darcy, catching on to her meaning.

He and Georgiana laughed merrily, catching Miss Bingley's attention and earning them a sour look for their temerity. Mr. Collins, however, took no notice and continued to ply her with his droning speech.

"She is the only lady here who might fit his criterion," replied Miss Elizabeth, this time her embarrassment replaced with a grin. "If she chooses not to encourage him, that is her business; I only provided the information he requested."

"Trust me, Miss Elizabeth," said Darcy, "I do not disagree. Perhaps, with Mr. Collins in attendance—and I feel he will be a constant presence whether or not she wishes it—I can enjoy a peaceful visit in the country."

In keeping with the impression she had given him as an intelligent woman, Miss Elizabeth caught his meaning at once. "You have a suitor, do you, Mr. Darcy? Given some of the comments she has made in my hearing, I never would have guessed she finds you to be a *very* agreeable man."

All three laughed together again. Their gaiety drew Miss Bingley's attention yet again, and Mr. Collins even deigned to look in their direction. Then the gentleman shrugged and began his monologue yet again, speaking of his parsonage—the stairs, unless Darcy misheard him. After another few moments of this, Miss Bingley's patience snapped.

"How fortunate you have such an excellent position, sir. It sounds like a perfect situation for one of your cousins; perhaps Miss Elizabeth is suited to become the mistress of your home?"

"Oh, I could never marry one of my cousins," said Mr. Collins, waving his hand with airy unconcern. "I require much more from a woman than they could provide."

Miss Bingley stared at him, her disbelief turning to anger, and she turned, stalking away from him in high dudgeon. Mr. Collins, however, was not about to allow her to escape, for he followed her, calling: "But Miss Bingley, you have not yet heard of my roses and petunias!"

This last sent the three companions into gales of laughter. "How fortunate for Miss Bingley that she has such an ardent admirer!" exclaimed Georgiana.

"How fortunate, indeed," replied Miss Elizabeth, her eyes shining with mirth.

It was at that moment Darcy saw the full measure of the woman's beauty. It was not mere physical comeliness, though Darcy's appreciation for what he was seeing continued to increase the more he spoke with her. No, it was the full measure of Miss Elizabeth which was so appealing. She combined a beautiful face with a lively manner, humor, intelligence, and the ability to speak about any subject. Darcy could not wait to know more about this intriguing creature.

The epiphany ended as soon as it began, and through no fault of Miss Elizabeth's. At that moment, a group of men wearing scarlet entered the room; among their number strutted the form of Darcy's detested nemesis, the man his cousin sought to reform.

Wickham became aware of Darcy's presence only a moment after Darcy discovered his, and the man paled, though whether it was with embarrassment or fear, Darcy could not say. It was fortunate he said nothing, for he bowed and turned away, joining Mr. Collins and Miss Bingley, though Darcy was uncertain he was acquainted with either.

"Georgiana," said Darcy, pointing across the room. "Wickham is here."

Darcy was proud of his sister, for her reaction was nothing more than a slight paling of her countenance and a glance at the officer. Wickham, Darcy was certain, noticed it, but he did a credible job of affecting ignorance.

"I hope he behaves himself," replied Georgiana, and then turned to Miss Elizabeth to speak again.

It was clear Miss Elizabeth had not failed to notice the exchange between them, not to mention that it was Wickham who had caught

Darcy's attention. Good manners, however, were ingrained in her, for she ignored the questions which must have leaped into her mind.

As Mrs. Bennet rose, doing her duty as hostess and introducing those who were not acquainted, Darcy considered the matter before him. Wickham would know better, he thought, than to attempt something with Georgiana, for he knew how Darcy—and perhaps, more importantly, Fitzwilliam, whom he had always feared—would react. Regardless of his cousin's assurances, however, Darcy was not convinced Wickham would behave himself; there was too much history between them for him to trust the cur.

Thus, Darcy determined that he would inform Miss Elizabeth of Wickham's conduct at the earliest opportunity. Better that she should be forewarned than to have her misled by anything Wickham might say or do.

"If I am not very much mistaken," said Georgiana, catching Darcy's attention, "it seems Miss Bingley now has another admirer."

Darcy followed her surreptitious motion and noted Wickham's proximity to the pair. Wickham, it seemed, had released his charm, as he had done so many times in the past, and was now speaking with an even more disgruntled Miss Bingley. Miss Bingley, it appeared was not any more pleased with his attention than she had been with Mr. Collins's.

"My cousin is not best pleased," said Miss Elizabeth.

Though Darcy had focused on Wickham, he saw in a moment that Miss Elizabeth was correct, for the parson was watching Mr. Wickham with barely concealed fury.

"Well, well," said Darcy, to no one in particular. "It seems this visit has become more interesting."

His companions laughed. For Darcy's part, he knew Wickham would bear watching, for the man could not be trusted to act with honor and integrity. Then again, any distraction he provided to Miss Bingley could not be unwelcome.

CHAPTER IX

$\mathcal{W}$eather was an unpredictable force of nature. Sometimes that unpredictability worked to the detriment of those who struggled under its influence, and at other times, it worked to their benefit. One of the latter occasions occurred on the morning after Elizabeth first met Mr. Darcy.

Arising early as was her custom, Elizabeth looked out her window that morning, only to see a low, grey sky, gloomy and uninviting. After looking at it for a few moments, Elizabeth decided she had too much energy to sit at home reading all day, and as a result, she decided to risk it. A few moments later, after tying her hair in a simple knot and donning one of her older dresses for her excursion, she slipped from the house and made her way down the lane toward the path which led away to the north.

For a time, Elizabeth watched the sky, concerned the heavens might open at any time to release its bounty on her head. But before she had gone more than half a mile, she noted a thinning in the clouds to the west, and soon the sun broke through, smiling down on her like a benevolent goddess full of warmth and promise. And soon after, the clouds were nothing more than a memory, conceding their power to some greater force than they. The morning began to warm, becoming more pleasant by the minute, a fine early September day to carry her along in its grasp.

When Elizabeth reached the furthest extent of her path and began the return loop back to her home, she heard the clopping of hooves against the hard-packed turf, and became aware she was not alone. Soon, from around a bend, a horse and rider appeared, tall and imposing in the morning sun. As they approached, the face of the rider came into focus, and Elizabeth saw that it was Mr. Darcy, sitting erect on a magnificent beast of a stallion, his top hat on his head making him appear even taller and more forbidding.

"Miss Bennet," said the gentleman as he cantered his horse close to her. With a smooth motion, he swung himself down from the saddle and bowed to her curtsey. "How are you this morning?"

"Very well, Mr. Darcy," said Elizabeth with a warm smile. "I see you were not exaggerating when you spoke of your interest in riding."

"Nor were you in your professed love of walking."

A smile passed between them, a sign of common interest. "What of Miss Darcy? Is she not riding, or does she prefer not to subject herself to the terror of such great creatures?"

Mr. Darcy chuckled and said: "Georgiana rides, but she is not an enthusiast like I am. This morning I left before she emerged from her room; her preference is to sleep a little later, time I often use to my advantage."

"Then your preferences are again similar to mine, Mr. Darcy, for I left before my family awoke." Elizabeth paused and amended: "Well, I am certain my father was already in his bookroom when I departed, for he is not accustomed to staying abed late either."

"A man after my own heart." Mr. Darcy paused and motioned to the path. "Shall we take this way together?"

Acquiescing, Elizabeth took the man's offered arm, noting he held his horse's reins in his other hand while the beast plodded obediently behind them. For a time, they spoke of nothing in particular — the land about them, the morning and the weather, typical subjects any recent acquaintances might discuss.

"If you walk these paths often, you must have an accurate notion of the lay of the land," observed Mr. Darcy.

"The land surrounding Longbourn, yes," replied Elizabeth. "As I ride little, I do not range far from home, but within the boundaries of my father's estate, I am knowledgeable."

"Are there any interesting features I might see during my morning rides?"

"There is not much of particular interest," said Elizabeth, thinking of the paths of her home. "Though I understand Derbyshire to be rugged, Hertfordshire is a much softer, friendlier sort of place. There are a few places where lovely forest streams flow, but the one particular favorite of mine is the low hill to the north."

Elizabeth turned and pointed to the prominence which they could see along the corridor of the path, adding: "That is Oakham Mount, though it is a grandiose name for what is nothing more than a hill. It is the tallest bit of land in these parts, and while the north is forested, one can see a fine view in any other direction, including toward Netherfield and Longbourn."

"Then I shall turn my mount's steps there when I have the opportunity," replied Mr. Darcy. Then he turned back to Elizabeth. "Have you ever seen Derbyshire, Miss Bennet?"

"No, though I have heard reports of it. My aunt lived there when she was a girl, and she is always going on about how lovely it is and how she would like to return. I believe she wished my uncle to purchase an estate there, but as Netherfield was empty so long and the price so low, it was an opportunity he could not refuse."

Mr. Darcy turned to Elizabeth with surprise. "Your uncle owns Netherfield?"

"He does," replied Elizabeth. "He made the purchase in the spring, but as his business interests are still demanding, he has not moved here yet. The year lease gives him the time to divest himself of the daily concerns and prepare to move his family."

The odd look which came over Mr. Darcy's countenance preceded the gentleman's chuckle. "Your uncle is a man of business?"

"He owns an import business that supplies many merchants in London," replied Elizabeth.

"It seems Miss Bingley knows of it, for when I first arrived, the subject of your uncle arose, and it was not palatable to her at all."

"I know, Mr. Darcy, for I informed her of the matter myself!"

A laugh arose between them, one of companionship and comfort. It gratified Elizabeth that Mr. Darcy did not appear to be a man who would look down on her for an uncle engaged in the detested realm of trade, even if he had purchased an estate. As Elizabeth's experience with Miss Bingley proved, not all were so minded.

"Then he is further along in his quest to become a gentleman than Bingley," remarked Mr. Darcy. "Bingley only leases an estate, whereas your uncle already owns his. Though Bingley still has interests in his family business, he no longer manages it, unlike your uncle."

"Perhaps Mr. Bingley will purchase his own estate next year," replied Elizabeth. "My uncle plans to move to Netherfield when the lease has expired."

Mr. Darcy nodded. "You mentioned your aunt lived in Derbyshire for some years. Do you know where?"

"In a town called Lambton, I believe," replied Elizabeth. "Her father was the parson there."

An expression of surprise came over the gentleman. "Why, Lambton is not five miles from my home!"

"Then you must know many of the same people," replied Elizabeth. "If you are here until Christmastide, my aunt and uncle always visit during the holidays. Perhaps you will have much to discuss."

"Believe me, Miss Bennet," replied Mr. Darcy, "I am eager to meet your aunt."

As they continued to walk, they continued to speak of such matters of interest, but this time Mr. Darcy spoke of his impressions of his home. It seemed to Elizabeth, however, that the reminder of Derbyshire caused a measure of quiet reflection to come over the gentleman, for his manner grew more introspective. After a time of this, he seemed to come to a resolution, for he turned to Elizabeth with purpose in his manner.

"Excuse me, Miss Bennet, but I believe I should speak of a matter of some import. There is a man in your midst, an officer you and your family should keep at arms' length."

The memory of the previous day flew back into Elizabeth's mind, and she recalled Mr. Darcy's reaction to the militia's arrival, and of one officer in particular. Elizabeth had exchanged few words with the man, and what little they had spoken, she had thought him to be a genial man. But the reaction of the two men to the other, and Mr. Darcy's solicitation to his sister, their departure soon after, had stayed on the edge of Elizabeth's thoughts.

"I must own, I had wondered about your reaction when he came into the room. Is Mr. Wickham known to you?"

Mr. Darcy nodded. "Please understand, Miss Bennet, that I would not speak but for the sincerest wish that you have the tools at your disposal to protect your family. Fitzwilliam has assured me he can control his officer and I believe he has his men watching too. I would prefer the matter did not become common knowledge, for I would not provoke Wickham to desperation, but I wish you to be forearmed against him."

"Thank you, Mr. Darcy. Is there anything in particular of which we must take care?"

With a sigh, Mr. Darcy looked away. "Wickham was the son of my father's steward, who was himself an honorable man. Unfortunately, Wickham did not live up to his father's example, being both a profligate spender and an indolent. Among his vices include gambling, accumulating debts without the ability—or intention—of honoring them, and an unfortunate tendency to use his manners to ingratiate himself with young ladies."

The thrust of Mr. Darcy's assertions Elizabeth understood at once, though fairness prompted her to clarify. "You suspect him of attempting seduction?"

"I have seen it many times," replied Mr. Darcy. "Though I do not think you and your sisters would be easy prey, he would find the challenge irresistible. Even your youngest sister's tender age would not protect her against him.

"It is true he plies his trade with an eye toward acquiring a woman's fortune, but that does not protect those lacking a substantial dowry. He is altogether without morals and thinks only of himself and his own desires. Though I trust my cousin, I would not have you defenseless against Mr. Wickham."

"Thank you, Mr. Darcy," replied Elizabeth. "I shall ensure my sisters know to take care when in company with Mr. Wickham."

That disagreeable subject behind them, they continued to walk, speaking of other, more interesting subjects. When Elizabeth parted from the gentleman some moments later, it was with a sense of regret. Though she had known Mr. Darcy only two days, she had already come to esteem him. In fact, Elizabeth wondered at the speed with which she had come to appreciate him.

Darcy accomplished his return to Netherfield with an absence of mind, as he considered Miss Elizabeth Bennet. There was an attraction between them, one which Darcy could not deny, though they had only met the previous day. Where it would lead, he did not know, for it was still too new. But Darcy was anticipating their closer acquaintance, for he knew he had discovered a rare gem here in the hinterlands of the kingdom where he would have expected to find little of interest.

Upon entering the sitting-room after changing his clothes, Darcy found himself the focus of Miss Bingley's gimlet eye. The woman was sizing him up, wondering where he had gone and if he had met anyone. That Darcy was not about to allow her to interrogate him became clear when he did not respond to her questions. That did not mean she would accept defeat.

"I see you appreciate this neighborhood, Mr. Darcy."

"On the contrary," replied Darcy, "I do not know enough of the neighborhood to be in any position to judge. However, the area is fine for riding, and as that is a pastime I enjoy, I do not doubt I will enjoy many more such mornings."

Miss Bingley fixed him with a critical eye. "Surely you do not suppose anything in this shire compares with Derbyshire. Is it not the best of all counties?"

"I believe so," replied Darcy with a chuckle. "But Derbyshire is my home, so I will own to bias. I am certain you prefer your home, and those who live here will give this place their allegiance. There is nothing surprising about that, Miss Bingley."

Miss Bingley sniffed with disdain. "There is nothing extraordinary about this place, and there is nothing special about anyone who lives here." Turning to her brother, Miss Bingley said: "There is nothing tying us to this place, Charles, for the lease ends next year, and you will not be purchasing. It would be best if we kept the neighbors at arms' length, for we would not wish them to influence us."

"I am sure I do not know what you mean," said her brother. "The people here are welcoming and obliging. I have never met friendlier people."

"What of the Bennets?" demanded Miss Bingley. "Were you so consumed with your interest in Miss Bennet that you failed to notice the poor behavior on display in Longbourn's sitting-room? Why, Mr. Collins was such a buffoon that I nearly lost my countenance more than once!"

"While I cannot disagree with you," replied Bingley, "you cannot blame the Bennets for their relations. As to the family, there is nothing the matter with them. I challenge you to point to any specific instance in which their behavior was lacking."

"What of the youngest girls wishing to take part in society when they are in no way ready to do so?"

"Has Georgiana not also been present during our visits?" asked Darcy mildly. "Is she not also to attend our amusements?"

"Your sister is far superior to those hoydens," snapped Miss Bingley, ignoring Darcy's second statement.

"There was little amiss with their behavior, Caroline," said Bingley in a tone which brooked no opposition. "Part of my reason for wishing to lease an estate was to learn what to do, but it is also, in part, to mingle in society with other gentlemen. Please desist, for I have no intention of snubbing my neighbors. We are to hold a ball next week; do you not remember?"

The scowl with which the woman responded told them all she wished to forget. It was a relief to them all when she rose, informed them all that she had much to do to show this backward society how a family of quality behaved and stalked from the room with her sister in tow. Bingley shook his head, informed Darcy he was returning to his study and left Darcy in his sister's company.

"I cannot understand Miss Bingley," said Georgiana, shaking her head at the antics of her hostess. "Though some members of the higher sets act like they are more important than anyone else, we do not associate with most of *them*. Why, then, would she suppose such behavior would endear her to us?"

"There is something in Miss Bingley which makes her wish to believe," replied Darcy. "It is because she wants to have the excuse of behaving that way herself."

Georgiana huffed. "She already behaves that way."

"So she does," replied Darcy with a grin. "That she has little reason for doing so must fill her with chagrin."

The siblings laughed together, after which Darcy was eager to leave the disagreeable subject of Miss Bingley behind.

"When I was riding today, I met Miss Elizabeth on the path."

"You did? I wish I had gone with you, for instead, I endured Miss Bingley's company here." Georgiana stopped and regarded him. "Was the meeting by chance?"

Darcy could not suppress a laugh. "Do you suspect me of meeting a young woman alone on a country path?"

"No, I know my brother would never do such a thing," replied Georgiana with a wink, suggesting she might wish he would. "I cannot be happier that you like her as much as I do, Brother."

"I did not expect to find her likes here, of all places," replied Darcy, his mind turning inward. A giggle alerted him to his sister's amusement, and Darcy fixed her with an amused grin. "What do you find diverting, Sister dearest?"

"That my taciturn brother seems to have had his head turned by a young woman of little prominence. Might it be that I am soon to acquire a sister?"

Darcy shook his head. "That, I believe, is a little premature. Miss Elizabeth, fine woman though she is, was unknown to me two days ago. I wish to know more of her before I contemplate such things."

"But you acknowledge it is possible?"

The eagerness with which his sister spoke alerted Darcy to her serious consideration of this matter. Then again, given her longer acquaintance with Miss Elizabeth, Darcy was not surprised she might be further on the path than Darcy was. Even so, she had not known Miss Elizabeth *much* longer than he had.

"Again, it is still premature," replied Darcy. "Now, there is something else of which I would like to inform you, for I spoke with her of Wickham when we were walking together."

Georgiana kept her composure at the mention of the libertine. "Oh? What did you tell her?"

"Nothing of Ramsgate, if that is what you are asking," replied Darcy.

"Oh," said Georgiana with unconcern, "we can trust Elizabeth with my secret, and I have no notion the knowledge would induce her to think anything less of me."

"No, I do not suppose she would speak of it. It would be better, however, to keep the matter in strict confidence, for the more who know of a secret, the more difficult it is to keep."

"That is true," replied Georgiana, though with less concern than Darcy might have expected. "Then you must have told her about Kympton?"

"No, I did not speak of the living," replied Darcy. At her questioning look he clarified: "Though Wickham is always eager to tell that story, I suspect he will not do so here, as Fitzwilliam will refute anything he says. The subject of our discussion was more general, as I informed Miss Elizabeth of Wickham's vices and the dangers to her sisters."

Georgiana sighed. "I do not suppose they will be as silly as I was."

Though Darcy thought to interject with a protest, Georgiana shook her head. "Do not concern yourself, Brother. I have come to terms with my culpability in that manner, and I have determined I shall do better. It is nothing less than the truth that I did not behave as I ought. If one good thing has come of it, I am much wiser than I used to be."

"Much wiser, I suspect, than the youngest Bennet sisters. They have not, as you have," insisted Darcy when Georgiana made to protest, "been the target of a man of Wickham's utter lack of morality. It seemed to me yesterday that they are still young and . . . immature, perhaps?"

With a sigh, Georgiana nodded. "So Elizabeth has told me." Seeing Darcy's look she smiled and said: "Kitty and Lydia can be great fun, but sometimes their immaturity shows. Mrs. Bennet and her elder daughters do their best, and they have a woman who gives them lessons, but I suspect they will not be the equal of their sisters when they are grown."

"What is your impression of Miss Bennet?" asked Darcy, thinking of Fitzwilliam's assertions of the woman and Bingley's interest in her.

"She is a lovely woman," replied Georgiana. "I do not find her as interesting as Elizabeth, but there is nothing the matter with her."

"Does she return Bingley's interest, do you think?"

Surprised, Georgiana gazed at him. "Oh, there is no doubt about that. I have never seen a woman so eager for a man's attention as Miss Bennet is for Mr. Bingley's."

"That contradicts Miss Bingley's assertion on the subject," replied Darcy, his wry smile informing his sister of the jesting nature of his comment.

Georgiana understood and laughed. "Miss Bingley wishes for advancement in society, and though Jane is everything good, she cannot provide that." Then Georgiana fixed him with a sly look. "If another were to display more interest in *her*, Miss Bingley would release her opposition to Mr. Bingley's interest."

"There you suppose wrong, Georgiana," replied Darcy. "Though I am her first priority, she still wishes her brother to make a splendid marriage. I doubt she will accept her brother's interest in Miss Bennet until he is waiting in front of the altar for her as his bride."

Proving Darcy's supposition, Miss Bingley continued to disparage the Bennet family whenever the opportunity presented itself, though in a manner which was a little less overt than her usual manner. She spoke of the neighborhood and the dearth of acceptable people, she waxed poetic on the difficult marriage situation in which the ladies found themselves, and more than once she referred to Mr. Collins as if the Bennets could choose their relations. By the time Fitzwilliam arrived for dinner, Darcy was tired of hearing the woman's voice and wished she would cease her diatribes.

There was a brief time in which Darcy found relief from her constant words, for Fitzwilliam had heard of the previous day's events. "I understand Wickham visited Longbourn yesterday," said he. Though she continued to speak, Darcy and Fitzwilliam ignored her in favor of the subject at hand. "My officers mention you were also present?"

"We were," acknowledged Darcy. "I was there when Bingley delivered the invitations to the Bennets for his ball, for I wished to be introduced to them."

Fitzwilliam gave a low whistle under his breath. "Bingley delivered the invitation to the Bennet family himself? That will do nothing to quell the rumors of his interest in Miss Bennet."

It appeared Miss Bingley heard the exchange, for she shot them a hateful glare. It was no trouble for Darcy to ignore her.

"No, I suppose it will not. That is Bingley's concern, however, and I mean to have no part in the debate."

"Good," said Fitzwilliam. "Did Wickham behave himself?"

"As far as I could see," replied Darcy. Then he grinned. "I would not suggest he is not up to his old tricks or that he cannot sniff out a woman with a dowry from one hundred paces. The moment he entered he singled out Miss Bingley for his attentions and did not leave her so long as we were there. It appears Miss Bingley has no dearth of suitors, for Mr. Collins also wished to make his presence felt."

"Mr. Collins?" asked Fitzwilliam, amused by Darcy's tone of voice.

"A cousin of the Bennets," replied Darcy. "If I had not seen him myself, I might not have believed it possible that he could be so ridiculous. I almost wonder if he is Aunt Catherine's parson, for he is the kind of self-important sycophant she might choose."

"Then Miss Elizabeth did not tell you?"

"Tell me what?" asked Darcy, confused.

"Your supposition is correct, for Mr. Collins is none other than the current parson at Hunsford."

Darcy groaned, regretting the quirk of fate which led to Lady Catherine's parson being the Bennets' cousin. "Once he realizes our connection with her, he will turn his attention on us."

"You more than I, old boy," replied Fitzwilliam "It would not surprise me in the slightest if he has heard of your engagement with Anne."

"That is a fool's wager, Fitzwilliam," growled Darcy. "When does Lady Catherine not speak of it as if it were an established fact?"

"Never," replied Fitzwilliam. Then he paused and chuckled. "This news of Miss Bingley is interesting. Who would have thought she would attract so much attention? I must see Mr. Collins courting her, for I know it must be a spectacle.

"As for Wickham, my senior officers know to watch him. Should he step out of line, he will not like my response."

Darcy nodded and their conversation ended when Miss Bingley approached. One thing the woman did not appreciate was Fitzwilliam escorting her to dinner whenever he dined with them, he, being the son of an earl, while Darcy was only a gentleman. Darcy knew she would prefer he did not come, but as Bingley had issued a standing invitation to Fitzwilliam, she could do nothing.

As the woman had one subject of which she wanted to speak, it was difficult for the other diners to speak between themselves, Miss Bingley being possessed of a strident voice. Fitzwilliam listened to her rants for some time before he lost his temper. That loss, however, he turned to a moment amusing to almost all.

"It is unfortunate you dislike the Bennets so much, Miss Bingley," said he when she paused to draw breath. "Getting on with one's neighbor smooths the path for a landowner."

Miss Bingley delivered a saccharine smile to her dining partner. "As my brother does not own this estate and shall not purchase it, our relations with our present neighbors do not signify. The opinion of such people would not concern me a jot anyway."

"Fitzwilliam nodded, his manner serious. "I suppose you are correct, Miss Bingley. For myself, I find the Bennets to be a good and interesting family, one with which I wish to deepen my acquaintance."

Fitzwilliam paused in thought. "If you are amenable to the suggestion, perhaps I shall suggest my father visit."

"Your father?" Miss Bingley's words were no less than a squeak.

"Yes," replied Fitzwilliam. "The earl appreciates people of intelligence, and I suspect he will like the Bennets as much as I do."

Miss Bingley's surprise changed to a flat stare. "The earl would like the Bennets."

"My father is not proud, Miss Bingley," replied Fitzwilliam. "He accepts others on their merits, not their standing. Yes, I believe my father would like the Bennets very much."

It seemed there was little more for Miss Bingley to say, for she remained quiet for the rest of the meal. Though Darcy could not speak for the others in the room, he appreciated her forbearance.

CHAPTER X

᠅

Visits were an important part of society, and Mrs. Bennet, as a woman who had not been born to the station she held as the wife of a gentleman, was careful to adhere to all such norms of gentle behavior. Elizabeth knew this about her mother. What she also knew was that her mother was a social woman, one who delighted in friends and family, in pleasant company and sharing news. That this rarely descended to gossip filled Elizabeth with a measure of gratitude, for it could have, given her mother's open temperament.

Mrs. Bennet demonstrated this facet of her character the day after Elizabeth met with Mr. Darcy on the paths of Longbourn. While her mother was cognizant of the polite forms of society, however, it did not mean she was blind to certain facts regarding those at Netherfield. It was the principal reason they had not visited the estate often since the Bingleys had come to the neighborhood.

"I suppose," said Mrs. Bennet that morning, "we should return the Bingleys' civility and visit Netherfield, for we are already several visits in their debt."

"Yes, that would be the proper thing to do," replied Elizabeth.

Mrs. Bennet, knowing Elizabeth's character well, noted the irony in her daughter's voice. "If Miss Bingley was more welcoming, we might go more often. As it is, as they have been so good as to deliver the invitation to the ball to us, it would be rude if we did not return the call."

"Miss Bingley is not *so* severe, Mama," said Jane from where she sat nearby.

It was a matter of some urgency for Jane to think well of Miss Bingley, though it was true she felt that way about everyone. In Miss Bingley's case, Jane's growing feelings for the gentleman and her desire for good relations with a woman she hoped would be her future sister provided the impetus for her wishes. Elizabeth could well understand, though she knew Miss Bingley would not return Jane's overtures. Elizabeth also felt, however, that Miss Bingley would, if faced with the reality of Jane as her sister, relent, though she was uncertain if the woman would accept Jane's position as mistress of Mr. Bingley's house, a position she held herself. In that instance, Jane's sweet demeanor could either be a benefit or a detriment, and only time would tell which it would be.

"I think Miss Bingley would prefer not to associate with us," said Mrs. Bennet, "but she will be gracious and accept us, I am certain.

"You consider the woman your friend, I know," added Mrs. Bennet when Jane would have protested again. "It speaks well of you that you do, Jane dear. I say nothing derogatory of Miss Bingley; I only wish you would take care and accept the woman's *sincere* overtures while seeing her with an eye free of any occlusion."

This Jane accepted with a nod, and Mrs. Bennet turned her attention back to Elizabeth. "The only matter which concerns me is the fact that the Bingleys are to host a ball next week. Would we impose on upon them when they are engaged in planning?"

Elizabeth pursed her lips and considered her mother's question, when Mr. Collins, who had been listening to their conversation, interjected with his own opinion.

"There can be no imposition. Why, my patroness, Lady Catherine de Bourgh, has always maintained that it is nothing to entertain guests whenever they deign to appear at her door."

"That is interesting, Mr. Collins," said Mrs. Bennet, her tone impatient. "Did Lady Catherine say as much when amid planning entertainment for the entire neighborhood?"

Mrs. Bennet's reply threw Mr. Collins into confusion, his mouth opening and closing in a vain attempt to speak. Then he closed his mouth, swallowed, and offered a spurious declaration, one Elizabeth thought would have been worthy of his patroness.

"Lady Catherine is of such consummate ability that it should not matter what she was planning. I have seen her act as a hostess for friends she invited to dine as easy as she has hosted me for a night of cards."

"In other words," said Mrs. Bennet, "Lady Catherine does not host balls."

"Well—" stammered Mr. Collins. "Not since I have been at Hunsford, though I am certain it is not beyond her capabilities."

"In this instance," said Elizabeth, eager to avoid an argument, "I believe I must agree with Mr. Collins's assessment."

The parson preened, but the smile ran away from his face when Elizabeth added: "But not for the same reasons. Were today the day before the ball, I believe it *would* be an imposition to interrupt their preparations. As there are several more days before the event, we can visit for a half-hour and not impose."

A beaming Mr. Collins fixed Mrs. Bennet with a satisfied smirk, to which Mrs. Bennet caught Elizabeth's eye and rolled hers discretely where the parson could not see. Elizabeth held in a laugh, knowing Mr. Collins would demand to know what was so diverting.

Amusement, when it came to Mr. Collins, however, was a fleeting emotion. After the private exchange between mother and daughter, Mrs. Bennet fixed Mr. Collins with an exasperated glare.

"I take it you mean to accompany us."

"Well," said Mr. Collins in his conceited tones, "one day I *am* to be master of this estate. As such, it behooves me to become acquainted with my neighbors."

"Perhaps it is true you will one day own this estate," replied Mrs. Bennet, "but you should remember that Mr. Bingley does not own Netherfield—my brother does. Thus, there is little reason for you to come to know him, for he will not reside there when you inherit."

A mask of confusion overcame Mr. Collins's countenance. Though she smirked at the point she had scored, Mrs. Bennet did not bother to revel in her victory. Rising, she fixed her three eldest daughters with a significant look.

"We shall depart in fifteen minutes' time."

Intent on accompanying them, Mr. Collins also left the room humming to himself, though his grasp of music was so poor that Elizabeth had no notion what he could be singing. Jane and Elizabeth shared a look, laughed, and then left the room to see to their own preparations, Mary following along behind.

The Bennet carriage was not a large vehicle and had been strained to capacity more than once since the Bennet sisters had become adults. With seven family members, Mr. Bennet was often obliged to ride on the box with the driver, for to seat seven in its confines was next to impossible. But the carriage had never seemed so small as it did that morning, though only five entered therein.

When one considered the relative sizes of the two men, there was no escaping the fact that Mr. Collins was a larger man than Mr. Bennet. The differences, however, were not so profound as to lead the Bennet women to suspect that Mr. Collins's presence in lieu of Mr. Bennet's would leave them all so cramped. Mr. Collins lolled about the carriage, unheeding of the family's discomfort, never saying a word of apology, or even so much as noticing he was making the journey difficult. Rather, he fixed his gaze outside the window, ignored them all, and continued to hum in his tuneless approximation of a song.

It was fortunate that Mrs. Bennet had taken it upon herself to sit on the same bench as the parson, for Elizabeth wondered if she or one of her sisters might be considered compromised because of their forced proximity to him. Though her mother pushed experimentally at the hand which lay on the seat a time or two, Mr. Collins took no notice and remained where he was. At length, she sighed, shook her head, and exchanged a heavenward glance with Elizabeth. And while there had been times when Lydia or Kitty had behaved in a like manner, never had they been this heedless.

The carriage pulled to a halt in front of the estate, and Mr. Collins, taking no thought for his duty as a man, bounded out of the carriage and up the stairs to the manor's entrance, leaving the four women behind. The surprised footman, who had not had time to open the door for him, looked inside at the mistress, uncertain of what he should do.

"Perhaps it is for the best," muttered Mrs. Bennet, as she allowed the footman to hand them down.

"Had Mr. Collins taken my hand, it might have forced me to ask for a room in which to wash it," said Elizabeth.

Her sisters snickered at her irreverent joke, while her mother turned a mock glare on her, joining with their jollity. John, the footman, was hard-pressed to keep his countenance and was not entirely successful if the snorts Elizabeth heard were any indication. When the four ladies alighted, they straightened their skirts and approached the door, where, even now, Mr. Collins was standing, arguing with the housekeeper.

"You shall take me at once to the mistress of the estate. Do you not know who I am?"

"I neither know nor care," said Mrs. Nichols, a woman known to the Bennets. "Wait for the rest of your party; I shall then convey you all to the sitting-room."

"Thank you, Mrs. Nichols," said Mrs. Bennet, giving the woman a smile and interrupting Mr. Collins's diatribe. "We are all gathered — please convey us to the mistress."

Mrs. Nichols curtseyed and turned to walk away, the five visitors following them. As she walked, Elizabeth could hear Mr. Collins muttering under his breath, promising to have her removed from her post. Annoyed with the parson as she was, Elizabeth could not help but snap at him.

"I suggest you allow the matter to drop, Cousin. Mrs. Nichols is an excellent housekeeper, and I know for a fact my uncle shall not part with her services, regardless of your opinion."

The sour look Mr. Collins fixed on Elizabeth spoke to his feelings. The parson, however, decided against speaking, a fact for which Elizabeth could be nothing but grateful. Within a few moments, they entered the sitting-room and greeted the gathered Netherfield party.

"Oh, Lizzy!" exclaimed Georgiana at the sight of her. "I have longed to see you!"

With those words, Georgiana and her brother commandeered Elizabeth's company, and she sat to speak with them. Jane joined Mr. Bingley, as was her custom, while Mrs. Hurst took on the office of greeting Mrs. Bennet. Miss Bingley, her hard gaze narrowing at Elizabeth's position between the Darcys, moved to intercept them but was herself intercepted by Mr. Collins.

"Miss Bingley," said the man in his arrogant and nasally voice. "How fortunate it is to see you again, for I must assume that you have wished to see me as much as I have longed for your company."

Had Mr. Collins possessed even a hint of sense he would have known at once that Miss Bingley might have wished to see a wild boar charging her rather than Mr. Collins. The parson, however, took no notice and spoke, rarely pausing to draw breath, never allowing her to say anything in response. Elizabeth did not know if the woman's forbearance would last in the face of her mounting frustration and fury when Mr. Collins began to speak of the dearest subject to his heart.

"My patroness, Lady Catherine de Bourgh, you see," the parson was saying, "is a woman of many abilities and talents. Why, she not only had the wisdom to send me here to search for my future companion, but she took the liberty of inspecting the parsonage to suggest changes to prepare it for her coming. These changes, I assure you, I have followed in every particular.

"'Mr. Collins,' said she in her usually condescending manner, 'the closets I see before me are horribly bare of anything resembling convenience. I would recommend you add shelves, for such items may be adapted in many ways for the use and comfort of your guests.' Thus has Lady Catherine proved her wisdom, making my parsonage the only one in Kent with such fine appointments."

Though Elizabeth was on the edge of bursting out into laughter. After what happened next, she almost wished she had.

"Lady Catherine de Bourgh?" asked Georgiana, not realizing the mistake she was making. "Why, Lady Catherine is my aunt!"

Mr. Darcy, it seemed, was not blind to the consequences of making such an obsequious toad aware of their family connection, but the damage was already done. Though Mr. Collins could not respond for several moments out of stupefaction, he recovered quicker than anyone might have wished.

"Lady Catherine is your aunt?" For the moment, no one could determine whether he was horrified or struck with awe. "Have I been in the presence of members of Lady Catherine's noble family and been unaware?"

Belated though it was, Georgiana seemed to understand what she had done, for she looked at her brother with uncertainty. Mr. Darcy, however, appeared amused at Mr. Collins's manner and was not unwilling to respond.

"We are related to Lady Catherine, though your ignorance of the matter is unsurprising."

"Of course!" exclaimed Mr. Collins. "Mr. Darcy! I have heard Lady Catherine herself speak of you and your sister in the fondest terms!"

"Family is of great importance to Lady Catherine."

"It is!" exclaimed a rapturous Mr. Collins. "Let me say then, Mr. Darcy, that Lady Catherine and her excellent daughter were in the best of health when I left Kent."

"Thank you, Mr. Collins, for that confirmation. I received word from Lady Catherine myself only last week confirming the same."

The vigorous nod with which the parson responded led Elizabeth to wonder if he was about to do himself permanent damage. The thought was so amusing, that Elizabeth turned away to hide her laugh with a feigned cough.

"Let me also say, Mr. Darcy," said Mr. Collins, "that Lady Catherine herself has spoken to me in the most animated terms of her anticipation for your upcoming union with her most excellent daughter. What a match it shall be! What felicitations shall be yours! What a splendid fortune you shall create together. One can scarcely contemplate it!"

Two things struck Elizabeth at once: the first was how ill Miss Bingley appeared at the parson's assertions, and the second was how a pang entered her heart at the same time. Before she could contemplate this thought, however, Georgiana leaned forward and caught her attention.

"Will my aunt never leave this subject alone? It is nothing more than her own hopes, for William does not mean to marry Anne, and I doubt Anne wishes to have William as a husband."

Relief flooded through Elizabeth, though the reason escaped her at the moment. Mr. Collins continued to speak without cessation of the wonders of his patroness and her expectations for Mr. Darcy, but when Elizabeth looked at the gentleman, she could see Mr. Collins's antics had ceased to amuse him. It is the mark of a gentleman to turn away from another when he is being ridiculous, and Mr. Darcy chose that manner of response, turning back to Elizabeth to resume their interrupted conversation.

"Pray, is there anything you wish me to tell Lady Catherine when next I write to her?' asked Mr. Collins, again interrupting their conversation. "It would be no trouble to include whatever comments you might have or include your felicitations to your fair betrothed."

"No, Mr. Collins," said Mr. Darcy. "That will not be necessary."

Then Mr. Darcy turned his attention back to Elizabeth and spoke again. Elizabeth did not know if Mr. Collins would have continued to importune Mr. Darcy regardless of his obvious disinclination for speaking with him; however, at that moment, Miss Bingley interjected herself into their conversation, drawing Mr. Collins's attention.

"A connection between the Bennets and your aunt's parson," said she in a voice brimming with harsh laughter. "How quaint! What other high connections do you Bennets have hiding in the woodwork? A tradesman, a parson, a country solicitor—perhaps you have an innkeeper or a blacksmith too?"

"No, Miss Bingley," said Mrs. Bennet, her annoyance spilling into her voice. "Respectable professions have we, but none of those you suggest."

"Let me tell you something of *my* connections!" exclaimed Mr. Collins, and Miss Bingley was once again forced into the parson's company.

"It seems Miss Bingley possesses the most ardent of suitors," said Elizabeth to her companions, unafraid to allow her amusement to show. Mr. Darcy and Georgiana laughed at her sally and Miss Bingley, though she had moved some distance away—attempting and failing to escape Mr. Collins—glared at them as if knowing of their conversation topic.

"That she does," said Georgiana. The girl turned her gaze on Elizabeth, and said in a playful tone: "Are you not jealous of her fortune? Shall you accept defeat at the hands of Miss Bingley?"

"Believe me, Georgiana," said Elizabeth, wryness seeping into her voice, "I wish Miss Bingley nothing but the best with Mr. Collins. Of the gentleman's society, a very little goes a long way."

Georgiana laughed and rose, giving them both a wink, before joining Mary, who had been watching the proceedings. Soon, they were engaged in a close conversation, concerning music, unless Elizabeth missed her guess.

"So, you are engaged already, are you Mr. Darcy?" said Elizabeth, regarding the gentleman with an arched eyebrow. "Perhaps you should make this known to the neighborhood, for you shall break the hearts of young maidens everywhere if you do not take care."

With a chuckle, Mr. Darcy said: "I am not engaged to my cousin, Miss Elizabeth, and I suspect you already understand that. It is true my aunt has long wished for the union; she does not possess as much sway with me as she might wish."

"There are many advantages to the match," said Elizabeth, "as Mr. Collins has stated, however ineloquent his words. Is your cousin's estate not extensive?"

"If I cared for nothing more than wealth, I might agree with you," replied he. "However, I have always hoped for something more in marriage than a cold union for the procurement of riches."

"And your cousin?" asked Elizabeth. "What does she think about the matter?"

"You must understand, Miss Elizabeth, that my aunt is of a forceful personality, whereas my cousin is not. Anne does not often volunteer an opinion of her own without my aunt interjecting, and given my particular . . . difficulties speaking to her, lest Lady Catherine assume more than I mean, I have not asked her opinion. Given her general demeanor toward me, however, I suspect she has no more interest in marrying me than I have in her."

"Then it seems to me, Mr. Darcy, that you have fulfilled your obligation to your cousin and your aunt."

"I have always seen it that way, Miss Elizabeth." Mr. Darcy paused and considered the matter for a moment. "As for Miss Bingley, she has long wished to be the mistress of my estate."

The way he phrased it told Elizabeth everything she needed to know of the situation. Miss Bingley had no interest in the man himself—or mayhap it was more correct to say her primary interest was the man's estate and his position in society, rather than his person.

"Yes, I see how that would disconcert you, Mr. Darcy, to be pursued for circumstances not in one's control."

Elizabeth turned and watched Miss Bingley, noting the woman's hateful glances in their direction coupled with her baleful glares at the still blathering parson. A thought crossed Elizabeth's mind and a chuckle escaped her lips, prompting a glance from her companion. Noting his questioning gaze, Elizabeth was happy to explain.

"It seems, Mr. Darcy, that Miss Bingley is experiencing the same frustration to which she has subjected you. Do you think Mr. Collins has any interest in her which is not due to her possession of a fine dowry?"

Mr. Darcy nodded wryly. "It seems you are correct, Miss Elizabeth. If my observation is correct, it does not appear Miss Bingley is enjoying the experience."

"Is it too much to hope that she will realize the truth and mend her ways?"

With a shaken head Mr. Darcy informed her: "In this instance, I believe it is too much to ask, Miss Elizabeth. I doubt she will see anything other than the obstacle placed in the path of her schemes."

"I suppose you must be correct, Mr. Darcy," murmured Elizabeth.

For some moments, they remained in companionable silence, watching those around them. Though Elizabeth watched, she did not see, for instead her thoughts were fixed upon the person of the gentleman at her side. It was a curious thing, she decided, that a man she had met only a few days before had become such a matter of interest for her. Did Mr. Darcy feel the same? Elizabeth could not be certain, but she soon realized she hoped he did; she hoped it very much, indeed.

"I hope you do not think I am being too forward, Miss Elizabeth," said Mr. Darcy, drawing Elizabeth's attention back to him. "It is on my mind that I should like to have your hand for a dance at Bingley's ball. Might I . . ."

Mr. Darcy paused and chuckled, and he fixed Elizabeth with a rueful look. "It has not been my custom to dance much at balls or assemblies, Miss Bennet. I would not have you think I am too proud or impressed with my position in society, but I have often found that young ladies will raise their hopes due to nothing more than the solicitation to dance."

Knowing this might be the sign of his regard, Elizabeth smiled and replied: "I hope you do not think *I* am one of those women, Mr. Darcy."

A broad smile came over the gentleman's countenance. "Perish the thought, Miss Elizabeth. That is why I feel comfortable asking you for your first sets, if you please."

"I am eager to accept. They are yours."

With those final words, they settled again into a companionable silence. While it was only a first step, Elizabeth thought it was a significant one, given her observation of the gentleman's reserve, coupled with his own testimony of the same. It was still premature, to be certain, but Elizabeth felt this man could be all she wished for in terms of a suitor. With that, she was content.

CHAPTER XI

$\mathcal{U}$pon returning home, Elizabeth found herself the subject of Jane's intense interest and interrogation. While Elizabeth might not have supposed her sister had been capable of any attention which was not focused on Mr. Bingley, it seemed her sister was more observant than she had expected.

"Lizzy," said Jane when they returned home, "I should like to speak with you.

While Mary entered saying nothing, Mrs. Bennet looked on, displaying her amusement, before announcing she must speak with Mrs. Hill, their housekeeper, and left them alone. Even that was not enough, for Jane grasped Elizabeth's arm and pulled her up the stairs toward their rooms. From the nursery, which Mr. Bennet had converted to a schoolroom when the Bennet sisters grew older, the sound of the woman who had been engaged to teach Lydia and Kitty reached them, but Jane ignored it, pulling Elizabeth into her room. Once the door was closed behind them, Jane turned a demanding look on her sister.

"I must own to having come to some interesting conclusions, Lizzy, though I would not have thought my sister capable of behaving in such an impulsive manner. Mr. Darcy, though we have only known him for a few days, appears to have made quite an impression upon you."

Feeling her cheeks heat, Elizabeth nodded, though she did not answer at once. It was clear from Jane's stance and the impatient tapping of her foot on the floor that she would not allow Elizabeth to retreat without the required explanation being offered.

"I do esteem Mr. Darcy," said Elizabeth after composing herself for a moment. "He is an excellent man, the best of men, I am coming to believe."

Jane appeared more surprised than ever, for she gawked at Elizabeth. After a moment, however, she came and sat by Elizabeth's side, regarding her with unfeigned interest

"For you to come to esteem a man with such speed is unlike you, Lizzy."

"Perhaps I have never met a man who is so easy to esteem," replied Elizabeth. When Jane pursed her lips, Elizabeth felt compelled to clarify: "I am not in love with Mr. Darcy, if that is what you are asking. The acquaintance is too new for that."

Elizabeth paused and laughed. "You would think me mad if I were to declare undying love for a man whom I have not known for a week."

"We have always declared we would marry for only the deepest love."

"And you are concerned with my affinity for a gentleman who was only just introduced to us this week."

"No, Lizzy," replied Jane. "If you say you love a man, I must allow you the knowledge of your own mind, regardless of the length of the acquaintance. I only wish to understand."

"How can you understand when I do not understand myself?" asked Elizabeth. "There are a few things I know, Jane, and that sustains me and gives me hope. Mr. Darcy is a man I would like to know better; I do not know how a man who has had such a hand in raising such a wonderful young woman as Georgiana, one who has been given a good character by men of the quality of Colonel Fitzwilliam and Mr. Bingley can be anything other than an excellent man himself."

"Yes, I suppose you must be correct," replied Jane.

"At present, I intend nothing more than to accept Mr. Darcy's overtures and learn more of his character. If he should prove to be what I expect he is, I would accept his proposal, should he offer it, with gratitude. But I stress it is still early in our acquaintance, and I do not *know* him yet."

"Then you will have my support," said Jane. For a moment, she regarded Elizabeth, as if attempting to make something out. "It seemed to me you were speaking of some weighty subject, Lizzy. Do you care to share?"

Elizabeth fixed her sister with a grin. "We spoke of Miss Bingley and Darcy's aunt, Lady Catherine, but of more import, Mr. Darcy *may* have asked me for the first sets at Mr. Bingley's ball."

"And *may* you have accepted them?" returned Jane.

"Perhaps," replied Elizabeth. "What better way is there to learn of a man than to learn how he dances?"

The sisters collapsed into laughter. It was a blessing to have such a close and wonderful sister as Jane, Elizabeth reflected. She had no better supporter.

Caroline Bingley was not happy — this was plain to anyone who cared to look, whether or not they were familiar with her moods. Though it could be said that she was not often happy, in the present circumstances, she had more reason than most for her discontent. That did not mean Darcy, though he empathized with her, meant to do anything to relieve her distress.

The reason for her current state, that of stalking about the room, gesticulating with wild abandon and complaining, was the continual and ineffectual attentions of one William Collins, parson. The scene that morning had been amusing, to say the least, for the parson had come before normal visiting hours — and this after visiting with the Bennets the day before — and had stayed for much longer than was proper, imposing himself on Miss Bingley and refusing to be moved from his objective. When he had left — Darcy thought Miss Bingley had been on the verge of ordering him thrown from the estate — Miss Bingley's explosion of temper had followed.

"Can the Bennets not keep their repulsive cousin at Longbourn where he belongs?" demanded Caroline in one loud burst of displeasure.

"He is a guest at their home, Caroline," said Mrs. Hurst, a rather surprising voice of reason. "Even if they wished it, they cannot control his movements."

In Darcy's opinion, the Bennets would have no interest in keeping their cousin at Longbourn and relished every moment he was away from them. 'Repulsive' was an accurate word for Mr. Collins, in Darcy's estimation.

Miss Bingley huffed at her sister's reasonable words. "I am sure they must push him out the door, for even they cannot stand him. What manner of man walks three miles of country roads to impose upon a woman who does not know him, and does not wish to?"

"It sounds much like accounts of our father's pursuit of Mother," said Mrs. Hurst in a dreamy voice. "Mama often claimed our father was a romantic."

The only reply Mrs. Hurst received to her wistful introspection was a sour look from her sister, who continued to pace. Though he sympathized with Miss Bingley in a general sense, Darcy found the situation amusing. The relief he received from Miss Bingley's insufferable attention was akin to the icing on the cake.

Be that as it may, it was clear someone would need to do something to rein in Mr. Collins's ardor. It was not Darcy's responsibility to be that voice of reason; however, Bingley was self-effacing and Hurst was so clearly on the edge of hilarity whenever the parson was present that Darcy knew it may fall to him. In fact, Hurst was not above tweaking his sister's nose at every opportunity, and this was one he could not pass up.

"I think you are not seeing the possibilities inherent in the situation, dearest Caroline. This Mr. Collins is, perhaps, not the most impressive of specimens I will grant you. If you were to marry him, you would have the constant attendance of Mr. Darcy's aunt. It sounds like he would be an excellent husband!"

"Perhaps we should go to Meryton for a time," said Mrs. Hurst, eager to avoid an argument, even as her sister whirled on Hurst and fixed him with a hateful glare.

Miss Bingley turned a horrified glance on her sister. "Why ever would we go there?"

"Caroline," said Mrs. Hurst, her tone reasonable, "it is clear this business of Mr. Collins is affecting you more than you realize. Would it not be beneficial to take your mind from your troubles?"

"If it was not *Meryton,* you may be correct," spat Miss Bingley. "What is there in that speck for us? I should not wish any of my friends to know that I went there except under the most extreme duress."

"If you do not recall," said Mrs. Hurst, "none of our friends are here. And what better amusements do we have? Our preparations for the ball are complete. Shall we sit about, bemoaning our fate, wallowing in our misery? I should much prefer to go out for a time."

"Oh, yes, let us go," said Georgiana, much to Darcy's surprise. "I should like to walk about for a time. Shall we not go Miss Bingley?"

"Yes, perhaps you are correct," said Miss Bingley. "It *would* be a relief to leave Netherfield for a time."

It struck Darcy that he had underestimated his sister. Georgiana, he saw, had learned how to deal with Miss Bingley in a way that eased her own experience with the woman. The simple mention that she would like to go to Meryton had the effect of changing Miss Bingley's opinion. Miss Bingley, eager as she was to impress Darcy, had always felt that acting the sycophant with his sister would garner his approval, as strange as that may sound. Georgiana had recognized that fact and was using it to her advantage.

Darcy wondered for a moment if he should be concerned that his sister was manipulating Miss Bingley into doing what she wanted. Then he decided there was no reason to do so. Having endured Miss Bingley's ways for the sake of Darcy's friendship with Bingley, he could not begrudge her any advantage she might gain.

"What of you, Mr. Darcy?" asked Miss Bingley, turning her predatory gaze on him. "Shall you not join us also?"

"Thank you, Miss Bingley," said Darcy, "but I think I will ride out today instead."

The woman's smile had grown larger when he first spoke but ran away from her face when Darcy declined. For a moment, he thought she might protest. The reality of her inability to direct him must have returned to her mind at that moment, for she hid a grimace and wished him a pleasant ride.

With a nod, Darcy smiled in parting at his sister and went to his room to change. Though it was later in the day, he wondered if he might see Miss Elizabeth again. Had Miss Bingley known of his thoughts at that moment, Darcy was certain she would not have been so willing to allow him to leave unmolested.

If there was one thing Fitzwilliam could not abide, it was poor behavior. It was one of the—many—reasons he had always despised George Wickham, for though Wickham affected the best manners and an amiable demeanor, his behavior was atrocious.

Fitzwilliam's father, the Earl of Matlock, and one of the best men Fitzwilliam had ever known, had raised both of his sons to believe in the basic principle of respecting one's fellow men. Though his father possessed a streak of pride for his family, his name, and his position, he was kind to all; he had never believed in his superiority due to his title, the accident of birth. Fitzwilliam's experience in the army had reinforced these lessons, teaching him that nobility was not confined to the "noble" classes. More than once he had witnessed men of impeccable descent flee in panicked terror at the first sign of enemy activity, where the common men would stand strong, defending their fellows to the very death.

Worse, in Fitzwilliam's opinion, were those persons who attempted to portray the possession of nobility when their claims were suspect at best. There were several among his acquaintances who fell into this category, but the one present who vexed him was Miss Caroline Bingley.

The town of Meryton, Fitzwilliam had decided early in his tenure there, was populated by good people. What the town lacked in the charm of some of the northern towns near his father's or Darcy's estates, it more than made up in the solid dependability of its citizens. Knowing the townsfolk had welcomed his company with open arms, Fitzwilliam made it a point to do business with them, drink with them, show them he and his men appreciated their welcome. It was when he was walking in the town that day that he heard Miss Bingley—well before he saw the woman, which spoke to how loud she was speaking, uncaring of who overheard.

"What a *quaint* town this is," said she, alerting Fitzwilliam to her presence. Stopping, Fitzwilliam found Miss Bingley—recognizing her at once due to her tall stature and the fineness of her dress. "I dare say I have never seen its like, and for that, I cannot but be grateful."

Walking by her side was her sister, and a little away, as if to inform anyone looking that she did not agree with Miss Bingley, was Georgiana. Mrs. Hurst, it seemed, was more aware than her sister of the difficulty a landowner could have if the townsfolk turned against them.

"Come, Caroline, let us enter this establishment. It appears charming."

The blazing look Miss Bingley directed at the inoffensive window— it was the town's milliner's—spoke to her wish to be anywhere else. Fitzwilliam turned toward the trio, intent upon saving Miss Bingley from making another mistake. Unfortunately, his hails went unheeded and he was too far away.

"Perhaps good enough for you, Louisa," said Miss Bingley with a loud, disdainful sniff. "But I require something more in the places *I* support. Should Lady Diane Montrose see me in such a place, she would rightfully abuse me as provincial and unworthy of notice in town."

Though Miss Bingley took no notice of the looks she was receiving from those nearby, it was clear from their nervous glances about that Mrs. Hurst and Georgiana did. One of these was the cobbler, a man walking nearby toward his shop, watching Miss Bingley as if she was something foul. The man had also done an excellent repair on Fitzwilliam's favorite pair of boots when the heel had cracked not long after his coming.

"Mr. Garner," hailed Fitzwilliam, distracting the man away from Miss Bingley and his dissatisfaction with her, "how do you do, sir?"

"Colonel Fitzwilliam," said Mr. Garner, turning toward him. "I am well, thank you. That boot I repaired for you is still sound, I hope?"

"Excellent work, sir," replied Fitzwilliam, raising his boot to emphasize the point. "Captain Carter informed me yesterday he has a pair of dancing shoes that have a hole in the sole."

"Then send him my way, Colonel. It will not take long to fix them, and I will give him a good price. We cannot have the men of the regiment unable to dance with the local ladies, can we?"

Fitzwilliam laughed and slapped the man on the back. "You have seen through to what is important. I shall be certain to tell him."

Smiling, Mr. Garner nodded and turned to leave, but not without fixing Miss Bingley with a disapproving stare. The woman did not notice, but her companions did. Then he departed, leaving Fitzwilliam in the ladies' company.

"Good afternoon, ladies," said Fitzwilliam, accepting Georgiana's girlish embrace with a grin. "How are you all this fine morning?"

"We are tolerable, Colonel Fitzwilliam," replied Miss Bingley. She did not see Georgiana rolling her eyes.

"Shall we walk this way?" asked Fitzwilliam, gesturing toward the end of town, offering his arm to Miss Bingley. While the woman would have preferred his cousin's arm to Fitzwilliam's, she could not refuse and remain polite.

"What brings you to town today?" asked he, thinking it might be beneficial to make a little light conversation.

"I have asked myself that question," replied Miss Bingley with a superior sniff. "There is little here of interest, and less of quality. We should better have stayed home."

Fitzwilliam gave the woman on his arm a glare, which she did not notice due to her expression of disgust at the sight of another shop they passed. It was then Fitzwilliam decided there was no reason to attempt diplomacy and every reason to prevent her from offending any other townsfolk.

"Perhaps it might be best, Miss Bingley, if you avoided affronting everyone in town." Fitzwilliam stopped and turned to face her, ensuring there was no one near enough to overhear.

"What can their opinions mean to us?" demanded the woman.

"This is nothing but a backwards speck of no significance in the hinterlands of the kingdom. No one of any import lives here. None of these townsfolk are of any consequence."

"It is people like this, Miss Bingley, who provide the goods many in positions of greater wealth and privilege take for granted. They provide clothing, accessories, foodstuffs, and other such items we use daily.

"Furthermore," said Fitzwilliam, ensuring she could not misunderstand his chiding tone, "not only do the townsfolk rely on the local estates for their custom, but the estates rely on the goodwill of the merchants, for they can make it very difficult if they take it into their minds to do so."

Miss Bingley gathered herself for a retort, but Fitzwilliam spoke again, not allowing her to make a larger fool of herself. "I understand your brother will not live here long, Miss Bingley, but he is bound to this neighborhood for the next nine months. Furthermore, is it not the height of poor manners to strut about as if we expect those around us to genuflect in our direction? Even my father, who has more reason to be proud than any of us, does not behave in such a manner."

Whatever she would have said remained unspoken, for Miss Bingley colored a little and looked down. Fitzwilliam had no intention to cause an excess of embarrassment, but her behavior must moderate if her brother was to find success in his first attempt to navigate the waters of a landed gentleman. A moment later she looked up, and against all hope, Fitzwilliam could see he had chastened her.

"You are correct, Colonel Fitzwilliam," said she in a small voice. "It is simply . . ."

"My sister is out of sorts today," said Mrs. Hurst. It was, perhaps, an oversimplification, for Fitzwilliam suspected Miss Bingley often behaved thus. "Mr. Collins came to the estate this morning and plied her with his attention. Nothing anyone says lessens his ardor."

"Then I sympathize with you, Miss Bingley," said Fitzwilliam. It was no exaggeration, for even a few moments in the parson's company was enough. "But let us not take our frustrations out on the townsfolk, for they have done nothing to earn our ire."

Miss Bingley nodded and allowed Fitzwilliam to lead her away again. They visited some few businesses, even the milliners which she had denigrated not a few moments before. In time, Fitzwilliam could see an improvement in her demeanor, and he thought she enjoyed her time in the dressmaker's shop. She was not a *bad* woman, he decided — often she was a misguided one, as she behaved as she thought those of the higher classes did. With women like Lady Diane Montrose for examples, it was no wonder she thought those of their level cared nothing for those beneath them in society's eyes!

It was well that her cousin had interrupted them, for Georgiana had been so embarrassed, she wished to sink into the ground in mortification. Anthony's stern rebuke had improved Miss Bingley's demeanor enough that Georgiana had enjoyed the outing thereafter. The other problem of the day presented itself after Anthony bowed and informed them of his intention to return to his office.

"Miss Bingley!" exclaimed a voice Georgiana had not heard since that summer. "How fortunate I am to have met you here today! How do you do?"

As one, the three ladies turned to see Lieutenant Wickham regarding them, his confidence in his charm never on display more than it was at that moment. At least it was until the man caught sight of Georgiana. He paled, but it was to his credit that he ignored her and focused on Miss Bingley instead.

It appeared to Georgiana that Miss Bingley was on the verge of saying something caustic to the officer. Her sister, however, nudged her, prompting a grimace. It did what she had intended, however, for Miss Bingley nodded and greeted the man in like kind, and for a moment they exchanged pleasantries.

Georgiana heard little of the exchange. The sight of Mr. Wickham, the sound of his voice returned her to those days in Ramsgate, brought back all the memories of a young, foolish girl, believing herself in love with a charming rake. For a moment, the shock of his appearance froze Georgiana in place, so much that she did not think she would have had the will to respond if Mr. Wickham had turned his attention on her.

Then a curious thing happened. As she watched the officer, noted his practiced replies to Miss Bingley's statements, watching him as he turned his charm on his chosen conquest, she realized that everything she had ever known about the man was untrue. Mr. Wickham was not an Adonis in the flesh, he did not possess everything a woman wished for in a man. In fact, Mr. Wickham was nothing more than a poseur, a man who used a superficial knowledge of the behavior of polite society and an ability to mimic charming manners to stalk his prey. There was nothing of substance in Mr. Wickham, nothing of use to any woman who wished for a man of dependable character for a husband, or even a friend.

At that moment, Georgiana released the last vestiges of her

previous infatuation with Mr. Wickham. The words Elizabeth had spoken to her some time before—the exact phrasing she could not remember—of her intention to marry a man of honor and integrity, a man she could love, returned to her. Georgiana wished for that also, and she decided she would take Elizabeth's example and find such a man for herself. A secret part of her also hoped William was that man for Elizabeth, for he was as good a man as Georgiana knew.

The result of Georgiana's musings on the subject was that she missed the entire exchange between Mr. Wickham and Miss Bingley. The woman extricated herself from Mr. Wickham's company and led them back to the carriage, her previous contentment gone in the face of *another* man who forced his attentions on her. When they arrived back at Netherfield, Miss Bingley exited the carriage and retired to her room at once, leaving Georgiana and Mrs. Hurst watching as she stalked up the stairs.

"Was Mr. Wickham's behavior that bad?" asked Georgiana.

Mrs. Hurst gave her a queer look, and Georgiana remembered too late that she had been there and to all appearances a witness to what had occurred. When Mrs. Hurst did not press the matter, she exhaled in relief.

"No, he was charming. Too charming."

"That is not a surprise," said Georgiana. "Mr. Wickham lives and breathes charm, but it is all a mask for he is an empty man."

The Bingley party all knew that Mr. Wickham had been connected to the Darcy family in the past, and Mrs. Hurst nodded in acknowledgment.

"Then I will ensure my sister knows. At present, she is out of sorts as neither Mr. Wickham nor Mr. Collins will leave her be."

"I understand where that might be frustrating," said Georgiana. "As I am not out yet, I have not experienced it much, but William sees such ingratiating behavior often."

Mrs. Hurst started, for Georgiana was not subtle with her admonishment. After a moment, she nodded and excused herself. Georgiana was eager to be alone, so she bid the woman farewell and made her way to the music room. Later, she would tell William of her epiphany.

As the three women moved away from him, Wickham watched them go, thoughts of the situation racing through his mind. The sight of Georgiana had almost caused him to lose his countenance; it was fortunate that a lifetime of presenting a mask to the world had allowed him to ignore her.

Miss Bingley, Wickham noted, was nothing like Georgiana. This was a woman full-grown, a woman cynical and calculating, one he knew meant to have Darcy at all costs. Wickham snorted at the thought—even if Darcy was not the prideful man he was, he would never have given the likes of Miss Bingley a second glance. Wickham would not have himself if she had not possessed a handsome dowry.

It was clear Miss Bingley did not like him. That had never stopped Wickham before. In fact, several feathers in his cap had come courtesy of ladies who had disliked him at first, including one particular woman who had declared him the worst of all men. Seducing women who did not like him was a specialty for George Wickham.

Wickham's thoughts then turned to Georgiana, and he shook his head before continuing on his way. Georgiana, he knew, he would always consider as the woman who evaded him, for not only did she possess even greater riches than Miss Bingley but taking her as a wife would have provided a fitting vengeance on Darcy. Underneath that, however, existed the residual affection Wickham had felt for her father—Wickham *had* esteemed the man, even though he had used him for everything he could get.

Wickham was not blind to the fact that he had betrayed the elder Mr. Darcy. The affection he harbored for Georgiana also informed him he had used her ill, and it did not sit well with him; it was strange, as he had never concerned himself with such matters before. Wickham mourned the loss of her fortune, now all his pretenses toward her were at an end, but he could not but rejoice that his actions had not permanently damaged her.

It occurred to Wickham that he owed her an apology. Though it was unlikely he would have an opportunity to offer it, should it arise, Wickham vowed he would beg her forgiveness.

CHAPTER XII

$\mathcal{S}$atisfaction was foremost among Darcy's feelings when Georgiana related the ladies' encounter with one George Wickham that afternoon. At least, it was after she had assured him there had been no trouble.

"Mr. Wickham said nothing to me, William." Georgiana, it appeared, was more than a little impatient with the question, and Darcy did not believe it was because she did not wish to speak of him. "In fact, I thought meeting me embarrassed him."

"And well it should," replied Darcy. "For a man who claims to hold our father in the highest esteem, he has not shown it with his actions."

"I would agree with you," acknowledged his sister. "Regardless, I believe I saw Mr. Wickham for what he truly is, and I did not like what I saw."

Curious, Darcy turned to look at his sister. That look proved enough of an invitation for her to speak.

"Mr. Wickham is nothing less than a peacock. He struts about and draws attention to himself when he plies young ladies with pretty manners, reveling in the longing looks and sighs he receives. But Mr. Wickham is all show and no substance, a man who does not even fill out the uniform he wears. It would not surprise me to know that he understands this himself, though he gives himself airs, congratulating himself on his ability to charm gullible girls. His pretty manners shall no longer mislead me. I am done with George Wickham."

Darcy, choked up at the evidence of his sister's growing maturity, grasped her hands and squeezed. "There is no greater blessing than to hear you say that, Georgiana. If Wickham can no longer affect you, we can put the mistakes of the summer to rest."

"I am ready, Brother," replied Georgiana, her voice soft, such that he strained to hear it. Then she brightened and fixed him with a smirk. "I believe Miss Bingley also sees Mr. Wickham for what he is, even though she is similar, in many respects. Regardless, she does not appreciate his actions. As soon as she returned to the estate, she took to her rooms and has not been seen since."

"Then I am sorry for her," said Darcy, "though I will note it is poetic justice."

Georgiana laughed and Darcy joined in with her. When their mirth had run its course, she turned her attention to Darcy's activities that morning and, in the process, discovered he had come across Miss Elizabeth during his ride.

"That is excellent, Brother!" exclaimed she. "Your time together was fruitful, I hope."

"If you mean to ask if I have proposed to her, the answer is no."

Not appearing amused, Georgiana swatted at him, much to Darcy's continued appreciation. Then he dropped the last piece of information she had not yet heard.

"But I am to dance the first with her at Bingley's ball."

Eyes wide as saucers, Georgiana gaped at him, and blurted: "You never dance the first!"

"On this occasion," said Darcy, "I shall make an exception. I have it on good authority that Miss Elizabeth will not see this as a sign I am about to propose to her."

"I should think not!" exclaimed Georgiana. Then she paused and chewed on her lip. "Can I assume Miss Bingley knows nothing of this?

"Of course not," said Georgiana, answering her own question. "Miss Bingley has not emerged from her room since our return."

"I solicited Miss Elizabeth for her hand yesterday during their visit to Netherfield, but no, I have not mentioned it to Miss Bingley. Nor do I intend to."

Though surprised at his admission, Georgiana fell into giggles. "No, that would not do, I suppose. We would not wish for Miss Bingley to attack Elizabeth when she comes."

Before dinner that night, another piece of unpleasant news was to come for Miss Bingley. A note arrived at Netherfield from Longbourn, brought into the room by the housekeeper and handed into Miss Bingley's hands. The woman read the note, paled, and tried to make light of it, but her brother would not allow it.

"Who is it from, Caroline?" demanded Bingley after his sister prevaricated for some moments.

Though Miss Bingley regarded the note in her hand again with some distaste, she realized he would not allow her to dismiss it altogether as she wished. Had it arrived and been brought to her alone, Darcy doubted it would ever have seen the light of day.

"Mrs. Bennet has invited us to dinner after church tomorrow," said Miss Bingley, though in as grudging a manner as possible.

"Excellent!" exclaimed Hurst. "Mrs. Bennet sets a table to envy — I look forward to it."

Trust Hurst to consider the matter with nothing but his stomach. Miss Bingley shot him a sour look and turned pleading eyes on her brother.

"I should prefer not to go, Charles. It is Sunday, and the ball is only two days after."

"And you shall not need to concern yourself for our dinner for one day," replied Bingley, unmoved by his sister's plea. "It will also free the servants from their tasks for the evening."

"Charles," said Miss Bingley, doing her best to maintain an even tone, "I do not wish to go to Longbourn for dinner. Anywhere else would be preferable. Can you not see how much I detest it? I will once again be subject to the inane attention of Mr. Collins, and you will be caught up with Miss Bennet. You will take no thought to my discomfort!"

"She is right about that," said Hurst with a snort. "That Collins fellow is persistent and has little notion of how to go about wooing a woman."

"Even if he did, I would not have him!" cried Miss Bingley. "He is altogether abhorrent!"

"Mr. Collins is not the most . . . impressive of specimens, it is true," allowed Bingley. "I suppose I should speak to him."

"Yes, speak to him! Inform him I have no interest and will not endure his company for even a single more minute, for I am at my wits' end! Perhaps if I beat him about the head with my reticule, he will cease!"

The image struck them all as amusing, for the entire company laughed, except for the woman who had uttered it. She seemed to think they were all laughing at her expense, which, Darcy considered, was not entirely untrue. Bingley, when he gained control of his mirth, gave his sister an affectionate smile.

"Then I shall speak with Mr. Collins, Caroline, and see about persuading him to back off. But as for dinner, we shall attend, for I do not wish to insult our neighbors."

Miss Bingley was not happy—this much was evident. However, she did not protest further, and she soon dashed off an acceptance note and sent it to Longbourn.

To Elizabeth's delight, she met the Darcys the following morning at church, and their greeting became an agreement to sit together. But while this arrangement was welcome to Elizabeth, not everyone in the congregation was fortunate enough to have such agreeable seating arrangements.

"Come, Miss Bingley, I insist," said the parson in his usually ponderous manner. "Let us sit together this fine morning, and I shall give you my opinion of the sermon we are about to hear. No one else present is in a better position than I to assist you to understand today's lesson."

Though Mr. Collins's invitation was not palatable to Miss Bingley, a fact understood by any who saw her reaction, Mr. Collins could see nothing of it. The parson grasped her arm and began directing her toward a nearby pew. For a moment, Miss Bingley, shocked that he had dared to lay his hand on her person, could not respond. Then she found her voice and tried to shake her hand free.

"Unhand me, Mr. Collins."

"That is going too far, Mr. Collins," echoed Mr. Bingley, who appeared at her side and glared at the parson.

"Not a bit of it!" was Mr. Collins's jovial reply, as if their protests meant nothing to him. "I was only attempting to be solicitous."

Mr. Bingley glanced about, noting they were attracting attention, and decided to avoid making a scene in the church. "We shall sit with you, Mr. Collins, but I would ask you to respect my sister and not treat her in this cavalier manner."

That Mr. Collins did not understand Mr. Bingley's objection was obvious, but he said nothing further, instead nodding and leading a now trapped Miss Bingley to the pew he had indicated. Mr. Bingley, having solicited Jane's attendance, led her to sit next to Mr. Collins and Miss Bingley, his sister and her husband sitting behind them.

Elizabeth, along with the Darcys, sat in the Bennet pew. It did not miss Elizabeth's attention that her father was regarding the parson, amusement written on his brow.

"I see Mr. Collins still makes love to Miss Bingley," whispered Elizabeth to her companions.

"And she greets it with peculiar fascination, I assure you," whispered Georgiana back, along with a giggle. "When we went into Meryton yesterday, Mr. Wickham appeared and began to flatter her also. It seems Miss Bingley has more suitors than she could have imagined, and not the one she hoped to attract!"

Georgiana's significant glance at Mr. Darcy left no doubt to whom she was referring, and while the gentleman shot her a quelling look, Elizabeth did not think he was unhappy with his sister's sally. A glance back at Miss Bingley showed her discontent with the parson's close attendance, though Elizabeth could see that Mr. Bingley was doing his best to distract him. This continued until the service started. Then it became worse.

Elizabeth did not know if Mr. Collins had ever attended a church service in which he did not provide the sermon; she knew within a few moments he had no notion one should listen in quiet contemplation. The disruption to the congregation was such that the dark looks speared the parson from all sides of the room. It was fortunate the elderly parson of Longbourn Parish, Mr. Jones, was more than a little deaf, for, in his own mind, the sermon progressed apace, his knowledge of the distraction nonexistent.

Elizabeth, who was sitting directly in front of Mr. Collins, could hear what he was saying. As the sermon progressed, Elizabeth became as disgusted with his interruption as anyone else in the room, for his words were nonsensical or in praise of his patroness.

"That is an interesting point, Miss Bingley, for my patroness, Lady Catherine de Bourgh, has often said . . ."

". . . what Mr. Jones means is . . ."

" . . . in that sense, I suppose he is correct, though I would have said . . ."

"Did you hear that, Miss Bingley? That is a direct commandment to . . ."

By the end of the service, Elizabeth could tell her father, a mild-mannered man who was more apt to laugh at the foibles of others, was sitting ramrod straight, his mouth set in a firm line.

The contrast with Mr. Darcy, however, could not be more astounding. As a young woman raised in the traditions of the Christian religion, Elizabeth would have called herself a believer, but not one who was as rigid in her beliefs as her sister Mary. Both of her companions proved themselves to be reverent and interested in what that parson was saying, singing the hymns and reciting the passages with an ease which spoke of long practice. Mr. Darcy, she found, possessed a rich baritone voice, while his sister was a light and sweet soprano. Elizabeth could imagine many more such occasions in the future, though she chided herself for putting the cart before the horse.

After the final hymn, Elizabeth was unsurprised when her father rose, turned around, and directed a baleful glare at Mr. Collins. "That was some interesting commentary, Mr. Collins."

"Yes, well, I have often been told I have a marvelous speaking voice, Mr. Bennet. My words were of benefit for Miss Bingley, but my gratitude at this evidence that it helped others understand is only equal to my humility in offering it."

It was clear from her father's raised eyebrow that Mr. Bennet was diverted all over again. Maintaining his purpose, however, he avoided laughing in the silly man's face, and said:

"That is interesting. Should you attend church with us next Sunday, I would ask you to restrain your comments. At Longbourn, we prefer to allow the parson to make his sermon and listen with respect."

Mr. Collins sniffed in disdain. "Then perhaps you should send your parson back to the seminary, for the man knows little of the Bible."

Mr. Bennet was on the edge of reaching for Mr. Collins's lapels and throttling him. "Mr. Jones has been the parson here for many years, and I have never heard so much as a whisper of complaint about him. Please keep your opinions to yourself, Cousin, or I shall have you removed."

Little though Mr. Collins appreciated being ordered in such a manner, Mr. Bennet gave his cousin no opportunity to further state his case, for he turned and moved away, leaving Mr. Collins with the Bingleys. Those who had been standing near enough to overhear were polite enough to refrain from commenting, but Elizabeth saw more than one satisfied nod of agreement for her father's words.

"Do you attend church often in Derbyshire?" asked Elizabeth of her companions. It was an inane question, for their performance told her they had; the situation demanded some conversation, however, and she did not know what else to say.

"We do," replied Mr. Darcy. "Pemberley is in Kympton parish; the Darcy family has attended there for many years."

The discussion evolved from there to a comparison of the church buildings, the styles their parsons used to impart their messages, and some of the charities in which they were involved and the assistance they offered those within reach of their influence. Before long, Elizabeth gained a clearer picture of Mr. Darcy as an estate owner and his sister as a young woman born to privilege. Mr. Darcy, she suspected, was a man of duty, one who cared for his estate like a mother might care for a child. Her father's sometimes more lackadaisical approach would be foreign to Mr. Darcy, for, through his words, Elizabeth learned he often rode his estate and was not afraid to roll up his sleeves and assist in the work.

Georgiana was more shy in nature and less inclined to put herself out, but Elizabeth suspected the tenants of Pemberley loved her for her sweet demeanor and willingness to assist. When Georgiana spoke of preparing boxes for the families the previous Christmas, and how she had sewn a dress for a young tenant's daughter, Elizabeth knew these were people who served others because it was right and proper and because it brought them joy to see others' pleasure. These were no publicans who made a show of the donations they were making.

Then Elizabeth contrasted what she learned from speaking with them and had observed with what she had seen of Mr. Collins. Mr. Collins, Elizabeth decided, was very much immersed in the activity of doing good for the sake of being noticed. His insistence on stating his own opinions—during a sermon, no less—and suggesting he knew better than a man of many years of experience, were the actions of a prideful man. Once again, Elizabeth thanked the Lord on high that Mr. Collins had not seen fit to punish her with the dubious favor of his attention.

A few moments later a familiar face entered Elizabeth's view, and she welcomed her friend with a warm: "Charlotte! Join us for a moment, for I do not believe you have met Miss Darcy's brother."

Right on cue, Mr. Darcy requested an introduction and Elizabeth did the honors, eager to ensure the man she esteemed was known to her oldest friend. Mr. Darcy did not disappoint.

"Miss Lucas," said he with a bow. "Yours is a name which often comes up when conversing with Miss Elizabeth, though I have only known her a few days. It is good to have a face to put with the name."

Charlotte smiled, saying: "I hope Lizzy has given me a good report, for we have been friends for a long time."

"An excellent account, Miss Lucas," assured Mr. Darcy. "Miss Elizabeth esteems you above all others not of her family."

The expressive smile Charlotte turned on Elizabeth seemed to suggest teasing, but Charlotte turned back to Mr. Darcy. "I do not see your cousin here today, Mr. Darcy. Could it be that he does not take his religious duties seriously?"

Mr. Darcy laughed. "Fitzwilliam will attend when he must, but many years in the army have rendered him lazy of a Sunday morning. There are no churches to attend when one is the target of French bayonets, or so he tells me."

They all laughed together. The four stood for some moments speaking in a lively fashion until Elizabeth noted her father preparing to leave to return to Longbourn. As the Netherfield party was to accompany them, Elizabeth knew she would have the pleasure of their company on the brief walk to the manor.

"Lizzy!" hissed Charlotte as they made their way from the church. "What a handsome man you have caught for yourself. Now is your chance to ensure he does not escape!"

"I do not yet know the gentleman, Charlotte," said Elizabeth, desperate to ensure Mr. Darcy did not overhear this exchange. "You know I cannot accept a man unless I love him."

Charlotte smiled and embraced Elizabeth, saying: "If you cannot see how he already looks at you, after so short an acquaintance, I must think you are blind. Give him a little encouragement, Lizzy—he will not disappoint you."

Then Charlotte turned and departed, leaving Elizabeth to follow. The Darcys were waiting for her when she exited the church, and she led them toward Longbourn, Charlotte's words echoing as she walked. After a time, she forced them to the back of her mind for later contemplation, for at present she wished to attend to her friends.

The walk to Longbourn was pleasant, the late summer morning warm, though cloudy, with a hint of a wind, presaging the future descent into autumn and winter. Conversation between them as they walked to her home was brief and inconsequential, the kind of discussion between friends who felt comfortable enough with each other that they did not require constant words between them. The only incident to mar the walk occurred, of course, at the instigation of Mr. Collins.

"What a silly thing to say, Mr. Collins!" exclaimed Miss Bingley, loud enough for the entire party, though they were spread out, to hear her.

"How charming you are, Miss Bingley!" exclaimed the parson. "I know that young ladies who admire a man will respond with a contrary opinion when all they wish to do is agree with everything he says. I am exceedingly charmed!"

Elizabeth exchanged looks with her companions and shook her head. "What manner of man believes a woman abusing him is playing the coquette?"

"Perhaps Mr. Collins is jesting?" ventured Georgiana.

"If you will pardon me, Georgiana," said Elizabeth, "I do not believe Mr. Collins is intelligent enough or possesses the imagination to jest."

"If he does not rein in his ardor, Bingley will be forced to call him out," said Mr. Darcy, his looks at Mr. Collins severe.

When they reached the entrance, the party entered, shedding footwear, bonnets, gloves, and other various items into the hands of the waiting Mrs. Hill and a maid. Mr. and Mrs. Bennet invited the company into the sitting-room to visit until their repast was ready, and while Elizabeth sat with Georgiana to further their conversation and acquaintance, she could not help but overhear what was happening in another part of the room. Mr. Bingley, genial man though he was, had had enough of Mr. Collins's misbehavior.

"That is enough of your insanity with respect to my sister, Collins," growled Mr. Bingley in as stern a voice as Elizabeth had ever heard from the gentleman.

"I do not understand your meaning," replied Mr. Collins his manner as short as Mr. Bingley's had been. "Now, if you will please excuse me, I wish to speak more to your excellent sister."

"Are you mad?" demanded Mr. Bingley. "What manner of man looms over a woman spouting nonsensical drivel in the hope she will find him irresistible?"

"I know not how you conduct your courtship, Mr. Bingley," replied Mr. Collins, "but I know how to court a woman. It is my distinct honor to have had Lady Catherine de Bourgh, my patroness, impart the best way to going about capturing a woman's heart, and I shall not shirk in putting her ladyship's expert advice into practice."

Mr. Bingley appeared fit to be tied, such that Elizabeth would not have been surprised had he beat the senseless parson about the head. Salvation came in the calming presence of Mr. Darcy. The gentleman rested a hand on his friend's back, calming him, and leant his voice to Mr. Bingley's.

"Bingley is correct, Mr. Collins," said Mr. Darcy in a tone which did not allow dispute. "A man courts a woman with the utmost in tenderness, but with an eye to assuring her comfort. If a woman does not wish for your presence or attention, you must bow out with more grace than you attended her. This looming over Miss Bingley is not endearing you to her."

"But Mr. Darcy —"

A hand silenced the parson, though he appeared the petulant child. When he was assured he had Mr. Collins's attention, Mr. Darcy continued:

"Perhaps today would be best spent admiring Miss Bingley from afar, Mr. Collins. For is it not said that absence makes the heart grow fonder?"

It appeared Mr. Collins had nothing to say, for he gaped at Mr. Darcy, his mouth moving with no sound emerging. Then an expression of cunning came over his countenance, and he nodded his head vigorously.

"Had I not already known you were Lady Catherine's nephew, I would have known it now, for those words might have come from her ladyship herself! What a wonderful notion you have suggested Mr. Darcy! I shall be certain to put it into practice, for the blessings of contemplation and reflecting on the delights to come cannot be underestimated!"

Mr. Collins might have gone on for some time had Mr. Darcy not turned away and rejoined Elizabeth. The parson, thereafter, was quieter than his wont, though his eyes did not often leave Miss Bingley's form. The lady, however, was in no way as ardent as the parson, for she refused to look at him, remaining close to her sister until it came time for them to leave.

One further moment of discord occurred when the company went into the dining room for dinner, and Mr. Collins discovered his position at the table was not near to Miss Bingley's. Again, Mr. Darcy called him to order and harmony was restored.

Elizabeth, for her part, did her best to ignore the parson, for he had proven himself to be less than contemptible. Besides, she was more interested in contemplating Mr. Darcy, for Elizabeth was beginning to wonder what the future might hold for her and if it might include a closer connection with him. Unlike Mr. Collins's chances, Elizabeth believed the possibilities of her association with Mr. Darcy were much better. If Mr. Darcy continued his charming behavior, Elizabeth thought herself well on the way toward being in love with him, the brief nature of their acquaintance notwithstanding.

CHAPTER XIII

*M*onday morning, Elizabeth woke with a start. At once she noticed the sun hanging higher in the sky than usual when she awoke, the sounds of birds twittering and calling filling the air outside her window. Luxuriating in the pleasure of a comfortable bed in a cozy room, Elizabeth stretched, throwing her arms high over her head, easing the stiffness from the previous night's rest.

A moment was all she allowed herself, for the morning and the outdoors beckoned, inviting her to savor the landscapes she so loved. So, Elizabeth threw off the blanket and rose for the day, choosing a comfortable walking dress and tying her hair back into a simple knot. Soon, a roll from the kitchen in her hand, she slipped out the front door and made her way down Longbourn's drive toward the freedom which lay beyond the gate.

If Elizabeth had tried to assert she was not hoping to see Mr. Darcy on her morning ramble, she would have been lying to herself. The thought of the gentleman, unknown to her only a week before, was a constant companion by now; Elizabeth was hard-pressed to remember what it was like before he came. The later than usual hour of her departure, coupled with the ball scheduled for the morrow made his appearance unlikely. It was not in Elizabeth's nature to be unhappy about such things, however, so she set to her walk with a will, determined to enjoy it as she ever had, regardless of Mr. Darcy's presence or absence. Sometimes, however, fate works in curious ways; Elizabeth was not to see Mr. Darcy during her walk, but that did not mean she would not see him.

When Elizabeth returned to her home and changed into a more appropriate dress, she visited the breakfast room for a more filling repast, and there she found her mother and her sisters, her father being nowhere in evidence. Upon entering the room, Elizabeth knew given the looks she was receiving from her family that teasing could not be far behind.

"You have returned late today, Lizzy," said Jane, giving her a knowing grin. "Did you, perhaps, meet someone on your walk who delayed your return?"

Elizabeth fixed her sister with a stare that suggested she eschew teasing as she was not proficient at it. "I awoke later than usual this morning. That is the only reason for my late return."

"It is not like you to sleep late," chimed Lydia. "Did you not sleep well, Sister dearest?"

"The thoughts of a certain gentleman must have kept her up during the night," said Kitty.

The rest of her sisters joined in with Kitty's giggles. Elizabeth, knowing Kitty's supposition was near to the truth, did not deign to respond. Instead, she fixed herself a plate of her favorite breakfast foods and set herself to it with a will.

"If Lizzy is meeting a man on a secluded path," said Mary, ever the stiff proponent of proper behavior, "that would be improper. I hope you are not indulging in clandestine meetings."

"Do not concern yourself, Mary," said Elizabeth with the warm and welcoming smile she used for her sister when she began to moralize. "Though I have encountered Mr. Darcy on my walks, I do not plan to meet him in advance."

With a smile of approval, Mary turned back to her breakfast. But that did not mean the rest of her sisters did not intend to take up the teasing standard.

"Oh, but you have met Mr. Darcy!" exclaimed Lydia. "How romantic!"

"And you have only known him for a few days!" added Kitty with a sigh. "How wonderful it is that you have already found your companion in life, and after so short an acquaintance!"

"Girls, that is enough," said Mrs. Bennet when the two youngest fell against each other laughing. "You know your sister is of better judgment than that."

Though Mrs. Bennet's admonishments quieted the sisters a little, the mirth was not at an end, for Jane continued to make comments to which Elizabeth was forced to reply. Soon, the merriment at the table was such that they were all in stitches. When they had finished their meal, Mrs. Bennet shooed away the youngest sisters for their morning lessons.

"I cannot be happier for you, Lizzy," said Mrs. Bennet. "Mr. Darcy appears to be such a good man. However, I am also worried, for you have only known him a few days. Is that long enough to have formed an attachment to him?"

"There is no need to concern yourself, Mama," said Elizabeth, pulling her mother into a warm embrace. "I do not claim to love Mr. Darcy. But I esteem him very much, and I am eager to come to know him better."

Mrs. Bennet smiled and patted Elizabeth's hands. "You are a wonderful girl, Lizzy. I knew you would not act without prior thought. Regarding Mr. Darcy, I agree with you in every particular and will support you whatever happens.

"I hope you will forgive me if I hope the gentleman turns out as you hope he does, for I believe he would suit you very well."

"Believe me, Mama," said Elizabeth, "my hopes are identical to yours."

When, a short time later, Mr. and Miss Darcy entered the room to visit them, Elizabeth was the subject of several expressive looks. Ignoring them, she stood to welcome their guests, embracing Georgiana like they were old friends and greeting Mr. Darcy with a curtsey to his bow.

"Good morning, Mrs. Bennet," said Mr. Darcy, greeting the mistress as propriety dictated. "I hope our visit this morning is not an imposition."

"Nothing of the sort, Mr. Darcy," said Mrs. Bennet. "Please be assured we are ready to welcome you and your charming sister at any time convenient."

Within moments, they sat in their usual positions, Elizabeth close to Mr. Darcy with Jane and Mary attending, while Mrs. Bennet had sent for Kitty and Lydia when Georgiana mentioned wishing to speak to them. The three girls were soon situated with their heads close together, speaking in low tones, with the occasional giggle, about the festivities scheduled for the following evening.

"Miss Bennet," said Mr. Darcy, turning his attention toward Jane, "I wish to pass along my friend Bingley's regrets which he charged me to carry to you. The ball tomorrow is occupying his time, rendering a visit today impossible."

"Thank you, Mr. Darcy," said Jane with no hint of embarrassment.

"And you, sir?" asked Elizabeth, fixing the gentleman with a playful look. "Are you and Georgiana not assisting with the preparations?"

"The benefit of staying at a house leased by another," said Mr. Darcy, "is the ability to cry off such activities. Though I offer my assistance to Bingley when required, in the business of hosting a ball I am not needed. Georgiana and I are not family, after all—we are nothing more than invited friends."

"Ah, then I salute your ingenious ability to beg off, for I would find planning a ball to be nothing less than tedious."

Mr. Darcy laughed, as did her sisters, though Jane gave her a sharp look. "I cannot claim that I am enamored with the notion either, though I have never hosted one myself."

"Then perhaps in the future, you will, Mr. Darcy," said Mrs. Bennet.

"Yes, my position in society guarantees it," replied the gentleman easily. "That, however, will not happen until I have married, and the burden will then rest with my wife."

It might have been a trick of her perceptions brought on by anticipation, but Elizabeth fancied Mr. Darcy spoke to her, or perhaps of her. The necessity of reminding herself that she had not known Mr. Darcy long was pressing, despite what she had told her mother. As such, Elizabeth turned her attention to other matters of interest.

"How is your cousin, Mr. Darcy? I have not seen him in some days."

"Fitzwilliam is well," replied Mr. Darcy, "though I have not seen him of late myself. There is much to do to command a regiment, or so he tells me. Though he often came to Netherfield for dinner after my arrival, these past days he has chosen to eat with his officers."

"Do you think he will remain long in the militia?" asked Elizabeth.

A frown settled over Mr. Darcy's countenance. "Though his mother may wish him to quit the army altogether, Fitzwilliam has always insisted on fulfilling what he thought to be his duty. When he has healed, I cannot say what he will do. I expect it likely he will return to the regulars." Mr. Darcy paused and sighed. "And this, though he possesses his own estate."

"Colonel Fitzwilliam has an estate?" asked Elizabeth, confused. "Then why did he join the army at all?"

"It was an unexpected bequest from a distant relation," explained Mr. Darcy. "When his father first purchased his commission, my cousin was a second son, one who knew he must make his own way in the world. Then three years ago, a distant relation—I do not recall the exact connection—willed him a small estate not far distant from mine."

"Then one would have expected him to resign his commission and transition to the life of a gentleman," said Elizabeth.

"One might," agreed Mr. Darcy. "That person would not know my cousin, for he is a man of duty; we could not sway him from his purpose." Then Mr. Darcy grinned and leaned forward as if imparting a secret. "Fitzwilliam has informed me several times that he considers the life of a gentleman too sedate."

Elizabeth laughed. "I suppose it is not surprising a man of action would feel that way."

The conversation turned to other subjects, and they continued in this manner for some minutes until another arrived. Elizabeth neither knew nor cared where Mr. Collins had been that morning, and the family had, by now, become indifferent to his very existence. But absent he had been, and when he entered the room that morning, he started when he saw the Darcys there; no one misunderstood his glance about the room and subsequent disappointment when he did not spy Miss Bingley.

"This is a wondrous surprise, Mr. Darcy," said the parson in his expansive manner, "but I do not see Miss Bingley here. Did she not accompany you?"

"Miss Bingley is busy with preparations for the ball tomorrow, Mr. Collins," said Mr. Darcy.

"Ah, that is unfortunate," said the man with a regretful shake of his head. "As I shall see her again tomorrow, I shall be content."

Mr. Darcy inclined his head but did not respond, turning back to Elizabeth. Their conversation continued for some more moments, but Elizabeth was not blind to the looks Mr. Collins was directing at them. The man's frown bespoke his displeasure, though she sensed a hint of concentration about him. It did not take long before they learned the reason for the gentleman's disapproval.

"Excuse me, Mr. Darcy," said he, interrupting their conversation. "It has come to my mind that I have often seen you together with my cousin in recent days."

"Yes?" asked Mr. Darcy. "What of it?"

Elizabeth did not believe that Mr. Darcy did not understand Mr. Collins's meaning. It seemed to her the gentleman was daring the parson to complete his thought. While most men would have recognized the warning inherent in his voice, Mr. Collins either did not, or he ignored it. He did so, however, in a hesitant matter, as if reluctant to state his case.

"Well . . . Do you think it proper, sir, to lavish such attention on my cousin?"

"First, Mr. Collins," said Mr. Darcy, beginning to sound testy, "I have no notion of what business it might be of yours. Second, I wonder just what you are implying; do you believe I am not behaving as a gentleman ought, or do you have some other purpose in mind?"

"A thousand apologies, Mr. Darcy!" exclaimed Mr. Collins. "I meant nothing of the kind! I am sure my noble patroness's nephew must possess an equal measure of superiority as her ladyship and would never presume to suggest anything of the sort. Thus, the fault must lie with my cousin."

It was clear Mr. Darcy did not know what to make of Mr. Collins's sudden declaration; Mr. Collins, however, was not bereft of words.

"Perhaps you do not know, Cousin," said he, affecting a stern tone, "but Mr. Darcy is engaged to Lady Catherine's daughter. Though I must assume you are attempting to entrap him into marriage, I must inform you it shall never happen, for who would choose a penniless, impertinent miss such as you, when he can have the jewel that is Miss de Bourgh? I abjure you to cease this objectionable behavior at once!"

So sudden was the attack that Elizabeth could not find her voice. Mr. Darcy was not in similar straits, and her mother looked like she would speak if he did not.

"That is enough, Mr. Collins! There is nothing you can say to censure Miss Elizabeth, as she has been the very model of propriety."

"Mr. Darcy, I assure you, I do not hold your inability to resist the siren call of my cousin, a woman who has used her wiles to entrap you."

"Not another word, Mr. Collins!" hissed Mr. Darcy. "This is none of your concern. I require you to be silent!"

It seemed Mr. Collins was cowed, for he nodded vigorously and did not speak another word. The moment ruined, Mr. Darcy decided there was nothing to do but depart, and as the time for their visit had more than elapsed, he gathered up his sister, made his excuses, and with one more piercing look at the sweating parson, departed.

When their visitors left, Elizabeth excused herself, unwilling to allow Mr. Collins any further opportunity to spew his drivel. The comfort and privacy of her own room was welcome, for it afforded Elizabeth the opportunity to consider what was happening between herself and the gentleman. Though it had only been a short time, Elizabeth was coming to the inescapable conclusion she was falling in love with him.

The realization that Mr. Darcy and his sister had gone to Longbourn filled Caroline Bingley with annoyance.

What could he want there, of all places?

Caroline could not answer her own question, but the thought that he had gone there often of late entered her consciousness and teased her with it. There was something happening, something of which Caroline felt, with the sure and unerring instinct of a fortune hunter, that she would not like. Had she not been so distracted by her twin suitors she might have had more time to devote some thought to the matter. Then again, there was still much to do for the ball on the morrow, and Caroline was determined to ensure it was the most sophisticated event that Mr. Darcy had ever attended.

Or as sophisticated as she could make it in this backward society. It would have been better, of course, had she had the ability to hold it in London and invite all the right people. These savages in Meryton could scarcely speak in polite English, let alone lend any distinction to her ball.

There was little choice, however, but to work with what she was given, for surely Mr. Darcy would not hold the lack of materials, good help, or people of quality against her.

That Mr. Collins had not bothered her that day was a blessing, for Caroline did not know if she could have withstood the man's inane ramblings. Though it galled her to confess it, perhaps it would be best if the man would get on with it and propose, then she could refuse him and have done with his attentions altogether. As long as no one in town ever knew she received a proposal of marriage from such an odious man, she was willing to endure one, if only to dispense with it altogether! What Caroline had not counted on was the other man who seemed intent on gaining her fortune.

"Miss Bingley," came a voice as Caroline was fixing the flower arrangements for the following evening's entertainment. "How fortunate that I have found you today, for I have missed your company of late."

So dismayed was Caroline to see Mr. Wickham that she almost groaned out loud. Would these men never leave her alone? Caroline Bingley had experienced her share of admirers, but never had they been so unsuitable. When could she escape them?

"I see you are hard at work preparing for the morrow's entertainment," said Mr. Wickham when Caroline did not respond. "It has been my pleasure to attend many social events in the past, but I dare say they will all pale compared to what I shall experience here. You are a talented hostess."

While such pretty words could not fail to stoke Caroline's vanity, the fact that the man she wished to speak them had not done so tempered whatever pleasure she might have felt. Caroline was in no mood to accept such simpering designed for no other purpose than to ingratiate.

"Why are you here, Mr. Wickham?" asked Caroline, deciding in a moment that bluntness was to be preferred.

"Do I need a reason to visit such a vision of loveliness?"

At Caroline's frown, Mr. Wickham laughed and shook his head. "You have my apologies, Miss Bingley. I should not have attempted to treat you like that idiot Collins. I have no desire to behave with such servility toward a woman I know to be intelligent."

"Then your reason for coming?" asked Caroline, only a little mollified.

"To request your hand for the first sets at tomorrow night's ball," replied Mr. Wickham.

Shocked, Caroline could only stare. The sight of his smug assurance raised her annoyance, for it seemed Mr. Wickham was a man of confidence in his own charm; Caroline would not about to allow him to escape without a deserved set down.

"I believe Mr. Wickham has you there," came the chortling voice of her sister's husband.

Confused, Caroline glanced at him, which Hurst took as reason enough to clarify his statement. "Mr. Wickham has asked you to dance, Caroline. You are aware of the convention concerning dancing for young ladies, are you not?"

"The dance has not even started yet," snapped Caroline. "You cannot hold me to such a ridiculous convention before the ball has even begun."

"There is also the matter of being a dutiful hostess," rejoined Hurst. The portly man was sitting back in his chair, hands clasped over his ample belly, regarding her with his usual brand of smug amusement.

"It would not do to offend one of your—your brother's—guests, now would it? It seems to me you have no choice but to accept."

"I think my husband has a point, Caroline," said Louisa, traitor that she was. "Though you may argue the ball has not started, he has made a request; it would not do to reject it."

Caroline stood, looking at her relations, her thoughts a jumbled mass of offense, annoyance, confusion, and wonder. Then the sight of Mr. Wickham, his smugness never receding for even a moment, entered her vision, and a new emotion found its way into her mind: determination.

"All your arguments neglect to consider one thing," said Caroline.

"Oh?" was Mr. Wickham's lazy reply. "What is that?"

"That I expect to be dancing the first with someone else," snarled Caroline from between clenched teeth.

"And who would that be?" asked Mr. Wickham, though Caroline was certain he knew to whom she was referring.

"Mr. Darcy," said she, her glare at the officer even unfriendlier than it had been before.

Whatever reaction she had expected, it was not laughter, and not from both men at once. Hurst was a man Caroline had never liked, for he was a glutton, a bore, and a man of little interest besides hunting, his dogs, and as much wine as he could pour down his gullet. Mr. Wickham, at least, was a better physical specimen than her brother-in-law, but his smug superiority made Caroline want to tear out her hair in frustration.

"My dear Caroline," said Hurst from between his wheezing guffaws, "you truly are amusing. I do not know when I have laughed so hard."

"I fail to understand how you would treat me so," replied Caroline, feeling more than a little sulky.

"Why, your assertion that you will dance the first with Darcy. Many times he has had the opportunity to solicit your hand for the first set, and yet he never has. Does that not tell you something?"

"Furthermore," said Hurst, preventing her from responding to his offensive words, "if Darcy is to dance the first with any woman, I will wager it will be Miss Elizabeth Bennet."

"Miss Eliza?" gasped Caroline.

"Of course," said Hurst, heedless of Caroline's consternation. "Why, have you not seen how they are always together whenever in company?"

"That is interesting," said Mr. Wickham, though Caroline hardly heard him. "I have known Darcy for many years; he is more liable to insult a woman than pay her attention, and only a week after knowing her."

"Darcy is rather stiff," agreed Hurst. "But had you seen them together of late, their closeness would surprise you, for I dare say they are rather cozy together. Had Darcy paid as much attention to Caroline as he does to Miss Elizabeth, my sister would have arrived at Netherfield wearing her wedding clothes, with her trousseau packed into as many trunks as she could find!"

The men burst out into raucous laughter, Caroline looking on with fury. Mr. Wickham, for all he claimed to admire her, attempting, as he was, to induce her to dance with him, to speak whenever nearby, to fall for his disgusting charm, was not put off in the slightest by Hurst's portrayal of her interest in Mr. Darcy. That it was the truth, Caroline pushed aside without considering—it was not as if she cared what either man thought.

"The richest part," said Mr. Wickham, still chuckling, "is all Miss Elizabeth's efforts will be in vain. Darcy is to marry his cousin Miss Anne de Bourgh."

"That is nothing more than a rumor," snapped Caroline.

"Perhaps it is," replied Mr. Wickham, not taken aback by her tone. "Darcy is a man who likes to have his own way, but that is nothing compared to how much Lady Catherine de Bourgh likes to have hers. If I were to place wagers on the likely outcome of the irresistible force of Lady Catherine against the immovable object of Darcy, I would choose the lady. It is my understanding she has the family on her side also."

"That is interesting, Mr. Wickham," said Hurst. "Perhaps I should enter it into the book at White's, for I suspect Darcy might just surprise you. When he looks at Miss Elizabeth, it is as if no other person in the world exists. I dare say the lure of a young, pretty woman such as Miss Elizabeth might just overcome whatever arguments Lady Catherine might summon, particularly as Miss de Bourgh is, by all accounts, in poor health."

The two men continued to banter while Caroline thought furiously of what she had just learned. Curse Mr. Collins and Mr. Wickham! Had they not distracted her, Caroline was certain she would have seen the danger; she might have acted to stop this infatuation! And Colonel Fitzwilliam had mentioned the possibility, but Caroline, certain Mr. Darcy would not fall for a woman as unsuitable as Miss Elizabeth, had discounted it.

All was not lost. What Mr. Darcy saw in Miss Elizabeth Caroline did not know, but it could not survive if she pointed out how poor his choice was. Could it?

"Well, what say you, Miss Bingley?"

Caroline glared at Mr. Wickham. It made no impression upon him, for the man was nothing more than amused. Her relations were no help at all.

"I suggest you accept, Caroline," said Hurst.

"Very well," said Caroline with a superior sniff. "One dance. I shall not dance with you again."

"I look forward to it," said Mr. Wickham.

The man then bowed and excused himself, proving he was not bereft of sense. It was just as well, for Caroline did not think she could have withstood anymore of his insincere flattery.

Of more importance was what she could do about Mr. Darcy. Now that the first was unavailable, she could not dance it with him, but Caroline acknowledged it had not been probable anyway. Miss Eliza was another matter altogether. If Mr. Darcy should dance the first with her, that would be a sign of a serious impediment in her designs. Then she would need to act quickly.

The problem was, Caroline was uncertain what she could do.

CHAPTER XIV

*T*he building the regiment used for its headquarters boasted a sizeable room, one suitable for meetings of the higher ranks of the regiment's commanders. Fitzwilliam was not a man who believed in an abundance of meetings. A close friend in the regulars had once branded meetings as a means by which one might escape from having to do something productive. While Fitzwilliam had thought it amusing at the time, that particular general had proven the supposition, as he had rarely decided on anything.

The morning of the ball at Netherfield, however, Fitzwilliam had made an exception, for there were several items of business he wished to discuss. The roster for that evening had already been filled by several good men who were to command the regiment in his absence in shifts—the first would remain behind when the rest left for Netherfield, while certain other officers would return to relieve them, allowing those remaining behind to attend the latter half of the ball. It was the fairest way to handle an event this anticipated, for the soldiers could not be left without someone in command the entire evening.

Of particular interest to Fitzwilliam, Wickham stood leaning against the wall, looking around with equal parts disinterest and boredom. Wickham had not been one of those who had volunteered to miss part of the amusement, not a surprise given his general proclivities. There was a matter Fitzwilliam wished to discuss with him before allowing him to depart; it was a surprise to Fitzwilliam, however, that it did not have to do with the performance of his duties, which Wickham's captain had informed him was adequate, though not exceptional.

As for the rest of this motley crew . . . Well, the best that could be said about many of them was that they were green. They were not bad sorts—but they were not the same caliber of men he had left behind in his last command. Then again, the regulars had no shortage of malcontents, dullards, laggards, and the like, so it was not all superior to the militia.

When the last few stragglers had entered the room, Fitzwilliam addressed them. "As you all know, tonight is the long-expected ball at Netherfield, to which we have all been invited. Now, as we cannot all attend at once, several of you have agreed to take partial duty for the evening. Is everyone who is staying behind aware of their assignments?"

A murmur of agreement reached Fitzwilliam's ears and he smiled in approval. "Excellent. To the men, this will be the same as any other evening. Should anything serious occur, you all know where to find me. I may make an appearance back at camp during the festivities, so you may bring any problems to me at that time.

"The next item of business I wish to discuss is that of our behavior at the ball tonight."

Fitzwilliam let his gaze rove over the room, fixing several of those he knew were a little boisterous or careless in their actions with a pointed reminder. Wickham's eyes he avoided—the upcoming conversation may come to the attention of the rest of the company, and there were already too many rumors about Fitzwilliam's history with Wickham.

"You are officers of His Majesty's army, and as such, a certain standard of conduct is required. Act in a manner that will not cast shade on the uniform you wear. Meryton, the same as any other neighborhood in England, has its share of silly young misses, eager to socialize with a man wearing scarlet. There will be no young ladies disgraced, no raucous revelry, and, in short, no behavior which would reflect poorly upon the regiment. Violators will be removed from the ball in disgrace and will face me on the morrow. Have I made myself clear?"

The general murmur of agreement prompted Fitzwilliam to nod.

They were, as he had considered earlier, a good lot, and they all understood by now that Fitzwilliam ran a tight ship. Fitzwilliam did not expect any lapses from the men, but it was important to remind them, for many were quite young.

"Very well," said Fitzwilliam with a smile. "Then let us enjoy this evening, for this community has welcomed us with open arms. Dismissed."

As the men filed from the room, Fitzwilliam caught Wickham's eye, prompting him to maintain his position against the wall. The rest of the men did not even bat an eyelash at the sight—Fitzwilliam suspected the excitement for the coming evening rendered most insensible of anything but the imagined delights. When the room had emptied, Wickham pushed himself away from the wall and approached, fixing Fitzwilliam with a sardonic sneer.

"There is no reason to take me to task, Colonel. I know not to get into any trouble."

Fitzwilliam fixed his cousin's nemesis with a slight smile. "One thing that has always impressed me about you, Wickham, is your sense of when to protect your own hide."

"For one in my position, such thoughts must be of paramount importance," said Wickham.

The suggestion that life—or Darcy—had denied him greater benefits was an old complaint and not one Fitzwilliam would waste any time debating. The thought crossed Fitzwilliam's mind that Wickham might have spoken of something else altogether. Whatever Wickham meant, Fitzwilliam did not mean to bandy words with him.

"There is another matter of which we should speak." Wickham raised his eyebrow, prompting Fitzwilliam to clarify: "I understand you went to Netherfield yesterday."

Wickham cocked his head to the side. "I suspected you have the men reporting on my movements."

"I do have two cousins staying at the estate," rejoined Fitzwilliam. They were not the source of his information; neither were the men who monitored Wickham's movements, but Fitzwilliam did not wish him to be aware of that fact.

"So you do," replied Wickham, like he did not care. "As I was not on duty, I cannot imagine why you would concern yourself with my movements. There is no one at Netherfield for whom you could concern yourself; I have not said two words to Georgiana."

"There is nothing of censure in my wish to speak of this, Wickham. I make no accusations. It is, however, interesting that you have chosen to ply Miss Bingley with your attempts at lovemaking, considering she possesses the greatest dowry in the neighborhood other than Georgiana."

"Are you warning me away from Bingley's sister?" asked Wickham, tired of exchanging words. "If I conduct my affairs properly, what does it matter to you if I woo a woman?"

"Nothing," replied Fitzwilliam with a chuckle. "It is more for your benefit I speak, for Miss Bingley is one of the worst examples of social climbing I have ever seen. You do know she has convinced herself that Darcy will offer for her?"

Wickham snorted, which was an echo of Fitzwilliam's thoughts on the matter with precision. "We both know that is unlikely," replied Wickham. "She is the opposite of the kind of woman Darcy would favor. Miss Elizabeth Bennet, however . . ."

The hackles on Fitzwilliam's neck rose at Wickham's predatory tone. Something in his countenance must have alerted Wickham to his tension, for the man laughed and shook his head.

"You may rein in your vengeful thoughts, Fitzwilliam. I have no intention of interfering with Darcy's courtship.

"However, I must say that I am surprised at Darcy; I never would have thought he had it in him. She is a wonderful lady to be certain; if I possessed a fraction of Darcy's wealth, I might even try my hand at her."

Wickham's comments, Fitzwilliam knew, were designed to provoke him to anger. There was little to do but ignore them.

"The point is that Miss Bingley is not likely to accept a proposal from a lowly soldier. Even I, who can claim to be the son of a peer and own an estate, am not good enough for her."

"You have your own estate?" asked Wickham with a raised eyebrow. "When did this happen?"

"An unexpected inheritance from a distant relation," replied Fitzwilliam. "It is not large, but it will support me when I put off the scarlet."

"Then why have you not done so? I might have thought the merest hint of such independence would have sent you fleeing from the army."

"Because, Wickham," said Fitzwilliam, "some of us possess a sense of duty."

The barb struck home, but, as Fitzwilliam expected, it did not injure Wickham. Quite the contrary.

"Then you have my best wishes. As for Miss Bingley, yes, it is very possible she will refuse my overtures. But that is my business—you can have no complaints if I do not misbehave. And as for Miss Bingley's pretensions, I know as well as you they are doomed to disappointment. The last I heard, Darcy was to marry Miss de Bourgh. Do you suppose he means to make Miss Elizabeth his mistress?"

The glare from Fitzwilliam informed him he had gone too far. True to his character, Wickham did not apologize or appear abashed, but he clamped his lips shut and waited for Fitzwilliam's reprimand.

"If you think that, you do not know Darcy at all," rejoined Fitzwilliam.

Wickham shrugged, relieved he had not provoked greater anger. "No, I suppose you are correct. I should not have said it, and I apologize."

Any apology offered by Wickham was worthless, and as such, Fitzwilliam decided against pursuing it. "I understand you are not fond of my cousin, Wickham, but I would ask you to avoid defaming his character in my presence. Darcy is one of the best men I have ever known; he has not dealt with you as many men would have, and that is just one of the examples I could cite as evidence of his goodness."

A tight nod was Wickham's only response.

"As for Lady Catherine's fantasies, I assume you understand they have little chance of ever being realized."

Again, Wickham showed his lack of interest. "Perhaps they do not. One way or another, however, Miss Bingley has no chance of eliciting a proposal from Darcy. If I am the one to fill the void when she is inevitably let down, am I to be despised because of it?"

"No, I have no objection. My only purpose was to inform you of the situation between the lady and my cousin. What you choose to do with that information is your concern."

"Then, if I may be excused?"

Fitzwilliam waved him from the room, watching as Wickham sauntered out the door. Of one thing Wickham was correct: there was nothing Fitzwilliam could do if there were no signs of impropriety in his pursuit of Miss Bingley. Wickham would discover the woman's character for himself, it seemed, and Fitzwilliam had little reason to prevent him from running over that cliff.

The animosity Wickham still held for Darcy, however, meant that it would be best for Fitzwilliam to avoid speaking to him more often than necessary. The cur's words had almost earned him a facer right there, which would not look good at all on Fitzwilliam's military record.

* * *

As evening fell over the county of Hertfordshire, the gentle families prepared for what many were calling the social event of the year. It was true, given the lack of large estates in the area and the recent emptiness of the one that boasted a ballroom. If those inhabitants could have seen some of the spectacles held in London during the season they might have thought otherwise; few were in that fortunate position.

At Longbourn, the preparations were little different from those at any of the other estates, though perhaps the activity was a little more frenetic. The simple reason for this was the composition of the family, for no other estate boasted a collection of five young ladies preparing to descend on the ball, leaving broken hearts and jealous lovers in their wake. Or at least that was the hope, laughingly spoken by the youngest more than once. The elder sisters had more sense than to think the whole of the community would fall down at their feet in awed silence. Mr. Bennet, in particular, was in a pleasant mood, for as he informed his closest daughter, he would not be attending the entire evening.

"In fact, I consider this Mr. Darcy to be a smashing chap," said Mr. Bennet. "For, in allowing his sister to attend, he smoothed the way for my youngest to also grace Mr. Bingley's ball with their presence. And since they will depart after dinner, someone must see them back to Longbourn. I, naturally, am more than happy to provide that service."

"Oh, Papa," said Elizabeth, shaking her head at her father's antics. "Only you could be gleeful at the thought of leaving a ball early."

"I am not the only one, Lizzy," replied Mr. Bennet, "for I am certain Mary is only a little more inclined to it than I. Regardless, I shall be happy to convey your sisters to their beds and retreat to my bookroom for a little well-earned rest from the excesses of society."

"I hardly think this is London, Papa."

"No, but I detest society all the same. You and your sisters may have your enjoyment in the ballroom — I much prefer my bookroom."

Hearing him speak in such a manner, Mrs. Bennet looked heavenward, and shook her head, smiling with affection. Mr. Bennet, she had long known, was not a sociable man, so his assertions did not surprise her. Elizabeth had heard stories from her mother, tales of her youth and courtship with her husband, in which she had painted a picture of a more open Mr. Bennet. Or perhaps it was that he had indulged the woman he was courting. Mr. Bennet had withdrawn over the years in keeping with his character, and Mrs. Bennet had supported him, saying she had had her fill of dancing when she was young and was content to sit with the matrons now.

Overseeing the preparations of the five Bennet daughters brought Mrs. Bennet much pride and joy, for she was proud of her progeny and made no effort to hide it. As they all gathered in the entrance, waiting for the time to depart, she inspected them, straightening fichu here, or pulling a ribbon a little tighter there. No imperfections escaped her keen eye, for they were laid bare before her, anything out of place promptly repaired; her girls were to look their best that evening. As she went to each, Mrs. Bennet shared a few words with them.

"My goodness!" exclaimed she as she deftly tucked a few strands of Elizabeth's hair back into her coiffure. "I declare you and Jane shall be the loveliest ladies at Mr. Bingley's ball. What lucky men Mr. Darcy and Mr. Bingley shall be to have you on their arms!"

"Thank you, Mama," said Elizabeth, noting that Mr. Collins was scowling at her. "We shall do our best to do you justice."

"There is nothing you could do that would make me any less proud of you," said Mrs. Bennet, touching Elizabeth's face. "You are all a mother could want."

"Perhaps," interjected Mr. Collins, his nose stuck up into the air, which affected his voice, making it sound as if he spoke through his nose, "you should speak less of Mr. Darcy, for I am certain the gentleman has only singled you out due to his unusual condescension for those of a lower sphere. He can have no designs on you, Cousin."

"Let us allow Mr. Darcy to make that determination, shall we?" said Mrs. Bennet, her mild tone belying her flashing eyes.

"I had given some thought to paying my cousin the compliment of my attention," said Mr. Collins, ignoring that which he did not like. "Distracting you away from your pursuit of Mr. Darcy would allow the gentleman to direct his attention to his betrothed as is proper."

"It would be best, Mr. Collins," said Mrs. Bennet, "if you removed such thoughts from your head altogether. Not only will my daughter not accept any assurances from you, but I would not allow you to make them."

Mr. Collins shrugged as if it were of no moment. "As she chooses. I have no interest in my cousin regardless."

"And for that," said Elizabeth in a low tone to her mother, "we may thank the Lord Almighty."

The women laughed together though Mr. Collins took no notice.

"You may do as you please," continued Mr. Collins, "but let me warn you, Cousin, that Lady Catherine will take a dim view of your actions with respect to Mr. Darcy. Her ladyship insists on keeping the dignity of rank in mind at all times, and as she has a stake in this matter, you should expect a catastrophic rebuke should you persist."

The parson then turned away, leaving Elizabeth regarding him as his tuneless hum rose over the group.

"What do you suppose he means by that?" asked Mrs. Bennet.

Elizabeth sighed. "I suppose it is possible he has written to Lady Catherine or will inform her when he returns."

The frown with which Mrs. Bennet regarded the parson might have frozen him. "Then you should speak to Mr. Darcy, Lizzy."

"Yes, I suppose I should," replied Elizabeth. "I would not presume to know what the gentleman is thinking, but he has made clear his position concerning his cousin. If it is possible Lady Catherine will journey here to confront me, Mr. Darcy will wish to know."

"Perhaps he has not made it clear by word, but by deed, he most certainly has."

Mrs. Bennet kissed Elizabeth's cheek and moved on to her next daughter. It had always been a bone of contention between mother and middle daughter about Mary's fashion choices. Mary, being the most pious and modest of the Bennet sisters, insisted on a conservative form of dress, one which had been called dowdy within Elizabeth's hearing more than once. With the assistance of her eldest daughters, they had convinced Mary to adopt a more fashionable dress, though she was still more modest than her sisters. Mrs. Bennet, knowing this, did not comment on her daughter's dress, which was pretty, and instead focused on her hair and accessories.

"You have your music with you, Mary?" asked Mrs. Bennet.

"Right here, Mama," said Mary, patting a small satchel.

Nodding, Mrs. Bennet reminded her: "Remember to wait until invited, Mary, for Mr. Bingley will ask his sisters to perform first. I believe you will do very well, for you have chosen a beautiful piece of music."

With a pleased smile, Mary nodded, and Mrs. Bennet moved further down the line, at length coming to her youngest two. "Remember to behave yourselves, girls," admonished Mrs. Bennet. "I will not have the Bennet family spoken of in whispers because you run about with no heed to our reputations. Your father will escort you home after dinner, and I expect you to find your beds when you arrive home."

The girls chorused their agreement, though it was clear Lydia was put out at being required to return home early. Having completed her inspections, Mrs. Bennet led her daughters out to the carriage, accompanied by the two gentlemen. There was one further disagreement when they were to set off, Mr. Collins objecting to being required to ride on the box with Mr. Bennet and the driver, one that Mr. Bennet resolved with a few pointed words to Mr. Collins.

"My carriage is not large, Mr. Collins; I doubt there is one in all the land that will seat eight in comfort. I have six ladies in my family, which limits where gentlemen may sit, as I have discovered myself many times."

"You should have thought of this in advance, Mr. Bennet," grumbled Mr. Collins. "To require me to ride on top with a common carriage driver is beyond the pale."

"I have done it many times," replied a firm Mr. Bennet. "If you dislike the arrangements, Meryton is a mile down that road." Mr. Bennet pointed past Longbourn village. "You may walk, or you may stay home. Would you have the ladies ride on top while we sit in comfort inside?"

"No, of course not," muttered Mr. Collins, though Elizabeth was uncertain he was at all sincere.

That little bit of drama behind them, the ladies entered and the men perched themselves on the top, and the carriage lurched into motion. Elizabeth, knowing her mother's increasing disgust for the parson, turned to her, noting that her gaze, from the front-facing seat to the box at the top, would have impaled Mr. Collins if he was not hidden by the carriage.

"What a truly excellent man Mr. Collins is," said she to no one in particular. "Such chivalry! Such solicitousness! Such a gentleman!"

"It is a relief that you did not require one of us to marry him to save the family," said Lydia, in a voice Elizabeth thought too loud. "Any woman who has Mr. Collins for a husband must wish to strangle him within minutes of saying their vows."

"I cannot say you are incorrect, Lydia," said Elizabeth, "but mind your tone. Mr. Collins is irksome and difficult, but we would not wish him to overhear."

"Oh rubbish!" said Lydia, though Elizabeth noted her voice was more modulated. "Mr. Collins cannot hear us in this carriage with the noise of the wheels on the gravel."

"Mind your sister, Lydia," said Mrs. Bennet. Then she gave her youngest an affectionate smile. "There is no need to save the family, Lydia. We are not wealthy, but none of us will know want if we must leave our home. Besides," added she, fixing Jane and Elizabeth with all the affection of a proud mother, "two eligible gentlemen have been paying their attention to your eldest sisters. It may be premature, but their behavior is such that I have high hopes for both."

With renewed purpose, the sisters teased their eldest, which Elizabeth parried with an expertise born of long experience, while Jane ignored them. Then with excited exclamations for the evening to come, they passed the rest of the brief journey to Netherfield. Within moments they had arrived, joining the line of carriages waiting to empty their passengers. And on the second floor, as Elizabeth stepped out, she noticed the commanding presence of Mr. Darcy looking down on her.

The look he bestowed on her could not be mistaken, for it spoke of promise and passion, love and devotion. Then the gentleman disappeared from the window, and Elizabeth knew he would join her within moments. With a deep breath, Elizabeth pushed her nerves aside and readied herself for the evening to come, convinced it would be as magical as she had hoped.

CHAPTER XV

$\mathcal{T}$he sight of Miss Elizabeth Bennet that evening, stepping daintily from her father's carriage with his assistance, was akin to an epiphany to Darcy. This was a beautiful woman, both inside and out, the likes of which Darcy was certain he would not find if he searched the length and breadth of England without ceasing for the rest of his days. What did it matter if he had only known her for a short time? They would have the rest of their lifetimes to come to know each other better if only they both possessed the courage to take that step. Perhaps it was a little premature, but only a little.

Regaining control over his limbs after first catching sight of her, Darcy hurried to the stairs, taking them two at a time down to the entrance hall where the Bennet family was just entering. The smile he received from Mrs. Bennet and the knowing look from Mr. Bennet informed him that both senior Bennets were aware of his interest, their smiles a testament to their approval.

Darcy greeted them both with pleasure, welcoming them to Netherfield, though he was aware it was not his duty to do so. Then they ceded Miss Elizabeth's company to Darcy and moved off toward the receiving line.

"I have waited for you, Miss Elizabeth," said Darcy. The sound of his own voice, speaking such drivel, almost provoked a wince.

"Waited for me?" asked Miss Elizabeth with feigned astonishment. "Why would you wait for me?"

The woman's jest calmed Darcy's beating heart just a little, allowing his mind to function again. "Do I not have the first dance? Or do you intend to foreswear yourself?"

"It is yours, Mr. Darcy. I have no wish to dance it with anyone else."

"Then I am well pleased."

They joined Elizabeth's family in the receiving line, chatting companionably as Darcy continued to calm, such that he could carry on a rational conversation. Miss Bingley, to Darcy's distinct lack of surprise, greeted Miss Elizabeth with words as cold as the driven snow. Bingley met Darcy's presence in the receiving line with his typical humor.

"I say, Darcy, I had thought you were staying at Netherfield. Did you, perchance, repair to the inn without my knowledge?"

"No, Bingley. I hope you do not blame me for not wishing to take more than two steps away from this lovely creature by my side."

Bingley laughed to Miss Elizabeth's self-consciousness and exclaimed: "Would that I could do the same. When all the guests arrive, I shall emulate you closely."

Darcy smiled and slapped Bingley's shoulder, and then guided Miss Elizabeth into the ballroom. Georgiana came close to ply Elizabeth with an excited greeting, after which, she left, giggling in the company of the two youngest Bennet sisters. Darcy watched her, happy this time in Hertfordshire had raised her spirits and putting a little of the girl she had once been back into her.

"Your sisters, it seems, are as excited as Georgiana for the evening," observed Darcy.

"Yes, the first taste of society is a heady experience."

Darcy thought to say something else, but Miss Elizabeth's countenance turned serious at that moment. "Pardon me, Mr. Darcy, but there is a matter I must bring to your attention. Before we left Longbourn, Mr. Collins had a few more choice words to say about our association."

"Did he?" said Darcy, his eyes finding the tall parson where he stood, waiting with unconcealed impatience for Miss Bingley to join them in the ballroom. "Perhaps I shall need to speak with the estimable Mr. Collins again."

"Of more importance," said Miss Elizabeth, "his words suggested he may have written to your aunt with his version of our acquaintance.

Or he will tell her as soon as he arrives home."

"And Lady Catherine, upon receiving such an account, will make for Longbourn with all speed," said Darcy with a sigh. He turned a smile on Miss Elizabeth. "You are correct, for that is exactly what my aunt would do."

"Do not concern yourself for me, Mr. Darcy," said Miss Elizabeth. "Whatever Lady Catherine says, I shall not wilt before her."

"Nor would I have expected it of you," replied Darcy, regarding her with an affectionate smile. "When the opportunity permits, I will take counsel with your father, for I have no wish to allow Lady Catherine to abuse you on the advice of her senseless parson."

Darcy's eyes found that parson again, and he shook his head. "I suppose there is no reason to confront him. My aunt has a distinct talent for choosing those underlings who are so sycophantic they will do anything for her. I may as well speak to my horse, for I might receive a more intelligent response."

The laughter which Darcy's comment provoked was a balm to his soul and lightened the atmosphere between them. By common consent, they put the objectionable subject aside and spoke of other matters. In this carefree manner, another fifteen minutes passed, and the trickle of revelers entering the ballroom ceased altogether.

"I do not know if you have noticed it, Mr. Darcy," said Miss Elizabeth, "but Miss Bingley has been watching me as if she thinks I have done her personal harm. Though she has never been friendly, I do not think she has been this hostile either. Do you know what offends her?"

Darcy followed Miss Elizabeth's eyes and found Miss Bingley, noting Mr. Collins and Mr. Wickham close by, vying for her attention. A chuckle escaped his lips.

"She appears cozy with her two suitors, does she not?"

The giggle with which she responded was an unusual occurrence, for she possessed a throaty laugh. "She does not look best pleased."

"As for the answer to your question, it seems she has had her eyes opened to the threat to her designs." Miss Elizabeth's eyes found his, a question within. "Mr. Wickham visited yesterday while Georgiana and I were at Longbourn and asked her for the first dance. When she told him she expected to be dancing those sets with . . . another, Hurst disabused her of the notion with great relish. Hurst does not get on well with his wife's sister and can be accused of tweaking her nose at every opportunity."

"Miss Bingley is to dance the first with Mr. Wickham?" At Darcy's nod, Miss Elizabeth laughed again. "How fortunate for her, for he is a handsome man, is he not?"

"That is not for me to say," offered Darcy. "My only concern is his other proclivities."

Miss Elizabeth nodded, but she did not wish to speak of Wickham and Miss Bingley. "I am interested in this mention of 'designs.' Of further interest is the possibility I could be a threat to them. Whatever can you mean?"

"You cannot be a threat to them, Miss Elizabeth," replied Darcy, "for Miss Bingley's designs have never had any chance of coming to fruition."

"Do you have designs yourself, sir?"

"Perhaps," replied Darcy.

"And will you inform me of what they are?"

"Do you wish me to ruin the chase?" asked Darcy.

Miss Elizabeth's eyes widened in seeming shock. "The chase? Am I nothing more than a hare and you the fox? Am I to become your dinner, Mr. Darcy?"

"Anything but, Miss Elizabeth." Darcy paused, sensing it was the time to become serious. "As to my 'designs,' you should know that such terms are as yet grandiose. If you are asking me if I appreciate what is before me, then my answer is an unequivocal yes. I am excited to learn the full measure of the possibilities that lie before us, and. I hope you are too."

"I am breathless with anticipation," said Elizabeth, though it was little more than a whisper. Surprised as she had been by the candor in his veiled statement, Elizabeth had not been certain she possessed the ability to respond.

"Then let us discover it together."

Unobtrusively, Mr. Darcy's hand crept from the side of his leg to find hers and grip it tightly. Moved, Elizabeth squeezed his hand with her agreement, soaring with pleasure when Mr. Darcy returned her gesture. The moment did not last long, for it was improper for an unmarried and unengaged couple to hold hands, but even when he released hers, Elizabeth could feel the warmth surrounding the appendage like a cocoon. She was well contented.

Their conversation returned to other matters, laughter flowing between them. Georgiana and Elizabeth's sisters joined them, and they spoke with others in the ballroom, including Colonel Fitzwilliam, Charlotte, and many of Elizabeth's friends. It seemed to her, however, that she and Mr. Darcy were the only two in the room; Elizabeth relished that feeling of utter closeness.

When Mr. Bingley gave the signal and the musicians began to play the opening strains of the first dance, Elizabeth took her place across the line from Mr. Darcy, curtseying to his bow. Then the dancers moved like flowing water in the first of the intricate steps, Elizabeth's heart beating in tune with the music. It may have been nothing more than her fancy, but she felt Mr. Darcy's heart beating alongside hers.

"I am gratified to see that I can call dancing one of your accomplishments, Mr. Darcy," said Elizabeth after admiring the precision of his steps for a moment. "I have heard it said that dancing is not your activity of choice."

"At present, Miss Elizabeth," said Mr. Darcy, "I must contradict you and say that I cannot imagine any activity I prefer to dancing. It is the partner that makes all the difference—would you not agree?"

"Oh, without a doubt," said Elizabeth, holding her blush at bay. "Then this is a pleasure I shall see repeated?"

"As many times as the occasion permits," replied Mr. Darcy.

The dance separated them and for a few moments, they danced apart. At that time, Elizabeth glanced about the room and noticed a few things. Kitty and Lydia standing by the side of the dance floor, eager for their turns to dance, with Georgiana by their side, Mary close by, watching over them. What was more interesting at the moment was that Jane and Charlotte were both dancing nearby, and another was just a little further on, wearing a thundercloud, hanging over all, threatening thunder and lightning.

"Mr. Wickham is dancing the first with Miss Bingley, I see."

Mr. Darcy showed her a grin. "That was the reason for his visit yesterday."

"Mr. Collins does not appear pleased."

"It will do him little good," replied Mr. Darcy with a shrug. "Miss Bingley will not marry a parson. But neither will she marry an officer, so they are both wasting their time."

Elizabeth nodded but had no interest in further talking about such objectionable persons. "Do you think Mr. Bingley is coming close to offering for Jane?"

"It is hard to say," said Mr. Darcy. "Though I have often seen Bingley in the throes of infatuation, I have never seen him this enamored with a woman." Mr. Darcy seemed to sense Elizabeth's surprise, for he laughed and added: "I do not accuse my friend of inconstancy, Miss Elizabeth. Though his head is often turned by a pretty face, I have noticed that when he is with Miss Bennet, he has eyes for no other."

Elizabeth nodded. "It may be that he did not know for what he was searching, and having found it, he knows instinctively there is no need to search further."

The smile with which Mr. Darcy favored her was gentle yet carried a wealth of meaning. "It is a feeling all men of good character understand, I believe."

The words were simple but carried so much more than Mr. Darcy could say in the middle of a ballroom. They spent several moments after gazing into each other's eyes until Elizabeth decided they must appear silly to those looking on. Then Elizabeth remembered one other item she had seen.

"Your cousin has chosen to open the ball with my friend, Charlotte Lucas."

Mr. Darcy's eyes roved the room until he found Colonel Fitzwilliam, speaking in an animated fashion with Charlotte.

"I have noted they appear comfortable together."

"Are you suggesting there might be something between them?" asked Mr. Darcy with a frown.

"I would not presume to say so much, Mr. Darcy, for my friend has vouchsafed no hint of admiration for Colonel Fitzwilliam, and I do not know the colonel well enough to know what he is thinking."

The slow nod with which Mr. Darcy responded suggested he had something more to say. The cautious way in which he spoke suggested to Elizabeth he did not wish to offend her.

"Many a time, my cousin has jested about his need to find a woman of wealth, or he must give up his lifestyle."

Elizabeth laughed. "Do not concern yourself, Mr. Darcy, for I have no intention of jumping to love and matrimony regarding your cousin and my friend. While I know Charlotte is an excellent woman who would make any man proud, I cannot say if they suit, or if there is any interest between them."

"Perhaps we should give them a push," suggested Mr. Darcy with a gleam in his eye. "We both know enough that we can give a good account to another."

The hilarity rose in Elizabeth's breast, and only the needs of the moment, where they were situated in the middle of a crowded ballroom, enabled her to keep her countenance. When she had mastered her humor, she fixed Mr. Darcy with a stern look.

"For shame, Mr. Darcy. Never would I have taken you for a

matchmaker!"

"I am not," said Mr. Darcy, echoing her mirth. "Then I suppose we must step back and permit them to find their own way. I shall note that Fitzwilliam, while his estate will not make him a wealthy man, will have enough to support a wife and any children he might have. Thus, he does not require a dowry."

"I shall be certain to let my friend know that," said an amused Elizabeth.

With such interesting banter, they passed the rest of the dance. When they were making their way off the floor at the end, however, Elizabeth was pleased to receive another request from the gentleman.

"If I might impose upon you, Miss Elizabeth—would you do me the honor of dancing the supper set with me?"

"I will," replied Elizabeth, "if you feel you are ready to accept the consequences it would bring."

"I have never been more ready for anything in my life," averred the gentleman.

Smiling, Elizabeth accepted and stood with him for several more moments until her next dance partner arrived. Having another dance to anticipate, parting from him was of less difficulty than it might otherwise have been.

Having secured Miss Elizabeth's hand for the supper sets, Darcy watched her leave with another man—Fitzwilliam—with regret, but no genuine sorrow. Matters were proceeding much more quickly than Darcy had ever had any right to expect, and while his innate sense of cautiousness suggested it may be best to take it slower, his heart was urging him on. There was no question which organ he would follow.

It was a peculiar night for Darcy, and at times he felt like a stranger in his own skin. Never one to enjoy balls and assemblies, he found himself mingling with these people more than was his custom. As the night progressed, Miss Elizabeth introduced him to more of her friends, and he found he could ask them to dance without hesitation.

In those moments when Darcy was alone and at leisure to consider the matter, he wondered why tonight was so different, why these people seemed more acceptable than those with whom he had mingled all his life. It took some time to determine the reason, but at length, Darcy realized what it was: there were no expectations of him. Miss Elizabeth's friends and family treated him with respect and friendship, but not with anything approaching covetousness or interest in his position beyond what was polite.

All Darcy's life since he had entered society and before, he had been hunted, stalked by young ladies and their mothers for the purpose of capturing him as a husband. Men sought him out, not for friendship but to claim they had made the acquaintance of Fitzwilliam Darcy, a man with connections to the nobility, whose family line was older than all but the most ancient of noble families.

These people, by contrast, seemed to accept him as he was, with no thought for anything more. For a time, Darcy wondered why that might be, why these people seemed to have the ability to put such things aside. Further deliberation gave Darcy the possible answer. For the gentlemen, the answer was that they were not part of the London set, and as a result, to them, he was another gentleman, albeit a wealthy one. For the ladies, however, it was his obvious interest in Miss Elizabeth that made all the difference. Though many might have wished he had singled them out instead, they had seen and noted his interest in her. Thus, he was another man who would dance with them, but they had no other expectations.

It was a heady feeling, this freedom. Darcy wondered if his forays into society would be more like this should he marry. The thought intrigued him, as did the notion that he might have found the woman with whom he wished to spend his life, in this of all places.

The one impediment to his complete enjoyment of the evening was Wickham's presence, though Darcy noted the officer took care to remain away from Darcy himself. Wickham's attentions to Miss Bingley remained unabated, though the woman did her best to make herself scarce — that was difficult, given her status as mistress of the estate. Wherever they two went, also went Mr. Collins. Fitzwilliam appeared to be enjoying himself with the local ladies that evening, but that did not mean he was not watchful of his officers.

"I assume you have noted our friend Wickham's activities tonight."

Fitzwilliam laughed. "I have. There are few, I suspect, who have not noted his persistence toward Miss Bingley. If you look about you, I suspect you will discover that Miss Bingley's misfortune as the focus of two ardent suitors is a source of amusement for most."

"Yes, I had noticed it, though I cannot account for it."

With a grin, Fitzwilliam related the recent scene in Meryton, and while Darcy had heard of the matter from Georgiana, Fitzwilliam's account was more comprehensive than his sister's had been, as Georgiana had been more concerned with the presence of one George Wickham.

"Many a time I have told her she should speak with caution," said

Darcy, shaking his head when Fitzwilliam completed his tale. "She is stubborn and will not listen."

"Of more consequence," said Fitzwilliam, "she is convinced she deserves to be treated as if she were royalty."

"It is difficult to understand," said Darcy with a nod. "To return to the problem of Wickham, however, what do you think of his behavior tonight?"

"There is little enough to say," replied Fitzwilliam. "Though I have ensured there are men to watch Wickham and have taken steps to curtail his ability to create havoc, there is only so much that I can do. If he does not stray from what is proper, there is little I can do to prevent him from paying court to Miss Bingley."

With a grimace, Darcy said: "Then it may be best if I were to speak to Bingley and have him warn Wickham off."

The laugh with which Fitzwilliam responded informed Darcy his cousin did not agree with him. "Why? If Miss Bingley wishes to be free of his attentions, she can speak to her brother. Should she refrain from doing it, is that not a sign she welcomes him?"

"You do not suppose she does, do you?" asked Darcy.

"No, I do not suppose it. It is clear she wishes for a man of greater consequence, and we all know who her first choice would be. As that choice will soon become unattainable, or so I suspect, she will soon learn that she must consider other men or remain unmarried."

"She will not marry him."

"Nor do I suppose she will. But if you consider it, Miss Bingley is the last woman I would suspect of yielding to Wickham's charm. There is little need for us to become involved, for the remedy against Wickham's attention is within her ability to summon, and I do not think she is in any danger, regardless."

"I suppose you are correct," conceded Darcy, though he continued to look at Wickham with distaste."

"Of course, I am," replied Fitzwilliam. "It may surprise you to learn it, but our friend Wickham has actually behaved himself since his arrival in Meryton. There is not a hint of scandal hovering about him; I even have reports that he owes no markers to his fellow officers."

"Do you trust him?"

"No," was Fitzwilliam's succinct reply. "I do trust him to do whatever he can to protect his own hide, and for now that means behaving himself. When he finds himself in a position where he is unrestrained again, I suspect he will revert to the old Wickham."

The conversation ended there, for Darcy knew Fitzwilliam was correct. For the moment, there was little to do but watch and stay wary. And the irony of Miss Bingley's being on the other side of the coin from her usual pursuit of Darcy was delicious, so he decided to enjoy it while he could.

CHAPTER XVI

When the supper hour arrived, Elizabeth was eager to sit with Georgiana, knowing her friend's evening would soon come to a close. Dancing the supper set with Mr. Darcy allowed Elizabeth the freedom to do just that.

Georgiana had attended even fewer functions than Elizabeth's youngest sisters, a circumstance Elizabeth put down to the family's higher consequence in society, where such societal rules were of more consequence. As such, the girl chattered throughout the meal, exclaiming over this sight, that dance, the impressions she had of the evening or the discussions she had with Kitty and Lydia.

"You do not wish you had danced more?" asked Elizabeth, amused by her young friend's enthusiasm.

"No, I believe I am satisfied," replied Georgiana. "I danced with William, Anthony, and Mr. Bingley, which I find enough for my first foray into the world of balls."

Elizabeth knew her sisters had complained at being denied more dances than this. Lydia had voiced her desire to dance with the handsome officers of the regiment loudly enough to be heard throughout the ballroom and could not understand why her father had not allowed it. When alerted to the ruckus she was creating, Colonel

Fitzwilliam had asked for permission to stand in for his men, to which Mr. Bennet—who had grown tired of Lydia's complaining—had agreed. After that, the girl had been easier to bear.

"Hurst would have danced with you," said Mr. Darcy, his grin displaying his own amusement. "If you had asked him, he would have obliged you, though he has less interest in the dance floor than even I."

"Could I have escaped with the toes of my slippers intact?" asked Georgiana with some wryness.

Mr. Darcy laughed. "It is my understanding that Hurst was light on his feet when he was a younger man. I cannot claim he is so now, but I do not think him deficient."

"Unlike some others, I could name," said Elizabeth with a shaken head and a glance to one side.

Georgiana giggled and Mr. Darcy shook his head. During the second dance of the evening, Mr. Collins had insisted on partnering Miss Bingley and had shown he was, perhaps, the worst dancer in the country. Stepping the wrong way, apologizing when he should concentrate on his steps, berating others when he had moved wrong, and lumbering up and down the line when he was actually moving according to the steps were just some of his offenses. Elizabeth was more grateful than ever that she had escaped Mr. Collins's inept attentions. Thus far, she had avoided the parson, reprieved from the fate of dancing with him. In fact, Elizabeth did not think any Bennet sister had partnered with him. None of them repined that loss.

After the supper hour had progressed for some time, Mr. Bingley stood to speak to the gathering, stating with enthusiasm how happy he was with the welcome the Bingley family had received. Then, after a few such words, he invited his sister to play for the company, which Miss Bingley did with a sense of pride and a sly glance in Mr. Darcy's direction.

"She is proficient," observed Elizabeth after a time of listening to the lady play. "Much more than myself, in fact."

"Oh, Lizzy," said Georgiana, "you are proficient too."

"Thank you for inflating my vanity, Georgiana, but I am not on Miss Bingley's level. Though I am proficient, I do not take enough trouble to practice, which limits any improvement I might attain."

Then Elizabeth turned to Georgiana and grinned. "As I recall, I have not heard you play, my dear. Shall you grace us with a song tonight?"

Georgiana paled and stammered, leading Elizabeth to laugh and put her hand on her friend's arm. "Do not concern yourself, Georgiana, for I will not insist. One day, however, others will expect it of you, so it may be best to become accustomed to it in smaller groups."

"Georgiana is skilled enough she could do it now," interjected Mr. Darcy, with a smile at his sister. "Her only issue is confidence."

"That is something which we may remedy," replied Elizabeth. "But I do not believe now is the time to insist on it."

Relieved, Georgiana nodded. "Perhaps we could play together, Elizabeth. Then you shall hear me play."

"That would be lovely, Georgiana," assured Elizabeth.

By this time, Miss Bingley was nearing the end of her song. As Elizabeth looked up again to observe the performer, she noted with some curiosity that Miss Bingley was staring back at her, a heated glare impaling her where she sat.

"What do you think offends Miss Bingley?" asked Elizabeth of her companions.

"I suspect she does not appreciate my brother's attention on anyone other than herself," said Georgiana.

With a laugh, Elizabeth could only say: "Then that is unfortunate for her, for I see nothing of your brother's admiration for her. Thus, she must be disappointed."

"Indeed, she must," murmured Mr. Darcy.

Miss Bingley's song came to a close and the company applauded, though their response did not seem to be as Miss Bingley wished, for she stood and swept away from the instrument, head held high but with a gleam of contempt in her eye for her guests. Mrs. Hurst succeeded her at the pianoforte, and then several others before Mary's chance to play for them all arrived.

Mary was also proficient, though Elizabeth had thought her sister often lacked a feeling for the music. That evening, however, Mary played well, a piece suited for her abilities and talents, and when she completed it, the company applauded enthusiastically. The blush which suffused her countenance was a testament to Mary's pleasure and evidence she had not always received such appreciation for her efforts. It seemed their efforts to induce Mary to play to her strengths were bearing fruit.

One who did not appear to appreciate Mary's efforts was their hostess. Miss Bingley glared at the girl, offended the applause for Mary had been louder. That Mary did not notice was a relief to Elizabeth. Miss Bingley said nothing disparaging, which was also a relief, but there was one in attendance who was not so circumspect.

"My cousin's playing is adequate, I suppose," said Mr. Collins in his superior voice. "But her modest efforts pale in comparison with the sublime efforts of Miss Bingley, for her song was the voice of an angel brought down to earth. What beauty in tone and execution! I dare say that should my patroness, Lady Catherine de Bourgh, have learned to play, she could not have performed any better, for all that her taste is as refined as any I have ever met."

While Mr. Collins continued to ramble on about his patroness, Miss Bingley, interspersed with comments about Mary, Elizabeth noted Mr. Bingley looking at him with utter annoyance. He must have decided against reprimanding the man, for he shook his head and turned back to Jane, who sat by his side. Mr. Bennet, so often amused by his cousin's antics, was glaring at the parson with unfeigned anger, and Mrs. Bennet was not hiding her disdain. It was fortunate that Mary seemed to be of the opinion that the parson's judgment did not matter a jot, for Mary's confidence was a fragile thing at times.

There were some few performers after Mary, but Elizabeth did not pay much attention to them, engrossed as she was in her conversation with the Darcys. Miss Bingley flitted about the edges of Elizabeth's vision, but the lady appeared to be attempting to avoid Mr. Collins and Mr. Wickham as much as she was intruding on her conversation. Thus, Elizabeth paid her little mind.

A minor incident arose toward the end of supper when Lydia began carrying on and laughing in raucous tones with a pair of militia officers. While Elizabeth glared at the girl, she was not obliged to rein her in, for another filled that role.

"Lydia, please come and sit with your father and me," said Mrs. Bennet. "You also, Kitty."

Though giving a put-upon sigh, Lydia rose and followed her mother, Kitty coming behind. Colonel Fitzwilliam approached the two officers and shared a few words with them, which had them nodding their agreement. As for her youngest sisters, they sat near Elizabeth, so she could hear everything they were saying.

"We were just having a bit of fun, Mama!"

Elizabeth did not even need to look to know it was Lydia speaking, for her whine was distinctive.

"Perhaps you were, my dear," said Mrs. Bennet, "but there is a proper way to have a bit of fun and a way which is not so proper. You crossed that line."

Lydia huffed and sat back in her chair, glaring at all and sundry with a childish pout. Elizabeth watched her sister and shook her head, and Mrs. Bennet, though she regarded her youngest daughter with fond amusement, held firm.

"It is clear to me, Lydia, that you are not ready for such events as this. No, I will not forbid you," interjected Mrs. Bennet when Lydia complained, "but I believe we should exercise caution when we decide what you will and will not attend."

"It is not fair," spat Lydia with a pout.

"Perhaps it is not, my dear," replied Mrs. Bennet. "However, embarrassing our family with your behavior is not fair either. When you prove you are ready for the responsibility, we will give you greater freedom, and not before."

"Excellent point, Mrs. Bennet," said Mr. Bennet, smiling at his wife. "And with that, I believe it is time for us to depart.

"Do not complain, Lydia," said Mr. Bennet when Lydia did just that. "You were aware of the rules long before the evening started. Say your goodbyes to your friends, so we may depart."

Though with little willingness, the two girls did as their father bid them while Mr. and Mrs. Bennet looked on. At her side, Mr. Darcy glanced at his sister, who understood his meaning in an instant.

"Yes, I understand, Brother. I shall retire."

"Thank you, Georgiana," said Mr. Darcy, kissing his sister's forehead. "I believe you have done well tonight. There shall be many such opportunities for further amusements."

Having said that much, Mr. Darcy rose and moved away to speak with his cousin, leaving Elizabeth and Georgiana together. They said their farewells, arranging to meet again two days after the ball, and Elizabeth moved away to talk to her sister, assuming Georgiana would make her way above stairs. She had not counted on the determination of a man who had been watching them, and in hindsight, Elizabeth wondered if he had been waiting for an opportunity to come upon Georgiana alone.

"Georgiana," said Wickham, alerting Elizabeth to his presence. "Miss Darcy," the man amended, his face screwed up in a grimace. "I apologize — my address should not have been so informal."

"Yes, Mr. Wickham?" asked Georgiana. Had Elizabeth not known her friend better, she might have thought Georgiana's tone was all haughtiness.

"I know I have no right to approach you and I do not wish to impose upon you. But I wished to apologize for my behavior in the summer."

"Oh?" asked Georgiana, her raised eyebrow showing both surprise and insistence he clarify his statement.

"It was unconscionable of me and an insult to the memory of your father. There is no excuse for what I attempted to do, and I apologize for it without reservation."

Only her friend's surprise prevented Elizabeth from joining her. It surprised Elizabeth herself. Mr. Wickham's words suggested a sinister plot against Georgiana, the truth of which Elizabeth did not even wish to guess. It was fortunate, Elizabeth thought, that no one else seemed to be listening, for she did not think her friend wished anyone to know of what they were speaking.

"Then I thank you for that, Mr. Wickham."

Without another word, the officer bowed and moved away, freeing Elizabeth to approach her young friend. It did not miss her notice that Mr. Darcy and Colonel Fitzwilliam were also hurrying to her side.

"I apologize, Georgiana," said Elizabeth, reaching her young friend first, "but I could not help but overhear a little of what Mr. Wickham said. Has he caused you discomfort?"

"No," replied Georgiana, her look and manner absent. "In fact, for the first time in his life, I believe Mr. Wickham has done something right."

"Georgiana, what did Wickham want?" asked Mr. Darcy as he strode up to them. His countenance was a mass of concern, his eyes searching his sister for any signs of distress. At that moment, Elizabeth thought he would find Mr. Wickham and call him out if the officer had caused any hurt to his sister.

"To apologize," said Georgiana, bringing the two gentlemen to a surprised halt.

"He apologized," echoed Colonel Fitzwilliam.

"Yes. He claimed his behavior in the summer was unconscionable, that he insulted my father's memory by it."

The gentlemen shared a glance. "At least he seems to understand that now," muttered Mr. Darcy, to Colonel Fitzwilliam's grim nod.

"He said nothing else?" At Georgiana's shaken head, Colonel Fitzwilliam said: "Then I suppose there is no need to call him out."

"Perhaps it would be best for you to go to bed," said Elizabeth, gently steering Georgiana toward the door.

The girl turned and flung her arms around Elizabeth, murmuring: "Thank you for your support, Elizabeth. Oh! You must be so confused."

"Do not concern yourself, Georgiana," assured Elizabeth. "It is clear Mr. Wickham hurt you in some way. More than that I need not know."

Georgiana nodded and bid her goodnight, then her brother escorted her from the room, but not before Mr. Darcy gave her a grateful glance. They soon exited, leaving Elizabeth in Colonel Fitzwilliam's company. After looking about for a moment, assuring himself that no one was near, Colonel Fitzwilliam addressed her:

"Please allow me to add my thanks to my cousin's, Miss Elizabeth. You have been an excellent friend and have helped her shed some of her shyness."

"You have a wonderful ward, Colonel Fitzwilliam," said Elizabeth. "I would support her, regardless of the circumstances. Whatever I overheard, I assure you no one shall hear aught of it from me."

"Of that, I have little doubt," said Colonel Fitzwilliam.

After a few moments, Colonel Fitzwilliam drifted away toward several of his officers, leaving Elizabeth alone to her thoughts. While she might have been excused for considering what she had just overheard, Elizabeth made a conscious decision to turn her thoughts to other matters. Georgiana, it appeared, was growing and maturing, and Elizabeth hoped she would be in a position to continue that friendship after her friend inevitably departed from the neighborhood. The thought of asking for a correspondence entered her mind, and Elizabeth determined she would speak of it the next time they met.

Then a low, unfriendly voice interrupted Elizabeth's musings.

"You seem to have become very close to dear Georgiana."

Turning, Elizabeth noted Miss Bingley's presence; the woman was watching her, a half glare fixed on her. While Elizabeth assumed that Miss Bingley was unhappy because of Mr. Darcy's recent attention to her and her friendship with Georgiana, she was not about to allow Miss Bingley to lure her into an argument.

"Did you not, yourself, laud her as an exquisite woman?" Miss Bingley made no response, and Elizabeth added: "In this, I must agree with you, Miss Bingley, for I like Georgiana very well."

"I am gratified you see her the way I do," said Miss Bingley. "If Mr. Darcy and his sister were not visiting here, it is possible you would not see them. Good manners induce Mr. Darcy to attend local events, for he can be reclusive in other places. He is careful of the society to which he keeps."

Amused, Elizabeth nodded. "Yes, I can see why a man of Mr. Darcy's consequence would prefer to choose his friends with great care, Miss Bingley."

Nodding, the woman leaned toward Elizabeth and said with great deliberation: "If I were you, Miss Elizabeth, I would refrain from seeing anything in Mr. Darcy's civility other than a true, generous courtesy. Many before you have hoped to induce a . . . a closer relationship with him and failed."

"I assure you, Miss Bingley, that I have no expectations for Mr. Darcy. I count Georgiana as an excellent friend and esteem Mr. Darcy. The gentleman may do as he pleases, and there is little I can or wish to do to direct him. I am content with friendship."

The way Miss Bingley searched her eyes, Elizabeth thought the woman did not believe her. Given what she understood of Miss Bingley's character, Elizabeth knew this was because Miss Bingley was doing everything in her power to attract the gentleman and could not understand another not doing the same. After a moment of this, she sniffed.

"You should also know that many others have tried — and failed — to use . . . underhanded means to attract the gentleman."

"That, Miss Bingley, is the furthest from my mind," said Elizabeth, doing everything she could not to laugh. "We Bennets are not a family given to such behavior. I would never dream of trying to force Mr. Darcy's hand."

With satisfaction that Elizabeth had heard and accepted her point, Miss Bingley opened her mouth to speak again when they were interrupted.

"Miss Bingley! Miss Bingley!"

The sound of Mr. Collins's voice rising over those assembled whitened the woman's countenance. Without excusing herself, she slipped away and out a door into another room, Mr. Collins rushing past Elizabeth to follow her a few moments later. When they were both gone, Elizabeth shook her head and looked about, her eyes resting on the person of Mr. Wickham, who appeared to be laughing at the scene. Elizabeth did not trust him, particularly not given the additional information she had gleaned that evening. But she was curious.

"It is interesting to see you laughing at Miss Bingley's distress, Mr. Wickham. I would have thought you would be angry, for are you not also eager to pay court to her?"

"Miss Bingley's distress does not amuse me, Miss Elizabeth," contradicted the officer. "It is the antics of Mr. Collins which cause my mirth. Who would not laugh at such a ridiculous man?"

"Who, indeed?" replied Elizabeth. "Then you have no concern for his interest in her?"

"Should I?" asked Mr. Wickham. The officer smirked and added: "There is little to suggest that Miss Bingley would ever accept an offer from a man such as Mr. Collins. Given that fact, I believe I have little to concern myself. I suspect Mr. Collins will offer his hand before long, but I am convinced she will reject him."

"Do you think it more likely she will accept a proposal from you?"

Mr. Wickham turned to regard Elizabeth, something more pensive in his mood now. "You are disposed to think she will not?"

Elizabeth laughed. "You do not misunderstand her interest in Mr. Darcy, do you?"

"No. But Darcy offering for her is even less likely that Miss Bingley accepting a proposal from Mr. Collins."

"That does not mean she will accept a proposal from you."

"No, I suppose it does not. However, I have confidence that Miss Bingley, when she comes to know me better, will see me in the correct light, and when she does, I believe my chances are as good as anyone else'."

There was something in the way he phrased his words that Elizabeth did not like, though she could not say what it was. Mr. Wickham, Elizabeth thought, was a dangerous man, a ruthless one. Even if she had not had Mr. Darcy's warning, she did not think she ever would have trusted him.

"Excuse me, Miss Elizabeth," said the man. "Unless I am mistaken, I believe you overheard my conversation with Miss Darcy a few moments ago?"

"I did," confirmed Elizabeth.

"Then I would appreciate it if you would maintain your silence and not speak of it. It would not do if any whispers about her came to the ears of even so small a society as this. The Darcys are a prominent family; if it were to become known in London, it would cause her immeasurable grief."

"Perhaps you should have thought of that before you did whatever it is you did," snapped Elizabeth, though she kept her voice low to avoid being overheard. "Though your attempt to apologize is laudable, to do so where anyone might hear you is more than a little careless."

Mr. Wickham, Elizabeth noted, did not deny anything she said.

"You need have no concern, Mr. Wickham, for I shall not tell a soul. I hope that you will take as much care with her reputation and that you will trouble her no more."

"Of that, you have my promise," replied Mr. Wickham.

The officer then sketched a bow and removed himself from Elizabeth's presence. Elizabeth was not unhappy to see him go. For a moment, she considered speaking to Miss Bingley and attempting to warn her about this dangerous man. Then she decided against it. Miss Bingley would not listen to her, and Elizabeth did not think the woman was in any danger from him anyway.

Those present soon migrated their way back to the ballroom and the latter half of the dancing began once again. Elizabeth stood up as much as she ever had, but her heart was not in it, for she was too full of weighty thoughts. Mr. Darcy and Georgiana crowded her thoughts, as did Mr. Collins and Mr. Wickham, and for a time, Elizabeth was insensible to the goings-on around her.

Of Miss Bingley, she saw little for the rest of the evening. Mr. Collins, Elizabeth saw often, for the gentleman wandered the ballroom and surrounding chambers, searching for Miss Bingley. Wherever the lady had hidden, it seemed successful in throwing the man off her trail.

It also meant that Mrs. Hurst stepped into the role of hostess for the rest of the evening, though the woman did not seem to mind. Elizabeth spent much of the remaining evening, when she was not dancing, in the company of Mr. Darcy, and for a time they stood with Charlotte and Colonel Fitzwilliam, laughing and speaking in animated tones. Charlotte, too, Elizabeth noted, was enjoying the ball as much as she had enjoyed any function in recent years. For a time, Elizabeth watched her friend, wondering if there was something between herself and the colonel.

Elizabeth pushed even those thoughts to the side in favor of her evening with Mr. Darcy. There were several times when the gentleman appeared absent-minded, and she wondered if he was thinking about Mr. Wickham and what had happened earlier that evening. If he thought to speak to her about it, Elizabeth was willing to listen. But it was only as a friend, for she did not need to know about Georgiana's misfortune.

CHAPTER XVII

ew were awake at an early hour the morning after the ball at Netherfield Park. This would be true regardless of the venue, for balls ended late, and beds sought in the wee hours of the morning.

This was true at Longbourn as it was in any other estate; some would say it typified Longbourn more so than other estates because of the preponderance of young ladies living there. It was true that Lydia and Kitty did not often rouse from their beds early, and even Jane could sleep late when the occasion permitted it, but Mary, and Elizabeth in particular, were early morning risers.

Yet even Elizabeth was abed later than usual that morning. Under normal circumstances, Elizabeth was awake with the sun and eager to go about her day. That morning, however, Elizabeth woke early as was her wont, but then dozed back to sleep for periods, her unconscious mind invaded by dreams which would have made her laugh had she remembered them when she woke.

When, at length, Elizabeth rose from her bed, she found the rest of the family likewise lethargic, shuffling with uneven steps, bleary eyes, and wide, exhausted yawns. Elizabeth suspected they would all nap for a time that afternoon, and even she, who rarely indulged in such things, thought it would benefit her that day.

That was what made the discovery that morning at the breakfast table that much more surprising. For some moments after the family gathered, they partook of the meal in silence, each eager to complete their repast and return to their rooms for a quiet day in the company of books or whatever caught their fancy. Thus, it was not surprising, perhaps, that no one noticed the absence of the visiting member of the family until they had been in the room for fifteen minutes.

It was Mrs. Bennet who noticed they were short one member of the party. Eyes narrowed, she looked down her table, and then at her eldest daughters.

"Has no one seen Mr. Collins yet this morning?"

"For a parson, he is reluctant to rise from his bed early," said Mary with a sniff. Mary was not one to excuse sloth, especially from one she thought should avoid it at all costs.

Mrs. Bennet thought on the matter for a moment. "Perhaps that is it." She paused and sighed, shaking her head and adding: "Though I could do very well without Mr. Collins's company, I suppose we should have him summoned."

Calling for Mrs. Hill, Mrs. Bennet instructed her housekeeper to send John, the footman, to inquire concerning Mr. Collins's plans for the morning meal.

"Mr. Collins is not here, Mum," said Mrs. Hill.

"Not here?" demanded Mrs. Bennet, confused by her housekeeper's intelligence. "Wherever has he gone?"

"I cannot say," replied Mrs. Hill. "Mr. Collins did not say where he was going or when he would return."

"When did he leave?" asked Elizabeth.

"Perhaps five and forty minutes ago."

Nonplussed, Mrs. Bennet dismissed her servant and turned back to her family. "That is rude of Mr. Collins, to depart and not inform us of where he is bound. I cannot imagine what he is thinking."

Though Elizabeth agreed the parson was lacking in proper manners, she thought she knew where Mr. Collins had gone. There was no reason to give voice to her suspicions, however, and she held her peace. They would all learn the truth when the parson returned, for if he succeeded, he would trumpet it from the rooftops. Should he prove unsuccessful, as Elizabeth suspected, his demeanor would tell them all they needed to know.

Though Kitty and Lydia returned to their rooms at once after lunch and Mary retired to the music room for some morning practice,

Elizabeth remained with her parents in the sitting-room, with Jane also in attendance. A book sat in her lap, the pages of which Elizabeth turned infrequently, for her mind was engaged in thinking of Mr. Collins's likely whereabouts, but more often considering her association with Miss Darcy, and even more, with her brother. After a time of sitting together, Mary joined them, and soon immersed herself in a book.

When Mr. Collins returned about an hour later, Elizabeth was certain her suppositions had proven correct, for the man bore an impression akin to a dark cloud bearing a fierce storm to beat the land with lashing winds and heavy rain. Had the gentleman returned to his room without comment, they might have avoided much unpleasantness. But Mr. Collins was not known for his sense.

Miss Caroline Bingley was as inclined to wake late the morning after a ball as for any other, accustomed as she was to town hours, having lived in London with her brother for much of the preceding several years. Town hours were considered fashionable. Since Caroline was eager to follow any custom which made her appear more like those of the highest set, she rarely rose early.

The morning after her brother had hosted the neighborhood, sleep was elusive, as thoughts and memories of Mr. Darcy and how he had carried on with Eliza Bennet plagued her waking moments, much as they had her dreams. Unable to find sleep, she rose, not to prepare for any useful activity, but to consider what she might do to return the gentleman's attention to where she, Caroline Bingley, felt it belonged.

The fact of Mr. Darcy's absence was both blessing and curse, for Mr. Darcy and his sister had requested a tray in his sitting-room that morning. While Caroline might have preferred a full day in Mr. Darcy's company, Caroline had to confess, if only to herself, that such tactics had not been successful in the past.

Soon after meeting the gentleman, Caroline had embarked on a campaign to show him how suitable she was to become his wife. She focused on his sister, flattering her whenever the opportunity presented itself, agreed with the gentleman in everything he said, learned his preferences, sought his opinion, attempted to adopt a sophisticated demeanor and to do everything she had seen others of society do to attract a wealthy gentleman's attention.

And none of it had succeeded. Caroline had thought many times she had reached the gentleman, had been certain he was close to offering for her. Now, as she considered her acquaintance with him, she realized she had only been lying to herself. Mr. Darcy had never shown her anything other than the courtesy he felt she was due as the sister of his close friend.

The question was what went wrong? Had she misunderstood how others of his set went about finding a wife? Or was Mr. Darcy a man who wished for something different? Though Caroline's only hope lay in the former, that he had shown interest in Miss Elizabeth with such alacrity was evidence of the latter. Caroline hoped it was not so, for if it was, she had lost the fight before it had even begun.

Into this maelstrom of fear and loathing came the detested and unwanted person of Mr. Collins. When the parson entered the sitting-room in which Caroline was sitting with her sister—Louisa had been quiet and thoughtful most of the morning—Caroline gaped at him, wondering why the silly man visited the morning after holding a taxing ball. This further evidence of the Bennet family's unsuitability prompted her lip to curl, as Caroline considered whether she could use this against Miss Elizabeth to injure her in Darcy's eyes. Would he believe for an instant that Miss Eliza was to marry Mr. Collins?

"Miss Bingley," greeted the despised parson. For a moment, Caroline had forgotten his presence as her thoughts had taken over again. "How fortunate I am to have found you at home this morning, for it is the most auspicious of all occasions. I see it now! You must have waited for me, eager for my arrival as a woman of delicate sensibilities can be!"

"What?" asked Caroline with less patience than civility, even as her sister gasped. "Where else would I be the morning after hosting a ball until the wee hours of the morning? Are not all sensible people in their homes recuperating from last night's exertions?"

"Your words are just," declared Mr. Collins. "Had I not been caught in the grips of a great tempest of feeling, threatening to overwhelm my senses, I might, even now, be in my room at Longbourn, contemplating your perfections. Alas, I cannot, for those affections have driven me here this morning."

"Perhaps it would be best—" attempted Louisa, only for the parson to interrupt her.

"If you will, Miss Bingley, I should like a private interview with you." The man turned a sickly-sweet smile on Louisa. "Though I cherish such sights as these, the bonds of sisterly affection, what I wish is to speak my mind to you alone."

"Of what are you speaking?" demanded Caroline, in no mood to listen to the parson's mewling. "What could you possibly wish to say to me that my sister cannot overhear?"

"Why, I am certain your feminine delicacy can only come to one conclusion, my dear Miss Bingley." The parson paused for dramatic effect and smiled at her, though his expression spoke of constipation rather than great feeling. "I have come, Miss Bingley, to offer you all that I have, all that I am, and all that I will be. I have come with a full heart and meekness of spirit only for you."

Though that last he spoke in a tender voice designed to make love, Caroline could only gape at the parson. Could he be saying what she thought he was saying? It was unfortunate she found no words, for the parson used her silence as an invitation to continue.

"Come, Mrs. Hurst, leave us alone for a brief time, though you may leave yonder door ajar. If you wait but a moment, you may return to a happy bit of news."

"Do you mean to propose to me?" demanded Caroline, finding her voice at last.

"Oh, your emotions have overcome you!" exclaimed the parson, his voice colored with what he thought was ecstasy. "I join you in your sublimity of heart, my dear Miss Bingley, for I feel it as much as you, down to the last degree. What felicity of heart and mind we shall have! What happiness! What commonality of purpose and opinion must be ours! My patroness decreed it must be so, and I see the hand of her greatness in your joy once again. What felicity we shall find under the wing of her protection until we must do our duty and take up Longbourn's management on that sad day when its current master shall go to meet his eternal reward.

"But perhaps before I am carried away on the wings of my feelings, I should explain to you, in some insignificant way, what has led me to Hertfordshire and to your heart. For, you see—"

Astounded as she was by Mr. Collins's stupidity, Caroline could not find her voice. His words of leading him to her heart, however, broke her from her shock and provided life to her voice.

"Why would you think I would ever marry you?"

The question hung in the air, halting Mr. Collins's copious words before he could utter them. The parson stopped and stared at her, uncomprehending, while she stood looking at him, her arms crossed while her foot tapped an impatient cadence on the floor. Louisa still sat in her chair, a look of utter horror etched on her countenance, one Caroline thought might be mirrored on her own, should she consider the possibility of marriage to an idiot on the order of Mr. Collins.

"Because I have asked for your hand," said Mr. Collins, as if that explained everything. "Given my attentions to you this past week, which you could not misunderstand, I am certain you must have been expecting my offer with every whit of your soul."

"No, receiving a proposal from you was the furthest from my mind," retorted Caroline. Then she grimaced and muttered: "I suppose I should have expected it from such a simple-minded fool!"

Though it was clear Mr. Collins had not heard the entirety of her statement, his frown suggested he had caught something of it. Louisa, traitor that she was, stood and hurried to the door, leaving Caroline alone in the dullard's company. Caroline did not concern herself with her sister's actions, for her concentration was on ridding herself of this man's odious presence at the earliest opportunity!

"But my dear Miss Bingley, you cannot be serious."

"I cannot?" asked Caroline through clenched teeth.

"Of course not! My offer is eligible, the best you are ever likely to receive, for—"

Mr. Collins's eyes bulged when Caroline laughed at the thought his offer was the best she would receive. Why, she, Caroline Bingley, mingled with the best society had to offer! The notion that such a disgusting man was the best to which she could ever aspire was laughable!

"Why do you laugh?" asked Mr. Collins. It was clear he was becoming perturbed.

"It should be clear I laugh at your idiocy, Mr. Collins," spat Caroline. "If you expect me to believe you and accept I shall never receive a better offer than that of a sniveling parson, you are without sense."

Mr. Collins sputtered and stammered and said: "But my offer is eminently eligible!"

"Perhaps for one of your cousins," sneered Caroline. "Perhaps you should offer for Miss Eliza. She can expect nothing better than squalor and she is not unsightly to look upon. There, I have resolved your dilemma for you, Mr. Collins. You may return to Longbourn and to your love."

When Mr. Collins did not respond at once, Caroline thought he had understood her, insulting though her words had been. The unctuous smile with which he regarded her disabused her of that notion.

"I am not discouraged, nor am I deceived, Miss Bingley, though I must wonder at your choice of words. I suppose you must be overcome by joy because of my application, for I understand it is usual for a woman to reject the hand of the man they mean to accept."

"By what convoluted reasoning have you come to that conclusion?" asked Caroline with a harsh laugh.

"To incite the increase of my love by suspense!" exclaimed Mr. Collins.

"The only suspense inherent in this situation, Mr. Collins," said Caroline, "is if I can avoid becoming ill because of the useless drivel you spout!"

"You must marry me!"

"There is nothing I must do, and certainly not with you!"

"Here, what is this?" a voice demanded.

The combatants turned as one and saw Charles hurrying toward them, Mr. Darcy and Louisa on his heels. Behind them, in sauntered Hurst, his usually bored countenance alive with glee. Never had Caroline so wished to slap him with every ounce of strength she possessed!

"What is the meaning of this, Collins?" demanded her brother again.

"Ah, Mr. Bingley," said Mr. Collins, bowing thrice in rapid succession. "It is fortunate, a sign from God that you have come, for there appears to be some unforeseen difficulty."

"Will you stand up straight and speak clearly! God did not bring me here, but by my sister's urgent plea to intercede. What are you doing?"

"Why, I am proposing to your sister! You must have expected it these past days, considering my incessant attentions to your sister."

Charles glanced about, and Caroline tried to inform him with nothing more than her scowl she had no intention of hearing this man sputter on for even a moment longer. She might not have concerned herself, for he was as bewildered as she had felt when Mr. Collins arrived.

"I have noticed something of your presence," said Charles. "Are you mad to have proposed to her after only a week of acquaintance?"

"He is mad to have proposed to me at all!" spat Caroline.

"Mr. Bingley," said Mr. Collins in a soothing tone, but one which carried an undercurrent of rising distress, "my patroness, Lady Catherine de Bourgh, Mr. Darcy's excellent aunt, has given me only a fortnight to be absent from my parish. As such, it is necessary that I conclude my wooing most expeditiously."

"I care not how long your patroness has given you leave to be absent," growled Charles. "Nor do I care if she is Darcy's aunt or the queen herself. To propose to a woman after a week of acquaintance is beyond the pale. To do so when she has not welcomed you is lunacy."

"Unwelcoming?" cried Mr. Collins. "She has never seemed to resent my presence!"

"That is only because you are witless!"

"You will not speak to me in such a way," retorted Mr. Collins. "I am to be your husband, and I will have your respect!"

"I will not marry you!" exclaimed Caroline.

"Oh, Caroline, you might as well accept him," said a chortling Hurst. "Life with Mr. Collins will not be dull!"

Caroline wished to give her sister's husband a piece of her mind. But she could not remove her sneer from the pathetic parson; Hurst was a secondary annoyance.

"Collins, it is time for you to depart," said Charles. "Do not suggest my sister is to marry you, for it is obvious she has refused to even consider your proposal."

"But Mr. Bingley!" wailed Mr. Collins.

"That is enough, sir," said Mr. Darcy, stepping into the conversation. Caroline could have wilted with relief—Caroline doubted this imbecile would hear anyone other than his patroness's nephew. "My friend has abjured you to leave the estate; you had better do so at once. A gentleman, Mr. Collins, does not continue to press the woman who has rejected him. To do so is gauche."

It was clear to everyone in the room that Mr. Collins wished to continue to protest the matter. As he appealed to her with his eyes, Caroline endeavored to inform him of every hint of her contempt. After a moment, he seemed to understand, though his silliness did not abate.

"Very well," declared Mr. Collins in a haughty tone. "It is your loss then, Miss Bingley, for I shall not extend the generous offer of my hand again."

Then the parson spun on his heel, staggering to the side as he almost lost his balance, and stalked from the room, the shreds of his dignity floating behind. It was Caroline's fervent wish she was never to experience the misfortune of his company again!

Elizabeth had little notion of Mr. Collins's sensibility before that day. Learning something of what had taken him to Netherfield that morning removed whatever doubts she might have still harbored as to his utter lack of intelligence.

Though one might have thought Mr. Collins would avoid any mention of any events detrimental to himself, it appeared he could not refrain. Whether that stemmed from an inability to understand why anyone would refuse to give him anything he wished, she could not say. What she knew was the mystery of his whereabouts that morning was soon vouchsafed to the family.

"It surprised me to learn you were absent this morning," observed Mr. Bennet upon spying the parson.

"Must I account for my comings and goings to you, Cousin?"

The terse question was almost an open accusation. Mr. Bennet regarded the parson for a moment, diverted rather than offended, and shrugged his shoulders.

"No, Mr. Collins, your activities are your own. I was speaking of nothing more than my surprise at your absence given our late night at the ball."

Mr. Collins's lip curled with anger and he spat: "Is everyone in Hertfordshire so improper as this? Is your whole county affected by this cursed disease? I wonder why I came at all if this is the reception I was to receive."

"If you refer to your welcome at Longbourn," said Mr. Bennet, his level gaze fixed on his cousin, "then I will remind you we have received you with open arms. Beyond that, I have no notion of your meaning. Perhaps it would be best to leave this conversation and speak of other matters."

"I am not certain I wish to speak of anything with you." Mr. Collins's tone was resentful, though no one of the family had any notion of why he would show bitterness to them.

"As you choose," replied Mr. Bennet, turning back to his paper. "Then we may continue in silence instead."

Mr. Collins stood glaring at Mr. Bennet for a moment, and Elizabeth was certain he was working himself up to some further exclamation. In this, she was correct, for the parson opened his mouth to speak several times and closed it again before he raised his voice.

"I have just been to Netherfield, where I have been summarily dismissed."

"That does not sound like Mr. Bingley," said Mr. Bennet, putting his newspaper aside again. "He is as genial a man as I have ever met. Are you certain there was not some mistake?"

"It was not Mr. Bingley!" Mr. Collins paused and added: "Well, it was not Mr. Bingley alone. It was his sister, who had the temerity to refuse my proposal of marriage! One might expect a loving brother to insist upon that which is for his sister's benefit, but it seems Mr. Bingley is not a man of moral character."

"Have you considered the possibility that Mr. Bingley does not agree with your assessment?"

"What could he believe is wanting?" demanded Mr. Collins. "I have a valuable living with the patronage of a lady of genuine quality attending to my every need, and I am to be the master of all this estate."

Mr. Bennet looked at the parson with amusement. "There are few men in England who are in a position to know, as I do, of the vagaries of determined young ladies. As men, we cannot know what a lady like Miss Bingley is thinking. It is our lot to accept it as best we can.

"If you wish for my opinion," said Mr. Bennet, a mocking note in his voice, "I could see no interest from the young lady in your suit. It has always seemed to me that Miss Bingley, in casting her net for a husband, was intent upon capturing a much bigger fish. I suggest, Cousin, that you endure Miss Bingley's refusal with whatever grace you possess and continue your search for a wife in other quarters."

Raising his newspaper once again, Mr. Bennet began reading, believing the conversation was at an end. The parson, however, was incensed, for Elizabeth could see his fists clenching, the muscles of his jaw working in anger. After a moment in which he stared at the paper, he opened his mouth to speak.

"I see how it is, Cousin." The parson's voice was raspy with emotion, prompting Mr. Bennet to appear from behind his paper yet again. "I see why I was brought here."

"If you recall," replied Mr. Bennet, his voice cool, "you requested an invitation to heal the breach between us. I did not 'bring' you here, as you suggest."

Mr. Collins was beyond reason. "Yet you accepted my request, brought me here and attempted to push your insipid daughters upon me."

"That is patently absurd, Mr. Collins," snapped Mrs. Bennet. "I have no desire to see you marry one of my girls."

"Then what was our discussion, where you brought up Mary?" Mr. Collins snorted. "As if anyone would want such a plain, colorless woman for a wife!"

Mary gasped and Mr. Bennet laid his paper on the table, rising to confront the parson. But the first to respond was Mrs. Bennet, who jumped to her feet and jabbed a finger at him.

"I spoke of Mary only because of your suggestion you wanted a wife. Mary is a good girl, and far too good for the likes of you, but she is suited to be a parson's wife if that is what she wishes for her future. I would never have worked upon her to accept you."

"And I would never have accepted you," added Mary, the utter contempt in her voice bludgeoning Mr. Collins. "You are no parson, Mr. Collins. You are nothing more than a poseur."

Mr. Collins's nostrils flared and he turned his glare on Mr. Bennet. "Is this how you allow your women to speak to me?"

"I do when you deserve it, Cousin," said Mr. Bennet. "If you dislike our hospitality, if you feel we have misused you or misrepresented ourselves, then you are free to leave. In fact, I believe it may be for the best if you did so at once."

"Very well," said Mr. Collins. "I hope you have provided for your improper family, Mr. Bennet, for they will receive no mercy from me when you die. That day cannot come soon enough."

And with those final awful words, Mr. Collins turned and stalked from the room. Within half an hour, he stomped out the door, disappearing from Hertfordshire. The next time Mr. Collins would return was the distant day of his inheritance.

CHAPTER XVIII

*S*everal things were clear when the Netherfield party arrived for a visit the following day, or they were to an observant observer. Elizabeth considered herself to be a studier of human behavior, as was her father, who watched the party come in with amusement written all over his brow.

The most obvious was Miss Bingley, who appeared to be nursing a foul mood, unsurprising considering what the Bennet family knew of the previous day's events. The way she glared at Elizabeth herself, she knew that on some level, Miss Bingley blamed her, perhaps for not drawing Mr. Collins's attention to herself. Given the woman's aborted attempt to intimidate her at the ball, Elizabeth knew it was almost certain she would have words for Elizabeth again if she had the chance.

The other matter which Elizabeth soon understood was that Mr. Darcy wished to speak with her. Their present position, in the sitting-room with the company, was not conducive to private conversation, yet the way he glanced at her suggested he wished to discuss something of some importance. Elizabeth was certain she knew what it was.

The last matter of which Elizabeth was convinced was Mr. Bingley's eagerness to speak with Jane in private. Elizabeth could not accuse the gentleman of wishing to propose, or anything else of that consequence. However, his eagerness for seclusion with Jane was clear in the words which were almost the first out of his mouth.

"The day is fine. Shall we not take ourselves out of doors to enjoy the day in the gardens?"

While Elizabeth thought certain members of the party were not eager for sunshine and clean air, they all agreed with alacrity. Even Mrs. Bennet agreed with the suggestion, chivvying her daughters out to the vestibule to gather their bonnets and gloves for their outing. Soon, they had attained the gardens and there, they broke into smaller groups. Elizabeth noted Kitty, Lydia, and Georgiana congregating around the swing affixed to a branch on one of Longbourn's largest trees.

Miss Bingley stuck to Mr. Darcy's side and refused to move away from him, foiling any plans the gentleman had of conversing alone with Elizabeth. While he accepted her presence with his usual patience as a gentleman, Elizabeth noted his exasperated looks at her. Elizabeth was not ignorant of Miss Bingley's knowledge of his annoyance, though the woman gave no sign of it.

"Yes, Mr. Darcy," said Miss Bingley when he mentioned the desire to walk in a specific direction. "There seems to be a quaint little corner away from the house there. Perhaps, Miss Eliza, you should keep your sisters company while Mr. Darcy and I explore what you must have seen many times over."

"But then you would not have a knowledgeable guide," said Elizabeth with humor, noting the way Miss Bingley said the word "quaint" made it seem like everything she saw was drab and lifeless and beneath her notice.

"Thank you, Miss Elizabeth," said Mr. Darcy. Elizabeth did not miss the dry note in his voice, nor, it seemed, did Miss Bingley, who shot a harsh glare at him. "We would appreciate your presence."

It was perhaps wise, given Miss Bingley's mood, that Mr. Darcy did not offer his arm to either, contenting himself instead with walking between them with his hands clasped behind his back. They said little as they crossed the lawn, though Elizabeth noted Mr. Darcy's surreptitious glances at her and noted the heavenward looks he cast from time to time. Underneath that, however, was a sense of seriousness that proved to Elizabeth he had something of which he wanted to speak. Thus, Elizabeth resolved to ensure the opportunity to speak in confidence would be available to them.

"Well, Eliza," said Miss Bingley after some time, "it seems there is little to see, after all. Or was there some notable location you wished to show us?"

"There are many excellent views I know well," replied Elizabeth, determined not to become pulled into a debate with this supercilious woman. "The crown of Oakham Mount, for instance, allows a fine view of both Netherfield and Longbourn, if one undertakes the exertion necessary to discover it."

"You have mentioned Oakham Mount before," said Mr. Darcy with interest, much to Miss Bingley's annoyance. "Is it far?"

"About two miles from Longbourn, though somewhat further from Netherfield. It is one of my favorite places, though there are several more I love."

"I did not know you rode," replied Miss Bingley with a sniff. "Or that your father kept enough horses to allow you the activity."

"We have several horses in our stables, Miss Bingley," replied Elizabeth. "Jane is the rider between us—I can ride, though I prefer to walk. To the determined walker, Oakham Mount is not far at all."

The sneering superiority with which Miss Bingley regarded her set Elizabeth's teeth to grinding. "You walk all that distance. How quaint. Given the dust of the road, I must assume you return home in a state which renders you unfit for company."

"There you would be incorrect, Miss Bingley," said Elizabeth, beginning to become annoyed. "Do you consider the outdoors to be unclean?"

"A woman who spends all her time out of doors becomes coarse and brown," replied Miss Bingley. "Those of us who know how to behave prefer to keep ourselves beyond reproach, for it is uncultured of a woman to appear anything other than to her best advantage."

"That is an interesting position, Miss Bingley." Elizabeth turned to Mr. Darcy and said: "I am curious about this portrayal of ladies of quality. Do ladies of a certain station prefer to stay inside all hours of the day? Such behavior can only be detrimental to their health, for such a life of sedentary pursuits suggest they would get little exercise."

"Though I cannot speak of all ladies of higher stations," said Mr. Darcy, his eyes gleaming with mirth, "I have never known the ladies of my family to be so delicate. Georgiana loves to walk and ride, and my aunt and cousins are much like her. Then there is the fashionable set's propensity to walk in Hyde Park, to see and be seen. Though perhaps their motives have nothing to do with exertion, they get it nonetheless."

"That is well," said Elizabeth, smiling sweetly at Miss Bingley. "As I do not concern myself with being fashionable, I believe I will continue as I have."

"Then you will never amount to anything in fashionable society," sneered Miss Bingley.

"Your thinking is laced with fallacy," said Elizabeth. "I have already said I do not care to be fashionable. What others think of me is a matter of extreme indifference."

"Yes, I can see that."

Elizabeth stopped and faced Miss Bingley. "I should much prefer, Miss Bingley, to remain true to myself and my character than attempt to pretend I am something that I am not. Such pretenses are dishonest, and I will have no part of them."

It seemed Miss Bingley did not misunderstand Elizabeth's meaning. When she did not respond at once, it was because she was too incensed to discover a suitable retort. It was fortunate that at that moment, Mrs. Hurst came to pull her sister into a discussion with Mrs. Bennet, for Elizabeth was certain Miss Bingley would have said something impolitic if she had been allowed to speak. Though Miss Bingley did not wish to leave them, she followed her sister away, first glaring at Elizabeth and Mr. Darcy in turn as she did so. When they were alone together, Elizabeth and Mr. Darcy breathed a collective sigh of relief.

"It appears," said Elizabeth, "given her behavior this morning, that Miss Bingley intends to stay nearby and prevent us from speaking together, Mr. Darcy. Can we expect this behavior always, or shall we have some reprieve from time to time?"

Shaking his head, Mr. Darcy replied: "I can only hope this does not become a common occurrence, Miss Elizabeth, though I suspect it might. Miss Bingley is a determined woman and not one to give up." The gentleman paused and looked at her askance. "I do not see Mr. Collins this morning. Has he sequestered himself in his room?"

The mention of Mr. Collins brought a laugh to Elizabeth's lips. "My father's cousin no longer remains at Longbourn, Mr. Darcy. Yesterday he made some unkind comments toward my sisters and me, and my father ordered him to return to his parish."

Mr. Darcy's amusement was clear. "Then might I apprehend that you know something of his errand yesterday morning?"

"If you refer to his intention to make Miss Bingley an offer, then yes, we know of it."

"It was the most ridiculous scene I have ever witnessed, Miss

Elizabeth. Though I hesitate to disparage any relation of yours, I have never seen such a specimen as Mr. Collins. That is saying something, as my aunt has employed underlings who all share some measure of silliness, given her desire for those who will not speak a word against her.

"Mr. Collins, however, outdid himself. Not only did he refuse to believe Miss Bingley's rebuff of his proposal, but he insisted that it was Bingley's duty to ensure she accepted. Though I was not present for it all, to hear Miss Bingley speak of it, it was the most inept proposal in the history of man."

"I can well believe it," replied Elizabeth, laughing at his account. "Since the first moment of the gentleman's arrival, I have known he was not sensible. I can only be grateful he decided, in his inflated opinion of his own superiority, the charms of my sisters and I were insufficient to tempt him to turn his attention on us."

"That is fortunate," murmured Mr. Darcy. The gentleman's countenance turned grave. "There is another matter of which I wished to speak with you. I am certain you apprehend that Mr. Collins's character is such that he will relate everything to my aunt the moment he returns to Hunsford—given his departure yesterday, it is possible he is doing it even now."

"Of course," replied Elizabeth. "As I mentioned to you at the ball, I realize this has always been a possibility."

"The matter of his dealings with Miss Bingley will serve no other purpose than to make him look ridiculous in my aunt's eyes, a truth she must already understand. If that were the only matter of concern, I should not bother myself, for Lady Catherine would not consider it worth her time to apply to Miss Bingley if she disagreed with her refusal. The same is not true of the matter between you and me."

Elizabeth found herself amused that Mr. Darcy referred to their connection, though they still had not known each other for long. "What can she have to say about that?"

"As you know," said Mr. Darcy, catching her irony and smiling, "Lady Catherine intends me for her daughter, and all my arguments to the contrary do little to dissuade her. Mr. Collins will relay his recent observations concerning our activities together to my aunt with relish, perhaps even with embellishment. While she would ignore this account of Miss Bingley, the same is not true of you."

"You believe she will come to Longbourn to confront me."

"It is inevitable," replied Mr. Darcy.

"And what do you think she will say?"

"No doubt the same thing she says at every gathering of our family." The grimace Mr. Darcy made suggested he had heard the arguments several times over and was annoyed by them. "It was an agreement with my mother, discussed while Anne and I were in our cradles, intended from birth, formed for each other, etc. It is well known in the family that her purpose is to consolidate the family's wealth and create a dynasty of greater power and influence. She may also have her eye on a title, though that is nothing more than speculation."

"Lord Darcy, Earl of Derbyshire?" teased Elizabeth.

Mr. Darcy's lips contorted into a lopsided grin. "I doubt even Lady Catherine believes it likely we can aspire to so lofty a title. But even a barony would be a feather in her cap. What need have I for a title? The Darcy family has owned our land for centuries and have never cared much for politics or titles. I am content to remain Mr. Darcy, if you please."

"Then I commend you, sir," replied Elizabeth, "for many men would be eager to do whatever it took to ensure they were ennobled."

The frown with which the gentleman regarded that statement informed her of his opinion if their conversation had not already done so. "That kind of man is the last who should receive titles, for they care for nothing but themselves."

"That is a statement with which I cannot agree more."

Mr. Darcy nodded. "Then we must prepare for the possibility of her coming. If you will wait for my return, I shall speak to your father to warn him."

"I believe he is in his study," replied Elizabeth.

The gentleman thanked her, and with a few more words, he turned and departed, his long, swift strides carrying him around the corner to the front entrance of the house. Again, the thought of how good a man Mr. Darcy was struck Elizabeth. Protecting her — a woman he had only met less than two weeks before — was a matter he considered to be his duty. Had it been Mr. Collins in his stead, he would agree with everything his patroness said and join in the chorus of censure against her. Mr. Darcy had more reason to do so because of his connection with the lady, yet it was the furthest from his mind.

"Have you driven Mr. Darcy away?"

Pulled from her thoughts, Elizabeth regarded Miss Bingley, noting the woman's sneer and the belligerence of her stance. Hiding beneath the bravado, however, was the woman's uncertainty, and in an instant, Elizabeth realized what it must look like. A mischievous thought came to her mind

"He has gone to speak to my father, Miss Bingley."

Eyes narrowed Miss Bingley hissed: "You lie! Mr. Darcy would never propose to the likes of you!"

"Who said anything of a proposal?" replied Elizabeth, feigning confusion. "There was a matter of some importance Mr. Darcy wished to discuss; that is all. I did not say he approached my father because of a proposal. I have not known Mr. Darcy long enough for that."

If Elizabeth thought Miss Bingley's eyes were narrowed before, now they were mere slits. Accompanied by the sneer of contempt she wore, it made her appear ugly, a virago of a woman intent upon having her own way.

"He never will, you know."

"Never will what?"

Miss Bingley growled her impatience. "Mr. Darcy will never propose to you. The reputation of the family name means too much to him to allow such a grievous lapse of judgment."

"And you presume I wish for a proposal?"

"Do you not?" Miss Bingley huffed with annoyance. "Every young lady in society wishes to secure Mr. Darcy's proposal."

"Including you, I presume."

"If he chooses me, I would be honored," was Miss Bingley's superior reply. "As I have been educated in all the finest seminaries and possess all the appropriate accomplishments, I would do him credit if he were to choose me for his wife."

"As would I be honored if Mr. Darcy proposed to me, Miss Bingley," retorted Elizabeth. "But that is not at issue. What is at issue is that I have not known Mr. Darcy long, and to suspect a proposal is imminent is premature."

"You wish me to believe you do not wish for a proposal." The disbelief in Miss Bingley's voice oozed from her, battering at Elizabeth like a ram.

"I did not say that," replied Elizabeth. "I said nothing more than that I have not known the gentleman long enough to know if I wish for a proposal from him."

"Everyone wishes for it!"

"As we have already established, I am not like everyone. Should Mr. Darcy propose now, I would be obliged to refuse him, for I do not know him."

"Then you are a fool," sneered Miss Bingley.

"It is not I who have pursued the gentleman without hope of his returning interest," retorted Elizabeth. "Who between us is the fool?"

"How dare you!" snarled Miss Bingley.

Weary of the conversation, Elizabeth attempted a conciliatory tack. "I have no intention to insult or offend you. But how long have you known Mr. Darcy? Two or three years, I understand? In all that time, has Mr. Darcy given you any hint of interest? Has he looked on you with the eyes of a man who admires a woman? Or has he kept his distance?

"You may do as you like, and I shall not gainsay you. But I would have you consider this: if Mr. Darcy meant to propose to you, do you not think he would have by now? Contrast that with his behavior toward me. Has he shown even a fraction of interest in you that he has in me?"

"Mr. Darcy will never offer for you."

Though Elizabeth knew the woman meant to show the conviction of her belief, it was more a hollow statement. There was no way of knowing her thoughts, but at the very least, Elizabeth thought she was taken aback.

"I do not know that he will, nor have I stated any belief in it. Neither can you say he will not. If you look at how he is behaving toward each of us, I think you will know which of us is more likely. You will if you are honest with yourself."

Having said that much, Elizabeth turned and strode away from Miss Bingley, and to her relief, the woman did not follow her. Mr. Darcy soon emerged from the house, approached Elizabeth and fixed her with a smile. At the same time, he noted Miss Bingley standing by herself, seeing nothing.

"Has something happened?" asked he, turning a frown on the other woman.

"Nothing more than a disagreement, Mr. Darcy."

It was Elizabeth's opinion that he would pursue the matter for a moment. Whatever he meant to say remained unsaid, however, for he shook his head and turned his attention to their recent conversation.

"I have spoken to your father, and he agrees with me. If Lady Catherine appears, he will send for me at once. We shall not allow you to speak in private with her."

"Very well," replied Elizabeth. "I will note that I am no coward who cannot face your aunt's displeasure, but I will confess to some relief."

Mr. Darcy grinned. "I should never have thought it of you, Miss Elizabeth. But this is for the best, for my aunt can be abrasive when she puts her mind to it."

The arrival of others interrupted further conversation, for several men wearing red coats came around the house and entered the lawn, among them Mr. Wickham. Following a short distance behind came Charlotte, escorted by Colonel Fitzwilliam. Eager to greet her friend, Elizabeth shot a glance at Mr. Darcy, which he understood as an invitation to follow her, and stepped forward with a grin.

"Charlotte!" exclaimed Elizabeth, stepping into her friend's embrace. "Why, if I did not know you better, I might suspect you of being enamored with these fellows in red. To see you arriving in their midst is a surprise, indeed!"

Charlotte grinned. "I am not Maria, Lizzy. I met these fine gentlemen at the juncture leading to my father's estate, and they offered to escort me here when they discovered our purpose was the same."

"Then I thank you for conveying my friend here, Colonel Fitzwilliam," said Elizabeth with an impish smile. "One can never know when she might be set upon by brigands on the dangerous stretch of road between Lucas Lodge and Longbourn."

The colonel guffawed, accompanied by Charlotte's playful swat. "It was no trouble, Miss Elizabeth. We men of the army are well accustomed to braving the dangers of bandit-infested roads."

"There is one who does not appreciate your coming," said Charlotte, gesturing toward the lawn.

Unnoticed in her eagerness to meet Charlotte, Mr. Wickham had taken himself to Miss Bingley's side and was now speaking with her, a wide smile for whatever she was saying to him. Charlotte's observation was correct, given Miss Bingley's annoyed look at the officer, but there was also something different about her. Maybe Mr. Collins was no longer present to bedevil her, leaving her with naught but one unwanted suitor. Mr. Darcy, however, posed another possibility.

"It seems Miss Bingley better tolerates Wickham's presence. Perhaps she has decided her favor for another man may induce me to jealousy, surprising, considering my lack of interest in Mr. Collins's clumsy attempts at courtship."

Mr. Darcy and Colonel Fitzwilliam exchanged looks while Elizabeth snickered her amusement. Charlotte, however, turned an interested look on the gentlemen.

"This is a tale I had not heard, though I suppose I should not be surprised." Charlotte paused and looked about. "Where is the inestimable Mr. Collins? Can I assume he has proposed and has slunk away with his tail between his legs?"

"That is a tale which may take both of us to relate," replied Elizabeth, her laughter growing at the thought.

Mr. Darcy and Elizabeth disseminated the story, though Elizabeth could tell her rendition was more willingly given than Mr. Darcy's. When they had completed it, both Colonel Fitzwilliam and Charlotte were in stitches. A surreptitious glance at the woman in question informed Elizabeth that though she was throwing them glances from time to time, Mr. Wickham had her attention, limiting her knowledge of their subject of conversation.

"That Mr. Collins is a wonder," said Colonel Fitzwilliam as he guffawed at the tale. "Aunt Catherine has outdone herself with him, for she could not have found a more ridiculous toad had she searched the length and breadth of England!"

Then he sobered and turned to Mr. Darcy. "Can I assume you expect a visit from Lady Catherine?"

Mr. Darcy grimaced and nodded. "Some of the comments Collins made before he departed all but assure it."

The speculative look Colonel Fitzwilliam directed to her suggested to Elizabeth that he knew something of their closeness and alerted Charlotte to the notion that something may be afoot. The colonel eschewed any teasing, however, and said nothing more than:

"If you require my assistance, Darcy, you need only ask.

"Thank you, Cousin." Then Mr. Darcy glanced back at Wickham. "What of our friend Wickham?"

Colonel Fitzwilliam shrugged. "His behavior does not differ from what it was a few days ago. Wickham little likes his position at present, I warrant, but he has given me no reason to reprimand him. He is not the perfect officer, but he is adequate."

Mr. Darcy nodded and allowed the subject to drop. The four stood and spoke together for some time after, their topics concerning the regiment, Miss Bingley, Mr. Wickham, among other subjects of interest to them all. It was, Elizabeth reflected, an excellent way to spend a morning in the company of friends. All was harmony at present, and she could not be happier.

CHAPTER XIX

*O*ne benefit to the uncertainty surrounding Lady Catherine's expected appearance was the presence of Mr. Darcy at Longbourn. While Elizabeth could not attest to her family's feelings on the matter—no one protested the gentleman's presence—the opportunity to be in his company, to speak of various subjects with the goal of coming to know him was heaven sent. The time she spent with him was not extensive, being only two days, but it was two days where the gentleman did not depart after thirty minutes, and where others, such as Miss Bingley, were not present to interfere. The second day, even Georgiana did not accompany him.

"Where is your sister, Mr. Darcy?" asked Elizabeth when the man entered the room and greeted them.

The grin which suffused his countenance spoke of true hilarity, the reason for which soon became apparent. "Georgiana decided it was best to stay at Netherfield today. Though I have judged my presence here necessary, it has taken me from my hosts, which has left Miss Bingley feeling neglected. In the interest of being an attentive guest, Georgiana is entertaining her today."

Elizabeth laughed. "Then you must give your sister my regards and inform her of my respect for her stamina."

A snort of amusement reached Elizabeth's ears, for it seemed Mr. Bingley, who had accompanied his friend that day, had overheard her. The gentleman, however, was aware of his sister's difficult nature, for he grinned at Elizabeth and turned back to Jane. Within moments, Mr. Bingley suggested a walk out of doors, and when Elizabeth and Jane accepted, they donned their outerwear and followed the gentlemen outside.

"What shall we discuss today, Mr. Darcy?" asked Elizabeth, favoring the gentleman with a bright glance when they attained the path outside Longbourn. Jane and Mr. Bingley had already lagged behind.

"I believe you will find I will discuss whatever you wish, Miss Elizabeth," replied Mr. Darcy. He looked about and added: "Is this the path to the famous Oakham Mount, of which you have spoken several times?"

"No, it is not," said Elizabeth, grinning at the gentleman. "That walk is too far for Jane. I must own to some disappointment, however, for did you not claim you would direct your horse thither at the first opportunity?"

"Yes, I did. The fact is, however, that I have ridden little of late. Something has prevented it, though I will own I am not complaining, for though I love to ride, the company with which I have been blessed of late is much better than that of my horse."

Elizabeth caught his meaning and to refrain from blushing, she turned to the gentleman and fixed him with a bold look. "Then I would encourage you to go there when you have the chance, for it is well worth it."

"I shall do so."

They spent some moments speaking of Derbyshire and the beauties of Mr. Darcy's distant home, and Elizabeth shared some of what she knew of Hertfordshire. After a time, the conversation turned to other locations, though Mr. Darcy carried the burden, as he had traveled far more than Elizabeth.

"The woods of my aunt's estate in Kent," Mr. Darcy was saying, "are extensive. Kent and Hertfordshire are far more tamed than Derbyshire, the land far less marred by rocks and valleys."

"But Kent is the breadbasket of England."

"That is true," agreed Mr. Darcy. "What my aunt's estate has in abundance it lacks in beauty, at least in my opinion. Were you ever to come to Derbyshire and my estate, I could show you a dozen locations that would astonish you for their beauties, and these are all within a few hours of my home. Kent is pretty, I will grant you, but the land is tame, flat, and without character."

"But Derbyshire must be a more difficult place to own an estate."

"That much is true," agreed Mr. Darcy. "In Derbyshire, the crops we grow are hardier, the soil, not as rich. Estates there tend to be more diversified. At Pemberley, we grow several different crops, we have sheep and cattle, fell timber for sale, and there is a small mine on the northwestern corner of my estate."

"Should one of these ventures produce less than you hope," observed Elizabeth, "the rest can keep you solvent."

Mr. Darcy nodded with obvious approval. "As has happened many times in the history of my family. It is one of the secrets of our longevity."

Conversation then turned to their families, Elizabeth sharing tales of her sisters, her aunts and uncles, noting that there were few Bennets left. Mr. Darcy's family was even smaller, with only Georgiana and himself. He also spoke of his extended family, of his cousin, Colonel Fitzwilliam's brothers and sisters, and his aunt and uncle, the Earl of Matlock. Through it, Elizabeth marveled that this man was not puffed up in pride and conceit, for though he was not a peer himself, he was descended from one and had every right to be proud.

"My uncle is the furthest from a self-important noble you could find," said Mr. Darcy when Elizabeth made some slight comment about his family. "The earl was a younger son, and, much like my cousin, served in the army himself. He has always said it taught him to esteem nobility in man that was not bestowed upon them at birth. He is quite the spectacle in society, for many cannot understand his views and consider him eccentric."

"I can well imagine it!" said Elizabeth with a laugh. "Then what of Lady Catherine? She is not like your uncle at all?"

Mr. Darcy sighed. "Few siblings have been less alike than my mother and uncle on one side, and Lady Catherine on the other. I should not denigrate her, for she is my mother's sister, and in intelligence, understanding, diligence, and prudence, she is not deficient. But she has received the principal part of the pride in the family — pride for the family, pride for our position, and an interest in protecting that position."

"Then I suppose I shall need to win her over when she comes," said Elizabeth. "Besides, we are not engaged, so at present, you have not contravened her directives."

With a chuckle and a shaken head, Mr. Darcy said: "If anyone can win her over, Miss Elizabeth, I declare it would be you. There is little you could not do if you set your mind to it."

Elizabeth blushed and looked away, pleased Mr. Darcy thought as highly of her as he did. Then a stray thought came to her, and she voiced it to the gentleman.

"Where have Jane and Mr. Bingley gone?"

A look about did not reveal the missing couple. Though Jane did not walk as much as Elizabeth, they were close enough to Longbourn that her sister could not become lost. A chuckle from her side caught Elizabeth's attention, and she turned to her companion, wondering what he was about. Seeing her watching him, Mr. Darcy shrugged.

"It may be naught but perception, but Bingley was as excited as I have ever seen him when we left this morning."

Surprised, Elizabeth could only gasp: "Mr. Bingley means to propose?"

"It is only conjecture," replied Mr. Darcy. "Bingley said nothing to me. I only observed a change in his demeanor."

"Then let us return the way we came."

Though they had walked for some time, their pace had been slow, meaning they were not far distant from Longbourn. Elizabeth had no notion of when her sister had disappeared, so she monitored the surrounding environs, hoping to glimpse them if they had left the path. The search proved fruitless, however, for soon they arrived at Longbourn without sighting them.

The commotion at the estate when they arrived, however, told Elizabeth something momentous had occurred. Giving the gentleman an expressive look, she hurried to divest herself of her bonnet and spenser, before hurrying to the sitting-room. There, she found her mother and sisters all crowding around Jane, giving her their hearty congratulations.

"I believe I am offended," said Elizabeth, fixing her sister with a grin. "Why did you not stop us and inform us of your marvelous news, Jane?"

"That would be my fault, Miss Elizabeth."

Turning, Elizabeth beheld a grinning Mr. Bingley, along with her father standing inside the door. "I was eager to gain your father's approval and rushed Jane back to Longbourn to make my case."

"It seems I have no choice," said Mr. Bennet, grinning at his eldest daughter. "Though I might have thrown this young buck from my house for the great sin of believing himself good enough for my daughter, I cannot refuse him if Jane has given her consent."

"Oh, Mr. Bennet!" said Mrs. Bennet, fixing her husband with an affectionate glare. "You do not fool us, for we know how happy you are for our Jane"

"I could not be happier," said Mr. Bennet, holding out his hand for Mr. Bingley, which the gentleman accepted without hesitation. "I believe you will do, sir, as long as you make my daughter happy."

Mr. Bingley pumped Mr. Bennet's hand with unmistakable enthusiasm. "That shall always be my priority, sir."

"I am so happy for you, Jane!" exclaimed Elizabeth, pulling her sister into an embrace.

Amid family and friends, happy tidings and lives destined to be entwined together, Elizabeth celebrated her sister's good fortune. It could not be supposed, however, that Elizabeth would not turn her thoughts, at least a little, to her own situation. A glance at Mr. Darcy revealed his thoughts to be nothing less than pure happiness for his friend. Then Mr. Darcy's eyes found hers, and Elizabeth thought she caught a sign of her own future in his countenance.

The return to Netherfield brought its own surprise. As they rode back to the estate, Darcy allowed his friend to wax elegant regarding the perfections of Miss Jane Bennet, not an onerous task. Bingley possessed the ability to speak with indefatigable zeal about a young lady, and his true attachment to Miss Bennet augmented that talent. It worked well for Darcy also; as Bingley did not require a response, Darcy could allow him to continue to speak while he considered the perfections of his own Bennet sister. That she was not his yet did not bear thinking about—Darcy was becoming convinced she would be his before long.

The arrival at the estate saw them leave their mounts with a groom and enter the house, Bingley eager to share his news with his family. Darcy was not eager for the fireworks he knew would follow their return but he did not shirk his duty to support his friend, though the thought occurred to him as he changed with his valet's help that it might be better to stay in his room.

His better nature coming to the fore, Darcy joined Bingley at the top of the stairs after he had changed, following his friend to the sitting-room where his sisters were waiting. It was clear to Darcy that Miss Bingley saw something in his demeanor the moment he entered the room, for her eyes narrowed as she regarded him.

"Your visit was enjoyable, I presume?"

"Far more than enjoyable," replied Bingley. "I have the pleasure to inform you all that I have made Miss Bennet an offer of marriage, which she has accepted. You see before you an engaged man."

Several emotions flitted across Miss Bingley's face at once, including anger, annoyance, contempt, and despair. While Darcy thought she might say something several times, she took some time to find the words to reply to her brother's sudden news. The response, when it came, was not what Darcy might have expected.

"Are you certain this is what you want, Charles?"

Bingley was so astonished that he did not reply, allowing his sister to speak again. "Against Miss Bennet herself, there is little enough to criticize. But you know her dowry is nonexistent and the Bennets have no connections worth mentioning. She will not assist you in society."

"I thank you for acknowledging there is nothing to hold against Jane herself," said Bingley, "for she is everything lovely."

Miss Bingley inclined her head to acknowledge his words but pressed him again. "What of my other points?"

"Acceptance in society has always been your wish, Caroline, not mine," said Bingley, not unkindly. "I am more than content with the welcome I now receive. It is much better to find happiness in marriage than to marry with every thought bent toward improving my standing in society."

Though Miss Bingley did not appear to like her brother's reply, she passed a hand over her eyes in weariness and nodded her acceptance. Darcy, who had thought she would rail against his choice, regarded her with some interest. Could it be the woman was less reprehensible than he had thought?

"Though I would not have made your choice," said Miss Bingley, "I cannot deny your right to make it. I hope Miss Bennet is worth what you are giving up, Charles."

"Worth that much and more," replied Bingley, giving his sister an affectionate smile. "You will see, Caroline. She may not be the daughter of an earl, but she will be a credit to me in society. My situation has never been enough to induce a woman of high society to accept me."

"Well do I know it," said Miss Bingley, though sounding regretful. "But another woman of greater standing and possessing the necessary connections might be within your reach. But you have done it, and I suppose it cannot be undone now."

How the conversation might have proceeded Darcy could not say but the sound of someone approaching caught his attention. From the voice demanding to see the residents, Darcy knew who it was, though he had thought she would go straight to Longbourn rather than appearing at Netherfield. The door swung open, and the lady barged her way into the room without waiting for the servant, her gaze falling on Miss Bingley with the force of a hammer.

"Are you Miss Elizabeth Bennet?" demanded she without preamble.

Diverted that Lady Catherine did not seem to realize she was at the wrong estate, and further that she had not seen him at once, Darcy said: "Miss Elizabeth is at Longbourn, Lady Catherine. You find yourself at Netherfield Park."

It was comical the way the lady's eyes swung to him and widened in shock. Then they narrowed, and she looked at him as if it was his fault she had gone astray.

"Netherfield Park, you say?" The woman huffed her annoyance. "I see Mr. Collins is as silly as ever. He informed me I would come to Longbourn if I took the right fork out of Meryton."

"Then perhaps you should confirm your parson knows right from left when you see him next," said Darcy, to the amused snorts of Bingley and Hurst. The ladies said nothing. "This is most definitely Netherfield. I have always taken the left fork to get to Longbourn."

Lady Catherine peered at him as if wondering if he was taunting her. Then she turned her attention on Miss Bingley.

"Then I presume your friends must be Miss Bingley and Mr. Bingley?"

"Yes, Lady Catherine," said Darcy.

Taking her words as a request for an introduction, Darcy performed the office, introducing those present to her ladyship's acquaintance. Lady Catherine accepted them all with better manners than Darcy might have expected. Before she could say anything more than a perfunctory greeting, however, the door behind them opened again and admitted Georgiana, who had not been present when Darcy had returned.

"William—" said she, though she stopped in astonishment when she caught sight of her aunt. "Aunt Catherine! What do you do here?"

The soft smile which came over their aunt's face was out of place on her stern countenance, but then Darcy remembered his aunt had always had a soft spot for her sister's daughter. "Georgiana, my dear. I did not know you were here, though I suppose I should have guessed. How are your studies?"

"Very well, Lady Catherine," replied Georgiana, approaching her aunt and bussing her cheek. "Mrs. Annesley has everything in hand."

"That is good to hear. Now, if you will be still for a moment, I have a matter to discuss with your brother's friends. Then I must pay a visit to this Longbourn of which I have heard. After that, I will be at liberty to visit with you."

Though Georgiana liked Lady Catherine's mention of Longbourn as little as Darcy did himself, she knew better than to contradict her aunt. With a smile, she chose a seat near to Miss Bingley as if to offer support. Georgiana knew, as well as Darcy did himself, what Lady Catherine's probable purpose was in wishing to speak with the Bingleys.

"As long as I am here," said Lady Catherine, "I may as well attend to one matter which drew me to Hertfordshire."

The lady fixed a gimlet eye on Miss Bingley and continued: "It has come to my attention that you, Miss Bingley, have rejected a very eligible offer of marriage. Given what I understand of your background and connections, I might wonder why you rejected Mr. Collins out of hand."

"I did not favor him," said Miss Bingley with a shrug, understanding it was useless to put the lady off.

"And why is that?" pressed her ladyship. "I hope, Miss Bingley, that you do not harbor other, more prestigious hopes."

No one misunderstood Lady Catherine's significant look in Darcy's direction, least of all Miss Bingley. It was fortunate she was also cognizant of the folly of declaring her interest in Darcy to his aunt.

"Whatever my hopes, I do not wish to bandy them about for the consumption of all. Though I am aware it must pale in comparison with what your ladyship must possess, I am blessed with a substantial dowry and am not limited to the choice of Mr. Collins as a husband. Furthermore, Mr. Collins was here for naught but a week, and if he did not consider the time too short to attach himself to me, still he ignored every hint I gave him of my lack of interest in him as a prospective husband."

"Miss Bingley," said Lady Catherine, her mien stern and unyielding, "your possession of a dowry is a point in your favor, but you must consider that it is by no means assured you will ever achieve your desire. Though it is possible you may attract some gentleman to offer for you, it is likely he will do so because he needs your dowry. Is that a situation you wish to obtain upon entering the marriage state?"

"Is that any different from marrying your parson?"

"Mr. Collins will not be a parson forever. Or do you not know of his position as heir to Longbourn estate?"

"He informed me of this." Miss Bingley's posture was as stiff as Darcy had ever seen.

"Of course, he did. I would not have supposed he would remain silent about it for even two minutes. Knowing that, I must wonder why you spurned him."

"Lady Catherine," said Miss Bingley, her patience exhausted, "let me ask you a simple question: would you be willing to marry a fool such as Mr. Collins?"

The lady was silent for a moment before nodding. "Yes, I understand my parson is not the most sensible specimen."

"That is an understatement," muttered Miss Bingley. Then she fixed Lady Catherine with a confident look, sensing the lady was not so severe as she had been before. "I could not accept Mr. Collins, your ladyship, and maintain my dignity. Mr. Collins fixed his attention on me for no other reason than the desire to acquire my dowry, imposed upon me despite my disinterest, proposed within a week of making my acquaintance, and refused to hear my refusal, claiming I was nothing more than an 'elegant female attempting to increase his love by suspense.' What say you? Should I—or any other woman—have accepted such an insulting application? If your parson continues to behave thus, I cannot imagine he will find a woman who will be willing to hear him."

Lady Catherine nodded slowly. "Your arguments are rational and cannot be contested, Miss Bingley. I came here, thinking to try you, to discover whether you were attempting to reach higher than you ought. It seems you had every reason to refuse Mr. Collins's suit, and I cannot blame you for it."

"Thank you, Lady Catherine," said Miss Bingley, no trace of irony in her voice. "I appreciate your understanding."

"Yes, well, it appears you are a genteel woman, despite your unfortunate descent. I am glad to hear it."

Darcy almost groaned at the lady's insolence, but Miss Bingley smiled. "I have attempted to use my education to improve myself, Lady Catherine. Should you stay with us, I hope to demonstrate my worth to you."

Lady Catherine nodded her approval. Then the other matter for which she had traveled so far intruded and she turned to Darcy.

"You know, the reason I sent Mr. Collins here in the first place was to secure one of his cousin's daughters for his wife. I do not know why the silly man instead focused on your friend's sister."

"To hear the Bennets speak of it," said Darcy, "it was because he wished to have a handsome dowry, as Miss Bingley suggests."

Lady Catherine huffed and shook her head. "What does Mr. Collins need with a large dowry? The man will never be anything other than a country squire. By creating closer ties with his cousin's family, he will ensure their support should Mr. Bennet die early."

"It is my understanding," interjected Bingley, "that securing their support is not required."

Lady Catherine fixed Bingley with an interested look, as did Darcy. As his friend had proposed to Miss Bennet that very day, he would have some notion of the extent of her dowry. Darcy knew little of the matter himself, though he had heard each of the girls had a small fortune with which they could support themselves if they never married.

"That is interesting, Mr. Bingley, for I had understood the estate did not generate much income."

Bingley shrugged and said: "It is not a large estate, that is true. However, Mr. Bennet has been investing in his daughters' futures for many years, and in this, he has his brother's assistance, a man whose knowledge of such investments is extensive, as I understand."

The notion of a possible tie to trade induced a tightening of Lady Catherine's mouth. "Perhaps I might induce my parson to release this silly desire for wealth and marry this Miss Elizabeth of whom I have heard." Lady Catherine turned a challenging glare on Darcy. "Or do you wish to refute what Mr. Collins has told me of your behavior with her?"

Though Darcy knew the conversation had been leading to this since Lady Catherine entered the room, Darcy could feel little more than mirth for the lady's predictable nature. "I should like to see you attempt it. Mr. Collins offended his hosts repeatedly after arriving, leading Mr. Bennet to declare he would allow none of his daughters to marry his cousin. Then, when he left, I understand they exchanged harsh words which have led to an irrevocable estrangement between them."

"Yes, I have heard of this too," said Lady Catherine. "But Mr. Bennet can be worked upon to change his mind for the good of his family."

"I believe, Lady Catherine, that Mr. Bennet would disagree with you as to what constitutes the good of his family. Much as Miss Bingley would not wish to marry a fool, I cannot imagine any of the Bennet sisters taking leave of their senses enough to accept your parson's proposal, even if he should be induced to offer it."

Lady Catherine opened her mouth to retort, but Darcy interjected, saying: "Given your words to Miss Bingley, you cannot blame the Bennets for espousing the same opinions. You will someday be rid of Mr. Collins, Lady Catherine; the woman who marries him must endure him as long as he lives."

"Very well," said Lady Catherine. "It seems I must go to Longbourn to speak with this girl who dares to imagine herself fit to fill the shoes my sister wore."

"That would not be wise, Lady Catherine," said Darcy.

"It seems I must since you have forgotten what you owe the family."

"Let me be clear on this matter, Lady Catherine," said Darcy. "There is no understanding between myself and Miss Elizabeth. At the same time, I am not bound to Anne, as you know. There is no contract, no engagement, and while you might wax eloquent on the matter, you have no leverage with which to force me to bend to your will. Can I not convince you to desist before there is a break between us?"

Lady Catherine peered at him, seeming to gage his determination. Why she should question it, Darcy could not say, for she had never turned him from his course, though she had tried many times. It seemed she came to that conclusion, for the look she directed at him was as sour as vinegar.

"You are your father's son, for he was as stubborn as you."

"Thank you for the compliment, Lady Catherine. To be compared to my father is high praise, indeed."

Lady Catherine's visage softened. "He was an exemplary man, your father, and he made my sister happy, though he was, perhaps, a little stiff. For that, I will always esteem and respect him.

"But I insist on being satisfied. I will speak to Miss Elizabeth. You may accompany me if you wish. But you shall not deter me from my course."

"Then I shall go," replied Darcy, knowing it was fruitless to argue with her.

CHAPTER XX

A visitor arrived at Longbourn late that afternoon, long after normal visiting hours had ended by any measure. The way the colonel entered the room Elizabeth might have suspected him of hesitance. Seated as Elizabeth was in the sitting-room with her mother and sisters, she noted at once he glanced about as if searching for someone, and thought she knew what he was about.

"Mrs. Bennet," said he, turning his attention on her mother at once, "I apologize, for I know this is an intrusion at an unconventional time. Please accept my assurances I would not come except at the direst of need."

Elizabeth's mother, who had risen at the colonel's entrance, understood his meaning at once. With a nod, she turned to her youngest daughters and sent them from the room, saying: "Mary, perhaps you would take your sisters to the other parlor. They would both benefit from some of your instruction on the pianoforte."

With a nod, Mary rose and guided Kitty and Lydia to the other part of the house. The younger girls, while they looked back with open curiosity and wished to stay, did as their mother asked, leaving Elizabeth with Jane and her mother in the colonel's company. Her youngest daughters now out of the way, Mrs. Bennet fixed Colonel

Fitzwilliam with a questioning look.

"Should I have Mr. Bennet summoned?"

"That would be for the best," replied the colonel.

Sitting when invited, Colonel Fitzwilliam waited while Mrs. Bennet called for Mrs. Hill and instructed her to request the master's presence. Then her attention fell once more upon the colonel, who, noting the question in her gaze, clarified his errand.

"It seems Lady Catherine has made her appearance at Netherfield, though why she went to Netherfield rather than Longbourn, I cannot say. Darcy delayed her long enough to send word to me in Meryton, and I came at once as I promised. I expect them to arrive at any moment."

Mrs. Bennet nodded with an absence of mind. "Do you know your aunt's mood?"

The grin with which the colonel regarded her was more grim than amused. "Darcy did not have time to say, though I can guess."

"Then what do you expect, Colonel?" asked Elizabeth.

"Fireworks," was the man's single word response.

"What sort of fireworks?"

They all looked up to see Mr. Bennet entering the room, an uncharacteristic seriousness about him.

Colonel Fitzwilliam spread his hands as if to disavow all knowledge of his aunt. "More of the same as usual, I should expect. Lady Catherine is nothing if not consistent. She has been touting this imaginary engagement between Darcy and her daughter for years now, never seeing reason, always intent upon carrying her point."

"Mr. Darcy is not engaged to Lizzy," said Mrs. Bennet.

"Given the attention he has been paying her, some of which Mr. Collins witnessed, there need not be an announced engagement for her to act."

"Shall I bar her from the estate?"

Frowning at Mr. Bennet's question, Colonel Fitzwilliam paused for a moment before shaking his head. "It would not be my recommendation to do so, Mr. Bennet, though you may act as you see fit. Though I see little chance of reasoning with her, all possibility will dissipate if you deny her the opportunity to state her objections. If we send her away without allowing her to state her case, I cannot say what will happen."

With a curt nod, Mr. Bennet said: "Then I shall allow it. But I will also make it clear to her that any misbehavior will prompt me to evict her."

The barked laugh with which the colonel responded betrayed a hint of diversion at the notion. "That is likely for the best, Mr. Bennet. Lady Catherine has not been known for her ability to remain temperate; the threat of removal might induce her to moderate her words."

At that moment, the sound of a carriage reached their ears, and as one, their attention turned toward the windows. Jane rose and went to them, pulling the curtains aside and looking out, though she stepped away at once.

"A large chaise and four," said she by way of explanation. "I cannot make out a crest, but it seems to be the possession of a person of wealth."

"Lady Catherine," replied Colonel Fitzwilliam. "It would be best to gird yourselves for battle."

While Mr. Bennet shot the colonel a sardonic grin, the ladies resumed their seats, Mrs. Bennet directing Elizabeth and Jane to sit close to her. A glance at her mother told Elizabeth all she needed to know of her mother's determination. Elizabeth smiled, signifying her readiness to meet any challenge the lady presented, prompting a nod from her mother, though her posture did not change.

A moment later, they heard the sound of voices from the vestibule, a soft masculine voice Elizabeth knew belonged to Mr. Darcy, and a louder woman's voice. Nothing of their words was audible, however, and soon the footsteps approaching the door signaled the imminent arrival, prompting the company to stand to receive them.

"If you please, mum," said Mrs. Hill, looking none the worse for wear, "Lady Catherine de Bourgh and Mr. Darcy to see you."

The gentleman preceded the lady into the room, likely by design, and the lady on his heels did not appear pleased. That first image of Lady Catherine, Elizabeth thought, would remain with her for the entirety of her acquaintance with her ladyship. She was tall for a woman, standing an inch or two taller than Jane, who was not a small woman. Draped about her was a dress of costly materials, over which she wore a pelisse, her feet clad with soft traveling boots. The cane in her hand was more an affectation than a need, Elizabeth thought, and it clacked against the tiles of the floor as she walked. As for the lady herself, she was, perhaps, ten years older than Mrs. Bennet, her hair a dark brown, showing strands of gray, her face long, dark, piercing eyes, and very little in the way of wrinkles or other signs of age. This was a woman to be reckoned with.

Before anyone could say a word, the lady caught sight of Colonel Fitzwilliam, eliciting an exclamation of surprise. "Fitzwilliam!"

boomed she, her voice strong, with nary a hint of a waver. "What do you do here?"

"I am happy to see you too, Aunt Catherine," said Colonel Fitzwilliam, giving her a jaunty salute.

The lady's eyes narrowed. "I am waiting, Fitzwilliam. Why are you here at Longbourn, of all places?"

"Perhaps you do not remember, Lady Catherine," replied Colonel Fitzwilliam, seeming to enjoy himself, "but I took command of a company of militia not long ago. That company is quartered in Meryton at present."

"Yes, I remember your letter informing me of that much." Lady Catherine nodded her approval. "I see you have seen sense; your mother was worried when news of your injury reached her. It is time you stopped playing soldier and took up the management of your estate, for the possibility of being called to active duty was causing us all concern."

"For the present, I believe I am in no danger," replied Colonel Fitzwilliam. Then a devilish grin fell over his countenance, and he added: "Unless it is from sleepless nights, lamenting the inability of my regiment to march in a line or their ability to shoot straight. From that last, I may be in more danger than if I stood against the entire French army!"

The entire company laughed, and even Lady Catherine chuckled and shook her head. The colonel grinned as if he had accomplished what he set out to do. Elizabeth thought it likely he had, for he was a jolly man, one who understood the efficacy of alleviating tension with a well-placed joke.

"Yes, well," said Lady Catherine, "perhaps it would be best if you stood behind these recruits of yours."

"I shall take your advice under consideration, Lady Catherine," replied Colonel Fitzwilliam.

With a nod, Lady Catherine fixed her gaze upon the Bennet family, seeming to catalog every detail about each one. Elizabeth returned Lady Catherine's regard with an undaunted air, something the lady noted, if the tightness around her mouth when she looked away was any indication.

"Which of your daughters, Mrs. Bennet, is Miss Elizabeth?"

The lady spoke her question in a calm, but firm tone, one which demanded response. The response she was to receive, however, was not to her liking, for Mrs. Bennet did not answer the question.

"I beg your pardon, Lady Catherine," said Mrs. Bennet, standing straight, "but if your purpose is to abuse my daughter, then it would be best if you leave."

"Where is your civility, Mrs. Bennet?" demanded Lady Catherine. Elizabeth did not think anyone had ever denied her ladyship in such a manner — or at least someone she considered lower than herself had not.

"We offer civility, your ladyship, to those who return it. As you must be aware, we know of the reason for your coming. I understand your position in society and your interest in my daughter, but I will not allow attacks against her."

"My wife is correct, Lady Catherine," interjected Mr. Bennet, stepping forward, though fixing Mrs. Bennet with a warm smile. "Because of the respect I hold for your nephews, I will allow you to make your point. I require civility, however; as Mrs. Bennet says, I do not wish to allow an argument or open impugning of my daughter's character. If we agree on this much, then we shall proceed. If not, it is best to desist at once. I should hate to feel it necessary to remove a lady of your obvious standing from my house."

The notion of being escorted from the estate did not sit well with Lady Catherine, but Mr. Darcy's cleared throat drew her attention when she might have retorted. Though not without a scowl, Lady Catherine nodded and said:

"I know not what my nephews have said of me, but I do not attack, nor do I behave without civility, Mr. Bennet. If you require my assurance, I shall give it without hesitation. But you must allow me to address these rumors which my parson brought to me, for there are concerns which I must make known to you."

"Thank you for your assurance, Lady Catherine," said Mr. Bennet. "Then let us sit and speak. Mrs. Bennet, shall you call for tea?"

With a nod, Mrs. Bennet gave the order to Mrs. Hill, who stood waiting in the door. Then when the door was closed and they were all seated, Mr. Darcy introduced the Bennets to Lady Catherine's acquaintance. The way her ladyship's eyes lingered on Elizabeth caused her a moment of concern. She said nothing at once, however, betraying, instead, a contemplation Elizabeth might not have expected.

"I am surprised, Darcy," said Lady Catherine, her eyes darting to where her nephew sat. "I might have thought you would have preferred Miss Bennet to her sister."

Mr. Darcy did not ask why. "Miss Bennet is a lovely young woman, but my friend Bingley holds her heart. They became engaged only two days ago."

"Then I offer my congratulations, belated though they may be," said Lady Catherine, nodding at Jane. "Though I have spoken but little with Mr. Bingley, my nephews' testimony suggests he is a good man, though his descent is a little unfortunate. With a gentleman's daughter for a wife, his position in society shall be raised accordingly."

It was a bit of civility Elizabeth might not have expected, both the congratulations and the lady's understanding of the benefits of the engagement. Jane murmured her thanks, to which Lady Catherine nodded, and then turned her attention to Elizabeth.

"Miss Elizabeth, I have heard from Mr. Collins that you have thrown yourself with no hint of shame at my nephew, intending to entrap him."

Elizabeth opened her mouth, intending to refute such a ridiculous charge, and noticed both her mother and father and the lady's two nephews engaged in the same. But her ladyship was the first to speak again.

"I shall not injure you by believing his account as he gave it to me. At the same time, I cannot believe Mr. Collins is capable of creating such a story out of whole cloth. Mr. Collins is not the most sensible of men—this I will own, I have not known him, however, to possess vicious tendencies—overzealous would be nearer the mark, I should think. Be that as it may, I wish to know what has happened between you and my nephew. Will you oblige me?"

The unexpected civility in Lady Catherine's manner surprised Elizabeth, as it did her nephews. Given her measured words, Elizabeth decided there was no reason to refuse to respond, though it was not, in the strictest sense, any of Lady Catherine's concern.

"As you expected, Lady Catherine, I have not thrown myself at your nephew. Though I will acknowledge my position in society is nowhere near as exalted as yours, I do know how to behave."

"Then what my parson said of you is without foundation?"

"In that sense, it is not." Elizabeth paused, considering what she should say, deciding she had best be open with the lady. "I shall not dissemble, Lady Catherine. I enjoy your nephew's company and have since I first made his acquaintance. Having said that, I am no Jezebel; I do not fawn over him, throw myself in his arms, or attempt to compromise him. As a woman, I am restricted to giving gentlemen hints of my regard. It is up to Mr. Darcy, however, to determine whether he wishes to pursue a closer connection with me, and I have never attempted to force his hand."

Lady Catherine, it appeared, was impressed by her response. The tender look from Mr. Darcy showed his own approval, and Elizabeth had never felt more certain he would come to the point than she did at that moment.

Their brief interaction did not miss Lady Catherine's attention either, for she directed a glance at both in turn, a slight frown marring her countenance. When she turned back to Elizabeth, she thought it was with a little softer mood, though it was possible she was mistaking the woman's manners.

"You speak well, Miss Elizabeth. That is a relief, for I would not wish to converse with someone who cannot string two words together. What you say is correct. What you may not know is that my nephew is already spoken for. Were you aware of that?"

Mr. Darcy opened his mouth to speak, but Lady Catherine raised a hand intended to silence him. Elizabeth shot him a look, informing him of her willingness to answer the question; Mr. Darcy subsided, though the way he looked at his aunt teemed with displeasure.

"There are two things I should like to point out, Lady Catherine: the first is that I am not engaged to Mr. Darcy, and the second is that I have it from Mr. Darcy's own mouth that he is not engaged. I would not wish to intrude upon a previous understanding."

Lady Catherine turned a displeased eye on Mr. Darcy. "You have spoken of this matter to those who are not members of the family?"

"Why would you be surprised I would speak of it?" asked Mr. Darcy. "It is well known in society that you wish for the match, though I have not contradicted it. With Miss Elizabeth, however, I did not wish her to misunderstand my actions, particularly when your parson spoke of it himself. His imprudence would leave me appearing like a cad at best—a bigamist at worst."

Once again, the lady's lips became a thin line. "You may be assured I shall speak to Mr. Collins on this subject."

"If you did not trumpet the matter for everyone to hear, he would not have felt obliged to speak up."

The lady had the grace to appear abashed. Mr. Darcy, however, was not finished.

"Lady Catherine, I would urge you to desist and speak no more of this cradle engagement. Though I will not presume to speak for Anne, I have no wish to marry her, and given her behavior with me, I do not believe she wishes to marry me either. That is the salient point, is it not?"

"I suppose it must be, though I will say that I do not appreciate the lack of respect of the younger generation."

Lady Catherine huffed and turned back to Elizabeth.

"You are yet full young, are you not, Miss Elizabeth?"

"I am not yet one and twenty," replied Elizabeth.

"And your standing in society? Have you had a season in London?"

"Though I have attended certain events, I have not had a season."

"You have not curtseyed before the queen?"

"No, your ladyship."

Pursing her lips, the lady regarded Elizabeth. "And what of your accomplishments? Do you play the pianoforte?"

"I do, well enough," replied Elizabeth, by now becoming diverted by the lady's manner. "It might be beneficial if I practiced more, but I do well enough."

"That is true," said Lady Catherine. "No true skill is acquired without practice. And what of other accomplishments? Do you sing? Paint? Can you sew and embroider?"

Elizabeth replied, indicating an affirmative to the first and last two, but denying the second; Kitty was the only Bennet sister who had any artistic ability. For several moments Lady Catherine continued to ask after Elizabeth's accomplishments, dispensing advice as she went. Elizabeth answered as honestly as she could, noting with some interest where the lady seemed to think she was acceptable, and where deficient. It was apparent that Mr. Darcy was becoming annoyed with the inquisition, and after the gentleman cleared his throat for the second time, Lady Catherine nodded and sat back, regarding Elizabeth.

"It seems, Miss Elizabeth, that you are well-spoken for one so young, though I will own you have a tendency to express your opinions in a decided fashion. You are a genteel, pretty sort of girl, as are your mother and sister, which bodes well for your future. I hope you do not consider my questions officious, for I do not intend to cast aspersions on you.

"The fact of the matter is that you have been little in society, so you cannot understand the attitudes of those of the level my family inhabits. I would not injure you by supposing you are incapable of standing up for yourself, for that appears to be untrue. I will, however, warn you that you will be the target of those looking for any perceived weakness, anything they can do to exploit that to your detriment, and that of my family."

"Again, I would remind you of the premature nature of this conversation—I am not engaged to Mr. Darcy," said Elizabeth. "This is all still nothing more than speculation."

For the first time since entering the room, Lady Catherine's mien softened. "No, you are not engaged at present. I hope, Miss Elizabeth, you will allow me the knowledge of my nephew. I have watched over Darcy and his sister these many years since my sister's death, and I can tell you my knowledge of him is as great as any. Darcy does nothing by half measures. He is forthright, a man who acts when he has made up his mind. When I came here today, I expected to meet with a woman who has captivated him, and what I have seen has not disappointed me by any means."

Though Elizabeth could not determine what she should say in response, she was flattered at the notion she had attracted a man of such character. The lady required no response, for she turned and spoke to Mr. Darcy.

"Please request a room for my use from your friend, Darcy, for I wish to stay in the neighborhood for some time."

Mr. Darcy regarded his aunt, his expression and that of his cousin suggesting they did not think allowing Lady Catherine to stay was wise. "Shall you not return to Kent?"

"No, Darcy. I wish to come to know your young woman better, and she shall need a guide. Though she is an intelligent girl, she still cannot know of the trials she will face in London. She will, I suspect, charm most of them, but she still requires some training to become a credit to our family. I shall do my duty by my sister and offer what advice and knowledge I can."

Elizabeth caught her father's eye and they shared a look of mirth while the lady was engaged with her nephew. For Elizabeth's part, she was no less than shocked at the way the discussion had turned, for, with Mr. Darcy's account, she might have suspected Lady Catherine of entering the room with guns blazing. Elizabeth had no notion that Lady Catherine had given up on her wish of marrying her daughter to Mr. Darcy, but she seemed to have pushed that desire to the side for the moment.

"Shall your ladyship stay for dinner with us tonight?" asked Mrs. Bennet. "Your nephews are invited also, as is your niece if you would like to send for her."

Lady Catherine regarded Mrs. Bennet and nodded. "Thank you, Mrs. Bennet. I should like that very much." Then she addressed Mr. Darcy. "As for Georgiana, I believe she is well where she is, at the moment, unless you disagree."

"With my unexpected absence," replied Mr. Darcy, "I would prefer to leave Georgiana at Netherfield, for I have not been a good guest of late."

It seemed Lady Catherine had some understanding of Mr. Darcy's meaning, but she was circumspect enough to avoid asking further. Instead, she fixed her attention on Elizabeth and began speaking to her again, and Elizabeth, interested to know this lady better, obliged her.

For a time, Elizabeth sat with Lady Catherine, exchanging conversation with her that was almost pleasant. Jane attended her and was not spared some of Lady Catherine's attention, though the lady reserved most of it for Elizabeth herself. Mr. Darcy sat close by, his concentration set upon them. For a time, Elizabeth thought him concerned, and a time or two he winced at some of his aunt's pronouncements. After a time, however, seeing that Elizabeth was comfortable and his aunt was behaving herself, he relaxed.

In time, Elizabeth thought she might enjoy having Lady Catherine as an aunt, though she reminded herself not to put the cart before the horse. It was also clear to her that whatever enjoyment she gained would best be administered in small doses. She knew Lady Catherine could be overbearing when she set her mind to it.

CHAPTER XXI

*C*ongenial man though he was, it heartened Darcy to see that Bingley possessed a backbone when necessary. In his dealings with his sister, Darcy had always seen a man who abhorred conflict and would go to any lengths to avoid it. Miss Bingley was, for all her other faults, an observant and intelligent woman, and she used her brother's trait to have her own way. It was a situation about which Darcy had always warned his friend, for the risk of her embarrassing him in public by her behavior was real.

In the matter of Lady Catherine, however, Bingley proved himself to be unyielding, a necessary stance given the lady's fondness for having her own way. When they returned to Netherfield that night after dining with the Bennets and applied for his permission for Lady Catherine to stay, Bingley agreed, but with conditions.

"It would be my pleasure to have you stay with us, and I am certain Caroline will agree with me."

Darcy thought Miss Bingley's eagerness to host Lady Catherine given the lady's behavior earlier that day was uncertain, but he refrained from commenting.

"But I must insist, Lady Catherine, that you do not persist in attempting to persuade my sister to marry Mr. Collins. Caroline has already made her opinions known and shall not move from them."

The way Lady Catherine regarded him, Darcy wondered if she thought he was to blame for Bingley's suspicions. Knowing it would do no good to point out it was her own behavior which led to his caution, Darcy kept his own counsel. With a huff, Lady Catherine nodded to her host.

"I understand your sister's reasons and have no intention to raise the subject again, Mr. Bingley. Though I have no notion of how you have come by this impression of me, there is no reason for concern."

Bingley nodded and smiled. "Then I shall have Caroline select a room for you. I believe she keeps a room or two ready at all times for unexpected guests."

The nod with which Lady Catherine regarded him spoke to her approval. "Just as she should, Mr. Bingley. I commend your sister for her diligence."

When informed of her ladyship's approbation, Miss Bingley's pleasure was, perhaps, more muted than might have been the case otherwise. Then again, she had probably expected much worse and had steeled herself as a result.

As Lady Catherine retired to her room soon after their return from Longbourn, there was little opportunity for misunderstanding, for which Darcy could not be more grateful. A night of rest would do wonders for her mood, an essential ingredient for civil coexistence. A tired and moody Lady Catherine was a recipe for disaster, and Darcy had no wish to lose Bingley's friendship.

The following morning passed without difficulty, though that might be in part because the Bingley family were not early risers. The way Lady Catherine glanced around the breakfast room with displeasure spoke to her opinion that those hosting guests should make themselves available at an earlier hour. It was a relief when she made no comment, instead turning to Georgiana and speaking with her about her recent doings.

Darcy had not informed Lady Catherine of the incident between Georgiana and Wickham; thus, Georgiana's recent recovery from that event was a matter of some relief. Miss Elizabeth and her sisters had done wonders for Georgiana, both for improving her outlook and helping her forget such a disagreeable experience. Darcy was grateful he had found such a rare and wonderful woman.

After breakfast, Georgiana took herself back to her room with Mrs. Annesley, intent upon attending to her studies, after which she would join Miss Bingley and Mrs. Hurst when they emerged from their rooms. Lady Catherine, after seeing her niece from the room, informed Darcy of her desire to speak with him. Darcy had expected this, and as a result, suggested they repair to the library as a location where they would be unlikely to be disturbed. Though it was not his intention, Lady Catherine read between the lines of Darcy's statement, and she did not refrain from offering her opinion when they entered the room.

"Your friend has graduated from university, has he not?"

"With excellent grades," replied Darcy with a grin, understanding Lady Catherine's inference.

"Then it is a surprise that Mr. Bingley should be so neglectful of his library. Why, I have never seen such a room so little deserving of the appellation. Have you not advised him of the need to stock his library with books?"

"I believe Bingley does not intend to see to it until he has purchased his own estate," dissembled Darcy, though he knew no such thing. "There is little reason to buy crates of books only to have to move them when the lease expires early next summer."

Lady Catherine pursed her lips, but she could not deny Darcy's point. "There is some merit to that, I think." The lady paused for a moment and then said: "He has no option to purchase when the lease has expired?"

"The owner has purchased the estate of late himself," replied Darcy, deciding the knowledge of the new owner as a man of business connected with the Bennets was a bridge too far for the lady at present. Though her eventual understanding of that point was inevitable should Darcy follow through with his intention to offer for Miss Elizabeth, her acceptance was still too new and fragile.

"Then he does not wish to sell so soon after purchasing," said Lady Catherine, showing her understanding. "What he means to do with it is irrelevant; he cannot realize a profit if he sells so soon."

Darcy did not respond, prompting Lady Catherine to sit in a chair near the fireplace, which had burned low, though it still cast a considerable amount of heat into the room. For a moment, the lady was silent, though her frequent glances informed Darcy she was attempting to formulate her arguments. Darcy was certain he knew what form they would take and was not surprised when she spoke at length.

"Though I have approved of Miss Elizabeth, I must say I am still disappointed, Darcy. As I am certain you know, I have counted on your marrying Anne for many years now."

"And I have told you for many years I do not wish to marry Anne," said Darcy. "Do you know if Anne even wishes to marry me?"

Lady Catherine huffed and fixed him with an annoyed glare. "Anne will do as she is told."

"Perhaps she will," said Darcy, returning her glare with a grin. "But I shall not."

"It was the favorite wish of your mother!" snapped Lady Catherine.

"That I do not know," said Darcy. "I was old enough to understand by the time my mother passed, and yet she did not see fit to inform me of any such wish."

Lady Catherine appeared on the verge of an outburst, leading Darcy to step into the breach to forestall her. "Lady Catherine, I understand your wish of uniting the two branches of the family, thereby keeping our wealth within the extended Fitzwilliam clan, but I have never had any such desire. I have no need of Rosings—managing such a large estate from a distance would present a difficult challenge."

Though he expected an immediate response, Lady Catherine regarded him for several moments. "You think my primary concern is to unite the wealth of the de Bourghs and Darcys?"

"Is it not? I have often heard you speak of it."

"That is a consideration," confessed Lady Catherine, "but it is not my primary motivation, nor is it even a concern. I have every confidence in your ability to manage your affairs, Darcy, and I do not doubt you could choose a proper woman." Lady Catherine paused and sniffed. "Then again, given you seem to have chosen a woman who does not possess dowry, lineage, or connections, perhaps I must revise my opinion."

"There is nothing the matter with Miss Elizabeth, Lady Catherine. I would also remind you that I have not yet made an offer for her."

The grunt with which the lady responded informed Darcy she had no wish to belabor the point. "My primary motivation in wishing you to marry Anne is to protect her."

Surprised, Darcy looked at his aunt askance, and she obliged him by explaining. "I am not blind, Darcy. Anne is a good girl, but she is not healthy, has few accomplishments, and has never had a season besides. I am very much afraid that when you marry, every fortune hunter in the country will fix upon my daughter as an easy mark."

"With all due respect, Lady Catherine," said Darcy, "I believe you are neglecting to consider two important points. First, if Anne is so ill the possibility exists that she cannot provide me with an heir, which is essential for a man in my position. The second is that the family would not leave Anne to fend for herself, regardless of my marital status."

"I know, and I thank you for that, Darcy. But you and my brother both live in Derbyshire, whereas Anne and I live in Kent." Lady Catherine paused and sighed. "It has seemed less likely to me every year that I could work on you to marry Anne, but my frequent commentary on it has also worked to my advantage; few men would risk offending you by attempting to steal that which was perceived to be yours."

"And few will risk the earl's displeasure by attempting to take advantage of Anne," said Darcy in a tone which allowed no rebuttal. "That I do not wish to marry Anne in no way affects my resolve to defend my family. Though taking care would be prudent, I do not think there is any overt danger. Perhaps Anne will surprise you, Aunt."

Lady Catherine regarded him for a long moment. "In what way?"

"Given the chance, there is no telling what she can do. If you allow her to spread her wings, it is possible she may even learn to fly."

A look of such hope came over Lady Catherine's countenance that it moved Darcy to compassion. Anne was not robust, but Darcy had always thought his aunt's tendency to smother her and exclaim over what she could not do was a self-fulfilling prophecy. One thing which had never been in question was Lady Catherine's love for her daughter. A careful attempt to direct her might bear fruit.

"Should we give her the opportunity to move in a society which is not demanding, perhaps Anne will become more comfortable. You know she is intelligent, Aunt. If allowed to exercise her body, she might grow stronger."

"You are suggesting I send for her."

"I believe she would benefit from being here. Miss Elizabeth has worked wonders with my sister who, you must acknowledge, has gained much confidence. Anne would also benefit from the friendship of those of the neighborhood. If you will forgive me, those near Rosings are too in awe of you to befriend her as she requires."

"Perhaps I shall consider it," said Lady Catherine.

"Please do. If you apply to Bingley, I am certain he will not disappoint you."

Lady Catherine laughed, one of the few times Darcy had ever heard a carefree note in the woman's manner. "He would at that. Your friend, I am convinced, can be induced to do almost anything if only you should ask."

"Bingley is that way with all of his friends. He is an excellent friend."

It did not take as long as Darcy had expected. As soon as Bingley appeared that morning, Lady Catherine applied to him for permission, which Bingley gave with his typical good cheer. To Hertfordshire, Miss Anne de Bourgh was to come.

Later that day, Fitzwilliam arrived at Netherfield for dinner. The invitation was an open one, which Fitzwilliam accepted several times a week, but Darcy knew on this day he was most concerned with how their aunt was behaving. When he arrived, however, it was to the sight of Lady Catherine sitting with Miss Bingley and Mrs. Hurst, speaking together with perfect civility. That the lady was a little uncomfortable in the company of those who were well below her in society was something only one well acquainted with her would understand.

"I will own that our aunt has surprised me," said Fitzwilliam when Darcy informed him of the day's goings-on. "Just when I thought I knew what she would do in any situation, she proves me wrong. And regarding a matter I would have thought was beyond argument!"

"I am just as much at sea as you, Cousin," said Darcy, shaking his head.

"Regardless," continued Fitzwilliam, "it is gratifying to see her behaving in a way that will not bring infamy on our family. I wonder, however, if her staying here will not bring out the worst in her before long. It would not do to offend Bingley."

"There is little chance of that," said Darcy. "Either way, I shall remain watchful."

Fitzwilliam grunted and turned his attention to another matter. "You know it is possible her agreement to send for Anne is nothing more than a final desperate attempt to throw her in your way."

"It is possible," said Darcy with a shrug. "If she espouses such designs, they are destined to fail. And it was I who suggested it, so you cannot blame it all on her ladyship."

"Then it will be on your head if she conspires to compromise you." Fitzwilliam grinned and slapped Darcy's back, an action which drew Lady Catherine's attention, though she said nothing. "I wish you the best of luck."

Another thought seemed to occur to Fitzwilliam and his grin became a glare. "Now that she appears to have accepted your refusal to marry Anne, I must wonder if I am to be the next target of her dynastic schemes."

Darcy replied with a grin. "Just remember, Fitzwilliam: I fended her off. If I can, I am certain you shall too."

Fitzwilliam grumbled but did not speak. Soon the company was called in to dinner, and their private conversation gave way to the demands of the evening in company.

If there was one thing Elizabeth learned in the ensuing days, it was that Lady Catherine was everything Mr. Darcy and Colonel Fitzwilliam had told her. While the lady had not seen fit to oppose Mr. Darcy's continued association with Elizabeth—the lady did not appear happy with it, regardless of her silence—she was still a woman of decided opinions, unafraid to share them with all and sundry.

The woman's target could be anyone; she dispensed advice to her nephews, her niece, Miss Bingley and Mrs. Hurst, and the Bennets with equal fervor and belief in her rightness. Elizabeth did not know what others thought on the matter, she did not care for the lady's meddling herself. When Lady Catherine opened her mouth to speak, Elizabeth listened, thanked her, and turned her attention to other matters, determined to ignore that which she did not find useful or sensible. Miss Bingley, she thought, liked the lady's ways as little as Elizabeth.

The only time in Lady Catherine's company that the lady did not speak incessantly was the first visit after she arrived. The Bennet ladies took themselves to Netherfield that day to pay a visit, and as she often did, Elizabeth sat with Georgiana and Mr. Darcy and spent the entire call with them. By that time, Miss Bingley's looks of annoyance had mellowed to something akin to melancholy, allowing Elizabeth to have an agreeable conversation with her friends.

Lady Catherine, though she was in nominal conversation with Miss Bingley and Mrs. Bennet, spent most of her time watching Elizabeth's interaction with her relations, and Mr. Darcy in particular. While Elizabeth might have become annoyed at the constant inspection, she decided it was best to ignore it. The lady would act the way she would; there was nothing Elizabeth could do to stop it.

"I believe you have impressed her," said Mr. Darcy in a low tone when he noticed Elizabeth's glance at his aunt.

"If that is so, I cannot imagine what meets her approval," said Elizabeth, choosing humor for her response. "I am neither wealthy nor prominent enough for her favorite nephew."

"Perhaps you are not," replied Mr. Darcy. "But you are intelligent and confident enough to stand up for yourself, and those are traits that the lady respects."

Though uncertain Mr. Darcy was correct, Elizabeth took this as a sign of his regard and changed the subject. The lady regained some of her volubility before the end of the visit, but not at all what Elizabeth might have expected.

During the return visit the following day, the lady reverted to what Elizabeth thought was her usual character. Nothing was beneath her notice. She questioned Kitty and Lydia on their studies, inserted her opinion regarding Mary's skills on the pianoforte, spoke of the proper method for one to manage a house, and commented on the tea service, the cakes, and whatever else crossed her mind.

Charlotte, who was also visiting Longbourn that morning, was a focus as well for the lady. Though Elizabeth had been much engaged with Mr. Darcy and Georgiana of late, it had not missed her attention that Charlotte was often with Colonel Fitzwilliam, who was also visiting that morning. The lady, it seemed, noted the same, for her gaze rested on them for a time, though she did not ignore Elizabeth and Mr. Darcy.

"Miss Lucas," said she after a time of this, "it seems to me you are a sturdy, practical sort of woman."

"Thank you, Lady Catherine," said Charlotte, already understanding much of the lady's nature. "In this, I think you agree with Elizabeth, who has made much the same observation more than once."

"Yes, well, Miss Elizabeth is as perceptive a young lady as I have ever met," said Lady Catherine, not sparing a glance for Elizabeth herself. "Pardon my intrusion, but it is my understanding that you live nearby. Does your father own a large estate?"

"My home is no more than a mile from here," said Charlotte. "Lucas Lodge is perhaps as large as Longbourn, or a little smaller."

The lady nodded, deep in thought. "Then your prospects cannot be great. It is on my mind that you would be an excellent wife to my parson, Mr. Collins. If you like, I shall recommend you to him, for I believe a practical wife is what Mr. Collins requires."

It did not miss Elizabeth's attention that the lady's words were a backhanded denigration of the parson's capabilities, not that she disagreed. The suggestion that Charlotte had no prospects was no more tactful, though Elizabeth caught sight of Colonel Fitzwilliam frowning by Charlotte's side and wondered if that was true. Charlotte, however, smiled at the lady and did not take offense, which was for the best, when faced by Lady Catherine's urge to be useful.

"I thank you for the offer, your ladyship. When Mr. Collins was here, he paid no attention to me, or to anyone who did not meet his requirements in a wife. As he did not see me as an acceptable prospect then, I suspect there is little we can do to change his mind now."

Miss Bingley, who was the only woman Mr. Collins had deemed acceptable, scowled at Charlotte, though Elizabeth knew her friend had not intended a slight. Lady Catherine, however, brushed Charlotte's words away as if they were of no concern.

"It is within my ability to persuade him, Miss Lucas. As you require a situation and he requires a good, intelligent woman for a wife, I cannot imagine there can be any impediment."

"Perhaps you are correct," replied Charlotte. "However, I will own that I do not wish to always be caring for a husband, directing him, always afraid he should say something imprudent to embarrass me. Thank you, but I believe I shall decline."

It cannot be supposed that Lady Catherine would take such a demurral with any grace, and for a moment, Elizabeth thought she would press the point. Whether she decided against it because of some well of restraint or because Colonel Fitzwilliam was glaring at her, Elizabeth did not know, but the lady did not speak on the subject again. Elizabeth was near enough to hear the lady mutter some choice epithets under her breath for the absent Mr. Collins.

For the rest of the visit, Elizabeth put the lady from her mind, grateful that Lady Catherine seemed to focus her attention on Mrs. Bennet. In this way her grand pronouncements were muted, allowing the others in the room to engage in their own conversations without interruption. When the Netherfield party left, however, Elizabeth found there was another issue of which she had not been aware.

"Do you see anything wrong with this room, Lizzy?" asked the Bennet matron after some time of silence. As the younger girls had retreated above stairs for their lessons, Mary was engaged on the pianoforte, and Jane had returned to her room, Elizabeth was alone with her mother.

"It has always seemed like a handsome room to me," replied Elizabeth, uncertain to what her mother was referring. "Was it not redecorated not long after you and Papa married?"

"One of the first things I attended to," replied Mrs. Bennet. "Your grandmother meant to do it herself, but funds were tight in those days, and your grandfather could not countenance an expenditure of such significance. The financial condition of the estate improved thereafter, and your father gave me leave to make the improvements."

"And they are lovely," replied Elizabeth, fixing her mother with a warm smile.

"Thank you, my dear," said Mrs. Bennet, returning Elizabeth's smile.

"What brought on these reflections, Mama?" asked Elizabeth. "Have the results of your efforts in this room not always pleased you?"

Mrs. Bennet's countenance darkened. "Lady Catherine informed me that the style was dated. It is my duty to my husband and my family to present the best front to our friends and neighbors, and part of that is to keep up with the latest fashions."

Shaking her head, Mrs. Bennet directed a plaintive look at Elizabeth. "The suggestions she made sounded costly; I wonder if your father would ever approve them. And do you know she also commented on our dresses, the dinner I ordered the night she dined with us, and the number of servants we employ? How we will ever afford all of her suggestions I know not."

Understanding flooded Elizabeth and she sent a dark thought in the absent lady's direction. Though Mrs. Bennet had been the mistress of Longbourn for over twenty years, Elizabeth knew Lady Catherine, with her experience and lineage, would impress her mother, forcing her to take notice of what the lady said. Mrs. Bennet was not above being insecure, regardless of her experience. Elizabeth had, for many years, attempted to bolster her mother's confidence, for she was an excellent mistress, despite her lack of formal education.

"Mama, I believe it is best to take care when considering Lady Catherine's pronouncements. What is best for the de Bourgh family may not be best for the Bennets."

Uncertain, Mrs. Bennet said: "What do you mean?"

"Just this, Mama: Lady Catherine is a wealthy woman, is she not?" When her mother nodded, Elizabeth continued. "The de Bourgh fortune is extensive, as I understand, meaning Lady Catherine possesses the funds to do whatever she likes. Though we live in comfort, the Bennets are not wealthy, meaning we must weigh the benefits of such actions as Lady Catherine might deem unworthy of much thought."

Mrs. Bennet paused, considering Elizabeth's advice. "Do you think her words have no merit then?"

"I think her words have merit for those who are able to concern themselves for such things. If we were a wealthy family, concerned with appearances, we might redecorate more often. As we are not, I believe the constraints of budget must have greater weight than the need to give a good appearance.

"You should believe me, Mother. Has Papa complained about this room? Have any of our neighbors? Does Lady Lucas not comment about how much she likes this room every time she sets foot within it?"

"Yes, I believe you are correct," said Mrs. Bennet with a nod.

"It would be best," said Elizabeth, fixing her mother with a knowing grin, "to listen to Lady Catherine's assertions and decide for yourself what would be best to accept and what we should decline. I believe Lady Catherine dispenses advice by habit and whim; she will not raise the matter again."

With a smile, Mrs. Bennet rose and kissed Elizabeth's head. "Thank you, Lizzy. You always know how best to ease my concerns. I believe I shall take your advice."

Then Mrs. Bennet left the room, allowing Elizabeth her thoughts. Perhaps it was best to speak with her sisters. There was no telling what nonsense Lady Catherine had imparted to them.

CHAPTER XXII

When Anne's carriage entered Netherfield's drive later that Saturday, Darcy watched it with mixed emotions. Anne was his cousin, was a member of his family, and yet he did not know her well. While due in large part to his aunt's insistence they marry and Darcy's wish to avoid provoking her to hope, he was aware he might have used other means to come to know her better. The primary concern between them was the only matter of which they had not spoken at all, though Anne had intimated on occasion that she had no desire to marry him. That sense had given him an additional reason to rebuff Lady Catherine's attempts to carry her point, and Darcy supposed he should thank her for that much.

"Cheer up, Darcy," said Fitzwilliam, standing by his side. "There is no need to look at Anne's coming as if it were a funeral."

"I am not regretting her coming, I assure you," said Darcy, unmoved by his cousin's teasing. "It is just that I do not know Anne well at all."

"She has not been close to any of us, and for that, you may put the blame on her mother. Perhaps this visit will benefit her if we can induce her to speak. Your young lady should do for that task — she possesses an astonishing ability to bring out the best in others."

The thought of Miss Elizabeth heartened Darcy, allowing him to look upon the upcoming visit with more equanimity. Fitzwilliam was correct; loosing Miss Elizabeth's joie de vivre and ability to charm upon Anne would help bring her out of her shell if there was anyone able to accomplish the feat. Perhaps Darcy might come to know his cousin at the same time.

As the carriage stopped and the footman positioned the step and opened the door, Fitzwilliam stepped forward and assisted Anne down from the carriage—even with Darcy's open acknowledgment of his interest in Miss Elizabeth, it was best he did not perform even such simple tasks. If Lady Catherine noticed it, she said nothing, instead reserving her attention for her daughter. The greeting between mother and daughter was affectionate, or with as much warmth as Lady Catherine could muster. Anne reserved her true emotion for her greeting with Georgiana.

"Anne! How wonderful that you have come!"

The two women embraced, and Darcy reflected that his sister had always been closer to Anne than he. It was Anne's presence that had drawn Georgiana to Rosings at times when she might have preferred not to go. Lady Catherine had always been much less severe on Georgiana than anyone else in the family, though that did not prevent Georgiana from fearing her regardless. The same was not true of Anne.

"Thank you, Georgiana dear," replied Anne, returning Georgiana's enthusiastic embrace. Then she turned to her other cousins.

"Fitzwilliam," said she. "I see you have deigned to share your insouciance with us all."

"Always, Cousin," said Fitzwilliam with a grin.

"And Darcy. What is this I hear of you attending a woman in this neighborhood? Is she a woman of sense? I had not thought you capable of wooing any woman who was not out of her wits."

Though Darcy had seen something of a teasing facet of Anne's character in the past, never had it been so overt. It appeared he was not the only one surprised, for Lady Catherine looking on her only child with something akin to astonishment. Darcy regarded his cousin with a speculative eye; perhaps Anne was shrewder than he thought.

"There is no engagement yet, so it is still possible I might frighten her away."

It seemed a return jest was the correct way to respond, for Anne's tinkling laughter lightened Darcy's mood, though Lady Catherine's severity grew apace. Anne, however, ignored her mother and stepped toward him, laying a hand on his arm.

"Then it will be Georgiana's responsibility, with my help, to ensure she does not run away screaming. We would not wish to throw away this chance we both have to be free at last, would we?"

"Anne!" chided Lady Catherine, having reached the limit of her tolerance.

"It is nothing less than the truth, Mother."

There was little the lady could respond, and she showed surprising judgment by choosing the expedient of remaining silent. Knowing it was best to put this matter to the side for now, Darcy motioned to their hosts, introducing Bingley, his sisters, and Hurst to Anne's acquaintance. The way Miss Bingley regarded her suggested to Darcy that she expected another Lady Catherine on a smaller scale. Anne, however, was quick to put her at ease.

"I thank you for inviting me to Netherfield on short notice, Miss Bingley," said she, "though I suspect my mother did not give you much of a choice."

"Anne!" was Lady Catherine's strident protest, though Fitzwilliam and Darcy sniggered.

"It was no trouble, Miss de Bourgh," said Miss Bingley, wisely choosing to ignore the byplay within the family. "We are pleased to have you stay with us."

The greetings completed, Miss Bingley escorted Anne into the house and showed her to her rooms. Darcy took himself to the library for a time where he read, knowing that Georgiana and Anne were reacquainting themselves in Anne's bedchamber. It was a surprise when he dressed for dinner and entered the sitting-room, that the next person to arrive was his cousin.

"Hello, Darcy," said Anne with good cheer. "Shall I join you? Or perhaps it would be best to summon Georgiana as a chaperone, lest mother use this last opportunity to engineer a marriage between us."

Darcy regarded her, wondering what this overflowing of mirth presaged; it was not something he might have expected from his quiet cousin. It had never been his opinion that Anne was unintelligent or unobservant, and she proved it by understanding his look.

"Do not regard me in such a way, Cousin," said Anne. "If I am feeling a little giddy, you cannot blame me. I am certain it will pass in time, and I shall be as I ever was."

That might not be welcome either, considering how quiet Anne had always been. "Was the prospect of marriage to me that onerous?"

"You have not had to live with my mother speaking about it at all times," retorted Anne. Then she paused and said: "That is not fair to

Mother either. When you were not before us, we often went days without my mother reminding me of my 'destiny.' But any time we were due to be in company with you, she would raise the subject again, and it seemed like she could speak of nothing else."

"It is best, then, that you are freed. Regardless of my future with Miss Bennet, I have made it clear that we shall not marry."

"And do you think Mother has given up altogether?" was Anne's pointed response.

The grimace which Darcy responded told Anne all she needed to know.

"There you have it. For me to achieve my freedom, I must ensure you are safely married to your young woman."

"Have you always been this way?" asked Darcy, hearing a hint of a plaintive note in his voice. "I would never have imagined it of you."

"Just as you have avoided me, I have avoided you," said Anne. "Now that we shall be free of Mama's machinations, I hope we can forge a relationship as cousins."

"To that, I can agree," said Darcy, deciding to ignore her behavior for the moment.

"Now, when am I to meet this Miss Bennet of whom I have heard so much?" At Darcy's pained look, Anne laughed and laid a hand upon his arm. "Do not concern yourself, Darcy, for I do not mean to meddle. Georgiana's letters have been glowing in their praise of her, and I find myself eager to make her acquaintance."

"Then I suspect you shall meet her tomorrow at church," replied Darcy.

"And I shall be spared Mr. Collins's droning pronouncements and nonsensical mutterings!" said Anne. "I have never heard such drivel in all my life. I suspect his subject for this week shall focus on a woman's reputation, for his anger at Miss Bingley's refusal knows no bounds."

"I can well imagine it," muttered Darcy. "It is fortunate the parson at Longbourn is a man much more in tune with his parish's needs."

"Excellent!" exclaimed Anne. "then I shall look forward to meeting your Miss Bennet and not falling asleep in church!"

The sound of Anne's laughter accompanied Darcy's shaking head. While he was not certain yet what to make of his cousin's astonishing change, he thought he might like her very well.

Miss Caroline Bingley was a woman of excellent character and impeccable manners. One did not eavesdrop at doors or listen in on private conversations, especially when one was the mistress of an estate and wished to make an impression upon the guests staying there. It was fortunate that no one saw her as she hesitated outside the door to the sitting-room, hearing the final few exchanges in Mr. Darcy and Miss de Bourgh's conversation.

Knowing she did not wish anyone to catch her there, she entered the room and greeted the occupants, asking after their comfort. Mr. Darcy had always been an easy guest to host, and Caroline suspected Miss de Bourgh would be similar, and if Lady Catherine more than made up for their civility, Caroline was not about to protest. When several other members of the party arrived soon after, Caroline allowed herself to fade into the background, grateful to be freed from meaningless small talk when she wished to think and ponder where she had gone wrong.

"Come and join Georgiana and me, Miss Bingley," said Miss de Bourgh soon after the former's arrival. "Perhaps you have something of use to say about Georgiana's regrettable insistence that she does not wish to play for the company."

"Oh, I agree with you, Miss de Bourgh," said Caroline, reflecting that it was no trial to do so. "I have been fortunate enough to have heard Miss Darcy play; her talents are nothing less than exquisite."

"It is not that," said Miss Darcy, coloring in embarrassment. "I do not possess the confidence to play before an audience."

"Confidence is gained by performing," replied Caroline, to Miss de Bourgh's approval. "Do you play, Miss de Bourgh?"

"No, I do not, though I should like to learn. Perhaps with you excellent musicians in residence I shall receive some training."

Flattered, Caroline promised her willingness to assist whenever Miss de Bourgh liked and fell silent, offering her own opinion when it seemed least likely she would be required to elaborate. On the other side of the room, Charles had gathered with Mr. Darcy and Colonel Fitzwilliam, while Lady Catherine sat with Louisa, speaking of what, Caroline could not say.

The sight of Mr. Darcy caused the now-familiar chagrin to well up in her breast again. While Caroline might not have wished to acknowledge her failure, it had been clear for some time that her campaign to induce Mr. Darcy to propose was not proceeding as she might have wished. Mr. Darcy's attentions to Miss Elizabeth had been the final nail in the coffin of her pretensions, and if it had not been, his words to his aunt upon her arrival had ended any possibility of another outcome.

Disappointed though she was, it surprised Caroline to find her vanity was little affected by his defection. Mr. Darcy was a good and upright man, but she had always been interested in his position rather than his person. Though the trappings of wealth and standing would have been welcome, life with Mr. Darcy would have proved dull, as opposed to society as he was. Perhaps it was better this way . . . .

That did not lessen the sting, of course, particularly the knowledge she had lost to a country nobody of no standing or fortune. Oh, Caroline was honest enough to confess that Miss Elizabeth was not without redeeming qualities, and she thought if they had met under other circumstances—and had she not attracted the man Caroline meant to marry—she might have found it tolerably easy to esteem the woman. Knowing what she did of Caroline's ambitions, she doubted Miss Elizabeth would ever see her as anything approaching a friend. That might also be for the best.

The question was what she was to do now. Caroline knew she had wasted the past two years, certain she could induce her brother's closest friend to offer for her. That possibility had not come to fruition, leaving Caroline three and twenty years of age and no closer to a marriage than she had been when she began her campaign. Her dowry was handsome enough to attract attention, but Caroline knew her background would be a detriment.

Yet there was nothing she could do. The next season she had little option other than to put herself forward in London society and attempt to find a husband. Whatever happened, Caroline did not mean to be an old maid. But she also meant to ensure her husband was of some standing in society.

The sound of a detested name sounded in Caroline's ears, and she turned to her companions, wondering of what they were speaking. "It is well that Mr. Collins has departed from the neighborhood, Miss de Bourgh. The Bennets could not countenance him in their home, for I understand Mr. Bennet ordered him from the premises and instructed him not to return."

"That I can well understand," replied Miss de Bourgh. The woman regarded her for a moment, and Caroline began to feel a little defensive. "I understand his presence was not palatable to you, in particular, Miss Bingley."

"No, he was not," said Caroline, her words sharper than she had intended. "I cannot imagine anyone of any sense appreciating Mr. Collins."

"Do not suppose I disagree with you," replied Miss de Bourgh, reaching out and resting a hand on Caroline's arm. "Though the man may yet find a wife, I cannot imagine a woman foolish enough to marry him."

"I thank you for seeing it that way," said Caroline, darting a look at Miss de Bourgh's mother. "Not everyone agrees with your assessment."

Miss de Bourgh noted her look and was diverted by it. "Do not concern yourself with my mother, Miss Bingley. I suspect she was merely annoyed that the world had not ordered itself according to her desires."

With a smile, Caroline nodded in agreement. Until dinner, they spoke of various subjects, and Caroline concentrated on the conversation rather than her own thoughts. Through it, Caroline remembered one pertinent fact: her chances in society would be improved by associating with these ladies. That was a boon, but Caroline enjoyed their company too. For the first time in many months, that was worth more to Caroline than all the societal prominence in the world.

Curious though she was to make Miss Anne de Bourgh's acquaintance, the opportunity was not afforded to Elizabeth before the start of church services. The Bennet family arrived at their usual time and sat in the family pew after greeting their friends and neighbors. There was no sign of the Netherfield party until a few moments before the service was to begin, and as a result, though Elizabeth noted when they entered, their late arrival afforded nothing more than the pleasure of a brief nod to her friends and a quick glance at the young lady.

Then the service began, and Elizabeth attempted to give the parson the compliment of her attention, though she was sorely tempted to consider the person of the young woman of whom she had heard so much. Miss de Bourgh and Lady Catherine's attendance was an improvement on the disruption the last visitor to their service provided, but almost anything was better than William Collins. When the service passed and the congregation rose, the awaited opportunity came to fruition.

Elizabeth's first impression of the young woman was nothing more than physical. Miss de Bourgh was small—her height more diminutive than Elizabeth's own petite stature, her form thin and waif-like, her brown hair an unremarkable color, her skin pale. These unexceptional features, however, were belied by the brightness of her dark eyes, and in the curious expression with which she regarded Elizabeth. Ill health might be the defining characteristic of Miss de Bourgh's life, but Elizabeth would not make the mistake of underestimating this woman.

"Miss de Bourgh," said Elizabeth, offering the other woman a curtsey when Mr. Darcy made the introductions. "I cannot be more pleased to make your acquaintance, for I have heard so much about you."

"Of course, you have!" intruded Lady Catherine. "For my daughter is another of the illustrious people with whom you have had the good fortune to associate of late. Making the acquaintance of another granddaughter of an earl cannot be a trivial matter for one in your position!"

The manic note in Lady Catherine's voice informed Elizabeth that whatever civility had passed between them, the lady was not resigned to Mr. Darcy's insistence against a match with Miss de Bourgh. Almost as one, Elizabeth could see the sighs and rolled eyes which comprised the reactions of the lady's family, though they were all hidden from the lady herself. Diverted, Elizabeth suppressed her laughter, unwilling to give the lady any fodder for criticism.

"If you have heard of me," said Miss de Bourgh, favoring Elizabeth with a wink, again hidden from her mother, "it cannot be anything in comparison with what I have heard of you."

This time the impulse to laugh was stronger, though Elizabeth's resisted it. The sight of Lady Catherine's huff of annoyance with her daughter was reward enough.

"Now that we have exchanged praises," said Elizabeth, "perhaps we may dispense with them."

"That would be much appreciated, Miss Elizabeth."

There was not much time to talk and become acquainted, for Mr. Bennet preferred to return to Longbourn immediately after church. Elizabeth had but ten minutes to speak with her new friend, and by the end of their time together, she had obtained the impression that Miss de Bourgh was an intelligent woman, though perhaps more reserved than she had shown at the outset. Elizabeth thought she could become a close friend to this young lady. The thought crossed her mind—suppressed, as the outcome was still unknown—that if she married Mr. Darcy, she would be in a position to provide Miss de Bourgh with a respite from her overbearing mother.

"Now, Anne," said Lady Catherine, inserting herself into the conversation after some minutes, "you know you should not tax your strength. It is time we returned to Netherfield, where you should rest a few hours."

The look Miss de Bourgh gave Elizabeth informed her this was a common occurrence, and that Miss de Bourgh had no intention of complying. As Mr. Bennet was showing signs of wishing to leave, Elizabeth decided they would have other opportunities to meet, and bid her new friend farewell.

"I hope we will meet again soon, Miss Elizabeth," said Miss de Bourgh. "I hope it very much."

The rest of the party said their farewells, including Georgiana's affectionate one and Mr. Darcy bowing over her hand. As he departed, Elizabeth thought she caught a hint of gratitude from Mr. Darcy, though whether it was because she had agreed to befriend Miss de Bourgh, or for some other reason Elizabeth could not be certain. It was unnecessary; Elizabeth could no more reject a woman of Miss de Bourgh's character than she could deny the gentleman who had crept his way into her heart.

"If you wish for my opinion," said Anne de Bourgh as the Darcy carriage drove away from the church, "it is that you have found a gem, Cousin. Though I only spoke to her for a few moments, I cannot imagine there is anything wanting in Miss Elizabeth."

As she said this, Anne noted the thin line of her mother's mouth. Calculated as her comment was to sow the seed that her dream of marrying Anne to her cousin was dead, it was not unexpected. Anne had no notion that she had persuaded Lady Catherine to relent, but the more doubt she created the better.

"Thank you, Anne," said Darcy, his knowing smile telling her he understood what Anne was doing, Georgiana nodding by his side. "I rather think so myself."

In fact, Anne considered herself to be an intelligent, observant woman. One needed to have their wits about them when dealing with her mother; living with a woman who spoke her opinion in a forthright manner allowing for no dispute had taught Anne to watch, form her own opinions, and keep them to herself. The ability to share at least an insignificant part of her opinions openly was liberating. Anne hoped it would lead to a greater ability to do so in the future.

"Well," said Anne's mother, "she is a . . . an intelligent girl, I suppose." Lady Catherine spoke the words as if Anne had pulled them from her mouth under duress. "Though she possesses a distressing impertinence which she must learn to curb before she will be acceptable in society."

"It is my opinion," said Anne, once again reveling in the ability to say those words, "that she will be a breath of fresh air to the dowdies of society. I should not call it impertinence, Mother. Call it instead a confident and forthright character."

"And yet she is not forthright to the point of being overbearing," said Darcy, betraying not a hint of irony despite the company. "If her observations are a little sportive, she charms rather than insults, intending no slight upon anyone, and in a manner which disarms reproof."

"Yes, that is it," said Anne before her mother could interject her opinion. "If you will pardon my saying, Cousin, you are not a loquacious man yourself; a little sportive conversation cannot help but do you good."

"No offense taken, Anne, for it is nothing less than the truth." Darcy turned to Georgiana and smiled, saying: "I dare say Miss Elizabeth has been a boon for my sister too."

"Oh, without a doubt," replied Georgiana. "And Kitty and Lydia, and Jane, though Jane is very reticent herself. I have also had many interesting conversations about music with Miss Mary, and I like her very well."

Lady Catherine huffed her annoyance, molding herself back into the seat and glaring at them all with arms folded. "To hear you speak of it, they are the very pinnacle of gentle families. I have never heard such nonsense!"

"No, Mother," said Anne. "I have not known them long enough to form an opinion that firm, and would not claim perfection, even if my acquaintance with them was longer than fifty years. Each is flawed as are we all, but on the whole, I like them very well."

"Well, I suppose you must be correct if you put it that way," muttered Lady Catherine. "But some improvement is necessary for them all if they are to be accepted in society. Else they shall embarrass us all."

Then Lady Catherine turned and glared out the window, finding some offense in the passing trees. Anne shared a look and a grin with her cousins and allowed the subject to drop. She had made her point, and her mother had not misunderstood it. Lady Catherine had always known she would not bend Darcy to her will; it was time her mother understood that Anne was no less stubborn than he. It was a lesson her mother would not appreciate learning, but it was necessary, nonetheless.

CHAPTER XXIII

*I*f there was one constant in Darcy's life, it was the unwanted presence of George Wickham.

It had seemed to Darcy in the five years since his father passed that Wickham was akin to a tax collector or a persistent headache—an unwanted manifestation that would not depart and leave him in peace. Though Wickham had preceded him to the neighborhood, Darcy had long planned to join Bingley at his estate, making Wickham's appearance another intrusion on his notice. Of late, Darcy noted that Wickham had not shown himself at Netherfield, and, consequently, the last time Darcy had found it necessary to endure his erstwhile friend was at the ball. Whether this was because Fitzwilliam had tasked him with duties or the man felt a little distance from Miss Bingley would soften her toward him, Darcy did not know. Whatever the reason, the officers paid a visit again to Netherfield on Monday, and Wickham strutted among their number as if he was master of all he surveyed.

Upon spying Darcy, Wickham shot him an insolent grin and a mock salute, before he took himself to the side of Netherfield's mistress and began plying her with his usual brand of charm. As he was not attempting the same with Georgiana, Darcy ignored him; Miss Bingley could see to her own concerns. With the officers came their commander, which prompted Darcy to join his cousin.

"I see your eyes have not left Wickham since we arrived," observed Fitzwilliam as Darcy approached.

"Can you blame me?" asked Darcy with more bluntness than tact.

"Not at all," replied Fitzwilliam. "I am the same way whenever we are in the same room, though I will note there appears to be little with which to concern myself of late."

Darcy turned a questioning eye on his cousin. "Have you let your guard down?"

"Of course not," replied Fitzwilliam with a snort. "A snake like Wickham bears watching—I doubt I shall cease as long as he slithers his way through Meryton society."

With an absent nod, Darcy said: "His behavior has been acceptable?"

"Exemplary, I should say," said Fitzwilliam. "It will shock you to hear that he is not diligent in the performance of his duties."

"Not at all," murmured Darcy.

"Many of my officers are the same." Fitzwilliam shrugged. "It is a mark of the militia when compared with the greater discipline of the regulars. In this, Wickham is no worse than any of his fellows. But in other matters, I have nothing of which to find fault. There have been no complaints of his behavior to any young ladies of the neighborhood, and his fellows report he owes no gaming debts.

"I am disgusted with how well he has behaved. When he came under my command, I thought it an even wager that he would desert within two weeks; then I could have hunted him down at my leisure and seen to his removal from England forever."

Darcy directed a sharp look at his cousin. "That is not what you told me."

"No, it was not," agreed an affable Fitzwilliam. "My reasons for keeping him here were accurate, and not because I wished him to fail. But I also said at the time that we could control him if need be. Given his history with our family, can you imagine I would have been anything less than vigilant?"

There was nothing Darcy could say to that and he did not make the attempt. Wickham seemed to have no notion they were speaking of him, though Darcy thought him aware of their position together. His full attention, however, was on Miss Bingley, and the man's laughter, which rang out from something she said, caught Darcy's attention. Knowing Wickham as he did, it surprised Darcy to realize it appeared genuine.

"Is it just me, or does Miss Bingley seem more receptive to Wickham's overtures?"

Fixed as his attention had been on Wickham, Darcy had not noted Miss Bingley's behavior. As he watched, however, Darcy noted the interest with which the woman regarded him, the way the words more easily flowed from her lips, not to mention how she had not looked at Darcy since Wickham had joined her.

"Perhaps she is," replied Darcy. "I cannot say she is in any danger from him, but she does seem more willing to allow him to speak with her."

"I had no intention of suggesting she was," replied Fitzwilliam. "Miss Bingley strikes me as a lady who would not be cajoled to run off to Gretna, no matter how persuasive his entreaties."

Fitzwilliam paused and then turned to look Darcy in the eye. "If asked, do you suppose Bingley would give his approval to a marriage between them?"

A sudden grimness coming over him, Darcy, glared at Wickham. "You should remember Miss Bingley is of age and does not need her brother's permission. Should Wickham request his blessing, I cannot imagine Bingley would be reluctant to give it, if it is something his sister wants."

Inclining his head in understanding, Fitzwilliam said: "I still think she is in no danger. It does appear, however, that Wickham is attempting to woo a woman in the traditional manner."

"That may be," agreed Darcy. "But Miss Bingley is set upon entering the upper levels of society, and that is something Wickham, with all the charm in the world, cannot give her."

With a nod, Fitzwilliam dropped the subject. At that moment, Lady Catherine entered the room, along with Anne, drawing the attention of the officers in attendance. As she had not been introduced to them, none did more than look with curiosity. But there was one among them who had known her before, and he started at the sight of her. Lady Catherine, it appeared, was no less surprised to see Wickham in Miss Bingley's sitting-room.

"George Wickham!" the lady's voice rang out over the room. "What are you doing here?"

"I am an officer in Colonel Fitzwilliam's regiment, your ladyship," said Wickham, gesturing at his scarlet coat. "It has been some years since I have seen your ladyship. How do you do?"

Eyes narrowed, displeasure shining in her eyes, Lady Catherine snapped: "I do well, though that is no surprise since I always do well. My wellbeing or lack thereof is not at issue, not when I remember some of your antics and how you have abused my nephew's family since his father's passing. What have you to say for yourself?"

The flicking of Wickham's eyes to his fellow officers, who were watching with interest, informed Darcy of his discomfort. Wickham was not bereft of wits, however, for he recovered soon and attempted to put her ladyship off.

"I have reformed, Lady Catherine. Now, I am a respectable officer in the militia, under the command of one of your ladyship's nephews. The vices of the past no longer hold sway over me."

It seemed it was the correct thing to say, for his fellows — not having known him before he came to the neighborhood — had nothing to hold against him. Conversation began again as an indistinct murmur, and Lady Catherine, though she pursed her lips, did not make any further comment. The way her eyes impaled him, however, informed Darcy she did not trust him, matching her nephews' feelings exactly.

"I hope you have Mr. Wickham suitably reined in, Fitzwilliam," said her ladyship. "That young man is a rotten apple."

"Have no fear, Lady Catherine," said Fitzwilliam with a grin. "George knows he may not step out of line lest the full weight of my authority fall upon his head."

"Very well. See that you remain vigilant."

Then Lady Catherine sought a nearby chair and sat, though she continued to watch Wickham. The lady did not request any introductions to any of the other officers, who did not seem to feel the lack of her civility.

What happened next was beyond Darcy's understanding, though he was watching Wickham the whole time. The man never took his attention from Miss Bingley that Darcy could see, continuing to ply her with the same flattery which had always marked his wooing. In the next moment, however, he was speaking with Anne, though Anne had been conversing with Georgiana and the first exchange of words had been a few innocuous comments.

"It has been some time, Miss de Bourgh."

"Yes, it has, Mr. Wickham. I believe it may be ten years since I last saw you."

Wickham thought about it for a moment and returned a slow nod. "The year before I went to Cambridge when you visited Pemberley."

"You never accompanied the family to Rosings."

There was no response for Wickham to make to that observation, for though he had been at Snowlock, the Fitzwilliam estate on occasion, Darcy's father had never tried to take him to Rosings, knowing Lady Catherine would not have endured it. Thus, Wickham changed the subject.

"I hope all has been well."

"There is nothing for which I can complain," replied Anne. "I hope you can say the same."

Wickham's almost imperceptible darting look at Georgiana nearly prompted Darcy to throw him from the house. Anne, he suspected, did not notice it, nor did anyone else in the room, except perhaps Fitzwilliam. For Wickham's part, he assured Anne that he had excellent prospects at present before he turned to other matters.

With a hint of Wickham's flattery making an appearance, they continued to speak, the subject of their conversation ranging from the past to the local neighborhood to Wickham's current situation in the militia. As they spoke, Darcy noted that more and more of Wickham's attention seemed fixed on Anne, rather than the woman he had been trying to charm these past weeks. Miss Bingley regarded him with a dispassionate stare, equally likely, in Darcy's opinion, to rail her offense as to sigh with relief.

Then Wickham paused, started a little, and seemed to recognize he had not been speaking with Miss Bingley for some time. The floodgates of his praise were once again opened on her, and Anne, taking his sudden defection with bemusement, returned to speaking with Georgiana.

Darcy was not the only one to witness the exchange, for his cousin leaned over and spoke in a soft tone. "If Miss Bingley has a fortune of twenty thousand pounds, Anne has Rosings itself. There is no question about which Wickham would find more appealing."

"Enough to allow him to live without restraint for a few years, or a lifetime of ready funds?" asked Darcy with a snort. "You have the right of it, Cousin."

"Then it would be best to monitor our lieutenant. This temptation might be more than he can withstand."

Darcy nodded, watching Wickham as he spoke with Miss Bingley. To a casual observer, his full attention was on her. Had Darcy not witnessed the darting looks at Anne, Lady Catherine, and even occasionally at Fitzwilliam and himself, he might have thought so himself.

"I do not suppose we may convince Lady Catherine it is for the best that they return to Rosings?"

There was no hope in Fitzwilliam's tone, so Darcy did not need to dash what did not exist. "Aunt Catherine considers herself fixed here, as much for the chance that I will notice Anne with her being before me as her stated desire to come to know Miss Elizabeth better."

A sour grunt was Fitzwilliam's response. Darcy felt no need to answer, choosing to stand in silence and watch Wickham. The danger that always lurked in the background whenever Wickham was present reared its dark and menacing head again, and Darcy resolved he would take care to watch him closely. He had become too complacent.

Elizabeth had always been secure in the knowledge of her mother's love. She had also long known her mother to be a woman of less than remarkable intelligence, but with a sensible, pragmatic outlook on life, a woman who was an excellent hostess and mistress of her husband's estate. Jane's engagement, however, taught Elizabeth that there was another side of her mother.

This creature, who, a voice brimming with excitement, spoke of lace and flowers, of weddings breakfast foods and guest lists with the fervor of a girl attending her first ball, was beyond Elizabeth's previous understanding of her mother. It seemed that Mrs. Bennet was intent upon celebrating the marriage of her daughter with the finest fete Meryton had ever seen. The energy with which she talked and planned and schemed was breathtaking in its breadth; Elizabeth soon became fatigued just watching. And they still had not even set a wedding date!

That Jane, rather than Elizabeth herself, was the center of her mother's planning was a blessing. Then again, with Mr. Darcy paying court to her in an ever more ardent fashion, Elizabeth knew she would be the center of her mother's attention before long. The mere notion of her mother turning her attention on Elizabeth in such a manner filled Elizabeth with the urge to shudder. At that point, Gretna would become a preferred option.

Mr. Darcy had an interesting bit of advice for Elizabeth. "Perhaps it is best to allow your mother her excitement. Your sister is, after all, the first of her daughters to marry. That must be a matter of great pride and anticipation."

With a sense of bemusement, Elizabeth regarded the gentleman. "How do you know what my mother is thinking?"

"I do not, Miss Elizabeth," said Mr. Darcy, catching the humor in her voice. "It seems best to me to attempt to think about it from her perspective; when one does that, it becomes obvious."

"You are a wonderful man, Fitzwilliam Darcy," said Elizabeth. "Yes, I understood this, but your words have made it more real to me."

Subsequent to that conversation, Elizabeth found she could bear her mother's excitement better, though she still allowed Jane to take the brunt of her attention. If her conscience whispered to her, Elizabeth quieted it, reflecting it would be her turn soon enough.

Those days in company, Elizabeth spent most of her time in Mr. Darcy's presence, the gentleman's regard no longer hidden to any but the most obtuse observer. As they already knew each other well, Elizabeth felt they were forging the final bonds of understanding, knowing it would not be much longer before the gentleman proposed. What Elizabeth had not expected was the gentleman's distraction, which would often manifest itself when they were in the regiment's company. It took no greatness of mind to know what had caught his attention.

"Is there aught amiss with Mr. Wickham?" asked Elizabeth, one night at a party at one of the houses of the neighborhood. "It was my understanding that his behavior has been better since he came under your cousin's command."

A sense of disquiet fell over her as she regarded Mr. Darcy, and the man said: "No, you are correct there, Miss Elizabeth. Fitzwilliam informs me Wickham has accumulated no debts, has trifled with no ladies, and has given him no reason for reprimand."

"And yet you watch him as if he were an asp coiled to strike."

The slight upturn of Mr. Darcy's lips presaged a hint of a lightening mood. "I know Wickham too well to trust him after a month of good behavior. While he has given me no reason to complain, I dislike his proximity to Georgiana, and I have noted his recent attention on Anne."

"Yes, he does seem to speak to her more than any lady other than Miss Bingley," said Elizabeth, her eyes finding Mr. Wickham. At that moment, he was speaking with Miss de Bourgh, though the woman walked away soon after. Elizabeth's eyes found Mr. Darcy again, and she said: "But Georgiana? As far as I can determine, he has not said two words to her all evening."

For a moment, Mr. Darcy regarded her, his manner absent, pensive. "That is one part of the tale of my family's troubles with Mr. Wickham that I have not shared with you."

Mr. Darcy glanced about, his eyes searching, perhaps attempting to determine if anyone was close enough to overhear. When he had assured himself of their privacy, his eyes once again sought

Elizabeth's.

"I apologize for leaving this out before, Miss Elizabeth—it is a tale of the most sensitive nature."

"If so," hastened Elizabeth to say, "you need not feel compelled to share it with me. I understand and believe your warning of Mr. Wickham—there is nothing more I need to know."

"I thank you for your faith, Miss Elizabeth, but Georgiana herself has suggested I relate this to you. By hearing of it, you will understand my disquiet."

The tale which followed disgusted Elizabeth, for Mr. Darcy spoke of betrayal of the worst kind, of a young man favored above any proper expectation, who attempted to steal that which did not belong to him to the detriment of a young woman of whom Elizabeth thought highly. The feelings of the gentleman by her side, Elizabeth understood at once, as did she comprehend part of the reason he was as reticent as he was. For Georgiana, she felt nothing but compassion, for Mr. Wickham nothing but contempt. When Mr. Darcy's words trailed off, she put her hand on his arm and give him a look which she thought expressed all the feelings she could not in front of the rest of the company.

"You have suffered, Mr. Darcy, and your dear sister has had her share in it. Your wariness for that despicable man is justified."

"Thank you, Miss Elizabeth."

"I shall keep watch with you, Mr. Darcy—we shall not allow him to hurt your cousin too. Now, if you will excuse me, I should like to speak to your sister."

With a bow, Mr. Darcy released her from his company; Elizabeth thought he might kiss her if he had the chance. As Elizabeth was crossing the room, intent upon joining Georgiana, she happened to pass near Mr. Wickham and catch his eyes. Though she had not intended to, the thought of what this man had tried to do rose in her mind, and she fixed him with a fierce scowl, such as shocked him. For the rest of the evening, Elizabeth felt his eyes on her. But she ignored him. Mr. Wickham was not worth the mud on her shoes.

Observant as she was, Anne de Bourgh noted the sudden coldness Miss Elizabeth displayed toward Mr. Wickham; or the greater coldness, for she had never looked on him with favor. Had Anne been at liberty to consider her friend's behavior, she might have wondered what had provoked it.

As it was, however, Anne had little time to spare for such

considerations. Though Mr. Wickham considered himself a charmer, Anne found the man so practiced as to be false. He betrayed an amusing conceit which diverted Anne for some time; soon, however, that grew tiresome too, and other concerns asserted themselves. Chief among these was her mother's growing dissatisfaction.

"I cannot understand what he sees in her," said Lady Catherine later the same night. "Miss Elizabeth Bennet is nothing special, and yet he treats her as if she were the first among women."

"Oh?" asked Anne, eager to provoke her mother to say more. "Why do you say that?"

Lady Catherine could not reply so she waved her hand, an ineffectual attempt to disapprove of what she was seeing, though she suspected her mother could not state with any coherence of what she disapproved. Anne, sensing the time was at hand, was not about to allow her to escape with so weak a demurral.

"Whether or not Miss Elizabeth is exceptional," said Anne, pulling her mother's eyes to her, "I cannot say. To Darcy, however, she is the most important woman in the world—anyone can see that. Or she will be as soon as he throws caution to the wind and proposes."

Lady Catherine scowled and muttered: "My task would have been far easier had you shown even a hint of interest in him."

"No one could accuse you of being mistaken," replied Anne. "If I had done so, I would have been lying to myself and you, Mother, and that I did not wish to do."

"I cannot imagine what you feel is lacking," said her mother, her tone exasperated. "Is your cousin not an exemplary man? Is he not well-favored? Can you not see that Pemberley is a jewel which, when united with Rosings, would make your situation the envy of many? What shall you do now for a husband?"

"Let me answer your questions in order, Mother," said Anne. "No, there is nothing wrong with Darcy or his situation. To the right woman—a woman who is standing with his sister at this very moment—Darcy would be an irresistible temptation. As for Pemberley and Rosings, Darcy has no interest in joining the estates, and I have no more interest than he.

"Now, Mother," continued Anne, fixing her mother with such a look that she had no choice but to respond, "shall we discuss this further? I think there is something more to this than the desire to join Pemberley and Rosings."

"My sister and I dreamed of uniting our children," said Lady Catherine.

"Perhaps you did, Mother," said Anne, "but you and I both know my aunt must have meant it in idle speculation, for she did nothing to formalize your agreement."

Lady Catherine glared, but she said nothing, proving Anne's supposition. Having put that to the side, Anne continued, saying: "I know you are not covetous, Mother, so it cannot be a desire for Pemberley. That leaves me as the motivation for your insistence."

"You understand better than I might have expected," said Lady Catherine after a moment's pause. "I told Darcy that very thing only a few days ago. Now that he is to make an imprudent marriage and remove the protection you have enjoyed all these years, we shall be inundated with every rake and fortune hunter within a month."

"Oh, Mother!" exclaimed Anne. "Am I not capable of fending off fortune hunters? Do you suspect me of wishing to run off with Mr. Wickham whenever he flashes his white teeth in a charming smile? Do you take me for a witless girl?"

At least Lady Catherine had the grace to appear ashamed, though her words did not reflect it. "Are you capable?" demanded she. "Do you possess the strength to fend off men who are much greater danger than the likes of Mr. Wickham?"

"I am not robust, Mother," said Anne. "This I know. But I am not witless. I have more than a little fluff in my head. Should all the rakes in London appear on our doorstep, I shall not fall prey to them. And I should think Darcy and Fitzwilliam, not to mention the earl and the viscount, would have something to say should they think a man was importuning me against my wishes."

"That may be, but I am still your mother," insisted Lady Catherine. "It is my duty to concern myself for my only daughter."

"Perhaps it is. The die has been cast; there is nothing you can do to change it. After a time, you will see that I am competent. I shall not walk for miles every day like Elizabeth does — but I am not so weak as you think.

"There was no passion between us, Mother," said Anne, catching her mother's hand and holding it, allowing her emotion to run free. "Even though you married my father for reasons other than genuine affection, I know you were fond of him."

"Your father and I got on very well," said Lady Catherine; Anne knew this was as close as she would approach to owning to loving her husband.

"And I wish for the same. Darcy and I are too much alike. I require a man more like Anthony for a husband."

"Do not suggest such a thing!" said Lady Catherine, though a smile arched her lips ever so slightly. "Anthony is far too unserious for his own good."

"Anthony is not for me," replied Anne, grinning at her mother. "I only said I require a livelier husband. Darcy is too staid, too reserved for us to do well together, though I know he would have treated me well. Allow Darcy to have his young lady and allow me to find someone of my own. We shall both be happier if you do."

No further words passed between them. A night of watching her mother, however, informed Anne that she was considering what she had heard, and not focused on her disappointment. Though neither spoke anything further on the subject, by the end of the evening, Anne knew the dream her mother had harbored all these years was dead and buried. It was about time.

CHAPTER XXIV

*I*mmature girls, not yet out in society, often clamor to attend events, and their pleas grow louder when those events offer the promise of an evening spent dancing. This truism could not be doubted, for Elizabeth remembered an element of it in her own behavior before she had come out. It is more prevalent, however, in younger sisters, those obliged to watch as their elder sisters partake in the enjoyment of their status, while the younger must wait their turn.

While Elizabeth loved Kitty and Lydia, it was often a trial to endure their complaining, Lydia more so than Kitty, for she was the leader in their protests and the louder in making their case. As their father had permitted them to attend the ball at Netherfield, this had set a precedent in their minds, a perceived precedent they were not hesitant to exploit. Whether such tactics found success in other families — whether they would succeed in their present objective — was something Elizabeth could not predict. Their mother was not insensible to their plight and their father was not a disciplinarian; but the fact remained that in Elizabeth's mind, they were not ready for society — Lydia in particular.

"We attended Mr. Bingley's ball," said Lydia that morning in a voice more grating the more she spoke. "Why you should prevent us from attending an assembly, a mere trifle in comparison, is beyond my understanding."

"There are many things beyond your understanding," said Mr. Bennet. He had joined them that morning in the sitting-room, his nose buried in his newspaper, though Elizabeth did not think he missed anything going on around him. "Just because you may not understand them, there are valid reasons you should not attend."

"I would understand them if you would explain," said Lydia, perhaps not the best way to make her case.

Mr. Bennet pushed his newspaper to the side and regarded his youngest, a suppressed smile causing his lips to twitch. "Have we not made the reasons clear many times? Lydia, you are still but fifteen years of age and not ready to take on all the society you wish. Age and experience will inform you of the truth of this, though you do not wish to accept it now."

"If anyone should be angry at being excluded," said Mrs. Bennet, regarding her youngest, a hint of displeasure hovering about her, "it is Kitty; she is two years your elder if you will recall."

"That is not fair!" exclaimed Lydia.

"Though you may not see it, there is nothing unfair about it," replied her mother. "Kitty is two years closer to being out than you are, Lydia, and you had best remember it."

When Lydia opened her mouth to protest further, Mr. Bennet interjected, saying: "It may be to your benefit if you refrained from saying whatever has crossed your mind. Your sisters all came out at eighteen but there is no rule which requires it; if we decide you are not yet ready, you may be nineteen before you make your official debut."

Laughter bubbled up in Elizabeth's breast at the sight of Lydia's mouth closing with haste. The girl's lips formed up in the rictus of a pout informed Elizabeth of her unhappiness, but she did not push the point, which was just as well. Kitty, by contrast, did not protest, though Elizabeth knew she wished to go as much as Lydia.

"For my part, Papa, I am eager to attend, but I shall wait until my turn comes."

Lydia's head whipped around toward her sister, the glare displaying her feelings of betrayal. Prevented from a sharp retort by her father clearing his voice, Lydia subsided, throwing herself back against the cushions on the couch with a childish pout, proving her continued immaturity. Mr. Bennet did not deign to give the girl any of his attention, instead focusing his approval on Kitty.

"That turn will come soon, Kitty," said Mr. Bennet. "Not only will you turn eighteen next year, but your eldest sister is to marry—and your second eldest, unless I miss my guess."

Kitty smiled and nodded, her countenance suffused with pleasure, a sharp contrast to Lydia's continued pouting. Nodding at his second youngest, Mr. Bennet turned a look on her sister, his expression pointed.

"As for you, Lydia, I do not wish to hear more of your silliness. Part of growing into a young lady who is a credit to her family is showing your mother you can understand what society expects of you.

"Next year you shall be sixteen years of age. At that time, you will find your participation in certain events increasing. You will not be out until you are eighteen, and perhaps not then if you cannot show yourself worthy of being in society. Remember how it was for each of your sisters—so will it be for you."

With a sulky nod from Lydia, they dropped the conversation in favor of other matters. Elizabeth, grateful as she was that her parents were taking a firm hand with their youngest daughter, could not have approved more. Lydia, she knew, was not a stupid girl. She would learn to behave, and if she proved difficult, she would learn through being obliged to stay home when she would otherwise be out.

Later that morning, Elizabeth was out on the estate, walking to enjoy the fine autumn day, the dry paths of the estate and the light breeze, bringing the delightful scents of the ongoing harvest. The month of September had passed and with it, the season had begun waning toward winter in earnest, though fine days were still in abundance.

It was with surprise and pleasure that she met Mr. Darcy on her walk, his tall steed appearing around a bend in the road, the clopping of the hooves announcing his coming. With a skip in her step, Elizabeth approached the gentleman, greeted him, and then with great relish, she related the events of the morning, injecting some anecdotes about the time before her own coming out, providing him much amusement. At length, when her recital drew to a close, Mr. Darcy turned to her and favored her with a knowing smile.

"The next time I see him, I must thank your father. Georgiana, as you might imagine, has been eager to attend. As I now know your sisters will remain at home, I can inform my sister she will also not attend and not leave her feeling ill-used."

Elizabeth laughed and fixed the gentleman with a mock glare. "It seems to me your sister was hiding her true self when she first arrived in Hertfordshire. Why, she is becoming more like Lydia every passing day!"

"Please, do not say such things!" was Mr. Darcy's dramatic reply. "I do not believe I could handle such a spirited young lady as Miss Lydia."

They laughed together and Elizabeth, an idea coming to her, suggested: "Perhaps Georgiana could stay at Longbourn that night while we are all at the assembly? That would help them all feel better about being excluded."

Mr. Darcy cocked his head to the side, regarding her with an air of thoughtful interest. "Miss Elizabeth, someday you will be an excellent mother, for you seem to understand how best to handle children."

It was an audacious statement, and Elizabeth felt her cheeks heating at the inference behind his comment. For once in her life, she felt at a loss for words, no clever rejoinder entering her mind to throw back at him to hide her embarrassment. In desperation, she blurted:

"Lydia and Georgiana are hardly children; they are on the cusp of being young ladies!"

The smile with which Mr. Darcy regarded her came easily to his lips. "No, but I suspect your facility with a child of three will be as great as with a girl entering society."

"Oh, and do you suppose I shall raise my own children?" asked Elizabeth, finding a hint of poise in his continued praise. "If I marry right, I might have the ability to leave them with nurses and governesses, bring them out to show off to society and ignore them at all other times."

The snort with which Mr. Darcy responded spoke without the possibility of error what he thought of her rejoinder. "If that be the case, then I do not know you as well as I thought. I cannot see you leaving the care of your children to another. You will be a loving mother, active in your children's daily concerns, nurturing, guiding, and adoring them far more than they could ever possibly deserve."

"And what sort of father will you be?" asked Elizabeth, turning the tables back on him. "Is it your intention to relegate your children to the nursery until duty calls them to your presence and that of your guests?"

"Nothing of the sort," replied Mr. Darcy, not daunted in the slightest. "Of my most cherished memories were those of riding with my father, learning of the estate business from him. Though my father was not a warm man by any measurement, it was during those times I felt closest to him. I wish to be more of a father than my own was, to guide my children to adulthood, to carry on my family's legacy in the manner of which I would be proud."

Moved, Elizabeth managed a smile, saying: "Then we are much alike, Mr. Darcy. I have always felt my mother's love, have always known my father cared for me, though he did not always know how to say it. I wish to pass that on to my children."

Both so moved by their conversation, they said little after that, content in the feeling of rightness which existed between them. When they parted not long after, Elizabeth farewelled him, content knowing that the proposal she now wished to receive as soon as may be would be forthcoming before long.

Monotony was Fitzwilliam's familiar friend those days, for there was not much of interest to find in the management of a company of militia. As an active man, Fitzwilliam could not understand how men like Colonel Forster endured it, for there was little of interest to be done, days stuck behind a desk. Fitzwilliam did not even have much to do with the training of the men, for his officers handled most of those tasks. Because of this, Fitzwilliam had learned to appreciate those times when local society allowed him to leave his cares behind. The militia was a different animal from the regulars — this he had known. But he had not known how different it would be.

The typical militia officer completed his duties as soon as may be, so he could focus on the more pleasant parts of his position. While this did not rise to the level which required official reprimands, the perfectionist in Fitzwilliam rebelled at the thought of work completed without attention to detail. It was like commanding a group of young women, intent upon gossip, feminine fripperies, and the time and location of the next assembly.

As the days lengthened to weeks, which became months, Fitzwilliam began to realize there was something missing in his life, something which he could not fill by returning to active duty in his former regiment. His arm was much stronger by now, the weakness surrendering to health and strength, and with it, the knowledge that he could set this unfamiliar task aside and move back into the familiar. The fact was Fitzwilliam did not know what he wanted.

Had he not had a certain libertine to watch, Fitzwilliam thought he might become distracted by his thoughts. As it was, he had little trust for Wickham and every incentive to keep the man in line, and Fitzwilliam did not shirk his self-appointed task to make something of him.

"I see Wickham continues to bestow his charm on Miss Bingley," said Darcy one day while they were attending a dinner in the neighborhood.

"Aye, he does at that," replied Fitzwilliam. "Bingley has warned his sister and watches Wickham as much as we do—I do not think she is in any danger. Anne is of far greater concern."

Darcy directed a sidelong glance at Fitzwilliam. "Do you suspect him more than the last time we spoke?"

"Do you not see how he is drawn to her?" Fitzwilliam snorted. "If it were not for his need to keep up appearances—to distract us—I doubt he would pay the slightest attention to your friend's excellent sister."

The sardonic quality in Fitzwilliam's voice prompted a snort from Darcy. Fitzwilliam knew Darcy tolerated the woman better because her insistence in putting herself forward to him as an excellent match had waned the closer he had become to Miss Elizabeth. Now Miss Bingley appeared to be aiming toward friendships with Anne and Georgiana, likely to improve her social position. It would not do to accuse the woman of having nothing else in mind than her own benefit in society; Fitzwilliam, however, was certain it was at least part of her thinking.

"I have not missed it," was Darcy's brief reply. "Wickham is careful to avoid showing Anne any preference while we are present, yet he is always nearby, always with a word or two, a compliment here and a jest there."

"What do you think of Anne's response to him?"

"It is difficult to say," said Darcy, his shoulders rising in a helpless shrug. "Anne declares that she will not allow him to tempt her into anything. You and I both know, however, that her exposure to society has been limited. She has never had to contend with a man of Wickham's ilk, so she cannot know what he is about."

"I suppose I must speak with him then," said Fitzwilliam.

At Darcy's look, Fitzwilliam nodded. "It would be better coming from me, for I am his commanding officer."

Darcy nodded and they dropped the subject. A few moments later, Darcy drifted away to put himself in the orbit of the lady who had captured his imagination. Genuinely pleased for his cousin, Fitzwilliam took himself to the side of the woman who interested him.

The confrontation with Wickham was of an urgent nature, Fitzwilliam decided, so he arranged to have it the following day. Wickham, though a man who had always been ruled by his lusts, was intelligent enough, and understood at once why Fitzwilliam wished to speak to him. It was fortunate for Fitzwilliam's temper that he contented himself with a knowing look and a smirk, allowing Fitzwilliam to raise the subject between them.

"You have been busy of late, Wickham. Every time we are in company, I can find you by the side of two ladies in particular."

Wickham shrugged. "Though I have no notion whom you mean by the second, I have noted a distinct thawing in Miss Bingley's manners of late. It is my hope she is receptive to my overtures, for I find her an intriguing woman."

"You mean you find her money intriguing," replied Fitzwilliam with a snort.

Having the temerity to laugh, Wickham replied: "Yes, well, that is part of her appeal. Perhaps you and Darcy might be less fastidious when you consider the financial prospects of your intended brides but those of us who do not possess your means must weigh that aspect with the other facets of a woman."

Though annoyed Wickham had dragged him into a different discussion, Fitzwilliam felt compelled to say: "If you think me a wealthy man, you are mistaken."

Shrugging, as if to show his lack of interest, Wickham fell silent, though his knowing look never abated. As it always did whenever he spoke to Wickham, Fitzwilliam's ire rose, though he tamped down on it with ruthless intent.

"Miss Bingley may take care of herself. As I informed you before, I doubt you have any chance of gaining her favor."

"She now understands Darcy is not an option. If she cannot have him, why not me?"

"I can think of several reasons," rejoined Fitzwilliam. "But I do not wish to discuss such things. Of greater concern is the second young lady to whom I referred. You do not suppose Darcy and I to be witless, do you? We have marked the interest you have shown in Anne, though you have attempted to hide it from us."

"Do you accuse me of misbehavior?" asked Wickham, though he appeared amused rather than offended. "I have done nothing wrong."

"No, your behavior has been acceptable, at least. There is little trust in me for you, but I will own I have had little cause to reprimand you."

"Then I would ask you to leave well enough alone." Wickham grinned at Fitzwilliam's level look and added: "Your protectiveness for your cousin is not hidden, Colonel. Why you would think I would risk what might befall me should I entertain such ideas is beyond my comprehension."

"As long as you understand we will not allow you to make off with Anne. If there is any such shade of an idea in your head, I suggest you dispatch it at once. Stick to Miss Bingley and woo her if you can, but remember: we will protect her as much as we will Anne. And Georgiana, for that matter."

The reference to Georgiana was deliberate, for Fitzwilliam wished to see if he could provoke a reaction. There was nothing he could see, for Wickham ignored the reference in favor of nodding and requesting permission to withdraw. Knowing he had done all he could at present to prevent Wickham from digging his own grave, Fitzwilliam allowed him to depart.

For some time after, he sat and thought on the matter; however much he considered it, Fitzwilliam could come to no resolutions. There was little denying that Wickham had focused on Miss Bingley at the very least, but whether he meant to get what he wished in the manner he had always attempted before, Fitzwilliam could not say. While examples of his integrity had been so rare as to be nonexistent, this time he was under the watchful eyes of two who could have a great deal to say concerning his future. That might make all the difference.

A few days later, Fitzwilliam reported his conversation with Wickham to Darcy. Sitting as they were in Bingley's library, which had become something of a study, where he attended to his correspondence and did what work there was for him to do, Darcy leaned back with a glass of Bingley's port; a similar glass was clutched in Fitzwilliam's hand. The discussion had proceeded as he might have predicted. There was something glib about Wickham's manner; then again there always was, for Wickham had a habit of minimizing such things whenever it suited his purpose.

"Then I suppose we must continue to watch him," said Darcy. "You have warned him as you can—the rest is his responsibility."

"Umm . . ." said Fitzwilliam, his mind not on the matter any longer

Darcy looked at his cousin, noting the slight frown on his face, the manner in which he swirled the liquid in his glass around, seeming to have no intention of tasting it. Fitzwilliam, Darcy had noted, had become far more thoughtful of late, almost pensive. Not that he was not introspective on occasion, for he was among the most intelligent men of Darcy's acquaintance. But he was not given to such reflexion as a rule.

"What would you say, Darcy," said Fitzwilliam, breaking the silence a few moments later, "if I were to tell you how tired I have become of living this life?"

"It would depend," said Darcy, choosing his words with care. "Is it the command of a militia company that is too tame for your tastes, or have you grown tired of the life of a military man?"

"Both and neither?"

Fitzwilliam laughed at his incomprehensible statement. "It has occurred to me that it is nothing more than the former, for the militia is different from the regulars, as I have told you many times. The more I think on it, however, the more I am convinced that matters have changed — that I have changed."

"Since I am not certain you know yourself what has brought on these feelings," said Darcy, "I will content myself to ask you if you are considering making a change because of them."

"Considering it? Yes, to a great degree."

"To the point of resigning your commission?"

Fitzwilliam turned and looked at Darcy. "Yes, even as far as that. Those who have never been in battle cannot understand, but there is a certain . . . exhilaration to a pitched battle. It is, perhaps, ironic that a man never feels so alive as he does when, at any moment, some enemy might end it.

"The thought of returning to that, however, has become distasteful, for everyone runs out of luck at some time or another. Would my turn come if I returned to battle? I cannot say. The thought of giving fate another chance is becoming less appealing by the day."

Lifting his left arm, Fitzwilliam clenched his fist, flexing it, showing no signs of his previous injury. "My arm has healed well and gives me little trouble now. I have been sending regular reports of my status, so my general knows my situation. The regiment has now received its orders and will depart for the peninsula in the New Year. If I wish it, I can be part of that deployment."

"And do you wish it?" asked Darcy.

"You know, I have always thought living quietly on an estate would be a tedious prospect." Fitzwilliam laughed at his own non sequitur. "Sometimes I have disdained those who live quiet lives. Such boredom has always seemed to be a terrible existence, a half-life, destined to do little, stagnate and die, accomplishing nothing.

"Now I begin to wonder if a little boredom would not be the best thing for me."

Diverted by his cousin's manner, Darcy pressed him: "I never thought I would hear the great Anthony Fitzwilliam, the man who could never stay in one place, say such a thing."

Fitzwilliam flashed him a grin. "Yes, well, I never looked down on you, for I saw the work you did at Pemberley, the part you played in the lives of people who struggle for something better. But many of our set are not men such as you, and to be honest, I despise most of them.

"Bingley is a good sort. He does not yet know everything, but he is eager and determined and he does not make the same mistake twice. Watching him, watching the other gentlemen of the neighborhood, I have concluded that there are other ways to be just as great as a general who leads his army to a glorious victory over a deadly foe."

"There are many kinds of valor," replied Darcy. "I shall not scruple to suggest you are incorrect about many of our set; you know my thoughts of them. Though men who fight and risk their lives to protect us all are to be revered, there is equal dignity in working one's land, in assisting others and ensuring their lives are as comfortable as they can be. There is also great value in finding a woman to love, in siring the next generation of children and teaching them to be responsible adults. It is they who are the future."

"Yes, you are correct."

"I know you have given it little thought, but perhaps it is time you begin the process of finding a woman of your own. You have an estate, one which will support you, a wife, and can look forward to any children you might have."

Fitzwilliam laughed and turned a teasing look on Darcy. "Speaking of boredom, with Miss Elizabeth by your side, I doubt you will ever have cause to be wearied unless it is because you must keep up with her."

"And I would have it no other way," replied Darcy. "Given the trajectory of this conversation, I suspect the time has arrived for you to find your own woman to keep you on your toes."

With a shake of his head, Fitzwilliam drained his glass and looked at Darcy. "I do not believe a spirited woman such as Miss Elizabeth is for me. In fact, I believe I might prefer a calmer woman, one more practical, for I am lively enough for us both."

Standing, he added: "Thank you, Darcy, not only for Bingley's excellent port, but also for allowing me my maudlin thoughts. I will bid you a good day, for I should return to camp."

"Then Godspeed, Cousin," murmured Darcy as Fitzwilliam left the room.

At the end of their discussion, Fitzwilliam had seemed like the cousin Darcy had known so long. That introspective man he had been recently was a mystery to Darcy. There was something in his statement about the kind of woman that would suit him which had pricked Darcy's interest, but for the life of him, he could not decide what it was.

The more important matter was that the family had been urging him to give up his commission for some time now, and Fitzwilliam had always laughed off their arguments. It seemed he was now open to the possibility, a matter of much gratitude for Darcy, for the concerns he had expressed about his cousin returning to battle were those espoused by all his family.

CHAPTER XXV

*P*reparations for four ladies were more easily managed than six. This was made further evident because one of the ladies preparing for the evening was not Miss Lydia Bennet. Lydia, though not vain to a large degree, was instead indecisive and had been known to ask her sisters for their opinions on her attire many times while preparing for an evening.

Displeased as she was to be excluded from the evening, Lydia had not deigned to descend to see them off, though Elizabeth thought she would not miss the actual moment when the carriage departed; the girl would look down on them with envy and spite, railing at her misfortune much as she had since her father had informed her of his decision that she should not attend. Kitty, of a more governable character, was on hand, exchanging a few quiet words with each of her sisters, perhaps wishing she would attend, but accepting nonetheless.

"You are a good girl, Kitty," said Mrs. Bennet on more than one occasion. "As your father promised, your time will come soon."

"It is no trouble, Mama," said Kitty, showing a brave face to her mother. "I shall be ready when my time comes."

Had Lydia been present, she no doubt would have abused Kitty for her betrayal. As it was, Elizabeth thought Kitty was being the more intelligent of the two, for Lydia did not understand that the more she fought the restrictions, the longer it would be before her parents lifted them. That Kitty seemed to realize it was an understanding Elizabeth would not have expected of her sister. Kitty had always been a follower and as Lydia possessed the more forceful personality, she had drawn Kitty along with her. Of late, she had been emerging from the shadow of her more energetic sister, and while she would never be such a person herself, coming into her own was no small step.

Soon the preparations were complete, and the Bennet ladies entered the carriage for the quick journey to Meryton's assembly hall. Kitty and Mr. Bennet walked out to see them off, he, being eager to dispense with the night in company for the more agreeable company—in his mind—of his beloved books. As the carriage jolted with the impact of the horses against the traces, Elizabeth saw Mr. Bennet escorting his second youngest back into the house and knew her sister would sit with her father for a time in his bookroom. Some of Elizabeth's happiest memories were of that room, the sound of her father's strong voice reading beloved passages to her while she sat on his knee. Georgiana Darcy was also to arrive with her companion to stay the night. Kitty would welcome the girl's arrival, as would Lydia, though Lydia's complaints would not cease. Elizabeth might have thought Georgiana would come before they departed, but word had come from Netherfield concerning a delay of some sort. As a result, she would arrive within half an hour but after their departure.

And there, in the window above the drive, Elizabeth caught sight of Lydia's glaring countenance in the window as expected. She soon disappeared, the curtains falling into the place where she had been. With a sigh of regret, Elizabeth turned her mind back to the amusement of the evening, leaving thoughts of childish girls and books at home where they belonged.

As they rode, the sisters listened to their mother's merry chatter, for Mrs. Bennet's tongue had been loosened these last days since her eldest daughter's engagement. On this occasion, Mrs. Bennet did not require much of a response, which was well, for Elizabeth preferred to think on the evening ahead, and the delights in which she would partake.

As they alighted from the carriage upon arriving, Elizabeth found her elbow grasped by her mother, who, as they were walking in, said: "Your young man appears to be as ardent as Jane's, Lizzy, though he does not show it as openly. Do you think he will propose soon?"

Feeling an unaccountable shyness fall over her, it was a moment before she could respond. "I believe he might, Mama. When I met him on a walk a few days ago, we spoke of our wishes for the future, and what we each thought about rearing children."

It was clear Elizabeth's report delighted her mother, for she said: "Mr. Darcy is an excellent man—I am sure you will find your happiness with him. If he should propose, you must suggest to him that Miss Darcy stay with us while you are on your wedding trip. She is such a dear girl; we would love to have her."

"When the time comes, I shall be certain to suggest it, Mama," replied Elizabeth. "Georgiana would appreciate the chance to stay with Kitty and Lydia, and with Jane and I gone, you would not lack for room."

Mrs. Bennet regarded Elizabeth with a gaze full of sentimentality, of happiness mixed with sadness. "Do not remind me, for the thrill of seeing a child well settled is always offset by the loss of her in the home. You and Jane will be very much missed."

"But you shall have Mary, Kitty, and Lydia for some time yet."

"That I shall. Then they shall leave me, and I shall be alone with your father."

Elizabeth smiled and touched her mother's hand. "Then you shall have grandchildren to anticipate, and I have no doubt you will spoil them to their mothers' frustration."

"If one of you settles close, I shall be well pleased."

"You may always travel, Mama," replied Elizabeth. "Think of the fun you will have visiting the homes of your five daughters in succession."

Mrs. Bennet laughed and nodded. "That is a wonderful prospect, Lizzy. I think I shall hold you to it."

As they gained the inside of the hall, Elizabeth parted from her mother, allowing Mrs. Bennet to seek her friends while Elizabeth searched for hers. The Bennets were punctual, often arriving fifteen minutes or more before the festivities began. There were few in attendance yet, though Elizabeth had the good fortune of spying Charlotte as soon as she entered the room.

"Lizzy!" exclaimed Charlotte upon seeing her. "I see you do not bring your youngest sisters with you tonight."

"Much to Lydia's chagrin," replied, Elizabeth, rolling her eyes. "It is fortunate my father and mother are united, for I cannot imagine the havoc that girl would create if left to her own devices."

"Maria too," said Charlotte. "She is finding it hard to be excluded now as she is coming so close to her own coming out."

They stood together for some minutes speaking about matters of little consequence. Having known Charlotte for as long as she had, Elizabeth could sense something a little . . . different in Charlotte's manner that evening. It was difficult to know what it was, for outwardly Charlotte was the same interesting woman she had ever been. There was a sense of anticipation about her that evening, though Elizabeth could not say why that might be.

When the Netherfield party arrived, Elizabeth's first sight was of Mr. Darcy, as he, tall and handsome, towered over the rest of the company except Mr. Bingley, who had left the others as soon as he noticed Jane standing some distance away. Though Mr. Darcy made his way toward Elizabeth, he was not the only one, as Lady Catherine and Miss de Bourgh accompanied him as he approached.

"Miss Elizabeth," said Mr. Darcy with a bow over her hand. "You are enchanting tonight."

"I must wonder at the effect you have on my cousin, Miss Elizabeth," said Miss de Bourgh, fixing Mr. Darcy with a mischievous glance. "I had not known Darcy could charm with such ease. If I had, I might have reconsidered my decision to never marry him."

Though Elizabeth laughed and Mr. Darcy grinned, Lady Catherine huffed in annoyance, as she often did when they raised the subject of her ill-fated wish for them to marry. Although Elizabeth might have expected her to say something more of the matter, she pushed it from her mind and addressed Elizabeth.

"Miss Elizabeth. For different reasons, I will echo my nephew's words. It appears I will not need to work as hard to bring you up to the standards required by my family."

Many might have taken Lady Catherine's words as an insult, but Elizabeth knew the lady by now, knew she did not mean her words as an affront. Mr. Darcy shook his head, while Miss de Bourgh turned a laughing smile on Elizabeth, the sight of which was almost her undoing. Knowing Lady Catherine would not allow her to escape without making a reply, Elizabeth thanked her, stating her confidence she would do very well in London.

"Yes, well, we shall see. Now, may I ask if your mother is present?"

Still amused, Elizabeth motioned to where her mother stood with some of the other ladies, after which Lady Catherine excused herself. Elizabeth had little hope the lady would find the company acceptable, but she would find more comfort there than with the younger members of the party who would dance before long.

"Is Aunt Catherine making her usual coterie of friends?" asked

Colonel Fitzwilliam as he strode up to them.

"Worse," replied Miss de Bourgh. "Were Elizabeth not so good-humored, she might have created undying enmity between them."

They all laughed at her sally. "Ah, well, no offense, Anne, but your mother has never gone five minutes in any gathering without causing some affront. Now, as Darcy will have Miss Elizabeth's hand for the first sets, I believe I shall ask for yours for those same dances."

Miss de Bourgh tutted and waved a finger. "If Mother were here, she would accuse you of conspiring to get Rosings for yourself."

"Perhaps I am," replied Colonel Fitzwilliam with a wink. "But I shall never own to it."

After securing Anne's acceptance, Colonel Fitzwilliam turned away and approached Charlotte, who was standing a little away speaking to another lady of the neighborhood. With interest, Elizabeth watched as the colonel joined them and was soon immersed in conversation with her, the other lady excusing herself thereafter. It appeared her companions did not miss their cousin's actions any more than Elizabeth did.

"Is it my imagination," said Miss de Bourgh, "or is Anthony paying more attention to that young lady than I have ever seen before?"

"Yes and no," replied Darcy, as interested as his cousin. "You have not seen him in company much—he can ooze charm when he puts his mind to it. In this instance, it seems to me he is paying her more serious attentions than I have ever seen, for his conversation is earnest rather than playful."

"Well, well," said Miss de Bourgh, "perhaps I was too hasty in accusing him of having his eye on Rosings."

It seemed to Elizabeth that Mr. Darcy was eager to keep Miss de Bourgh by his side. That this protective attitude coincided with the arrival of the militia was much as she might have expected. Mr. Wickham was among them, resplendent in his pressed scarlet coat, his deep blue eyes flashing in his alluring manner whenever they met the eyes of a woman. There were more than a few who sighed in his wake, their hearts set aflutter by his manners and his handsome countenance. Mr. Wickham did not come near to where Elizabeth stood with Mr. Darcy and Miss de Bourgh, his destination none other than Caroline Bingley, as was his wont.

"I wonder if Mr. Wickham shall ask me to dance tonight," said Miss de Bourgh, her manner studied in nonchalance, her words designed to pull a response from Mr. Darcy.

"Of course, you may dance with him if you wish," replied Mr.

Darcy, refusing to rise to the bait. "As I recall, he is not deficient in the activity."

"Unlike the absent and unlamented Mr. Collins," said Elizabeth, pulling a chortle from Mr. Darcy.

Miss de Bourgh, not having attended the ball at Netherfield, looked on with interest. "Surely the estimable Mr. Collins is capable of guiding a woman through the steps of a dance for a half-hour."

"There you would be incorrect, Miss de Bourgh," replied Elizabeth. "Mr. Collins is as inept at dancing as he is at most other things. I, myself, was fortunate to have escaped unscathed, as I took the simple expedient of avoiding him so he could not solicit my hand, not that I possessed those qualities necessary to tempt him. But I am aware of more than one young lady who suffered grievous harm because of his clumsiness!"

It was clear Anne knew of whom Elizabeth was speaking, though she avoided looking in Miss Bingley's direction. In this manner, they continued to speak between themselves, and before the first dance of the evening, Miss de Bourgh insisted that Elizabeth call her by her first name. It was a joyous day, Elizabeth decided, whenever she was afforded the opportunity of calling anyone she esteemed friend. There was more, she thought, to Anne de Bourgh than anyone in the lady's family had ever known.

Under normal circumstances, hearing his name bandied about by those present at a society function would have incensed Darcy. It was amazing what a change in perspective did for one's temperament, for though he would still have been annoyed had he been in London and heard whispers of his attentions toward this gentleman's daughter, or that young woman of pedigree, the name he heard on the lips of those present that night was not one to whom he did not wish to be connected.

It was no surprise that others should talk when the young lady in question was known to these people and had been so all her life. The way he stood with her that evening when she was not engaged on the dance floor, or watched her as she glided through the steps with another, rendered his preference no less than obvious. The ladies oohed and ahhed, the gentlemen sighed and looked on with envy, and the matrons spoke of their sure knowledge of the engagement which he would soon solemnize. None of it bothered Darcy, for he was far too focused on Miss Elizabeth.

Even overhearing Mrs. Bennet's comments that evening was not enough to prevent his enjoyment; innocuous though they were, they would have offended the old Fitzwilliam Darcy.

"He is such a good and handsome man," said the woman, not understanding how close he was when she spoke. "And so very attentive to Lizzy."

"His income does not do him any harm in your eyes, I wager," said another lady, the envy clear in her voice.

"A man's position is a consideration," said Mrs. Bennet; Darcy could hear the distinct coldness in her voice. "But it is not the only one. A woman must consider whether a man can support her — none of our daughters should marry militia officers with little to their names. Mr. Darcy, however, is more than a man possessing worldly goods. He is a man devoted to my daughter, and that is the most important consideration."

"It is fortunate your daughters have caught the attention of such fine men," said another woman, though her words sounded more wistful than envious. "They are such agreeable girls; I am prodigiously happy for them."

"Do not concern yourself, Flora," replied Mrs. Bennet. "Your nieces are lovely girls too. I am certain they will attract some gentleman before long."

As Darcy moved away, he could not help but reflect how fortunate it was that Mrs. Bennet was a rational woman. If Miss Elizabeth had been cursed with a shrew for a mother, he did not know what he might have done.

During a break in the dancing, Darcy stood by the side of the dance floor with a cup of punch, speaking with Miss Elizabeth. Not far away, he noted Fitzwilliam speaking with Miss Lucas again, something which had seemed to have become something of a habit of late. When Miss Elizabeth excused herself for a moment, leaving Darcy standing by himself, Bingley approached with mischief in mind.

"Well, Darcy," said he, taking in Darcy's position by the side of the dance floor, "it seems you are intent upon standing by the dance floor in your usual stupid manner. I might have thought you would be more active tonight, given the inducement."

It was a conversation that had played out many times between the friends. Whereas Bingley might abuse him for his lack of interest in being social, tonight he had not been so reticent, a fact his friend had not misunderstood.

"Perhaps I should prance about, eager to approve of all and sundry?" returned Darcy. "There are others in the present company who do just that, appearing silly while doing it."

Bingley guffawed. "Perhaps there are. But that is no reason to be a misanthrope, Darcy. I declare, I have not seen you stand up more than a few times tonight. Are there not young ladies enough to tempt you here tonight?"

"Only one," replied Darcy. "And she is more tempting than ten other ladies."

"Indeed, she is. It is also fortunate she can talk her way around most men and will challenge you, for I am certain that is what you have been looking for in a woman all these years."

"Are you suggesting she is a bluestocking?" asked Darcy, noting that Miss Elizabeth had come close enough to overhear their conversation.

"I doubt you would be interested in any other sort of woman!" replied Bingley, his laughter growing louder. "For what is a woman if she cannot debate politics, the situation on the continent, and the evils of the Luddites?"

"What sort of woman, indeed. Do you not wish for a woman of that ilk yourself?"

"Oh, no, for I must prefer a gently flowing river to one with raging rapids along its length. I shall stay with the sweetness of Miss Bennet and leave you to the archness of her sister."

"Then I suggest you get back to her, my friend, for you would not wish her to become lonely."

Bingley slapped his back and agreed. "What a pair we shall make, Darcy. I dare say we shall be brothers, though perhaps not by the means certain members of my family might have preferred!"

Then continuing to laugh to himself, Bingley departed. Lady Catherine, who had also been close enough to overhear, shot Darcy a look, but Darcy caught sight of Miss Elizabeth and had no attention to spare for his aunt. She stepped toward him, her gait light and her expression teasing.

"Well, Mr. Darcy, it seems like you have understood my character. It may be best for you to recall that it is better that I am a bluestocking than an imbecile."

"If you were an imbecile, my dear Miss Elizabeth, I should not have looked at you twice."

"Of course not! For who wishes to have an insensible wife? And what woman wishes for a dullard for a husband? If I had wished for that, I might have induced Mr. Collins to propose to me, for he fits the description!"

Soon the dancing began again, and Darcy was treated to the sight of Fitzwilliam dancing a second time with Miss Lucas. It could be said that he had the benefit of anonymity, considering the fact that there were many in attendance wearing scarlet. But Darcy had not missed his attention to her, nor had Lady Catherine remained insensible, though he was not certain of her thoughts on the matter. Fitzwilliam, in Lady Catherine's opinion, had never been as important as Darcy himself for the simple reason that she wished Darcy to marry Anne. That did not mean she was sanguine about the possibility of another nephew marrying a woman of less than acceptable breeding.

When the dance ended, Darcy situated himself near to where Fitzwilliam led her, and when her next partner led her away, Darcy approached his cousin. Fitzwilliam knew what was coming, for he grinned when he caught sight of Darcy.

"Have you perhaps found the woman of whom we spoke the other night? Miss Lucas is sensible, but I suspect certain elements of the family will not appreciate your choice."

"Do not be silly, Darcy," came the voice of Lady Catherine. Darcy had not noticed her presence nearby. "And do not speak about me as if I am not present."

Darcy regarded Lady Catherine with a look of all innocence. "If you recall, I mentioned no names."

The withering look Lady Catherine shot him left him in no doubt of her feelings. Having had her say, however, she fixed her attention on Fitzwilliam.

"I hope you have not lost your head as Darcy has."

"If you are referring to Miss Lucas, I would suggest the man who gains her hand would be a lucky one." Lady Catherine's mien darkened, and Fitzwilliam chuckled while holding out his hands in surrender. "There is nothing imminent with Miss Lucas, Lady Catherine. Be aware, however, that if I decide she will do for me, your arguments shall not sway me, and the objections of anyone else will mean nothing."

Lady Catherine's look was as sour as curdled milk. "It seems you and Darcy have spent much time together, for you are united in your desire to vex me and inflexible when I attempt to guide you."

"I apologize if you feel that way, Lady Catherine," said Fitzwilliam, sounding anything but apologetic. "However, I am almost thirty years of age and may keep my own counsel. Again, I shall remind you I have made no decisions. This conversation is premature at best."

Nodding, and perhaps understanding that she would get no

further with Fitzwilliam than she had with Darcy himself, Lady Catherine directed her attention back at Darcy. "As for you, my understanding was that you favored Miss Elizabeth. Do you mean to propose to her before the end of the year, or have you reconsidered?"

"No, I have not reconsidered, though I will note that I never said I would propose. Let us say that the situation will progress before long and leave the subject be."

Fitzwilliam grinned while Lady Catherine nodded, unable to say anything more. What might have been said after that Darcy could not know, for his attention was suddenly arrested by an unwelcome sight across the dance floor.

"Anne!" said Lady Catherine seeing the same thing Darcy had seen.

The grin ran away from Fitzwilliam's face as he glanced across the room and saw what his relations had already witnessed. Anne was standing on the other side of the dancers, speaking with Wickham. Given the smile Wickham was giving her, indulgent yet a little predatory, Darcy knew he was up to no good. Anne knew all about Wickham, other than the incident with Georgiana last summer. Did she know enough to avoid allowing him to charm her into something she should not do?

"How long have they been standing thus?" asked Fitzwilliam.

At that moment, Wickham broke away from her and exited the room, leaving Anne by herself, looking contemplative. Whatever the subject had been, Darcy sensed they would not approve of it.

"I do not know but it seems we must speak with her again."

"Tomorrow," said Lady Catherine with no hint of hesitation. "Darcy and I shall speak to her. I shall not have a daughter hoodwinked by the libertine son of a steward!"

"And I shall speak with Wickham tomorrow myself," said Fitzwilliam. "For now, we should not leave Anne alone for the rest of the night."

Lady Catherine took it upon herself to stay with Anne. While she said nothing of her mother's attention, Darcy was certain from her knowing smile that Anne knew something of why she was so attentive. Of Wickham, they saw nothing else that evening. Darcy did not know if he left, or for what reason, if he did so. But he was determined that Wickham should fail with Anne where he failed with Georgiana. Perhaps it was time to persuade Fitzwilliam that they should ship him off to Botany Bay. He could not do any harm to them if he was on the other side of the world.

Chapter XXVI

*B*eing united with Lady Catherine about anything was an unfamiliar sensation.

The thought crossed Darcy's mind and he grimaced. It was not fair to Lady Catherine—this Darcy well understood. The lady was not deficient in understanding and she was not one who delighted in contrary behavior, radical ideals or opinions, or intentionally causing harm to others. Darcy had spent so much time avoiding her, keeping her at arms' length to avoid her constant proclamations of his destiny with Anne, that it had jaded him. In fact, Darcy remembered possessing great esteem for her before the matter of Anne had come between them.

This morning, however, seemed the first time in many years in which they had been united with no division between them. Lady Catherine was concerned for her daughter to the point of fear. Darcy considered himself more rational. The potential for Wickham to use Anne in one of his schemes existed, but while Lady Catherine was considering taking away her daughter's freedom to protect her, Darcy preferred to help her see the man was a libertine. This supposed she was under his thrall or in danger of being so. Darcy wished to give her the benefit of the doubt; it was difficult to do so, as Darcy had seen

Wickham charm many women he had never thought were in danger. It sobered him.

Anne was showing a side of her character none of them had ever seen, and Darcy could only conclude she had hidden it because she had always felt dominated by her mother. When they confronted her that morning, she regarded them with a knowing smile, her manner more flippant than Fitzwilliam at his most infuriating. While Darcy did not think she was treating the matter as a lark, he was still worried.

"What did Wickham say to you last night, Anne?" asked Lady Catherine, as direct as ever she was.

"What does Mr. Wickham ever say?" was Anne's rhetorical question in reply. "Serious thoughts are foreign to him, for he concentrates on compromising women and procuring fortune to the exclusion of all other considerations."

"So, he attempted to charm you," said Darcy.

"When does he not? I dare say Mr. Wickham spends most of his waking moments attempting to charm."

"Anne, this is not a laughing matter," reproved Darcy. "Have Fitzwilliam and I not warned you of Wickham's character?"

"You have," replied Anne. "Ad nauseam."

"For good reason. Wickham is a derelict of the first order, his recent enforced moderation notwithstanding. His only thoughts are to gamble, carouse, and engage in his debaucheries without restraint. If you allowed him to charm you into running away with him, how long do you think Rosings would remain solvent under his management?"

"You are progressing quickly, are you not!" protested Anne. "Mr. Wickham has made no such references on the few occasions I have spoken with him."

"Anne," snapped Lady Catherine. "You cannot be this senseless. Of course, he would not speak of such things to you. That will come later when he feels he has you in his control."

"Control which he shall never procure," replied Anne. She paused for a moment considering them, and then added: "This has made me curious, for I do not see such warnings given to Miss Bingley, and she has been more the focus of Mr. Wickham's attention than I."

"Miss Bingley's brother can concern himself for her welfare," snapped Lady Catherine. "Our concern is for you."

"Bingley has spoken to his sister," said Darcy, trying for a more tactful reply than Lady Catherine had given, "for she is his responsibility. There are also differences between you. Miss Bingley is a woman long in society and intent upon marrying a man of wealth—

this as much as anything protects her from Mr. Wickham."

"She is also not a coddled young woman held out of society."

The hint of bitterness in her tone surprised Darcy, though he reflected he should not be. While he thought of saying something in support, Lady Catherine, who heard nothing of Anne's tone, was quick to respond.

"She is a woman full-grown, Anne, and may take care of herself."

"As am I," replied Anne, the hint of coldness in her voice such that even Lady Catherine could not misunderstand. "So you both know, I have not and will not allow Mr. Wickham to charm me, regardless of what he attempts. I have no desire to lose control of Rosings to a libertine. There, will that do?"

Spinning, Anne turned and stalked from the room, leaving Lady Catherine staring open-mouthed at her retreating back. The way her gaze became flinty, Darcy knew his aunt meant to follow her and make the matter worse, so he intervened to prevent it.

"It would be best if you allowed the matter to rest, Lady Catherine."

The lady turned her sharp glare on Darcy, belligerence in her very stance. "She has not given us the assurances we require. Do you believe those flippant words she spoke?"

"We will get nothing more from her," replied Darcy. Determined to keep her here, Darcy fixed her with a look he knew had always given her pause, one he reserved to persuade her to his way of thinking for some important estate matter. "Do you not see how Anne became offended when we spoke of the comparisons between Miss Bingley and herself? If you approach her now, it will only make the situation worse."

"I cannot understand her!" growled Lady Catherine, frustration coloring her voice. "Can she not see we have her best interests at heart?"

"Yes, we do, and I am certain Anne sees it too."

Darcy paused, uncertain whether he should speak further. Then the memory of Anne's offense, of the truth of her words, no matter how much anger had provoked them, filled him. Lady Catherine was incapable of seeing anything other than what she believed, but Darcy knew he needed to make the attempt for Anne's sake.

"Do you not concern yourself with Anne's words about being coddled?"

"Of what do you speak?" demanded Lady Catherine. "What does Miss Bingley have to do with this?"

The temptation to roll his eyes was strong, but Darcy refrained.

"Anne was not only speaking of Miss Bingley, Lady Catherine. Can you not see that she was also speaking of herself?"

"Herself? What nonsense is this?"

"The nonsense to which you refer is that we have all coddled Anne all her life! Can you not see this, Lady Catherine? Do you not understand that she is a woman full-grown, yet she has not had a season, has little experience in society, has had no opportunities to live the life expected of one of her station?"

"Are you attempting to blame me for this?" Lady Catherine's voice was growing shrill, rising to grate on his senses like the screeching of a crow. "Do you not know how ill she has been all her life? Had you done as I asked, she would have no need of such things!"

"I do not blame you," replied Darcy, holding his temper in with the force of will alone. "Anne has been ill—this I understand. However, as I told you once before, if you allow Anne the opportunity to live, she may surprise you with what she can accomplish."

Such a statement, so close to condemnation, might have provoked Lady Catherine to rage not long before. With all the changes that had occurred of late, however, it was clear she was only taken aback.

"I do not intend to berate or accuse, Lady Catherine," said Darcy in a calmer tone, eager to attempt reconciliation. "You did what you thought was best to protect your child, and I commend you for it.

"Having said that, you must see that Anne has a legitimate complaint. Is it not best that we allow her the chance to live her life in a manner she sees fit?"

Darcy's words moved Lady Catherine, for he could see it in the deflation of all her anger. Swiping a hand over her face, she appeared like an old, tired woman rather than the force of nature she had seemed all his life.

"I am willing to allow Anne to live, Darcy. But what of Wickham? Do you believe her beyond his reach?"

"It seems to me that Anne understands what he is, and she claims she will not allow him to charm her. I will not let down my guard if that is what you ask. At present, however, it may be best to watch and wait, for she will not respond well if we further importune her on the subject."

"Then I will rely on you to safeguard her, Darcy. Now, if you will excuse me, I believe I shall find my daughter for a long-overdue conversation. It seems we must decide what we are to do now; I would not make any plans without discovering her wishes."

As Lady Catherine left the room, Darcy reflected on the good that had come of their discussion that morning. Though he was yet unconvinced of Wickham's inability to harm his cousin, Darcy thought Anne had a greater chance of happiness now than she had at any time in the past.

"It seems to me we have had this conversation before, Colonel," said Wickham as he walked into Colonel Fitzwilliam's office. "Or, at least what I expect this conversation will be."

"Close the door, Wickham," said Fitzwilliam, setting his pen in the holder and looking up at his officer.

Wickham complied without comment, easing himself into the indicated chair like a boy being brought before the headmaster. Fitzwilliam regarded his officer, wondering at his game, for it was not the Wickham he knew. And Fitzwilliam did not like it. In any other man, he might have thought he was intent on not provoking a superior officer. In Wickham, Fitzwilliam suspected it was nothing more than an act, a show to prove he was not the danger Fitzwilliam knew him to be.

"Since you have already divined the reason I summoned you, perhaps you would explain your actions."

When Wickham did not respond at once, Fitzwilliam watched him, alert for any deception. The only thing he could glean from Wickham's behavior was uncertainty. What that might portend, Fitzwilliam did not know, but it did not make him trust the man any further.

"I know why you suspect me, Colonel," said he, opting for the safety of formality. "I have not always behaved the best in my dealings with your family."

"That, Wickham, is perhaps the understatement of the century."

Though the man attempted a hesitant smile, it fell away from his face when Fitzwilliam did not respond to it. Now nervous, Wickham nodded, a little jerky, but he did not speak again.

"I am still waiting for an explanation, Wickham."

"Do you consider me witless?" asked Wickham, a little of his courage returning. "I am not ignorant of the power you hold over me, and I know Darcy can have me put into prison on a moment's notice. Why should I risk that?"

"Then you were not attempting to charm my cousin."

"We were both attending an assembly. Though I have attempted to keep my distance from G . . . Miss Darcy when I have been in company with her, I know of no reason I should refrain from speaking with Miss de Bourgh. Our conversation lasted only a few moments; you may ask her if you doubt me."

Fitzwilliam considered Wickham, leaning back in his chair to give him more time to think without responding. "Then you deny having any designs on my cousin."

"I believe I am allowed the ambition to improve my lot in life," growled Wickham, showing a little spirit.

"Do you believe we—her family—will have nothing to say of that?"

"With all due respect, Miss de Bourgh is of age and may make her own choices."

Fitzwilliam snorted. "You say that, knowing her mother?"

Wickham shook his head. "If Lady Catherine allowed Miss de Bourgh to go her own way, she may surprise you all. Regardless, if I was interested in her as a potential wife, it is her choice whether to allow me to make my case or send me away. I have no intention of attempting to spirit her away and provoking your vengeance."

"So you deny any interest in Anne."

The grin with which Wickham regarded him was unfeigned, as far as Fitzwilliam could determine. "Her situation is an excellent lure, as you know, but her mother is the trump card which prevents any contemplation of her as a bride."

A barked laugh was Fitzwilliam's response; well did he know it!

"And what of Miss Bingley?"

Again, Wickham's manner became colder. "That lady is none of your concern, Fitzwilliam. As I told you, I have no desire to provoke you or your cousin to act against me. If I woo Miss Bingley, if I resolve on proposing to her, it is none of your concern. Perhaps she will accept, though I suspect otherwise. Either way, it is my concern, as long as I do nothing underhanded."

"You understand I will not relax my vigilance."

"I did not expect you would. My only request is that you do not interfere."

"Then you may go," said Fitzwilliam.

Nodding, Wickham rose and departed from the room, leaving Fitzwilliam alone with his thoughts. The man was a slippery one and no mistake. While Fitzwilliam had attempted to watch him to determine if he was lying, it was unclear. Though he had always considered himself a good judge of such things, Wickham was a man for whom lying was as natural as breathing.

He was also correct. If Wickham did nothing objectionable, there was nothing Fitzwilliam could do to stop him from paying his addresses to Miss Bingley. That did not mean he would cease watching him. Further vigilance was required, for Wickham was too much of a known quantity for that.

Elizabeth was aware of the concerns of Mr. Darcy and Colonel Fitzwilliam the previous evening, for Mr. Darcy had informed her of what he saw. A part of Elizabeth thought the gentlemen were overreacting, for she saw no sign of Miss de Bourgh's imminent infatuation with the officer. However, she understood their history with him and knowing much of it herself, Elizabeth could not say they were not right to worry.

The pledge she had given to watch Wickham herself whenever required had earned her a tender smile and a heartfelt thanks from the gentleman. There was little desire in Elizabeth to see Miss de Bourgh hurt or married to a man who wished to have her for nothing more than her inheritance. Though Mr. Darcy would not say much of the matter, Elizabeth suspected she had been the victim of an overbearing mother all her life. What Miss de Bourgh needed was love and support, the devotion of a husband when the time came, a man who would treat her as a woman ought to be treated. Until that happened, Elizabeth meant to offer her whatever friendship and support she could.

The morning after the assembly, the youngest Bennets were restless in a manner Elizabeth had rarely seen. Georgiana, sweet girl that she was, had provided a distraction for them the previous evening, for which Elizabeth—and the rest of her family—were grateful. After she departed, however, Lydia's mood grew restive again.

"Oh, how this house is dreary!" groused Lydia for perhaps the fifth time. "How I long to leave it for a time."

Lydia looked to Kitty as if demanding her support. "Do you not wish to go out?"

"I would not be opposed to it," was Kitty's diplomatic response.

Though Lydia scowled at her sister, she turned to Elizabeth, hope shining in her countenance—so much so it was almost pathetic. "We have not walked into Meryton for a time. Shall we not go there today?"

"Have you completed your studies?" asked Mr. Bennet.

"Before luncheon," replied Kitty to Lydia's enthusiastic nod.

"Perhaps it would be acceptable to go to Meryton today," mused Elizabeth. "It is a fine day, and the exercise would be beneficial."

"If you are to go," said Mrs. Bennet, "Cook mentioned something of wishing to restock some of her spices from Mr. Hodge."

"Then let us go!" exclaimed Lydia.

Elizabeth exchanged a shrug with Jane and agreed to the outing, much to Lydia's excitement. Kitty, given the praise she had received the previous day, exhibited a demure pose of a girl of seventeen, though Elizabeth could see she was also excited. They rose from the room, gathering spensers and bonnets, gloves and instructions from Longbourn's cook, and then set out for the town little more than a mile distant.

What Lydia found so exciting about Meryton, Elizabeth could not say. Though she had always thought it a fine town, more so because of its friendly inhabitants than its physical beauty, there was nothing special about it. Lydia, if her sisters allowed it, could walk the length of its principal street from sunup until sundown and never grow tired. While the shops were quaint, like old friends Elizabeth had known all her life, they were small and often dingy and did not contain the treasures one could find on Bond Street, or even those in Luton or Stevenage.

It was not long before the reason for Lydia's current fascination with Meryton became clear, though Elizabeth thought she should have guessed. For here and there along the street, they could see the red coats of the officers, their bright attire marking them without the possibility for error against the drab background of fading paint and cloudy windows.

And those dashing fellows were not reluctant to stop and flirt with young ladies of the neighborhood either. Here and there, all over the town, they stood in groups of two or three, with young ladies speaking with eager anticipation. It was thus that Lydia's wishes were revealed, for while the girl remained composed, the first pair of officers to greet them—Lieutenants Denny and Sanderson—received an excited greeting as they stopped to talk to them.

The officers of the militia, Elizabeth knew, were a reflection on their commander, who was such an upstanding man himself. Of the Bennet sisters, they knew little and had spoken even less, for none of the eldest, though they would speak if the occasion demanded it, were enamored of their bright coats or eager to hear the stories laced with exaggeration and outright falsehoods which fell from their lips. The lieutenants, therefore, were impressed by the youngest, who gave them much more consequence than the elder, and soon the flirting became more overt and suggestive.

"Thank you, Lieutenant Denny," said Elizabeth after a moment of this. "I believe it is time we must now depart."

The look she gave to the officer seemed to remind him of the proprieties of the situation, not to mention with whom he spoke. Both bowed, spoke of their pleasure, hoping with little disguise that the acknowledged future fiancée of their commander's close cousin would not bring this minor lapse to the colonel's attention, and departed.

"Lizzy!" hissed Lydia as they were leaving. "Why did you chase them away? Do you mean to keep every officer to yourself?"

"I mean to keep none to myself," snapped Elizabeth, hitting Lydia with a sharp gaze, the kind which informed her sister of her displeasure and warned her to refrain from any further protest. "You should remember, Lydia, that you are not yet out. If you persist in flirting with every officer we meet on the street, it will be longer before Papa will allow you the freedom you so desperately crave."

Though Lydia muttered, Jane, ever the diplomat, interjected: "Let us visit a merchant or two. The milliner and the haberdasher, perhaps?"

Brightening at the promise of ribbons and bonnets, Lydia agreed, and they all turned to make their way down the street. It seemed to Elizabeth that word had spread, or they had been observed, for though they came across other officers, most offered a polite word of greeting and a bow, and continued on their way, much to Lydia's disgust.

At length, Elizabeth decided she would take the purchase of Cook's spices upon herself, knowing Lydia would not have the patience for it. After a quick word with Jane, she left them and visited Mr. Hodge's shop, acquiring the necessary items, before making her way outside again. There, the most unwelcome sight of Mr. Wickham standing speaking to her sisters greeted her.

"Mr. Wickham," said Elizabeth as she strode to the small party.

"Ah, Miss Elizabeth," replied the gentleman with a bow. "How do you do?"

"Very well, sir. I see you are taking advantage of the fine weather we have been having."

The lieutenant seemed to understand Elizabeth's reason for choosing the weather as a subject, for he gave her an easy and knowing smile. "It is a benefit we must take when we can, for winter will soon be upon us and such opportunities will be lost. I understand you are of a like mind in this opinion."

"Perhaps," replied Elizabeth.

Though Mr. Wickham understood her succinct reply, he remained undaunted, turning his attention back to her youngest sisters. There was something flirtatious in his manner, his vanity stoked by adolescent girls hanging off his words. As his manners did not go beyond that which was proper, Elizabeth allowed them to speak without interrupting, considering the man before her.

Mr. Darcy's words had taught her to be cautious against him, and Elizabeth did not think it was unwarranted. Mr. Wickham was all ease in company, his charm on display for all to see. While he might appear to be a true and jovial man, Elizabeth thought she understood something about him, for while he wore his civility like a well-worn glove, it seemed it was an act he put on to impress others. Even the comments exchanged with Kitty and Lydia were peppered with little compliments such as would impress an unwary and inexperienced girl, practiced, though delivered with a casual ease which bespoke true confidence.

Was there anyone in the world who knew the measure of this man? Elizabeth doubted it. In fact, she doubted that Mr. Wickham possessed much self-awareness, for the façade he put up for the world was so tight about him as to be a second skin, one which had been there for so long that it was now unnoticed. When Elizabeth compared his affable manners with Mr. Darcy's fervent reticence, one man appeared to have all the substance, while the other was in possession of it. How fortunate she had been that Mr. Darcy had shown her his very soul and exposed this man in the process! Mr. Wickham might have duped her, the same as her younger sisters.

Soon, another pair of officers joined them, and Lydia, being eager to make the acquaintance of them all, began speaking to them, though Elizabeth appreciated she had waited for the introductions. This left Mr. Wickham displaced by the newcomers, a circumstance which he seemed to accept with good humor. Why he spoke to Elizabeth she could not know, though she wondered if it were some notion of portraying himself to the best advantage to the woman he was certain his former friend would soon connect himself.

"Miss Elizabeth," said he. "I thank you for bringing your sisters to town today, for I have not had the opportunity to speak with them."

"That is no surprise," replied Elizabeth, "for they are not yet out."

"Yes, I gathered that much. Still, they appear to be wonderful girls, and with such excellent examples as you and Miss Bennet, I cannot imagine they will be anything but poised and confident when they come out."

Elizabeth returned a faint smile at the man's praise. "Thank you, sir. I confess I have high hopes for them myself."

What followed was a stilted conversation, for Elizabeth did not wish to speak with the man, and he could not seem to find anything to say. There was not much of consequence of which she wished to speak to him, as most topics seemed fraught with danger or off-limits altogether. This all changed when Mr. Wickham made some slight comment of the Netherfield party.

"And how is it, to meet again with those whom you must not have seen in years?"

"Agreeable, indeed," replied Mr. Wickham with what Elizabeth saw as a false smile. "I have missed Pemberley, for it is a lovely estate."

"So Miss Darcy has informed me."

The mention of Georgiana was deliberate, for Elizabeth wished to know if he would betray any remorse over how he had misused the girl. There was nothing for her to see in his reaction, however, for he smiled and nodded.

"Yes, the Darcys are proud of their estate, and one cannot blame them. Should you ever see it, I am convinced you will count it the most beautiful of estates in the most beautiful of counties."

"That is what my aunt says," replied Elizabeth. "She is from Lambton, which I understand is near Pemberley."

"Very near," replied Mr. Wickham. "Why, Darcy and I used to go there every day in the summer. Perhaps I have met your aunt."

"It is possible," was Elizabeth's noncommittal reply. "Then you must have known Lady Catherine also, for her sister was Mr. Darcy's mother, I understand."

Mr. Wickham made a face. "Lady Catherine is not a woman one could forget, and her sister was much like her in essentials."

Not knowing enough about Lady Anne Darcy to know if that was true, Elizabeth agreed with respect to Lady Catherine and changed the topic. "It is interesting that Miss de Bourgh is so unlike her mother, given their close connection. I count it fortunate that I have made her acquaintance."

"Oh, Miss de Bourgh is a good enough girl," replied Mr. Wickham, his mask slipping just a little in the moue of distaste which hovered about his mouth. "It is unfortunate that she is been so sickly. It has left her wallowing in insipidity and left her uninteresting in most respects."

"Except in her inheritance?" demanded Elizabeth, feeling offended for her new friend.

Mr. Wickham attempted to correct his mistake, but Elizabeth was in no mood to hear it. After a moment, he gave up attempting to explain himself.

"It is not my purpose to judge you, Mr. Wickham," said Elizabeth, "but I must speak as I find. It seems to me that you have lived your life in such a way that you have become jaded. Is it proper to see those around you as nothing more than pawns you can use to benefit your own selfish desires? People do not live their lives to benefit you, sir. Anne is an excellent young woman, and I should tell you that I now consider her to be a friend, one whose society I hope to have for many years to come.

"I cannot tell you how to live your life," continued Elizabeth, raking a disdainful glare over his form. "What I can tell you is that selfish people rarely find happiness, for genuine happiness is in giving of yourself as much as receiving from others. All your desires and lusts can never make you happy. They will only make you lonely."

With those words, Elizabeth gathered her sisters, informing them of their need to return to Longbourn, and departed. Though she wished for Mr. Darcy's proposal, she hoped that Mr. Wickham would never be a part of their lives. The man was unendurable.

CHAPTER XXVII

"$\mathcal{C}$ ontinually looming over me is not what I would call useful, Cousin."

The voice startled Darcy from his thoughts and he blinked, fixing the woman in front of him, feeling as if she had roused him from a deep sleep. It was heartening to note that Anne regarded him without anger, favoring instead the cynical amusement which had characterized her interactions with him since the day he and Lady Catherine had confronted her. Darcy shook his head to remove the confusion, hoping he would gain the wits to respond intelligently.

"I hope you do not find our interference officious, Cousin," was the limit of what Darcy could muster at present.

"Officious?" asked Anne, as if testing the word. "No, perhaps not officious, though there are other unflattering words I could summon. It has not missed my attention that you seek to protect me; if I did not feel like a naughty child watched so she keeps out of the mud, it might be easier to endure."

"It is not you that we watch, Anne," replied Darcy.

"Mr. Wickham," mused Anne, nodding her agreement. "Yes, I think I begin to have the measure of the man. He is slippery, I will grant you, and he seems to have all the confidence in the world in his possession of the necessary charm to do as he wishes.

"At the same time, I will also point out that his ardor seems to have cooled to a certain extent. Had I not had every confidence in his lust for riches, I might think he has lost interest in me, to say nothing of Miss Bingley."

A scowled settled over Darcy's countenance, and he gave his cousin one clipped nod. "That is my concern."

As one, their gaze found Wickham from across the room. Standing as they were in Lucas Lodge along with the officers and almost every gentle family in the district, the sound of conversation flowed about them, the rooms so heavily populated that Darcy could not hear Anne's voice unless she raised it. From what Miss Elizabeth had told him, this was typical for one of Sir William's gatherings; the man was so fond of company that he could countenance leaving no one out of his invitations.

"Look at him," said Anne, drawing Darcy's attention back to Wickham. "The way he stands, I might almost think he was contemplating momentous thoughts, for his attention is all inward and he holds his cup of punch as if he has forgotten it."

"I cannot account for his behavior," said Darcy, noting the same of his former friend. "There is little he allows to stand in his way when he fixes on a woman to charm; his failure to charm some lady out of her fortune has not dimmed his confidence in his abilities even a jot."

Anne snorted and said: "No, I do not suppose it has, considering his behavior when he first turned his enchantments on me."

"What do you mean?" demanded Darcy, turning a sharp gaze on his cousin.

The way Anne laughed annoyed Darcy, though he kept his temper long enough to allow her to respond. "Do not suppose that because I informed you of my determination to avoid being charmed that he did not make the attempt. The man uses it as a bludgeon without even thinking about it, so ingrained is it in his personality.

"But I am curious. Do you know what provoked this change in him?"

"I do not know," confessed Darcy. "It was not something I said."

"That is interesting," replied Anne. "Then perhaps he has learned something about himself, though how he managed it I cannot say."

"That would be something new," muttered Darcy.

"Yes, it would be at that," said Anne with a laugh. "You must own, there is an unforeseen benefit to your increased attention to me in light of the threat of your former friend."

When Darcy turned on Anne askance, she nodded to another side of the room and said: "My mother's hope for our eventual marriage seems to have been raised as a result of your recent proximity to me. I know you will find that insignificant fact to be highly diverting, as do I myself."

Then Anne fixed him with a crooked grin and moved away, leaving Darcy to ponder the truth of her words. Darcy had noticed Lady Catherine's eager attention whenever they were together but had not thought it necessary to speak to her about it. Lady Catherine was adept at seeing what she wished to see—no protests on his part would induce her to see reason.

Fitzwilliam also did not know of the genesis of Wickham's changed behavior. "I have noted his introspection myself, though if you are suggesting I provoked it, you are incorrect. Wickham appeared as serious as I have ever seen him when last I spoke with him. That does not mean he listened where he has never done so before."

"Do you think he is planning something?"

"Is he not always planning something?" asked Fitzwilliam with a shake of his head.

"I suppose you are correct," conceded Darcy.

"Do not worry, Darcy," said Fitzwilliam. "Our watching him serves to protect Anne, and I believe her claims of wariness are genuine. Let us not borrow trouble."

Then Fitzwilliam grasped Darcy's shoulder and walked away, his destination the side of the woman with whom Darcy had often seen him of late. Darcy could not consider that fact any further, for Miss Elizabeth joined him at that moment. Whenever she was near, Darcy could spare no attention for anyone else. Miss Elizabeth's intellect was keen and her powers of observation prodigious, for she could see there was something concerning him and drew it from him in short order.

"That is curious, Mr. Darcy," said she, her attention fixed upon the officer. "I wonder if my words had some effect on him."

Confused, Darcy said: "You have seen Wickham of late?"

"The day after the assembly," replied Miss Elizabeth, her eyes finding his. "My sisters and I happened across him in Meryton."

Miss Elizabeth related what had occurred that day, and while it seemed innocuous enough, Darcy was interested to hear how she had berated him. The thought of this diminutive woman scolding Wickham diverted Darcy, for Wickham considered ladies such as she to be his for the taking.

"Then," continued she, "I informed him his attitude and his

tendency to consider others to be his playthings did not impress me. Then I informed him he would never find happiness if he did not change his ways."

Though amused, Darcy forced himself to put aside her words and examine her account of Wickham's reaction to better understand him. "Wickham listening to anything he does not like is beyond my experience, and he would not like a set down such as you describe."

"Then perhaps there is something else at work. I assume that is why you have been looming over Anne—to force him to reconsider any notion of attempting to make for Gretna with her in tow?"

Darcy grinned. "Anne made that same point—she also used the word 'loom,' as I recall."

"Then it appears our turn of mind is uncommonly similar," replied Miss Elizabeth.

"Yes, it does," replied Darcy, for the moment forgetting about Wickham in favor of the wondrous creature before him.

On the day it happened, Elizabeth had had no notion it was in the offing. If pressed, she might have asserted it was unlikely, considering the amount of attention Mr. Darcy was giving to ensuring Mr. Wickham attempted nothing with his cousin. Though she understood and did not begrudge his attention, there was a part of her, a small distant voice which whispered jealous murmurings and knocked her mood a little out of sorts.

That day, however, was different, for the ubiquitous presence of the regiment—other than the excellent Colonel Fitzwilliam—was absent, and with them, Mr. Wickham. The Netherfield party had come to Longbourn, and as Charlotte was also present, there was quite a crowd within Longbourn's sitting-room. While Elizabeth might have been unaware of Mr. Darcy's intentions, and though the gentleman had not meant to do anything himself, later, in hindsight, she thought she could point to a specific moment that made his actions inevitable.

Sitting as she was, speaking with Anne, Elizabeth had thought nothing out of the ordinary was occurring. Mr. Darcy had approached Mr. Bennet as soon as he arrived, and as he had stood with her father for several moments in earnest conversation, Anne related some interesting stories to Elizabeth, including the behavior of the absent Mr. Wickham.

"I spoke with Mr. Darcy two days ago and informed him of a recent conversation I had with Mr. Wickham," said Elizabeth, then proceeding to explain the basics of the exchange with her friend. When she finished, she added: "Perhaps Mr. Wickham has never had his behavior explained in such terms before and it has caused him to pause."

Anne laughed and rested a hand on Elizabeth's shoulder. "If anyone could explain the matter in terms blunt enough that even Mr. Wickham would understand, I declare it would be you, Elizabeth."

"Perhaps he is not so terrible," said Elizabeth. Then she grinned and added: "Now I sound like Jane."

Again, Anne's merriment rang throughout the room, drawing others' attention to them. In particular, Mr. Darcy seemed to regard her with wonder, as if he had not heard her laugh in such a manner before—it was possible he had not—and Lady Catherine, who also appeared surprised, but not as happy with it as Mr. Darcy.

"Your sister's attitude is refreshing," said Anne. "There is little enough of seeing the best in others in the world, and yet she will not allow others to deceive her. It is a strange mixture, both the ability to see the best and to refuse to be drawn to the worst. There are few capable of it, I think."

"It is well that you see it my way, Anne, for I consider Jane to be the dearest person in the world."

After some moments of speaking together, they were joined by Georgiana, and Anne drifted away. That was when the situation changed, at least from the perspective of one who was intent upon having her own way. For Mr. Darcy finished speaking with Mr. Bennet and began making his way toward Elizabeth.

"Darcy, come and sit with Anne and me," rang out the voice of Lady Catherine.

It was a simple statement, one Elizabeth might have thought innocuous. But it was not so to Mr. Darcy, who directed a hard look at his aunt. Anne, Elizabeth noted, shot him an apologetic grin.

"It seems Lady Catherine has fallen back into her old ways," whispered Georgiana to Elizabeth. "It has always been thus—she attempts to put them together at every instance, hoping to browbeat them into surrendering to her desires."

Before Elizabeth could respond to her friend's words, Mr. Darcy responded: "On the contrary, Aunt, I thought that perhaps a visit to the back lawn would be just the thing, for the weather is fine."

Lady Catherine seemed to see something in his demeanor she did not like, for she frowned. There was nothing she could say to oppose the plan, however, and she did not make the attempt. Soon, the younger members of the party rose and were preparing to take themselves outside. Elizabeth thought Lady Catherine, from the displeasure she directed at them all, might join them, but she remained inside, speaking with Mrs. Bennet, while the Hursts also elected to remain within.

Though the weather was fine, as Mr. Darcy had stated, it soon became clear that his purpose in taking them out of doors had nothing to do with that fact. Instead, while the younger girls congregated around the rough swing hanging from the branch of an old oak and Colonel Fitzwilliam obliged them by pushing all who wanted to use it, Mr. Darcy, throwing Elizabeth a significant look, captured her hand and dragged her away toward another part of the lawn. The amused looks she received from most of the rest of the party did not miss her attention.

"This is rather precipitous, is it not, Mr. Darcy?" asked Elizabeth as he was leading her away. By this time, Elizabeth had something of a notion of what he intended, and while a woman might wish for a man to declare his undying love without being provoked by his aunt, the prospect of being engaged was appealing.

"I think it is not precipitous enough, Miss Elizabeth," said Mr. Darcy.

When they reached a part of the garden around the side of the house from the swing where they could not be observed, he turned and regarded her. Tenderness brimmed in that gaze, as did longing, desire, love, devotion, and many other emotions Elizabeth could not name.

"It has crossed my mind that I have allowed this situation with Wickham to distract me, and I hope you will forgive me for my lapse."

"That depends upon what manner your restitution will take, Mr. Darcy," replied Elizabeth. "It has also occurred to me to wonder if your aunt's ill humors will always rule you."

The teasing tone of Elizabeth's reply took any sting out of her words if Mr. Darcy had thought to take offense. That he had not was clear in his grin and in the manner in which he grasped her hands and brought them to his lips.

"I think, Miss Elizabeth, that we can lessen her interference, though I suppose there is nothing we can do to change her ways."

"Then it is fortunate that Derbyshire and Kent are so far distant, is it not?"

Mr. Darcy laughed. "Yes, fortunate, indeed."

"You have my complete attention, Mr. Darcy. How do you propose that we prevent your aunt from interfering in our lives?"

"By joining them together," replied the gentleman. "It has been my greatest fortune that not only did Bingley lease this estate in a forgotten corner of the kingdom but also that my cousin assumed command of the local regiment. I cannot imagine I would ever have met you had these events not come to pass, and it would have been to my great detriment.

"I am not a masterful speaker, Miss Elizabeth. But when I speak, you know it will be from the heart. Thus, I must ask you to allow me to tell you how ardently I admire and love you, and I beg you to accept my proposal and consent to be my wife."

"There is one thing with which I must disagree, Mr. Darcy." At his quirked eyebrow, Elizabeth laughed and said: "When you say you are not eloquent. What woman could hear such exquisite words of love and not be moved by their eloquence? Yes, Mr. Darcy, I would be happy to bind my life to yours forever . . . and to put an end to your aunt's scheming."

A chuckle rumbled in Mr. Darcy's midsection, and Elizabeth discovered she had no choice but to join him, little though she had any intention of demurring. When their laughter had run its course, they spent some minutes in close proximity, murmuring words of love and devotion, sharing little nipping kisses, Elizabeth's first—she would never kiss another man!

At length, however, their privacy was interrupted. It could not be supposed that the rest of the party, whose company they had left in such a hasty fashion, would not wonder where they had gone. Then again, Elizabeth suspected they all knew what was occurring, and their patience to hear the news was likely at an end.

"I think they went this way," Georgiana's voice floated to them from around the house.

"It is just like Lizzy," Lydia's voice followed her. "She lectures us about our behavior and then leaves a party to be alone with a man."

Elizabeth shared an amused glance with Mr. Darcy. Then they righted themselves, which only took a moment, turned, and began walking toward the voices, Elizabeth's hand ensconced in Mr. Darcy's arm. That was when the girls—including Kitty, Lydia, and Georgiana—came into sight around the corner of the house. The looks they received were alive with suspicion.

"Why are you here by yourselves?" demanded Lydia, seeming the most obtuse of the three girls.

"Is it not obvious?" said Kitty, turning an incredulous glare on her sister.

"Brother," continued Georgiana, "have you obtained a sister for me at last?"

"A sister for you?" asked Elizabeth. "Is that what matters to you, Georgiana?"

"Oh, I suppose a companion for my brother is also desirable," was Georgiana's flippant reply. "But from my perspective, a sister is much more important."

"I think perhaps it would be best to limit the contact between you girls," said Mr. Darcy. "Your behavior is degrading by the minute."

"Do not tease, Brother!" exclaimed Georgiana. "What news do you have for us?"

Though he attempted to present a stern façade, Elizabeth could see the exact moment when it cracked, leaving nothing but happiness in its wake. The truth of the matter revealed, the three girls let out cries of delight and crowded around them, congratulations flowing without hesitation. Above them, however, the sound of Lydia's voice rang out.

"Two older sisters married! Perhaps I shall be out soon, after all!"

The amused glance Elizabeth shared with Mr. Darcy revealed their similar thoughts—whatever Lydia's pretensions, there would be no early coming out for her. The happiness of the occasion, however, was such that Elizabeth had little desire to provoke the girl's protests. Thus, she kept her own counsel, knowing her father would have something to say on the matter.

When the company returned to the house, everyone who had been outside already knew what had happened. Fitzwilliam, happy for his cousin, gave them both as hearty congratulations as he felt on the occasion, and he noted that most everyone else was equally delighted. Even Miss Bingley, who had pursued Darcy for many months, swallowed her pride and offered her felicitations; it seemed to Fitzwilliam the woman had prepared herself for this, making it easier than if the news had caught her surprised.

The drama, of course, occurred when they entered the house. For while Miss Elizabeth's parents were as excited for the match as the rest of the company, there was one who did not greet the news with excitement. Fitzwilliam had known that Lady Catherine still harbored hopes that Darcy would "come to his senses," little though her observations must have supported that hope.

In the end, she offered her congratulations along with the rest of them, though with much less enthusiasm. And the lady's ability to turn a merry occasion into an opportunity to direct others was no surprise to anyone.

"Then we must begin your training as soon as may be," said the lady with a put-upon sigh. "We must preserve the honor and credit of the family."

The lady turned to Mrs. Bennet and added: "I shall assist you with the preparations for the wedding breakfast. And a ball, where all Darcy's friends and relations shall be invited to become acquainted with his future wife, would also be advisable."

Whatever Mrs. Bennet thought on the matter, she chose the wisest course of nodding to her ladyship and turning the conversation to other matters. Whether Lady Catherine would carry the day, Fitzwilliam did not know, but he thought Mrs. Bennet might prove to be a match for his aunt. Fitzwilliam decided he would allow them to argue over the matter, for there were other considerations for him to ponder.

"It seems to me your friend is incandescent in her happiness," said Fitzwilliam to the woman by his side.

Miss Lucas smiled and nodded. "It is just what Lizzy has always wanted, for she has always wished to marry for love."

"It appears she has found her dreams in my cousin. I have never seen Darcy laugh so much as he is now, for he has always been a serious man."

"Lizzy will suit him as he will suit her," agreed Miss Lucas. Then she paused and laughed, saying: "It seems your lady aunt did not get what she bargained for, or do I misunderstand her desire to pair Mr. Darcy with Miss de Bourgh?"

"I would have been surprised if you had not noticed," replied Fitzwilliam. "These past few days, she rekindled that hope, though Darcy and Anne both told her in no uncertain terms of their decision that they would not oblige her."

"Then all has worked for the best for everyone except your aunt."

Fitzwilliam chuckled and shook his head. "Even Lady Catherine may come around. Depending on whom Anne marries, it may even turn out for the best. Lady Catherine has a habit of directing all within range of her influence; Darcy, however, is not a man to accept such direction."

"Shall she search for a man of a retiring temperament then? That seems like a curious criterion for a husband."

"I suspect Anne will not stand for it. Lady Catherine is not yet accustomed to her daughter having her own opinion, but recent events have informed me that Anne will not allow her mother to dominate her any longer."

"That is well, for people should be free to choose their own paths."
Fitzwilliam turned to face Miss Lucas, thanking her in his own
mind for the opening she had just given him. "What of you, Miss
Lucas? Is there a chivalrous knight in your future?"

The rosy hue which stained her cheeks provoked Fitzwilliam's
heart to skip a beat. "I am not like Lizzy, Colonel Fitzwilliam. She has
always been the romantic between us, where I am the more pragmatic.
In my situation, I would be happy with a man of good character, one
who can support me and any children with whom we might be
blessed."

"A large estate is not a requirement then?"

"I do not need riches, Colonel Fitzwilliam. Comfort is what I would
like to attain, not the wealth of Midas."

"You say you are not romantic, Miss Lucas," said Fitzwilliam.
"Given the proper inducement, do you think you could become a
romantic?"

The woman's eyes rose to meet his, and she inspected him as if
looking for some hint of his intentions. Fitzwilliam had never been a
man known for hiding himself behind a wall—he was open and
honest. It had never seemed so important to him to show that openness
as it did now when his very future might depend upon it.

"Yes, Colonel Fitzwilliam," said she. "It is possible the right man
might persuade me to adopt a more romantic attitude. I hope he does
not require me to relinquish my practicality, however."

"If he did, he would be a fool," replied Fitzwilliam. "Being romantic
is an excellent attribute to the right man, but he will always desire
practicality."

Once again, Miss Lucas's mien flushed a little and she nodded,
though words appeared to be beyond her at the moment. Perhaps,
Fitzwilliam thought, she was more susceptible to romance than she
thought. If no one else had seen the benefits of encouraging that trait,
Fitzwilliam could only call them fools. He would not be so foolish
himself.

CHAPTER XXVIII

*T*he happiness Darcy's engagement provoked was to a degree that he had not felt in some time, and Darcy reveled in the feelings of new love, of having that love requited in every particular. While he thought he would grow tired of talk of breakfasts, flowers, ribbons, trousseaux, and all the other accouterments that accompanied a wedding, the thought of what would follow after would sustain him until that joyful day.

Lady Catherine was resigned, if not accepting, which is all Darcy had wished from his aunt. For a time, he had worried she might offend Mrs. Bennet with her officious pronouncements; his betrothed's mother proved well able to handle her, removing Darcy's concern, leaving him at liberty to concentrate his attention on Elizabeth.

Elizabeth! How wonderful it was to now claim the privilege of referring to her in a more familiar manner. Already Darcy was coming to understand the blessings she would bring to his life, provoking in him a returning determination to ensure she never had cause to regret her decision.

A few days after his engagement, however, the other matter which had occupied Darcy's attention of late was once again brought to his notice, in a manner which he would never have expected. Attending to some correspondence that morning so he would be at liberty to visit Longbourn after, the housekeeper announced a visitor to the library where he was at work. It was Wickham, to Darcy's surprise.

"Wickham," said Darcy with more wariness than civility. "Why are you here?"

True to the man's character, he looked about the room with interest for some moments before deigning to respond. "I have come to see you, Darcy."

Darcy paused and considered the man before him. "Our most recent conversations have not been at all cordial, Wickham. I might have thought you would avoid me."

"And you would not be incorrect. At present, however, there is no one else who can give me what I wish. Thus, I must come to you."

"Give you what you wish?" echoed Darcy, the familiar feeling of contempt for this man's grasping manner filling his breast. "Why would I give you anything?"

Rather than answering, Wickham chose a different approach. "If you will pardon me for saying so, I have noticed you seem happy of late—disgustingly so, if you will permit me to observe."

"I am certain you will forgive me if I will not confess to anything disgusting about it. If you refer to my recent acquaintance with and engagement to Miss Elizabeth Bennet, then I suppose you must be correct. I *am* happy—happier than I can remember being since long before my father passed away."

Wickham nodded, his manner filled with introspection. Then he grimaced and said: "Your father would not be happy with me for the way I have lived my life, would he?"

A snort conveyed all Darcy thought he needed to say, though he added: "What do *you* think? You could not fail to have heard some of his lectures on the matter. Do you think it would please him to know what you have become?"

"If that is the case, then I must wonder why you never told him of me. Would it not have made your life easier had you done so?"

"Perhaps," allowed Darcy. "But my father was a severe man, one who had no joy in his life. You were one of the few who could provoke a smile from him. I did not wish to destroy that."

Wickham cocked his head to the side, curiosity written upon his countenance. "I might have thought you would worry that I would take your place in his heart."

"My father did not possess much of a heart," said Darcy with a sigh. "The most important things in his life were his duty, his lineage, and his desire that I uphold the honor and credit of the Darcy family."

"For a time, I thought he might confer upon me a gentleman's income."

Shaking his head, Darcy glared at his former friend, wondering if the man had ever seen anything other than what he wished to see. "If you thought so, you did not understand my father. He was a creature of duty, a man stiff and unyielding in his observance of it. Had you been a second son, it is possible you might have inherited Appleton or Blackfish, but for a steward's son? It shocked me to learn he went as far as to recommend you for the Kympton living."

"Perhaps *you* did not know him as well as you thought."

For the first time in their conversation, a note of contempt had entered Wickham's voice. Darcy, however, ignored it without difficulty; Wickham's opinion had long since ceased to have any effect on him.

"It seems you are correct. Now, what do you wish, Wickham? You had best make your request, so I may reject it and have done with your company."

Wickham smirked. "Charming to the last, Darcy."

He paused for a moment, marshaling his thoughts, and then spoke again. "It seems, Darcy, that your morality has infected me, little though I desire to have it."

"My morality?" asked Darcy. "I am sorry, but I have not the faintest notion of what you speak."

"To be exact," replied Wickham, "I suppose it is not *your* morality; rather, it is the morality of your betrothed, which I assume must be a match for yours."

When Darcy did not respond at once, Wickham appeared to become impatient. "Might I assume you have heard from Miss Elizabeth of our discussion on the streets of Meryton?"

Darcy had heard her speak of the exchange. Given his knowledge of Wickham, however, he had discounted it, preferring the safer assumption of Wickham he had held all these years. Nothing anyone said to him had ever made an impression.

"I see you understand," observed Wickham. "I cannot explain why her words affected me as much as they have, for she was not the first to say them. You yourself have made similar accusations more times than I can count. Perhaps it was the way she delivered them, or it may be her perspective, that of an attractive young woman, made all the difference."

Darcy bristled at his words of Elizabeth, but Wickham cut him off before he could say anything. "I was paying her a compliment, Darcy; I do not desire to come between you.

"In fact, Miss Elizabeth's words have informed me most forcefully how young ladies—those who possess intelligence and beauty in equal measure—see me. And I do not like it; I do not like it at all."

Darcy was uncertain whether he should believe his former friend. A part of him—a large part—screamed at him to ignore Wickham, to accuse him of falsehood and see him escorted from the property. But something stayed his hand, though Darcy could not understand what it was himself. The desire to believe that the boy he had known had not disappeared beyond all retrieval? Perhaps, though Darcy had long despaired of the return of that friend.

"You know," said Wickham in a casual voice, one laced with self-congratulation and no small measure of provocation, "it strikes me that I could have had what I wished. I know you and Fitzwilliam both consider Miss Bingley to be a scheming social climber with no interest in anything other than herself. I could have had her eating from the palm of my hand if I had expended any effort. And as for your cousin . . . ."

There was little doubt in Darcy's mind that his wish was to provoke Darcy to anger, though for what purpose he could not divine. It was, perhaps, nothing more than reflex, a reflection of the man he had been for many years. Whatever Wickham meant by it, Darcy regarded him with passive disinterest; at one time Wickham might have tempted him to lose his temper. But at present, he felt nothing but curiosity for how this conversation might proceed.

"In fact, before your affianced interfered, I had decided to give up my interest in Miss Bingley in favor of Miss de Bourgh."

"Do you think I would have allowed you to take her from us? Do you think Fitzwilliam would not have had something to say of it? Or the earl?"

"You would not have allowed an elopement," replied Wickham with his typical dismissiveness. "Would you have prevented her choice if she accepted a proposal offered in good faith? A choice made of her own free will? It is not as if she is still underage."

Several thoughts passed through Darcy's mind at that moment, but he refrained from contradicting Wickham's statement. Wickham would meet anything he might have said with the same indifference with which Darcy was so familiar.

"Then why did you not do it?" asked Darcy. "If you were so confident of your success, I might have thought you would jump at the opportunity."

"Yes, you might have thought that of me. The truth is, now that your young woman has opened my eyes, it has come to my mind that I might actually prefer a woman who feels something for me instead of a cold union based on nothing but money, societal advantage, and primitive lust."

Of all the things Wickham might have said, that was a surprise to Darcy, for it was so unlike everything he knew of his one-time friend. "And you think you will find that?"

"Not in stodgy old England, I will not." Wickham huffed with annoyance. "The class system is too entrenched in England for me to have any chance of success. I have spent many years fighting against it, but I believe I have now come to that conclusion. Even if I were to persuade some young lady of fortune, her family would despise me, and she would learn to regret accepting me. The fortune she possesses would keep me company for a time; I have learned it would be cold comfort in the end."

"Then what do you propose?" asked Darcy, curious how far his former friend intended to take this.

"The possibilities are remote here," said Wickham, "but in the New World, I believe I could make a go of it. Perhaps I could find some wealthy man's daughter who cannot live without me and will not concern herself for my descent. The notion may seem unlikely, but I suspect it is far more likely there than here."

"I presume you wish me to fund this adventure for you."

Wickham grinned. "I have little to my name at present. The sale of the commission will help if we can persuade Fitzwilliam to relent and allow me to leave. If you prefer, we could call your support an added . . . incentive to encourage me to stay in the Americas when I arrive there."

As much as Darcy wished to throw the man out, inform him that the Darcy family's support of him was over, and to abjure him to fund his own journey to America, something held him back. Fitzwilliam might suggest it was Darcy's continued inability to take decisive action against Wickham due to his father's memory, and Darcy owned that may be correct. Of more importance, however, was Darcy's disinclination to continue to endure what had always been a millstone around his neck. This was the opportunity to remove Wickham from his life once and for all. It was a chance, he realized, he could not allow to pass.

"Very well, Wickham. Where do you wish to begin?"

"He asked for far more than you would give, I will wager."

Sour though Fitzwilliam's tone was, Darcy thought he detected relief also. Fitzwilliam had been urging him to deal with Wickham for many years now, but his own actions in accepting him into the regiment with the express purpose of seeing to his reclamation had left him incapable of promoting many other solutions he had championed over the years.

"If he had not," replied Darcy, "I might have sent for a physician. It would not be Wickham if he did not extort as much as he could. He settled for much less than he wanted."

"More than you wished to give, I assume?"

"It is a price well worth paying," said Darcy, wishing to cease speaking of the financials of the situation. "As part of our negotiations, I informed him I would keep his debt receipts and would use them should he ever cause me trouble again."

Fitzwilliam snorted. "He did not like that, did he?"

"No, but he understood it." Darcy paused and reflected on his confrontation with Wickham. "There is something . . . different about Wickham, something I never thought to see. Underneath, his character has not changed, for he is still the same thoughtless wastrel he ever was. At the same time, he has acquired a hint of hesitance in his manner, which lends credence to his assertions."

"That is the most surprising factor of all. For Wickham to care for another's opinion is shocking. I have no notion of whether to believe this conversion is real."

"I cannot blame you. Until he is aboard a ship, I shall not breathe easily."

"For that, I pledge my own services." Fitzwilliam's look was as determined as Darcy had ever seen. "I will escort him to the harbor, see him on the ship, and ensure he does not leave it before it departs. If you can, it would be best to book his passage on a ship bound for the Americas without a stop at another port in England. Let us not give him a chance to disembark."

"That is why I intend to book his passage from Bristol," replied Darcy, nodding to his cousin's suggestion. "There should be no other ports of call once he departs."

Fitzwilliam looked on him with approval. "Good. With any luck, we shall rid ourselves of him once and for all."

"I had not the slightest notion that Mr. Wickham had taken my words in such a way."

Confused though Elizabeth was, her fiancé's obvious regard warmed her. The story of Mr. Wickham's confession to William—as she was now allowed to call him—and the subsequent decision to assist him in relocating to the Americas, Elizabeth put aside; she knew of the man's worthless character, but he had done nothing to harm the Bennet family, so Elizabeth did not think much of him at all. As she had never thought the Bennet family appeared in his thoughts much, it was beyond surprising he would listen to her where so many others had failed to reach him.

"I had not the slightest notion Mr. Wickham would listen to *anyone*," replied William. "How it came about, I cannot say, and Wickham was not explicit, even if he knows himself. What is clear is your words struck him in a way no words ever have before."

"That is astonishing," replied Elizabeth. "When I spoke to him, I was angry and spoke without thinking. There was no purpose in my criticisms other than to inform him I found him to be a repugnant creature."

"There, I suspect, is the reason for the efficacy of your words, Miss Elizabeth," said Colonel Fitzwilliam with a chuckle. "For as long as I have known him, Wickham has possessed supreme confidence in his abilities, and, in particular, in his ability to charm women. To hear your criticisms delivered in a manner which made clear your disgust for him must have been no less than a shock."

William nodded and said: "That is my thought too. It showed to Wickham not only what you thought of him but informed him what a woman who knows something of him other than his charm and gentlemanly manners would find wanting in his character. That, as much as anything else, must be intolerable."

Unable—and not wishing—to refute what they were saying, Elizabeth nodded. "When will Mr. Wickham leave these shores?"

"We have not decided the exact time of his departure," replied William. "I have sent for a schedule of departing ships and destinations from Bristol—once I have that, we can make some choices. As Wickham is going to the New World of his own free will, I am allowing him to choose his own destination, which he has determined will be Baltimore."

Colonel Fitzwilliam grinned and added: "What our friend Wickham does not know yet is the assistance Darcy has agreed to provide is in the form of a bank draft which Wickham cannot cash until he arrives in Baltimore. It will at least ensure he retains the funds until he sets foot on the Americas, denying him the ability to gamble them away on the ship."

Knowing this was Colonel Fitzwilliam speaking from experience, Elizabeth accepted his words without comment. She allowed herself to feel gratitude that Colonel Fitzwilliam had been on hand to control Mr. Wickham, for given what they were saying about him, an unfettered Mr. Wickham could have caused great havoc in their small community.

The most amusing part of Mr. Wickham's upcoming emigration to the former colonies was the man's behavior in the days leading up to his departure. Mr. Wickham was no more liked than any other officer of the militia. As he had gained no great notoriety in the neighborhood, there were those who appreciated his company and his handsome countenance; there were as many young ladies who favored Lieutenant Denny or Captain Carter or other members of the regiment.

And yet, when the time of his departure approached, Elizabeth saw the true measure of the man unleashed, for the way he acted, one might have thought he was the most beloved officer in the company, such that his departure would cause the heartbreak of every young maiden in town. Though Elizabeth was not present at every visit, Mr. Wickham went on a tour of the houses of the district, saying his farewells amid self-congratulation and false regret.

The one occasion at which Elizabeth was present was the visit the man paid to Netherfield, and while she could not say how the other visits proceeded, his leave-taking there provided much amusement for all. Or perhaps not for all, for there was one who did not appreciate his resolution.

"It is a hard decision to make," said Mr. Wickham to the company which included the regular Netherfield inhabitants, along with Elizabeth and Jane, who had been invited to spend the day with their future families. "Though the welcome I received here in Meryton is far more than I might ever have expected, new lands and adventures call me away. There is little I can do but succumb to the calling."

Exchanging a look with William, Elizabeth covered her mouth, trying to stifle a laugh. With such words as these, he seemed to fancy himself the equal of Columbus or Magellan, rather than a man bound for a tamed land filled with many who would seem little different from those of England.

"Is that so?" asked Anne, herself diverted by his dramatic retelling. "Well, then we must wish you luck, Mr. Wickham, and pray for your safe arrival there. We would not wish you to run afoul of the hydra or other such monsters of the deep and untamed sea."

It was clear that Mr. Wickham caught the ironic undertone in her comment, for he smiled and said: "It is said that large sections of the Americans are yet wild and untamed, Miss de Bourgh, but I shall brave the vast wilderness nonetheless.

"There is only one thing I shall regret leaving behind, and that is the lovely countenances of all the young ladies, especially you, Miss de Bourgh, and you, Miss Bingley. I shall pine for your smiling faces for many months."

"Well, that is unfortunate for you," said Anne. "But I am certain you shall rally tolerably. As your mind is made up, I shall not attempt to persuade you. Rather, I shall wish you Godspeed and good fortune and future blessings of health and prosperity."

The smirk with which Mr. Wickham regarded Anne suggested some suspicion she might be laughing at his expense. He fixed her with a gracious smile and turned to Miss Bingley, who had remained silent.

Uncertainty was something Elizabeth had not expected to see in Miss Bingley's response to Mr. Wickham's flirting. The woman had so often met his overt attentions with caustic comments and innuendo that Elizabeth might have thought she would greet news of his going with relief, if not eagerness. None of these were present, however, and Miss Bingley's response was all that was surprising.

"I am surprised to hear of your departure, Mr. Wickham," said Miss Bingley. "Your actions of late had led to the belief of . . . Have you no reason to remain in England?"

"Many reasons," said Mr. Wickham with the ease of a man who believes he has the upper hand. "The more pressing reasons, however, propel me on. As for our connection, Miss Bingley . . . ."

Mr. Wickham trailed off, though Elizabeth had thought his mien had suggested he was about to say something caustic. His glance at that moment at Mr. Darcy had revealed to him that the gentleman was not pleased, and he amended whatever he had been about to say.

"There is no lady in the land more tempting than you, Miss Bingley," said Mr. Wickham with all the charm at his disposal. "But fate, it appears, will not allow us to come together. My future is in the Americas. I hope you will wish me good fortune and allow me to go with no ill will; my own wishes for your future happiness, I give without reservation."

Miss Bingley responded with a monosyllabic answer, unintelligible, which Mr. Wickham took as the highest praise anyone had ever afforded him. The man's flattery continued for some moments toward them all, including some choice comments for both Jane and Elizabeth. Then he excused himself and went away to the relief of them all. When he was gone, however, Miss Bingley was not her usual voluble self, instead caught in some well of introspection which consumed her every thought.

"I will own that I cannot understand Miss Bingley," said Elizabeth after some moments of observing the woman. "She never received Mr. Wickham's attentions with anything approaching acceptance, and yet she appears unhappy to learn he is going away."

"I believe you are failing to consider this from her perspective, Elizabeth," replied William. When Elizabeth glanced at him askance, William considered his words for a moment before speaking. "I have never had any ill will toward Miss Bingley, and I do not dislike her. However, it is nothing less than the truth that she thinks well of herself and possesses ambition aplenty.

"My defection to you—as she must see it—must be a blow to her vanity, one I believe she struggles, even now, to understand. In Miss Bingley's mind, I was her door to high society, all she ever wanted to have. When I did not fall in for her schemes and chose someone she considered unsuitable, it caused her to question her own worth. Mr. Wickham, in a way, vindicated her perception of herself, for even if she had no interest in accepting his overtures, it proved to her that someone who was not only handsome in his own right, but also possessed a connection to me, albeit nebulous, could find her irresistible."

"In that way, Mr. Wickham *was* you," said Elizabeth, understanding Mr. Darcy's point.

"Perhaps he was," replied Mr. Darcy. "Wickham upheld her belief in herself, that had matters differed only a little, she would have succeeded in her quest to elicit a proposal from me. Miss Bingley does not wish to consider where her plans went awry, but she did not need to if she could assume there was nothing lacking in *her*."

"Now that Mr. Wickham has withdrawn his attentions, it is causing her to consider that which she does not wish to consider."

William chuckled and shook his head. "Yes, I expect that is so. But you should not concern yourself for Miss Bingley, Elizabeth. There is little doubt she will right herself and continue on as she has, though this time she will need to find someone else upon whom to pin her hopes."

"Do you believe that is likely?" asked Elizabeth.

"Bingley has many friends, though most are not as close as we are. There are several who are single and looking for a wife, and even if those will not suit her, Miss Bingley's twenty thousand pounds will ensure some interest. I suspect that she will settle for less than she wishes; that might just make her happier in the end."

"Then I can do naught but wish her the best," replied Elizabeth. "For I have already found that which will make *me* happy; I am relieved she did not pluck it from me before I even found it."

The smile with which Mr. Darcy regarded her made Elizabeth feel warm all over. "That was never an option, Elizabeth. But I join you in your happiness. I believe we shall do well together, for I cannot imagine a better mistress for Pemberley."

EPILOGUE

*I*n the months and years that followed, Elizabeth's thoughts only returned to Mr. Wickham when her husband's thoughts directed her there. That William thought of his erstwhile friend often was not a surprise, though, with distance, such occurrences lessened. It was also very much a surprise to Elizabeth that Mr. Wickham wrote to William at various times to inform him of the happenings in his life.

"No, I never would have expected Wickham to be so thoughtful," said William one day after finding a letter from Mr. Wickham in his morning mail. "If anything, I would have expected to receive requests for more funds, for that has ever been a characteristic of our relationship."

Grinning, Elizabeth motioned at the still unopened letter and said: "Are you certain it does not contain such a request?"

With a laugh, William agreed and broke the seal. "Right you are, my dear. Just because his first letter did not, does not mean this one is not more typical of his correspondence."

For a few moments, William was silent while he read the missive which appeared to comprise only one piece of paper, written on only one side. When he finished, he looked up at her and returned her grin with one of his own.

"Perhaps Wickham has learned some prudence, for there is no mention of requiring funds. It seems he has decided to make his way south from Baltimore toward the Carolinas; he mentions some opportunity in that direction, though he is not explicit."

"Then I wish him the best," said Elizabeth.

Word from Mr. Wickham was sporadic over the years, a letter here and there when least expected, most containing only snippets of news and no actual information. It soon became clear that Mr. Wickham had settled in the Carolinas, though much of his doings there remained shrouded in mystery. Then one day above three years after his departure from England came a letter which shocked Mr. Darcy.

"Wickham is to be married!" blurted he after opening Mr. Wickham's letter.

"Is he?" asked Elizabeth, looking at her husband with interest.

"According to Wickham," said William, still perusing the letter, which appeared longer than most of Mr. Wickham's missives, "he has found a woman without whom he cannot live. Given the dates he mentions, it seems he is already married, for the letter took some time to arrive."

Mr. Darcy then paused and smiled, shaking his head. "It seems Wickham found a woman whose father owns a substantial plantation south of Charleston; she the man's only child."

Elizabeth could not help the laugh which escaped her lips. "Then he has obtained his life's wish."

"It would appear to be so," replied William. "He was correct, to an extent—a woman here was not likely to accept him, given his descent, whereas a woman there would have fewer reservations over the same. It seems, from his words, that Wickham might actually have some affection for this woman, rather than just her father's money."

"That is well then," said Elizabeth. "I can only wish Mr. Wickham the best."

As congratulations, Mr. Darcy shipped his former friend two bottles of French brandy, for which a thank you note arrived in due course. Communication remained sporadic thereafter, limited to announcements of the birth of children and other significant events. Neither Elizabeth nor William noticed when a few years later word stopped coming from the now-successful and wealthy Mr. Wickham, and thereafter they never heard from him again. Word arrived some years later of a massive hurricane that swept through the area, and while Mr. Darcy hoped his former friend was well, there was no way of knowing. That letters had ceased long before suggested there was no correlation between the two events.

As for the eastern side of the great divide, life went on for all concerned. Elizabeth took to her new life with aplomb and assumed the reins of the Pemberley's management with skill and dedication, leading William to exclaim that the house had never run so well as when Elizabeth was managing it. In time, they were blessed with children—three strapping boys and two lovely girls, who lived to adulthood—and the family grew in happiness and contentment.

Jane married Mr. Bingley, and they settled not far distant from Pemberley, adding this happiness to all others in Elizabeth's life. While the Bingleys were not as blessed with as many children as the Darcys, they had two fine boys, both of whom grew to be a credit to their father and adored their mother.

The remaining Bennet sisters all found their own paths in life, which resulted in families and situations for them all, Kitty and Lydia remaining in the south not far from their childhood home, while Mary followed her elder sisters northward. If the reader might assume cynically that Lydia never outgrew her tendency toward wildness, they might be forgiven, for it was true. Lydia's husband adored her, and her vivacity and good cheer did not mislead him. On the times they were in company with her, Elizabeth could see that he encouraged that vivacity and acted to ensure her behavior never exceeded that which was proper.

For Georgiana's part, she continued to grow in confidence and maturity, entering society the year after her brother's marriage to Miss Elizabeth Bennet. Elizabeth was accepted in society and provided much guidance to her young sister, such that Georgiana determined to find a situation akin to that of her brother with a man she could love and respect. When Georgiana left Pemberley for her husband's home, she did so with happiness, knowing her association and friendship with her sister-by-marriage would last her entire life.

Anne de Bourgh too found her own way in life, proving William's words about her capabilities were no less than prophetic. While it was true she would never be robust, she found a man who filled all her dreams and married several years after her cousin set her free. While Lady Catherine was not enamored of the match, she too came to appreciate the man, and even more that her daughter was happy, which was all she ever wanted. If Lady Catherine was obtrusive and meddling in Elizabeth and Darcy's lives, they recognized the lady's actions as benign and remained close to her throughout the rest of her life. Her brother, the earl, commented on several occasions that the dissolution of her hopes had rendered his sister easier to bear than she had been before.

To his family's great relief, those few months spent as the colonel of the regiment in Meryton were the last of Colonel Fitzwilliam's career. Soon after the New Year, the colonel informed his friend and former superior, General Berger, of his intention to resign his commission, to which the general sent him a lengthy letter, wishing him well and abjuring him to stay in contact. What influence Miss Charlotte Lucas had on this decision shall be left up to the reader's imagination to determine. What is not in question is that the colonel married Miss Lucas six months after his cousin's marriage, after which they retired to his estate to live out their lives with children and love of their own. At long last, Elizabeth induced her friend to relent and agree that she was a romantic after all. If one thought Elizabeth would ever allow her smugness to recede, it is clear they did not know her at all.

Miss Bingley also found the great blessing and felicity of marriage, though it took her some months of finding her way after the shock of being rejected by Mr. Darcy. Though the man she married was, by all accounts, one who adored her, he remained unknown to the Darcys. Word of the former Miss Bingley came to the Darcys via her brother, and the Darcys wished her well, though neither wished to associate much with her.

Of Mr. Collins, they knew much but cared little. The parson continued as Lady Catherine's parson for many years after his ill-fated visit to Longbourn. Mr. Bennet, blessed with good health and long life, prevented Mr. Collins from exacting his vengeance until long after there was anyone upon whom to revenge himself. The parson remained unmarried for some time as he stubbornly held to his desire to marry a woman of fortune, long after it became clear none would have him. He was finally forced to acknowledge the truth when he proposed to a young lady of a situation much like Miss Bingley's, several years later. When the lady laughed in his face and told him in no uncertain terms what she thought of him, Mr. Collins slunk away and married a young, unintelligent lady of the neighborhood some months later. Perhaps the only agreeable things which could be said of that union were that the lady gave him two sons and that neither took after their parents, being both sensible and intelligent.

For her part, Mrs. Bennet took great delight in informing Mr. Collins as each of her daughters married, punctuated by one final missive which reminded him they all entered that blessed union, contrary to his prediction. Mrs. Bennet was beloved by all her daughters and spent much time with them over the years with her husband by her side. Elizabeth remained her favorite, and of her second daughter, she was often heard to say that she would not be the woman she became if not for her. Elizabeth, who had always esteemed her mother, credited her with her own fortunate situation, for Mrs. Bennet had raised five good and beautiful girls and taught them well. It was her mother's influence, great throughout the course of her life, that had made Elizabeth Darcy the woman she was.

The End

MORE GREAT TITLES FROM
ONE GOOD SONNET PUBLISHING!

PRIDE AND PREJUDICE VARIATIONS

By Jann Rowland

Acting on Faith
A Life from the Ashes (Sequel to
Acting on Faith)
Open Your Eyes
Implacable Resentment
An Unlikely Friendship
Bound by Love
Cassandra
Obsession
Shadows Over Longbourn
The Mistress of Longbourn
My Brother's Keeper
Coincidence
The Angel of Longbourn
Chaos Comes to Kent
In the Wilds of Derbyshire
The Companion
Out of Obscurity

What Comes Between Cousins
A Tale of Two Courtships
Murder at Netherfield
Whispers of the Heart
A Gift for Elizabeth
Mr. Bennet Takes Charge
The Impulse of the Moment
The Challenge of Entail
A Matchmaking Mother
Another Proposal
With Love's Light Wings
Flight to Gretna Green
Mrs. Bennet's Favorite Daughter

By Lelia Eye

Netherfield's Secret

By Colin Rowland

The Parson's Rescue

ALSO FROM ONE GOOD SONNET PUBLISHING
A COLLECTION OF COLLABORATIONS

PRIDE AND PREJUDICE VARIATIONS

By Jann Rowland & Lelia Eye

WAITING FOR AN ECHO

Waiting for an Echo Volume One: Words in the Darkness
Waiting for an Echo Volume Two: Echoes at Dawn

A Summer in Brighton
A Bevy of Suitors
Love and Laughter: A Pride and Prejudice Short Stories Anthology

By Jann Rowland, Lelia Eye, & Colin Rowland

Mistletoe and Mischief: A Pride and Prejudice Christmas Anthology

PRIDE AND PREJUDICE SERIES

By Jann Rowland

COURAGE ALWAYS RISES: THE BENNET SAGA

The Heir's Disgrace
Volume II Untitled*
Volume III Untitled*

OTHER GENRES BY
ONE GOOD SONNET PUBLISHING

FANTASY

By Jann Rowland & Lelia Eye

EARTH AND SKY SERIES

On Wings of Air
On Lonely Paths
On Tides of Fate*

FAIRYTALE

By Lelia Eye

The Princes and the Peas: A Tale of Robin Hood

SMOTHERED ROSE TRILOGY

Thorny
Unsoiled
Roseblood

About the Author

Jann Rowland

Jann Rowland is a Canadian, born and bred. Other than a two-year span in which he lived in Japan, he has been a resident of the Great White North his entire life, though he professes to still hate the winters.

Though Jann did not start writing until his mid-twenties, writing has grown from a hobby to an all-consuming passion. His interests as a child were almost exclusively centered on the exotic fantasy worlds of Tolkien and Eddings, among a host of others. As an adult, his interests have grown to include historical fiction and romance, with a particular focus on the works of Jane Austen.

When Jann is not writing, he enjoys rooting for his favorite sports teams. He is also a master musician (in his own mind) who enjoys playing piano and singing as well as moonlighting as the choir director in his church's congregation.

Jann lives in Alberta with his wife of more than twenty years, two grown sons, and one young daughter. He is convinced that whatever hair he has left will be entirely gone by the time his little girl hits her teenage years. Sadly, though he has told his daughter repeatedly that she is not allowed to grow up, she continues to ignore him.

Please let him know what you think or sign up for their mailing list to learn about future publications:

Website: http://onegoodsonnet.com/
Facebook: https://facebook.com/OneGoodSonnetPublishing/
Twitter: **@OneGoodSonnet**
Mailing List: http://eepurl.com/bol2p9

Made in United States
North Haven, CT
11 February 2023

32423797R00176